Rasel's Song

Stories in thw World of Nardva

Under the Mountain Series:
Heart of the Mountain
Blood Crystal
Stone of the Sea
Shadow Crystals
Caverns of the Deep

Akrad's Legacy Series:
Akrad's Children
Rasel's Song
Lumi's Allegiance
Mannok's Betrayal

Short Story Collections
Ruhanna's Flight and Other Stories
Space Triage and Other Stories

Also:
Shadow Queen in *Starlit Realms*
Shadows of the *Deep in Tales from the Underground*
The Princess and the Messenger *Glimmer anthology*
Full Moon Rising in *Like A Woman*
Maroon Sanctuary in *Gods of Clay*
Space Triage in *Challenge Accepted*
Project Chameleon in *The Quantum Soul*

Rasel's Song

Book 2 Akrad's Legacy Series

Jeanette O'Hagan

By the Light Books

Rasel's Song
© Jeanette O'Hagan
Book 2 in the Akrad's Legacy series

Copyright Jeanette O'Hagan © 2021 © 2023 © 2024
http://jeanetteohagan.com

Cover design: Jeanette O'Hagan © 2021© 2023 © 2024
Typesetting and Layout: Jeanette O'Hagan

Cataloguing-in-Publication entry (CIP) is available at National Library of Australia

NATIONAL
LIBRARY
OF AUSTRALIA

A catalogue record for this
book is available from the
National Library of Australia

ISBN-978-0-6485859-1-6
Published through By the Light Books

By the Light Books
Brookside Post Shop, PO Box 2520, Brookside Centre, Qld 4053
Email: Bythelightbooks@gmail.com

To my sister Kathleen Hillenberg who lights up my life. I love your enthusiasm, encouragement and ability to see the good in everyone. It was worth waiting twelve years for my dear sister for life. .

Note to Reader

A map, genealogies and a list of character names are included at the end of the book.

***

This book follows Australian style conventions for spelling, punctuation and grammar.

***

Subscribe to *Jeanette O'Hagan's Newsletter*
at http://eepurl.com/bbLJKT for the latest on new releases, giveaways and other news and receive story set in the world of Nardva.

Tarka, royal city of Tamra

Chapter One: The Children of Tamrak

Rasel

Rasel stretched her wings to catch the rising air and glided over the next mountain ridge. Far below, a river cut across the valley like a curling silver thread dividing a deep green bowl. To the north, the snow on two mismatched twin peaks glowed powdery pink against the pale sky. Their flanking ridges, extended by tall stone walls, encircled a great city. Adobe houses and a scattering of massive grey-stone buildings huddled together like chicks in an eagle's eyrie.

A thrill, half-fear, all-wonder, spiked through her.

'Is that Tarka, city of Tamra?' she keened to her brother, Semian, flying half a wingspan ahead. It had to be. The legendary city of the Children of Tamrak.

'I hadn't realised we'd come so far south.' Semian's chest feathers ruffled and his protective translucent eyelids flicked across his coal-black eyes. 'We should veer to the north.'

'The city is beautiful.'

Even from this height, Tarka loomed larger than she'd imagined. Bigger even than Silantis in the distant Lonely Isles was reputed to be or the fabled Pelinor from the ancient lands.

'Come, youngest sister, there will be no welcome for our Kin here.'

Despite her brother's warning, Rasel hovered on the wind. The tiled roof of the large building halfway up the hill shone like molten gold in the growing daylight. Rows of windows winked back in silvery flashes of light. How many people lived in that stone mansion set

1

like a jewel within its own high red walls? How many more in the multitude of tiny houses clustered like passionfruit seeds? How many of the mountain dwellers walked those hard-stone streets, jostling against each other in the shade of the towering city ramparts?

'Come, don't tarry, littlest sister.'

'I'm not a youngling anymore. Besides, you've seen Tarka, walked its streets and spoken to its people. I haven't. Why should we always avoid the city?'

'Rasel! You know why. Would that I had never done so, nor seen the blood of our Kin staining the streets. Would that our Kin had never befriended such a violent and contrary people.' Semian's eagle-voice thinned.

Rasel snapped her beak and half-turned, regretting the distress she'd caused him. She grew up hearing the stories of how Akrad, the man from the West, had tricked the Tamrin into betraying her Kin. What had been lost was irreparable, yet it happened before she was born.

'Isn't it time we left such sorrowful memories behind? Those bloody events happened over seventy song-cycles of the sun ago. Akrad the Betrayer died nine solars past.'

'At the cost of Da-Baba's life.'

A long mournful sound blared out from the gate towers in front of the gold-roofed building. The gilded gates swung open and a cavalcade of young warriors poured out on prancing steeds. They cantered along the paved road, following the wall before turning and galloping down the hill. Sunlight flashed off chest adornments and the tips of sharp bronze spears.

Rasel tilted her body and dipped down lower to get a closer look.

With a flash of russet hair and nod of a green-plumed headdress, a broad-shouldered young man pulled out a full horse length in front of the others. The jaunty and proud warrior seemed the very embodiment of a future unfettered by the hurts and sorrows of the past.

Semian looped around and waggled his wings. 'Youngest sister, come away,' he keened, his eagle-voice insistent. 'The Kinleader has forbidden contact with the children of Tamrak and for good reason. They are still a people of blood and strife, not to be trusted.'

Rasel sighed. She didn't want to believe that. The Tamrin were friends and allies once. Now that Akrad was dead, could they not be so again? Yet none of her Kin thought peace with the Tamrin possible. Even someone as peaceful and genial as Semian became heated when they were mentioned.

With a powerful downstroke, she regained height and angled her flight feathers to follow her cautious, rule-keeping brother. 'Shouldn't we give them a chance to do better? "Believe the finest in others and they will rise to it." Isn't that what Baba says?'

'Perhaps, but how many more lives should we risk? It's not wise to poke a sleeping jaguar. Come away, impetuous one.'

Why not take the risk, when she could shift to the jaguar-form as easily as donning her tari? Like her baba and da-baba before him, she learnt new forms with ease. Tamrak's children were short-lived and confined to their human forms. She would not be deceived by them so how could they harm her? Her Kin, the Forest Folk, were more than a match for these people. How long would the Kin stay hidden among the green songlines of the Great Forest?

A sudden snow-chilled wind swirled from the slopes of the Younger Twin. Rasel wobbled in the turbulence before regaining her balance.

Maybe one day she would see how the children of Tamrak lived in their stone and mud houses or learn more of the young warrior now galloping down the hill toward the massive city gate. Maybe she would find out what happened to that brave, lonely lad—the boy, Dinnis, who had helped free her da-baba from Akrad's chains—and his funny prickly sister, Ista. Afterall, it was a Pathfinder's job to determine the dangers and the opportunities for her people.

With one last lingering look, Rasel banked and followed Semian over the protective slope of the Elder Twin, leaving the sight of the famed city of Kapoks, Kupannas, warriors and artisans behind.

Whatever happened, she knew in her heart's song that this wouldn't be her last glimpse of the city and its people.

Chapter Two: Seizing the Victory

Mannok

Chilled air rushed against Prince Mannok's face, ruffling his hair and feathered headdress and snapping his cloak out behind him. Exhilaration raced through him like a rain-choked stream rushing down the mountain. A whole morning with his age-mates stretched out before him. Free time after ten-days of constant storms and drenching rains.

Two white-crested eagles wheeled on invisible air currents high in the newly washed sky and feathery clouds gathered above razor-edged mountains to the east, already promising more storms to come. But, for these few sweet hours, he could forget his father's crafty strategies of state, juggling clan loyalties like pieces in a game of Conquest. He could forget his mother's never-ending parade of suitable brides. This princess or that noble lady, not one of which could compare in intelligence and grace with his Ista.

Heat mantled his cheeks. His half-sister in fact, as Papa decided to reveal a couple of alume ago, to Mannok's deep humiliation and devastation. What other secrets lay hidden behind Papa's urbane manner and fierce smile?

Mannok tightened his jaw. To lose his sister the moment he'd learnt their true connection, to have her bustled off to Silisea like a wrongdoer, to not know when, if ever, he would see her again ... it rankled. Mannok took a great shuddering breath. He shouldn't let such bitter memories sully these few short hours of freedom.

He leaned over his stallion's arched neck. 'Run with the wind, Shadow,' he whispered.

'Slow down, Your Highness,' Garvin called from a horse length behind him. 'At least until we get outside the city gates.'

Mannok's shoulders tensed and then relaxed as he banished the flicker of annoyance at Garo's caution. 'Straight Street is empty this time of morning,' he yelled back.

Soon enough it would be choked with the usual crowds of city folk and the influx of peasants from the surrounding areas, the constant stream of humanity that flowed in and out the gates during the daytime like the air in a giant bellows.

Further down the paved road, a pack yarma whistled a warning and a dog yapped behind courtyard walls. Children, circling the public fountain in a game of warriors and mourners, splintered the early morning peace with piping voices.

The lower door of one of the three-storey stone houses lining the street banged open and a young woman with a basket on her head stepped out in front of him. Turning and calling to someone inside the house, she walked into Shadow's path.

'Watch out!' Mannok roared.

Shadow snorted and his powerful muscles bunched beneath Mannok's thighs. Mannok shifted his balance in rhythm with the abrupt change in gait and shortened the reins. 'Whoa, there my beauty.'

The stallion danced to the side and missed trampling the startled lass by a jaguar's whisker.

Mannok's heart rapped like frenzied war drums. That was close.

The young woman's basket had toppled, spilling rounds of yarma cheese out onto the cobblestones and sending them rolling down the hill.

'Be careful, you ruffi ...' Her voice faltered and her mouth fell open as her brown eyes met his. 'Your Highness.' Her tan face paled. She dropped to the cobblestones and lowered her forehead to the stones.

Heat mantled Mannok's neck and face. Why hadn't the woman looked? He could have been thrown. Shadow could have broken his leg. His hands tightened on the reins. She could have been killed.

Garvin and his other age-mates caught up in a breathless rush of horses, creaking tack and loud voices.

'Are you alright? The lass isn't hurt?' Garvin asked.

Mannok's stomach squirmed. 'Yes. No, no, Garo, she's unharmed,' he said, his voice gruff.

Garvin was right. He shouldn't have ridden so fast within the city.

He turned toward the woman kneeling on cobblestones. 'Please, stand. There is no need to bow. If you would accept my apologies,' Mannok said. 'I'll ... I'll send someone from the Palace to make recompense for the cost of the goods.'

'Your Highness, you are too gracious.' The woman's voice trembled and she kept her gaze lowered.

'No, I insist.' He singled out one of the guards. 'You, see that it is done.'

Papa would come down on him like a landslide if he injured someone in a mad rush to get out of the city. Besides, he didn't need another death lying like a weight-stone on his conscience. Not that he could've done much to prevent Redrik's death when the rope bridge was sabotaged last year. A shiver spread across his back and up his neck. A trap most likely meant to take Mannok's own life.

And then there was Uson and Asik's attack on Papa over an alume ago. He wasn't responsible for their actions, but he had shared meals and sleeping quarters with them, hunted and trained with them. He should have known they harboured such treacherous thoughts, but he was too busy suspecting Dinnis, then too angry at Ista's betrayal.

'So,' Estolik, Lord Haka's son, urged his roan gelding forward, pushing past Garvin. 'What have you in mind for us this morning, Mannu? Apart from sudden encounters with lovely peasant women?'

Mannok prickled at his older second-cousin's tone. Still, maybe something of the morning could be salvaged. He straightened in the saddle and ran his gaze over the band of young warriors.

'We'll head for the lower slopes of the Elder Twin for some rounds of Seize the Shield.' He leaned over and slapped Estolik's shoulder. 'You lead the Dolphin team, and I'll lead the Jaguar.'

'Yes!' Garvin punched the air.

The others whooped, their horses pirouetting around him.

Only blue-skinned Dinnis kept his usual half-bored, non-committal look in his smoky grey eyes.

Feeling less than gracious and more a fool, Mannok urged Shadow forward into a slow trot down the hill, his band close behind him. Arriving at the plaza in the outer ring of the city, Mannok edged around the cluster of townsfolk waiting in front of the massive main gate. He signalled to the duty officer to unlock the smaller postern gate.

Moments later they left the city, galloping past the fields of half-grown maize spreading out beyond the paved road, coating the valley and terraced hillsides with hopeful green. At the markstone, he turned away from the fertile jade basin to the shattered grey slopes of the Elder Twin. The two eagles to the north lifted high on the wind and disappeared between the double triangular peaks.

Shadow stretched out into a gallop. A slow grin spread across Mannok's face and all thoughts of the troublesome past and present regrets shredded in the wind.

* * *

The brittle sunlight splintered off the gravelled sides of the Elder Twin. The sun's slow ascent burned away all traces of dawn softness and small white clouds smudged the jagged line where the circle of mountain peaks met the lapis sky. Mannok nudged Shadow with his knees, directing him through the underbrush above the broad ledge Estolik had chosen for the Dolphin base at one end of the makeshift arena. Garvin followed close behind on Glacier.

Once in position, Mannok squinted through the bushes screening the ledge. Estolik's shield, sporting a leaping dolphin, hung on an anchor spear buried in the ground. Good. Estolik hadn't hidden it. Mannok cupped his hands and mimicked the musical call of the tarrawong, the agreed-upon signal.

Moments later, Hasuk and young Trasin from his Jaguar team broke from cover below the ledge some fifty tanis away and galloped up the slope towards the shield.

Estolik and most of his fellow defenders rode out to meet them with hoots and war cries. 'Dolphin, Dolphin, Dolphin!'

Only Durrin remained circling the shield, his bulk and that of his sturdy brown and white mare blocking possible attacks.

Mannok held up three fingers, folding them down—one, two, three. As one, he and Garvin burst out of cover, hurdling over a small ridge and converging on the sole defender.

Durrin roared, his face flushing muddy-red. He jerked on the

7

reins, turning his horse, and rushed at them. The mare bared her teeth and neighed a challenge.

Shadow sidestepped the burly warrior's onward rush and pivoted in a tight turn. Following Mannok's signal, he shouldered Durrin's mount, using his greater muscle to herd man and horse against the low cliff face.

'Garo, now!' Mannok yelled. 'Go, go, go!'

Garvin dashed past, riding low and slanted along the flank of Glacier. He lifted the shield from the anchor spear in one seamless motion. With a flick of a tail, Glacier trotted down the slope to the long flattish area stretching out towards the Jaguar base at the other end of the arena.

Mannok turned to follow, countering Durrin's frantic attempts to get past him and recover the shield. Shadow stretched out his legs in a gallop, his great heart drumming in rhythm to Mannok's own.

Durrin's mare stumbled, increasing the distance between them.

'Ware, ware, they have our shield,' Durrin shouted.

'Back to base,' Estolik yelled.

He and his band disengaged from the Jaguar decoys and raced back, gravel and fine dirt flinging like ash with each strike of the horses' hooves.

'To the gully on the right.' Mannok nudged Garvin to the south, using a line of boulders and a creek bed as a barrier between them and the oncoming Dolphins. Deeper into the gully, Mannok lost sight, but not sound, of those in pursuit.

A flash of movement close to their own base caught Mannok's eye. The hairs on his arms and neck prickled. Two Dolphin players soared over the jumble of boulders lining the creek and shot like released arrows toward Garvin.

Too late to turn back. Besides, they needed to get the captured shield to their base to win.

'Garo, change to the plover manoeuvre.' Mannok pulled wide of the Dolphins, continuing to head for the Jaguar base.

The Dolphins glanced between him and Garvin, until Garvin raised the Dolphin shield. 'Eat my dust, jaguar-bait.'

With a snarl, their opponents fixed their eyes on Garvin and their blue and silver prize. Mannok rode to the side, putting distance between them.

'Mannu.'

A moment before the Dolphins intercepted him, Garvin tossed the shield to Mannok and ploughed straight into the two young warriors, sending them careening off in different directions.

Mannok pushed up against the saddle horns, twisted and caught the shield with his left hand. His grip held and Shadow sailed over the boulders lining the gully and streaked toward the Jaguar base. The stallion's long legs devoured the distance like a starving man, his ash-grey mane flying and muscles rippling with power.

Hooves thundered behind him. Estolik and his gang changed direction and closed in on him.

'Dolphin, Dolphin, Dolphin.' A victorious cry went up from his own base.

Mannok's heart hitched a beat. That didn't sound good.

Durrin's younger brother, Kontar, burst around the large boulder screening the Jaguar base, the green and gold shield, Mannok's shield, in his left hand. Two of Mannok's team pursued, a couple of horse lengths behind. None of the other Jaguars were close.

Mannok gritted his teeth. With both teams in possession of the opposing band's trophy, a gruelling standoff would ensue.

'Not on my watch.' Slinging the Dolphin shield over his back, Mannok angled to intercept the opposing rider holding the Jaguar shield.

Shadow was tiring but he rose to the challenge, his ears flicking forward. The rest of the Dolphin team converged behind him.

Kontar's eyes widened when he saw Mannok riding straight for him. He turned his horse and cut diagonally across the makeshift arena.

Shadow, the Maker bless him, increased his speed.

Got him.

Mannok pushed himself up, anchoring his legs on the saddle horns, and snatched the shield from his opponent. Shadow peeled away and they charged back toward the Jaguar base, drawing on every last kernel of energy.

The melee converged on him. Hands reached out grasping and grabbing at both of his prizes. Shadow turned and twirled and twisted, as elusive as high mountain fog. Mannok kicked out at the pack, jabbing with his elbows and moving his body out of reach.

'Over here, Mannok!' Trasin called.

'We've got you covered,' Garvin yelled.

The Jaguar team arrived in a rush, playing interference with the Dolphins, clearing a path for him to their own base.

'Jaguar, Jaguar, Jaguar,' they chanted, eyes wild and teeth flashing.

In five big-heated strides, Shadow reached the empty anchor spear. Mannok brought Shadow into a tight circle. He rose up in the saddle, knees against the saddle horns, and held both the Dolphin and the Jaguar shields high. Shadow reared up and pawed the air and trumpeted a challenge that echoed across the valley.

'Seleste!' Mannok's chest swelled with pride, victory humming through him like a swarm of new season bees. He stroked Shadow's sweat-dark neck, murmuring praises into the long, alert ears.

'Mannok, Mannok, Mannok.' Garvin and the others circled him, flushed with victory.

This. This was what he was good at. Not books. Not subterfuge. Not diplomacy. At seventeen years, it was time he escaped the stratagems of the Palace and joined the patrols guarding the northern border with the Nolmec. His older cousin, Waren, already had his own command. Why not the Prince of Tamra?

'Seleste, Your Highness.' Garvin pummelled Mannok on the back.

Dinnis flashed a cynical half-smile. 'Brilliant, Your Highness. A miracle you didn't break your neck or Shadow's leg in that mad dash.'

Mannok frowned. He never knew when the fellow was teasing him. 'Thanks, I think.'

Estolik rode up to him, his chest heaving. 'Seleste, your Highness. You're as reckless as your father is reputed to be.'

Mannok stiffened. 'No, I'm not.' Besides, Papa may have been a brilliant military commander once, but all he did these days was calculate odds and placate this noble or that, including Estolik's own haughty sire, Lord Haka.

'He got lucky,' Durrin mumbled, rubbing his shoulder and wincing. 'Besides. The sun was in our eyes. It's only fair to swap sides.'

'Durrin, some respect for the Prince,' Estolik moved with his horse, his face unreadable.

Mannok smirked. His win might irk Durrin —the young noble was a sore loser— but he should get used to losing to his prince. 'We can swap ends if you think that will help you.' He lifted his eyebrows. 'Best of three games?'

'Bring it on, Your Highness.' Estolik's grey-green eyes glittered in a dust-smeared face.

Mannok grinned and tossed him the Dolphin shield. 'Fifteen minutes to rest the horses and check equipment. Then we'll see who's lucky.'

* * *

The warning horn sounded from the timekeeper, young Yalik, sitting on his horse midfield. 'Next game starts in five.'

Mannok tightened Shadow's girth strap and checked his other tack, before vaulting into the saddle.

He swiped his brow with his arm. The humidity was ramping up. White scalloped clouds with dark-grey undersides towered above the mountains, sending tendrils of mist down their slopes and casting inky shadows skimming over the terraced fields and the valley floor.

His band completed their last checks and walked toward him, leading their horses. Dinnis straggled in, last and alone.

'Mount up, Jaguars and huddle close,' Mannok said.

Garvin stroked Glacier's neck. 'Any change in tactics, Your Highness?'

Mannok nodded. 'Let's mix it up. Go in, go fast and go hard, then high tail back to base. Trasin can lead the attack team this bout. Kimsak and Hasuk can run interference.'

'Will the sun be an issue?' At fourteen, Kimsak was one of the youngest in the group, included as a special favour to Uncle Lukarn.

Mannok raised his eyebrows. 'No warrior can guarantee perfect conditions in battle. Keep your eyes on our opponents and the shields. Be alert to Dolphin slip-ups and use them to our advantage. Garvin and Dinnis will be on defence with me. We'll hide the shield this time round.'

'Good plan. Should keep Estolik's team off balance.' Garvin pushed his modest blue and brown feathered headdress higher on his forehead, approval in his teak-brown eyes. Whatever happened, Mannok could count on his closest friend.

'The Dolphins would have already scouted out the best hiding spots last bout.' Trasin fiddled with his reins, his horse restive beneath him. Lord Challak's second son was shaping up as a fine warrior. He would calm down once in action.

Dinnis leaned back in the saddle, a thoughtful look in his smoke-grey eyes. 'What about the small cave on the slope above us?'

Mannok gave Dinnis an extra hard stare. Did his often-elusive age-mate spend the last game in such a hiding place? No, he'd seen his blue-skinned face and tall form midfield, though on the edges of the ruckus.

'Brilliant.' Hasuk snorted, his roan gelding circling. 'You can't fit a horse through that tiny opening and it only goes back a tanis or two deep.'

Dinnis wrinkled his nose, his cheeks darkening. 'True. You'd need to dismount.'

'Right.' Mannok tilted his head. It was rare for Dinnis to be caught out, though when it came to horses ... he didn't know how to ride when he'd first arrived in Tarka. Mannok never understood why Papa chose the older half-Nolmec lad as one of his age-mates, except that he had been orphaned by the war, like Uson and Asik.

Garvin coughed. 'So, forget hiding the shield?'

Mannok snapped his attention back to the game. It was a crazy plan, but then Estolik avoided risk and was unlikely to suspect such a ploy.

'No, let's do it. Your idea, Dinnu, you take the shield.' Mannok met his age-mate's sceptical gaze. 'Garvin and I will stay at the base as decoys. Get back to base the instant Trasin brings in the Dolphin shield.'

Dinnis' eyes narrowed a fraction before he brought his fist to his chest. 'Your command Your Highness.'

Balooo. Baloo. Baloo. The timekeeper blew the starting horn.

After a flurry of fist bumps, the Jaguar attack team urged their horses down the slope and past the boulders, eyes squinted against the sun, Trasin in the lead.

Mannok and Garvin circled around their new base, blocking both shield and Dinnis from sight.

'Now, Dinnu.'

Dinnis slid out of the saddle and slapped Pumice's rump, encouraging the gelding to take cover in the bushes. He grabbed the shield, slung it over his back, scrambled up the slope and disappeared behind the straggle of vegetation covering the cave entrance.

Several moments later, the midfield erupted into tumult. Cries of 'Jaguar, Jaguar, Jaguar' and 'Dolphin, Dolphin, Dolphin' splintered the air.

Mannok eased his tight grip on Shadow's reins. He'd much rather be in the mad scramble on midfield directing the action than waiting for the Dolphin attack. But he needed to give others a go at command and the plan would work or it wouldn't.

A soft breeze sighed off the snow further up the mountain slope, cooling his face and rustling the strappy grasses and leaves. Mannok scanned the shrubs, hollows and ridges, alert for any sign of ambush. Shadow circled the spear instinctively, picking up his feet and shaking his mane.

Time crawled like chilled honey.

A flash came from the south of the arena; sunlight reflecting off metal. Mannok's tension ramped up like the towering thunderheads.

Yet, nothing untoward moved, the slopes and what he could see of the arena remained empty. He relaxed.

Another stab of light and this time he noted it came from across the Tari valley. He shielded his eyes against the glare. A blur of movement, like a river of ants, crawled along the Royal Road leading from South Ridge Village into the valley. 'That's strange.'

'What?' Garvin followed Mannok's gaze. 'Oh, that.' He shrugged. 'Some out-of-season merchants bringing crafted goods from Silesia.'

Mannok clicked his tongue. Maybe. The group seemed too broad, too big and disciplined to be a train of pack yarmas or a merchant convoy. Besides, it was the wrong time of year for merchants to travel far. The Heavy Rains brought the risk of thunderstorms and floods and landslides, even blizzards in the higher mountain passes. Perhaps it was Durrin's father, Lord Durak, Markan of the Southern Marches. Durrin's younger brother was old enough for the Trail of Tears. Yet, two alume remained until the New Beginnings Festival.

'Your Highness.'

What if the group came from Silisea? His heart sped up and warmth mantled his cheeks. Silisea. Papa had taken Ista to Silisea. Would she come back without Papa's permission? And how would he deal with it if she did?

'Mannok!'

Papa's revelations about Ista had come like a raging forest fire sparked in a drought. She was a close friend, as close as Garvin, though different. And now things could never be the same between them. That didn't mean that he didn't miss her every day she was gone.

13

'Mannu! Watch out.'

Mannok pulled his attention back to the game. Durrin and Estolik barrelled toward him from opposite sides. They were close, too close.

'Slide it, the shield's not here,' Estolik yelled, turning his chestnut stallion and scanning the area. 'Check the gully.'

Durrin kept coming at a dead gallop, head down and leaning forward, aiming straight for Mannok, the gleam of revenge in his pebble eyes.

Mannok snapped into action, urging Shadow to move.

'Durrin, what are you doing? The shield's not there,' Estolik screamed.

Garvin angled towards Durrin, altering his path enough for Shadow to swerve past the murderous charge.

'Durrin, check the gully to the south,' Estolik roared. 'Now!'

Durrin shook his head, as though dazed, and grunted. 'We've got you,' he growled. 'We'll win this round.'

The two of them took off in different directions.

Signalling Garvin to stay, Mannok set off after them. Got to make it look like the suckers could be right.

A roar came from further down the field. Trasin emerged from the screen of bushes and galloped toward them, the Dolphin shield held high. The rest of the field, both Dolphin and Jaguar, hurtled behind him.

'Dinnu,' Garvin shouted, 'Now!'

The bushes thrashed above them. Dinnis emerged, twigs in his hair and clutching the Jaguar shield.

Estolik gave a wild shout and turned his horse to scramble up the slope and block Dinnis' only path down.

'Run!' Mannok screamed. He turned Shadow to intercept Estolik. With his age-mate on foot, he'd need all the support he could get.

Dinnis teetered on the edge, his nostrils flaring. He launched forward and half-ran, half-fell down the low cliff face, bushes whipping about him. He jumped the last couple of tanis and landed in a crouch some six paces from the anchor spear. Garvin urged Glacier toward him. Trasin rode toward them, several tanis away, and the pack closing in behind him.

'Go! Go! Go!' Mannok yelled.

With the crash of hooves on stone, Durrin on Fist barrelled past Shadow and headed straight for Dinnis.

'Got you, bluey!' Durrin swung low to the side to grab the Jaguar shield, with no apparent thought to what his powerful horse would do to a dismounted player.

Mannok flinched but forced himself to keep watching. 'Dinnu, throw the shield to me,' he yelled.

Dinnis stood, oblique eyes stunned as the barrel-chest steed thundered toward him. His voice-nub bobbed once and then, with a sharp nod, he hugged the shield to his chest, tucked his head in and rolled under the horse's belly. His shoulder hit the gravel and he slid between the flashing hooves just tinas from his head, and out the other side.

Durrin pulled up in front of the cliff, head whipping from one side to the other, the look of confusion on his face almost comical. 'Where'd it go?'

Behind him, Dinnis staggered up, first onto his knees, then to his feet. He turned about and stared, his nostrils flaring, his chest heaving, the left side of his face grazed and the shoulder of his tunic ripped and bloodied.

Mannok's eyes locked with Dinnis' grey ones. 'Don't stand there! Go!'

Dinnis' blue face split into a crooked grin. He sprinted with the speed of a spooked yarma. He reached the anchor spear at the same time as Trasin. Together they hung the shields on the spear—Dinnis on foot, Trasin on horseback.

'Seleste!' Mannok punched the air. They'd done it. Dinnis had done it.

Mannok turned his horse, right into Estolik's flinty glare.

Mannok cocked an eyebrow. 'So, another rest before the third rout, I mean bout?'

His cousin rubbed the sweat out of his eyes and snarled. 'No point.' With a visible effort he pulled himself together. 'Best of three, you've won, Your Highness.'

Durrin's broad face collapsed into a scowl. 'He was on foot, that's a foul.'

The burly young warrior had to be kidding. Mannok folded his arms. 'Nothing in the rules says you have to be on horseback.'

'Afterall, only a fool would be on foot in a field of horses.' Dinnis raised an eyebrow and cradled his shoulder.

Garvin shook his head. 'I'd say. I thought you were dead meat or at least maimed for life. You're as reckless as Mannok, Dinnu.'

'Didn't know you had it in you.' Trasin slapped Dinnis on the back.

'You did well.' Mannok turned Shadow in a circle, catching the eyes of all his age-mates, 'You all did well.'

The young men erupted into a cheer. 'Jaguar. Jaguar. Jaguar.'

The voices echoed off the mountainside, startling a flock of doves. A wind whipped up from nowhere, rattling the shrubs and bringing the smell of distant rain. Purple clouds towered above the mountains in tall columns, flashes of lighting silvering their underbellies.

Mannok glanced over the valley at the southern ridge twenty lek away. The grey line of travellers flowed along the broad road winding beside the river that divided the valley. Sunlight glinted on metal, like fireflies at dusk. At the centre of the group, the flutter of colourful material suggested the presence of a couple of palanquins. Someone preferred to be carried by others in a litter rather than ride, a rich old merchant or perhaps his womenfolk.

Ista preferred to travel that way. She'd never learnt to love horses ... or dogs, an aspect of her character Mannok found hard to fathom. Though that didn't explain the other litters. Unless it was the Silisean Queen come to announce Ista's engagement to that annoying fellow, Prince Tolteal. Mannok's shoulders clenched tight and his head throbbed. If Papa had told the truth from the beginning, his friendship for Ista would never have been tainted by unattainable dreams. His heart would never have shattered into a thousand shards like a storage jar ransacked by thieves.

'So, what next, Your Highness?' Garo's cheerful voice broke into his thoughts.

Mannok pulled his attention back to his age-mates. Most were rubbing down and watering their horses, wide grins and jocular exchanges with only the occasional broody face in the Dolphin team at losing.

He'd planned a ride to the stand of pine trees in the valley or maybe even a trek to the Bridal Veil waterfall, but his heart had gone out of it. The mysterious party would arrive at the city gates in a couple of hours with the storm chasing them across the valley. Mannok wanted to be there to greet them, to find out who they were and what they wanted.

'Let's get back to the Palace.'

Garvin and a few of the others groaned. 'Come on, we've an hour or two before the rains arrive, Your Highness,' Hasuk said.

'Besides, what's a little rain for a true warrior?' Trasin smiled.

'All fun and games until the lightning strikes. Besides, it looks like we have some unannounced visitors.' Mannok tilted his head and grinned. 'Last one through the city gates, gets to clean the winner's tack.' Without waiting for a response, he leaned forward and squeezed Shadow's flank. The stallion shook his mane and galloped down the slope without hesitation.

A few moments later, the sound of hooves rumbled behind him like an avalanche.

Mannok's heart gave a half-hitch of hope. If it was Ista ... Perhaps he could salvage something from last season's debacle and forge a new relationship as brother and sister.

Chapter Three: New Arrivals

Mannok

Mannok paced the length of the audience Throne Room, his ceremonial cloak swirling behind him. Grey brooding light filtered through the tall glass windows above the thrones lined up along the southern wall. It muted the large tapestries and cast gloomy shadows over the mosaic stone floor.

His heavy headdress gripped his temples tighter with each impatient stride. The humid air pressed down on him like a heavy cloak. Three or was it four hours already! It's only a mere twenty lek across the valley. Why weren't the strangers here by now?

At one end of the spacious room, his royal parents stood at the centre of a group of nobles. A smaller group than it might have been, for most of the clan leaders and all four Markans had returned to their clan lands at the beginning of the Heavy Rains, the season of storms. Kaptan Jakan of the Palace Guard stood at alert to one side and guards flanked the doors and lined the walls.

Papa—tall, broad-shouldered and big-chested—dominated the group in his hastily donned ceremonial headdress and fine yarma wool cloak embroidered with polished citrine and chalcedony. His golden pectoral plate, embossed with a green and gold Jaguar emblem, gleamed with royal power even in this dull grey light. Papa's expressive face seemed watchful rather than concerned or surprised at the news of these unannounced arrivals. Could Papa have recalled Ista from exile, despite Mama's hard attitude toward her? But then, he was rarely startled, taking everything in his long stride.

If it was Ista, if Papa had planned this, Mama would be seething. Instead, she smiled and sparkled in a robe seeded with sapphires, pearls and diamonds, a patch of bright sky among dark storm clouds. The top of her crystal headpiece, balanced on her intricately arranged hair, barely reached Papa's shoulders, but no one could doubt she was the Kupanna. She laid elegant fingers on Papa's arm, as though the two were in perfect accord. Yet what if Papa hadn't told her? It was the sort of unpredictable thing he might do, only to let shards of a shattered pot fall where they may.

A white flash of lightning lit up the room, followed moments later by a bone-shaking crash of thunder. Mannok's skin crawled with static and sweat beaded his forehead. Hopefully, the afternoon storm would break soon, clearing the air.

'Your Highness, what gives?' Garvin whispered as Mannok passed his friend for the hundredth time. 'You're as restless as a caged jaguar.'

Mannok checked his stride. What could he say? Both his parents insisted Ista's connection to the royal house remain a state secret, one that not even his best friend could know. Lord Haka might use it to undermine Papa's position as Kapok. Besides, Mannok needed to sort out his own turbulent feelings. Angry at his parents, yes. Sad she wasn't here, but also ashamed, embarrassed and confused. How could he explain all that even to Garo?

'Mannu?'

Mannok flashed his friend a crooked smile. 'I hate all this waiting.'

'Do you think they mean to attack?' Hasuk asked, his slate-brown eyes crinkled with worry. 'The City and Palace Guard are at minimum strength.'

'Exactly! No one starts a war in the middle of the Heavy Rains.' Estolik sauntered over to them, his pompous voice cutting through the gloom. 'Moving armies and their supplies would be a nightmare.'

'No one else normally travels either.' Dinnis said in his quiet voice, his face grazed.

Mannok tugged at his too tight tunic. 'I wish we could ride out and find out ourselves. Why are they taking so long?'

The doors leading to the Great Hall swung open and the Palace madomo, Bitjarnan, bustled into the Throne Room. 'Your Majesties, Kaptan Kaspin and the Master of Scouts, Sparak.'

The esteemed Kaptan of the City Guard strode into the room, his snow-white hair in stark contrast to the creased sun-darkened copper of his face. The Master of Scouts followed close behind, rake-thin and morose, his gaze flicking about the room as watchful as a grey mountain fox.

Now he'd get some answers. Mannok made a spearline to the small knot of people circling his parents.

'So, what have you discovered about our mysterious visitors, Kaspin?' Papa said, his voice rough with displeasure.

Kaspin bowed low. 'Your Majesty. They are a largish party with a mixture of nobles and warriors.'

Papa's eyes narrowed. 'How many warriors?

'Fifty. They have two palanquins with them and they approach the city gates openly. It's not a war party, sir.'

Papa turned to Sparak, his face grim. 'I do wonder how they slipped past your scouts, Sparro. It's unacceptable for a large group of unknown origin to approach the very fringes of Tarka with no warning.'

Sparak's sharp cheekbones darkened, the scar that slashed across his left cheek deepening until it stood out against his tan skin like a silver thread. 'Nobody travels …'

Papa raised an eyebrow. 'It seems they do.'

'Yes.' Sparak dipped his head. 'An oversight on my part, Your Majesty. My deepest apologies.'

'And now that they are under your pointy nose, dear friend, do you have any idea who they are?'

'Some, Your Majesty. They have no visible insignia, but they have the height of flatlanders …'

Mannok's spirits rose. 'Silisean?' he asked.

'… and pale skins and light-coloured hair. Their attire is more flowing. My guess, they come from distant Limar or one of the smaller principalities east of the Vilka mountains.'

Mannok gripped the hilt of his hunting knife. Not Siliseans. Not Ista, but Limarians? The most distant of the three surviving nations of the Five Lands. Sometimes, a Limarian merchant came this far to trade, but it was rare. Normally, the prospect of meeting such unique guests would spark his interest. Instead, he felt flat.

A staccato blast of a horn echoed from across the city—the call that signalled the arrival of strangers at the Gate.

'You should let me question them before you allow them into the city,' Sparak cautioned.

Mama frowned at him, no hint of worry on her still beautiful face. 'You treat the strangers as though they are a threat, Master Scout, yet most likely they come in peace.'

Papa waved a hand. 'The Kupanna is right. We will receive our mysterious arrivals as guests, not enemies, at least unless they prove otherwise. Kaspin, take fifty warriors to escort them here. They can leave their weapons at the Palace door.'

Kaspin bowed low and strode out of the room.

Papa pushed out his cloak and took his place on the large central Golden Throne, Mama sat on the embossed bronzed one beside it. The great carved wooden chairs for the Markans and Markanas flanking the royal thrones on either side remained empty. Uncle Lukarn and the other Markans were spending the season in their clan lands with their families.

Mannok smoothed down his tunic, readjusted his Jaguar ceremonial breast plate and stood behind his father's throne.

Papa tapped his long, sturdy fingers on the golden armrest while Mama lay her hands in her lap and twisted the gemmed rings, their golden bands and bright jewels shining in contrast to the bronzed-tan of her skin.

The moments slid by, slow and sluggish. The afternoon bustle in the corridors and rooms outside the Throne Room seemed to hush, as though the Palace was holding its breath. Outside, the sky darkened though sunset was hours away. The lightning accompanied by thunder in its train, flashed and crashed in increasing tempo. With a sudden rush, a deluge of rain drummed against the Palace walls.

Servants hurried into the room, lighting the large candelabras standing against the walls.

At last, strident voices and approaching footsteps sounded from the Great Hall, signalling the arrival of their guests. Mannok stood straighter. At last. The golden doors swung open, two guards entered and moved to either side of the entrance. Kaptan Kaspin followed, Bitjarnan one step behind him.

Bitjarnan opened his mouth, no doubt to announce the visitors, but a young man, slender, with robes of rich midnight-blue cloth, splotched from rain and mud, pushed past the portly madomo. The room lit up in a dazzle of white light and, bare seconds later, shook with a boom.

Behind the stranger, two-bare chested men and a group of unarmed warriors escorted a veiled woman. More nobles hovered behind them.

Bitjarnan cleared his throat and started again. 'Your Majesty—'

The young man stepped forward and spoke over the madomo. 'My Lord Kapok, I am Prince Dashon, oldest and favoured son of His resplendent Majesty Kwetok, Sulkan of Limar, Lord of the Green Forest and the highlands, wise and noble father of his people.'

'Er, yes.' Bitjarnan gave the self-proclaimed prince of Limar a frustrated look. 'Yes, Your Majesty, and ... ah ... his sister, the Princess Kerri of faraway Limar.'

The veiled woman stepped forward, her jewelled bangles tinkling. Her pale hand with long slender fingers, covered in rings, pulled aside the gauzy purple scarf sparkling with tiny crystals, to reveal the most unusual face. Beautiful as a bone statue, framed in sandy-gold hair and eyes like chips of lapis lazuli. Only a petite nose and an air of disdain marred her seeming perfection.

Mannok swallowed hard. A princess of Limar and, no doubt, another contender for his hand in the marriage game. This day was rapidly unravelling from brilliant to awful. Instead of the return of his sister and friend, he had another simpering palace beauty to avoid. Mannok folded his arms. He was not going to be herded into marriage to some simpering and empty-headed beauty. Not now, not so soon after Ista. Maybe not ever.

'Your Royal Highnesses, Prince Dashon and Princess Kerri.' Papa nodded at the visitors, the soft burr of wry amusement lurking in his booming bass voice. 'I am sure we are pleased to receive such illustrious guests, children of the Great Sulkan. I hope your esteemed father is well.'

Dashon's cool grey-blue gaze swept the court and settled on Papa. He gave a flourish with soft pasty hands. 'My father, the most resplendent Sulkan, long may he live, is in perfect health and sends his greetings to his royal brother of Tamra.'

'Ah, yes, that is marvellous to hear.' Papa waved his hand. 'May I present my resplendent Kupanna, Marra of the Puma Clan, as sweet and beautiful as a Marosa blossom, as ...'

Mama's bronzed cheeks pinked and she cut in. 'Your Highnesses, Prince Dashon and Princess Kerri—you are most welcome. We'll find accommodations for such honoured guests and, please, you must join us tonight in a welcoming feast.'

'... and my son, Prince Mannok,' Papa continued, quite unabashed, the twinkle in his amber eyes intensifying. Normally not one to stand on ceremony unless absolutely required, he seemed to be enjoying teasing the ostentatiousness of their guests.

Dashon turned toward Mannok, his gaze sweeping over him. 'Your Highness.'

Princess Kerri parted painted lips, showing a set of white, even teeth, and placed a dainty hand on his arm. Her bangles slid, jangling down her arm. 'Prince Mannok, it is a pleasure to meet you. You are more handsome than rumoured.'

'A pleasure to meet you, Princess Kerri.' Mannok gave a flourish and shifted his gaze away from her intense stare. Not Ista, except for the uncommon paleness of her skin, though even that was different. No, nothing like Ista. This could be a long afternoon.

Chapter Four: Abrasions

Dinnis

So, who be it this time?' Anna shot Dinnis a disapproving look. 'One day, you'll keep out of trouble.'

Dinnis snorted and stretched his long legs in a vain effort to find a comfortable position on the rough wooden stool. 'Trouble finds me as certain and swift as a trained message hawk finds its target.'

With a click of her tongue, old Anna dipped the spatula into the tar-like, red paste, her movements slow and methodical. The sunlight picked up the wrinkles in her brown face and highlighted the growing strands of grey in her once dark hair.

Dinnis lifted an eyebrow. 'You know, Da-Matu, I can apply the kino paste myself. I'd run out, is all.' He searched the fold in his tunic. 'Here, I've three copper rods.'

Anna glared and knocked his hand away. 'I'll not let you leave with skin still raw and bleeding. You'll be ruining my reputation!' A hint of gentleness seeped into her brown eyes. 'Keep still, boy. This will sting.' Leaning on her gnarled bloodwood stick, she spread the paste over his left ear and jawline.

Dinnis ignored the sharp bite and focussed on the calming aroma of chilli bean and cavy stew bubbling away on the hob. Afternoon light slanted through the small window above him, burnishing the painted adobe walls and hardened clay floor. The rhythmic strike of the pestle on mortar and Tilli's melodious voice speaking to a customer filtered through the door dividing the herbal shop's front from the family's living area. A feeling of being where he belonged seeped over him.

'Who you be scrapping with this time?'

He let out a wry chuckle. 'The mountainside. The Prince decided to spend the first fine morning in a ten-day playing Seize the Shield.'

Anna leaned in closer and gripped his shoulder. He flinched at the sudden searing of pain.

Anna released her hold and scowled at him. 'Not your face only then.'

'It's nothing. A small scratch.'

'Don't you try to cozen me, son. Take off your tunic.'

'What? No!'

'That not be a request.' She waved her sturdy walking stick at him.

'What, are you going to beat me into submission if I don't?'

She stared at him, not even a hint of a smile in return. 'Maybe, or ban you from the shop.'

Not that she would, surely? 'Then who would supply you with the best herbs this side of Mokka or Shanta? Besides, you tried that once before and it didn't work.'

She maintained her glare. Anna might look like a plump mountain sparrow, feathers puffed up to impress, but she still managed to scare him. Besides, he knew she wouldn't give up. He let his breath out and slipped his injured left arm and shoulder out of the tunic.

'Dinnis!' Anna's old eyes focused on the long abrasion running from the tip of his shoulder down his arm and wrapping around the left side of his back as far as the shoulder blade. Even though he'd cleaned it up as best he could, it surely must look a mess.

'By the Maker, what did you do? Seize the Shield, did you say? You fell off a horse?'

'Not this time.' Her eyes bored into him. 'I slid downhill between the hooves of a vicious beast and his mount.'

'Argh, you young blades and your games!' Anna leant forward and eased his tunic off his other shoulder, letting the garment fall to his waist. 'I see you've done a half-decent job in cleaning this, but you've missed bits. The salve will stop infection.'

'Yes, I applied mountain-sweet, briarweed and honey. But I thought the kino paste would be advisable.'

'Hmm, yes. And removing the bits of gravel you missed.'

'It's hard to reach.'

She gave a curt nod. 'Best get started cleaning this mess up. Asking for help not be a weakness, boy.'

She had a point for ordinary folks, at least, but asking for help made him vulnerable. Besides, he didn't like exposing his back and chest. The old scars invited too many unwanted questions.

Anna moved over to the hob, placed some meadowsweet in a clay bowl and poured steaming water from the kettle over it. She covered a jar and placed bronze tweezers in a dish of maize spirits. 'I can give you some keka leaf to dull the pain.'

'Thanks, but no. I want to stay alert.'

'Humph,' Anna grunted. Taking a soft cotton cloth, she dabbed at his back with the mountain-sweet infusion, before picking up the tweezers and tugging at the gravel.

He slowed his breathing and counted the different coloured threads in the rough woven tapestry hanging on the opposite wall, shutting the door on the pain. A trick he'd honed in his years as Akrad's hostage.

Finally, Anna took up the jar of paste again.

Light footsteps sounded in the passageway from the outer shop. With a jolt, Dinnis grabbed his tunic and tugged at it. Anna slapped his hand away.

'Do you want the salve smeared all over your fine tunic?' she growled.

'Ma,' Tilli's clear voice floated across the room, 'Do we have any kwina bark? There be none out front and the potter's youngest daughter has the shaking fever.'

Tilli, Anna's oldest daughter, stopped at the door, her rich chocolate eyes rounding. 'Dinnis. When did you get here?' Her face broke into a sunlit smile. 'It's been days.'

She glanced at him, flushed and studied her hands.

'I'm sorry, Tilli. It's been hard to get away from the Palace with everyone shut in due to the incessant rains.' She looked lovelier each time he saw her, with flowers tucked into her hair and a long dark plait swinging on her shoulder.

'I would think having nothing to do would make it easier.'

'There's always something to do. Ride, fight, eat, polish weapons.' Read, sketch, study herbs if he got a chance.

Tilli looked sceptical. 'And why didn't you come out front to speak to me, instead of slipping over the courtyard wall?'

Anna placed the spatula on the tray and took strips of clean cotton cloth from the shelf. Tilli's bright eyes moved from his face to his chest. She sucked in a breath.

'You're hurt!'

'A few scrapes. I got a bit too enthusiastic in one of the Prince's games.'

'It looks worse than a few scrapes.'

Anna clicked her tongue. 'Don't make a fuss, girl. It'll heal well enough, though be adding to your scar collection, lad.'

Dinnis shook his head at her.

'Scar?' Tilli's eyes widened further as they racked over his chest, back and arms, seeming to catalogue every stripe, burn and mark. 'Dinnis, who did that to you? Did those bullies at the Palace ...'

Here came the questions. 'Well, I did get a beating for bothering the Herbalist a few years ago.'

Anna cocked her head. 'I'm sorry about that Dinnis, but you acted like a pest, turning up uninvited again and again.' She spread out her hands, joints knotted with age. 'And I not be expecting them to thrash you.'

Tilli shook her head. 'Whoever did this ... it looks like torture. Be it the Prince?'

'No, he would never do something like that. It was before I came to the Palace. I don't like to talk about it.'

'But you been at the Palace since you were a young boy.'

'I was eleven when I came here.'

'Yes, when the rebellion led by Naetok and Akrad ended, the war that killed Da...' Tilli stopped. 'Who be doing that to a child?'

Dinnis shivered at the emerging memories. He closed his eyes. Six long years he and his sister Ista were held under Akrad's noxious care. 'My kidkna ... my da-baba, if you must know. Now, please, can we talk about something else?'

Tilli's lower lip trembled, then tightened. 'You know everything about me but, after all these years, you still be a riddle. You cradle secrets like life, as though you didn't trust me ... us. I thought we be your family.'

'You are. I do.' But maybe his life did depend on keeping his secrets. Maybe Rokkan wouldn't have the stomach to harm him, but his protectors, Markan Lukarn or Master of Scouts, Sparak, would. They would end him in a heartbeat if they thought he'd told anyone about his true parentage.

'Tilli, enough. Dinnis be...'

'... never here. He has no time for us anymore, or only when he needs something.'

Tilli palmed tears from her flushed cheeks.

Dinnis' heart squeezed. 'I'm sorry, Tilli. It's that ...' Maybe the prospect of some Palace gossip would mollify her. 'The Palace is in uproar with the arrival of the Limarian royals. I'm sure I can get away more often, now. Well, after the banquet tonight.'

But instead of asking for more details, Tilli reached up and grabbed a sealed jar of powdered kwina from the high shelf. Soft lips pressed together into a thin line, she turned and walked back into the shop without another word.

Dinnis smashed his thigh with his fist. 'Slide it.'

'Give her time, lad. Between the Palace and your apprenticeship with Laetil, it be a wonder you have any time at all.'

Dinnis looked up at the old woman, who had filled a lonely orphan's empty heart with a gruff mother's care. His own mother died giving birth to his sister, leaving precious but fleeting memories.

'And do you want to know my secrets?' That came out more bitter than he'd intended.

'No, lad. I know who you be.'

Dinnis tensed.

She leant in on her stick. 'A young man too clever for his own good, a young man with a warm heart and healing hands, a young man with many irritating habits,' the corners of her mouth twitched and her eyes twinkled, 'but be always welcome at my hearth.'

Chapter Five: Courting Limar

Mannok

Mannok jogged along the third-floor balcony of the royal atrium, Garvin following behind. Half-melted candles guttered in the candelabras spaced along the inner wall. Hours ago, the nobles straggled to their beds in royal guest rooms or to homes and lodgings outside the Palace. Hours since, Madomo Bitjarnan escorted the new arrivals to a guest suite on the ground floor of the royal atrium. The sounds of servants clearing the remnants of the feast faded. Now, the Palace slumbered. Only the slow tread of the guards in the hallways, Garvin's breathing a step behind him, and the gentle patter of rain on the tiled Palace roof disturbed the night.

Reaching the entrance to the Royal suite, Mannok turned and faced his friend. 'I'll be safe enough now, Garo.' He raised his eyebrows. 'Hardly at risk in the heart of the Royal Palace, after all.'

Garvin tilted his head, his strong teeth flashing in a grin. 'No doubt, Mannu, but can't hurt to be cautious. Not with the attacks on you and the Kapok last year and now the sudden arrival of these outlanders.'

'The miscreants responsible for the attack on Papa are in chains awaiting their final sentence. No need to worry.'

'And the saboteurs of the bridge? Were Uson and Asik behind that too?'

Mannok moved uneasily. 'Perhaps.' Though it seemed unlikely. 'But either way I doubt the Limarians had anything to do with it.'

The normally genial Garvin gave a sharp nod. 'Can't be too careful, Your Highness. Who knows why they are here? As your friend, age-mate and loyal subject of your father, it's my job to worry.' Garvin bowed and turned toward the courtyard gardens to access the bachelor quarters in the adjoining atrium.

Mannok drew in a lungful of rain-soaked night air. With any favour, his parents would be asleep. He nodded to the guards flanking the door into the entrance of the suite and angled toward his own rooms. Since the Trial of Tears last year, he usually slept in the bachelor quarters with his age-mates. Tonight, he felt the need for solitude.

A murmur of voices came from his parents' antechamber, the rich alto of his mother and the dulcet tones of Lady Lumi, Estolik's sister. Ever since Ista's exile to Silisea, Mama preferred one of the young ladies of noble birth to attend her. The rumble of his father's bass voice was absent. Perhaps Papa was already asleep, though more likely he'd retired to his office to sift through state papers or consult with his Kaptans even at this late hour.

Mannok pulled the handle of his private bedchamber. The door swung toward him with a loud creak.

'Mannu, is that you? Come, say goodnight,' his mother called out.

Suppressing a groan, Mannok turned away from the haven of his own space and walked across the outer room into his parents' receiving room come dressing room. Mama sat, back straight and head erect, as Lumi carefully removed the gems and golden ornaments from Mama's cascade of dark hair. The soft candlelight smoothed out the lines developing between her brow and the corners of her mouth. She seemed young and beautiful, an echo of his memory of her before Naetok's rebellion, when life was simpler and safer. Behind Mama, Lumi looked ethereal, her silver-grey eyes shining like two lakes reflecting Argenti's light. She caught his eye and her cheeks dimpled into a smile.

Mannok looked away. 'You look lovely, Mama,' he said.

'No need to flatter me like your golden-tongued father.' Mama's coffee-brown eyes searched his face. 'What do you think of our guests?'

He grimaced. 'Tiresome and haughty. They act as though they are the only cultured people north of the White Wastes and east of the Lapis Sea.'

30

'Limar is a great nation and Kuza is a grand and fabled city.'

'Tarka is more ancient.' That at least he remembered from the endless lessons in history and culture. 'Big is not always better.'

Mannok met Lumi's eyes briefly. She dimpled a smile. Laying the golden marosa flower in a carved soapstone box, she picked up an ornate brush and pulled it through Mama's hair. He looked away and shifted the balance of his feet.

'Tarka is incomparable,' Mama said. 'Still, they say Kuza is ten lek from one end to the other. It sits beside a lake so large you cannot see the other shore.' Mama's tone grew dreamy. 'They say it is rich beyond compare, the very streets made of gold.'

'They say a lot of things.' Papa entered unannounced through the outer door. 'But you shouldn't believe everything you hear.' For a big man, Papa moved with the silence of a jaguar.

'If even half of what they say is true, Rokkan, Limar is a power to be reckoned with.'

'That, my dear, I do not doubt.'

Mama turned back to Mannok. 'Prince Dashon does seem somewhat pushy, but what did you think of the Princess Kerri? She has an unusual beauty, maybe one that appeals since you prefer pale beauties?'

Mannok stiffened. Mama didn't think that he and the Princess of Limar...? No way was he going there. 'Her nose is puny, her voice high-pitched, and so many bangles jangling. And she drips false sweetness like a honey-soaked inka berry.' He stretched his tired muscles, tight from the morning's bout of Seize the Shield and the long hours lounging in the banqueting hall. Up since dawn and now past midnight, all he wanted was sleep.

Papa's unruly eyebrows crunched together in a frown. 'I hope you did not speak your opinions in the hearing of the Princess or her retinue. Whatever we may think of our guests, we will be polite and courtly.'

Mannok rounded on him. 'Do you want me to woo her too?'

'By the two moons, no! We have no need to be entangled in Limarian affairs, but—'

Mama frowned. 'Really, Rokkan, then who do you suggest would be a suitable bride for your only son? It's bad enough that Mannok vetoes every contender without you adding your own caveats.' She glanced at Lumi and took the brush from her hand. 'That will be all, Lumi my dear, thank you.'

Lumi lowered her eyelids, hiding a spark of interest in her lovely eyes. She bowed and left the room with a quick glance at Mannok over her shapely shoulder.

Papa unfastened his cloak and dropped it on a chair. 'Mannok is free to choose his bride ...'

'... which is half the problem ...'

'... from among the noble women of Tamra and Silisea but no first cousins, none of Haka's daughters or any other political—'

'All of whom, he's rejected. If not a Limarian princess, who is left? Do you suggest a Nolmec princess?' She gave Papa a long hard look, as though sending an arrow to its target. Mannok sighed at the undertow of unspoken secrets he often felt around his sparring parents. Most likely his mother hinted at Papa's liaison with Ista's Nolmec mother, a secret he now knew.

'Kiprissa, not Princess. And no, an alliance with the Nolmec would be almost as disastrous as one with the Limarians.'

'Well, you would know. You are certainly intimately acquainted with our northern invaders.'

Papa lifted a shoulder. 'And so I should be, since my late father sent me to be his ears, eyes and hands in the north among Akrad and the Phoenix Nolmec court for years.'

Mama looked away. 'Yes, between Silisea in the south and the Nolmec in the north, it was a wonder you spent any time in Tarka.'

'True enough, plus the half-year he sent me to Limar when I was barely twelve. It was as though my own father could not take pleasure in my company.' Papa ran a large hand over his face as though to banish painful memories. 'I know I never met his exacting standards.'

Mama's face softened. 'No, he cared about you, Rokku, just ... It was unfortunate that he expected so much of you yet could see no fault in your treacherous younger brother.' She took a deep breath. 'I'd forgotten you'd been to Limar.'

'Did you invite them, Marra?'

Mama coloured. 'No, of course not. Or not exactly. The Sulkan did send a message while you were in Silisea last year, which I answered favourably, but I had not thought anything was arranged and certainly didn't expect an official party to arrive at such an unfortunate time of year.'

'Hmm, you know that they are after our tin mines.'

Mama pulled herself taller, though she still looked small against Papa's tall, broad-shouldered and barrel-chested frame. 'Which no doubt, we can exchange for Limarian goods.'

'Feathers, smoked fish and fripperies.'

Mannok bridled at Papa's tone. 'Gold, woven cloth and fine timber. Maybe increased trade between us is not a bad idea.' Not that he could imagine marriage to Kerri, but if Papa was set against it …

'Hmm.' Papa looked at Mannok between narrowed eyes. 'Well then, there might be something in it. No need to rush into a decision before we can explore all paths. Besides, the hour is late and we're all tired. Certainly, this year's Heavy Rains will not be dull or lacking in diversions.'

Argh! Attending dinners, soirees and pleasure outings until the roads begin to clear in time for the Festival of New Beginnings with the advent of the Lesser Rains. Two alume fending off Kerri's charms along with the other palace beauties. Mannok bit down on a groan. What else could go wrong?

Chapter Six: Witness

Dinnis

The gong for the eighth hour since dawn sounded from the Great Hall. Dinnis picked up his pace along the breezeway connecting the royal kitchens with the main structure of the Golden Palace. He was late for his meeting with Jakan at the western duty room. Over the last ten-day, the demanding Limarian Princess and her overbearing brother could be counted on to distract his prickly half-brother, Mannok, thus avoiding awkward questions about his absences to visit Anna's shop or to attend Laetil on his rounds. Today, Princess Kerri's late rising had delayed the departure of the pleasure ride out to Bridal Veil waterfall till after midday, which, in turn, had complicated his own slipping away from the Prince's age-band.

Dinnis nodded to the stone-faced guards flanking the tall double doors and strode unimpeded into the western atrium. Dinnis' skin prickled.

The tall, cavernous space stood empty of the normal bustle of servants, petitioners and courtiers. Hot white sunlight flooded down from the rectangular opening in the high atrium roof, splintering off the surface of the central pool and splashing the limewashed walls in wavy lines and chevrons. Humid air beaded his upper lip and steamed off ornamental plants and colourful mosaic tiles damp from the morning rain shower. A distant door slammed deep in the Palace complex, dishes clattered in the smaller dining hall across the way, and languid voices droned from the library level above him.

Not unusual during the siesta time, yet the niggling sense of unease remained. He scanned the long atrium a second time, searching for something, anything, untoward. His eyes widened.

The door of the guard duty room gaped open, devoid of the guards usually flanking the entrance, wielding bronze-tipped spears and bristling with annoying questions.

Icy fingers massaged his spine. Dinnis approached the door with slow, cautious steps and peered into the dim-almost-cool of the duty room. Sunlight spilled through the lattice above the door and fell in a net-like pattern on the flagstones.

'Kaptan Jakan?'

No response. No one stood behind the desk or at the entrance to the lower levels. The room lay empty. Empty of guards. Empty of Jakan.

Every instinct urged him to leave, but he couldn't afford to let the Kaptan down. Dinnis skimmed the flat of his hand over his tunic, his shoulders relaxing as his fingers scraped over Kaptan Jakan's package, secure in a fold of his tunic. His age-mates might draw on the need to visit family or attend clan matters and celebrations, but for someone like him with no known ties in the city, running errands for Kaptan Jakan and others in the Palace gave him a legitimate pass for his forays beyond the red walls. And a pass limited the need for more secretive and risky means of escape.

Dinnis stole through the spartan room and down the stairs into the gloom of the lower levels. Wall-bracketed torches flared against lichen-stained walls at long intervals along the empty corridor. Thick stone walls muted the everyday Palace sounds above him. Only the distant drip drip drip of trickling water and the faint splutter of the torches teased his ears.

'Kaptan Jakan?' he called.

His voice rolled back to him, distorted and stuttering. 'Jakan, akan, akan.'

He ducked into the discipline room on his left. The long room remained as bare as a poor widow's treasure chest.

'Slide it! This is ridiculous.' Where was everyone?

The morning was developing a dark dream-like quality. A dream of foreboding, of being abandoned to terrors of the night. Dinnis spun around, his heartbeat stuttering. Was this someone's idea of a joke? He gave himself a shake. While others in the Palace thought it funny to bait him, Jakan had treated him with respect from the moment he'd found Dinnis in the aftermath of the battle for North Pass.

A sudden soft whisper of distant voices echoed from the lower levels of the holding cells.

Dinnis let out a puff of air. That was it. The Kaptan and the guards were dealing with some prisoners, perhaps the Kapok's would-be assassins, Asik and Uson. Uson in particular, might put up a fight, with his heavy build, mean abrasive attitude and the realisation of no hope for a reprieve.

Dinnis rubbed his large nose, the most Tamrin thing about him. Perhaps, he should wait in the duty room. But the sooner he could leave for the library, the better. With a resigned shrug, he set off along the narrow corridor toward the whispering echoes.

The uncertain torchlight cast stripes of ruddy-light and dense shadows through the bars of the empty cells and played over the straw-strewn flagstones and mottled stone walls.

A bizarre dark shape snagged Dinnis' gaze.

Shivers ran down his spine. An almost human shape, though twisted and grotesque.

A stench full of body wastes, mildew and smoke buffeted him. He gagged. Among the foul stinks, an unexpected floral undertone lingered, more like a memory than a sensation.

He took a torch from the nearest wall sconce and thrust it between the bronze bars. A distorted face stared back at him, the contorted body sprawled out in the shadows and rucked-up straw.

A jolt of recognition ran through Dinnis. Uson!

The stubby hands of his former tormentor clawed at the dank shadows, his head arched to meet his back, his lips peeled back in a mirthless grin, his glittering eyes stared into the dark.

Dinnis swallowed down hard. Cold sweat mottled his forehead. He shook the bronze gate of the cell. 'Uson!'

No response, not the flicker of an eyelid, not the twitch of a muscle, not the flutter of the chest, not a wisp of breath. The waxen skin and rigid limbs said it all. His age-mate would never stir again. Dinnis rested his forehead against the rough metal bars. He had no reason to mourn this relentless bully. But no one deserved to die like this.

The voices of the unknowns in the lower levels increased in volume as if they drew closer.

'Guards! We need help here,' he called out and immediately regretted the impulse.

He could do nothing for Uson now and, as recent events had shown, few of the Palace people could see beyond his smoke-blue skin, high cheekbones and oblique eyes inherited from his Nolmec mother. Would they blame him? Of course, they would. Hadn't the guards, Bitjarnan, Mannok and Lukarn all immediately accused him of poisoning the Kapok, despite the fact he was trying save the man's life? A man who had once been his father, until the war had stolen him away.

Time to leave.

Dinnis replaced the guttering torch in its sconce and headed back to the bright light and fresh air of the upper levels.

He'd taken only a few steps when the clatter of boots boomed out from the stairs leading to the duty office. Slide it! Someone was coming this way, blocking his one chance to escape.

Dinnis' first impulse was to head deeper into the prison, but that would only delay discovery. The one secret passageway he'd discovered in this part of the Palace started in the discipline room, close to the entrance off the western atrium. He was caught between the guards above and the guards below and his presence close to Uson's corpse would be harder to explain the longer he lurked down here. Better to tell the truth and hope he'd be believed.

A burly warrior careened around the corner of the corridor leading to the upper levels. A ruddy light gleamed on his bronze chest plate, upper arm rings and a sharp-bladed spear. Lutan Atorak, one of the surlier regulars, a minor noble from the northern Puma clan.

Not good. Not good at all.

Dinnis resisted the urge to edge backwards.

Atorak lunged forward and clamped a meaty hand around Dinnis' arm. 'Hey! What are you doing down here, bluey?' He craned his compact head past Dinnis' shoulder and peered into the cell.

Dinnis gritted his teeth against the man's grinding grip. 'Lutan, I'm glad you heard me. The prisoner, Uson, is in a dire way.'

'Dead, you say?'

'Most likely. Is this the way to treat an age-mate of Prince Mannok?'

'If you murdered the prisoner, it is. Speak up!' Atorak shook Dinnis as though he were a rebellious street urchin in need of chastising.

Stay calm. Stay calm. Stay calm. Dinnis lifted an eyebrow. 'And why would I kill him?'

'You tell me.' Atorak thrust his blunt face forward, the sour smell of maize beer making Dinnis' eyes water. 'Maybe revenge. You can't pretend you were friends. Or to silence him, so he couldn't implicate you in the plot against the Kapok?'

Dinnis' lips thinned into an ironic smile. 'So, I'm his friend *and* his enemy?'

'Don't give me lip,' Atorak growled. 'Why are you here and not with your Prince?'

'I have business with Kaptan Jakan.'

The Lutan's mud-brown orbs glittered. 'In trouble, are we?'

'Always.' Dinnis clenched his teeth. 'But in this case, I completed an errand for the Kaptan in the lower city.' He patted the small parcel with his free hand. How ironical that Atorak blamed him just as the other guards had when he'd attempted to save his father from drinking poison.

'Wipe that smirk off your stinking blue face.' Atorak slapped Dinnis' cheek.

Dinnis' head jerked backwards and a sharp pain splashed over the side of his face. His hands curled into fists. Stay calm. Like a stone.

'Why didn't you leave the package with the duty officer at the entrance?'

Dinnis' lips thinned. 'Perhaps because he wasn't there?' How could Atorak not realise that, since he'd just come through the duty room? Unless, perhaps, the guards were back in position.

'And because, Lutan, I charged Dinnis to hand it to me personally.' Kaptan Jakan strode along from the corridor that led deeper beneath the Palace. The portly quartermaster followed behind him.

Dinnis' tight shoulders relaxed. He could hope for a fair hearing from Kaptan Jakan. A younger son of a minor noble family from the Deer Clan, his jungle green eyes attested to a connection, however tenuous, to the Tamrin royal family. Yet, he was one of the few in the Palace who saw past Dinnis' Nolmec heritage.

Jakan gave Dinnis a brisk nod before stopping in front of Atorak. 'Report, Lutan!'

Atorak brought his fist to his chest. 'Sir, the prisoner Uson is dead. And I found this blu ... er ... delinquent about to escape from the scene.'

Dinnis clicked his tongue. 'I'm a bit slow at it, don't you think, Lutan? The body has cooled and starting to stiffen. Uson must have been dead an hour already.'

Atorak snorted. 'What? Now you're a medic?'

'Lutan, Dinnis makes a good point. Let go of the lad.'

Atorak scowled, but released his grip.

Dinnis rubbed his throbbing arm before pulling out the package and handing it to Jakan. 'What about Asik, Kaptan? Could he be in danger too?'

The drumming clatter of bronze-studded boots hurrying towards them grew louder. Two guards sprinted from the upper corridors. They shoved past Dinnis and came to a standstill before Kaptan Jakan.

The young mop-haired guard banged his fist against his oval chest plate. 'Sir, we've just come on shift and found the duty room unguarded. What orders?'

'We have a dead prisoner.' Jakan pointed his chin towards mop-hair. 'You, fetch the garrison surgeon. And you,' he faced the other taller guard. 'Check on the other prisoner, Asik.'

'Yes, sir.' The guards split up, the one heading towards the duty room and the western atrium, the other heading toward the short dead-end corridor on the right.

Jakan grimaced. 'Let's have a closer look. Dinnis, get us some light.'

Dinnis stepped away from the wall and grabbed the closest torch. 'Lutan, the door.'

Atorak unlocked the cell gate and then stood to one side. 'Phew! What a stink,' he grumbled.

Kaptan Jakan covered his nose with the corner of his cloak before entering the cell. He stepped over the grimy straw on the floor.

Dinnis followed, holding the flickering torch high.

Uson lay in the pall of his own filth. His enlarged pupils swallowed up the brown irises and reflected back the twisting orange flames of the torch. Sullen light skittered over a bare plank bed, a wooden stool, a jug of water and an overturned waste bucket. A tray with food lay slanted against the stool. A reddish-grey mess of half-eaten bean stew congealed at the bottom of a rough clay bowl.

Jakan crouched down and brushed Uson's forehead with the back of his hand. 'Cold as mountain ice.' He placed his ear close to the blue-tinged lips. 'Not breathing either. He's dead alright. The body shows no obvious injury. Looks like poison to me. The same one Uson used on the Kapok, perhaps.' Jakan leant over and slid the eyelids over the sightless eyes.

Dinnis moistened dry lips. 'No, sir, not breathstill.' The mottled bluish tinge of the skin, the dried froth at the mouth and cheeks, the vomit in the straw, the dilated pupils and contortions of the limbs suggested another poison. 'Striken, most likely. Death would have taken an hour with agonising spasms. I'm surprised he didn't call out for help.'

Atorak cleared his throat. 'The prisoner often made a racket over the staleness of the maize bread or the thinness of the blankets or some such silly matter.'

Jakan turned and gave the junior officer a steely look. 'Not such a minor matter this time, Lutan.'

The man's voice nub bobbed in his thick neck. 'No, sir.'

'But why kill Uson now? Everyone knows his sentence will be a walk off Red Leap Cliff.'

Jakan tapped his calloused fingers in a rapid rhythm on his thigh. 'Once we can be sure of why and how, it's a short trip to discovering who.'

Atorak shifted his grip on the shaft of his spear. 'If not murder,' he shot a smouldering look at Dinnis, 'maybe bad food or he caught some weird disease.'

Jakan rubbed his chin. 'Possible, I suppose.'

The Lutan slapped his chest with his fist in salute. 'The ... er Dinnis could help me clean up this mess, sir, and make remains decent for his family to collect.'

Dinnis' lips tightened. 'You forget, he's a war orphan. He has no family.'

Atorak sneered. 'That's right, clanless—like you.'

'Uson's father was a good man, a brave warrior, from the Peccary clan. You didn't fight against the rebellion, did you Lutan?'

Atorak's lips twisted. 'No, sir. Too young, but I remember the war.'

'Who could forget.' Jakan edged around Uson's corpse and headed for the corridor. 'Make sure no one disturbs this area until the garrison surgeon examines him. He might discover more clues.'

Dinnis followed behind Jakan, smothering the itch to find out more. The less he had to do with the investigation, the better.

Something different in the play of light on the straw caught his eye. Despite himself, he stooped to look. A handful of white crumbs glistened in the dirty straw spilling out into the corridor. He scooped up a couple. Red granules clung to the creamy white fragments He rubbed them between his fingers. Oily and pliant. He sniffed them and stifled a sneeze at the spicy bite. Strange.

'Hurry up,' Atorak growled from behind him.

'I found something.'

Jakan turned back, sudden interest in his green eyes. 'What is it, Dinnis?'

'Chilli-coated castana nuts.'

'Is that how the poison was given?'

'Probably in the stew, sir. These nuts wouldn't be the best way to transfer poison. Besides, it's an expensive taste Uson never developed.'

'Hmm, perhaps our assassin likes chilli-coated castana nuts,' Jakan said.

Dinnis nodded. 'Someone stood here a while.' He stopped as the younger guard ran around the corner from the corridor leading to Asik's cells. On reaching them, he stopped to catch his breath. A greenish shade tinged the tan of his face.

'Kaptan, the second prisoner is dead.'

Dinnis' chest tightened. Both dead, most likely poisoned. Both murdered, he was sure of it. If they could be murdered under the noses of the Palace Guard, then both the Kapok and Mannok were under threat. And as hard as he attempted not to, he cared.

Chapter Seven: At the Waterfall

Mannok

Mannok sighed and shifted in the saddle, as frustrated as Shadow with the slow pace of the expedition to the nearby Bridal Veil waterfall. The aroma of rain-soaked earth and pine needles from the nearby stand of trees hung heavy in the air. A perfect afternoon for a gallop, but royal protocol required him to match the pace of their Limarian guests. Now, half the afternoon eaten up, they hadn't yet left the Tari valley.

Prince Dashon rode beside him, his white knuckled hands gripping the reins as though his life depended on it. The Limarian Prince seemed more awkward than even Dinnis on his first ride at the Palace nine years ago. Not that Dashon's glacier-slow pace mattered, as Princess Kerri's massive palanquin progressed at the pace of an algae-tinted sloth from the lower slopes of the Mist Forest. Ten bare-chested bearers carried the ornately carved and heavily curtained litter on broad and calloused shoulders. Even so, the contraption swayed and lurched at each dip or rise in the road. The Princess' Limarian attendants, including her aunt acting as her duenna, and a handful of the noble young ladies of Tamra, followed in lighter, less ornate and more practical litters. Lumi and Rizanna preferred to ride; a custom started by Kupanna Tula and continued by Papa's younger sister, Princess Lakwi. With Dashon's retinue, Mannok's age mates and two-tens of guards, some six-tens of people rode or walked or were carried along the road.

Mannok suppressed a groan. First, his mother had deflected his cobbled-up excuses to avoid this torturous outing she'd proposed while dining with the Limarians last night. Then, this morning, she'd used preparations for the upcoming soiree in honour of the Prince Dashon and Princess Kerri as an excuse to withdraw, leaving 'the young people to enjoy themselves.' Could Mama be less blatant in signalling her wishes?

A sudden breeze ruffled the leaves of the avocado trees edging the fields of maize, giving some relief from the humidity of mid-afternoon. Beside him, Dashon jumped as his mount, a gentle old mare, swished her tail and flicked her ears forward.

Dashon's mouth tightened. 'Is this waterfall much further?'

'Not long now, Prince Dashon.' Mannok pointed with his chin. 'See the dip in that ridge, where the river cuts through to the lower valley? Almost there.' He glanced again at the palanquin struggling to negotiate a bend. 'We could ride ahead—'

'No ... no, this is fine.'

Sometime later, they reached the pass. A screen of trees hid the river but couldn't mute its throaty roar as it plunged over the cliff two hundred tanis high. Dashon pulled his horse to a jerky stop and peered down the path zigzagging its way down into the narrow and less cultivated valley. 'You mean, down there?'

Mannok bit down on a smile. 'It's quite safe.' He pointed with his chin to the forest further down the western side of the valley. 'Madomo Bitjarnan has arranged a small repast in the glade across to the river.'

Dashon's straight nose wrinkled. 'I see. It's .... It's all rather ...'

'Quaint?' Mannok supplied, one eyebrow raised. He grinned. 'Come on.' He encouraged Shadow into a fast walk. The stallion snorted and tossed his head, straining to break into a canter, He should have ridden Mirror this morning as the grand old dame would have fretted less at this tedious pace. Dashon's horse fell in step with Shadow and the Limarian Prince focused on the ride, quiet for a few minutes, apart from a series of sharp intakes of breath.

On one bend, halfway down, they glimpsed a long drop of white water feathering down from the head of the valley before it was once again hidden by trees.

They paused a moment to look and to allow the cumbersome palanquin to catch up.

'Oh, qua … pretty, I guess.' Gripping the horn of the saddle, Dashon scanned the steep rocky sides of the valley. 'Are your famed mines around here?'

Mannok frowned. 'Mines?'

'Yes. Tamra is renowned for its tin and copper mines, after all.'

'Of course, and gold, silver, precious stones, even some rare iron. The mountains give us many riches.' So Papa was right, the Limarians were interested in Tamra's mineral wealth such as tin, essential for the making of bronze-tipped weapons wielded by warriors. But what could these pale cousins from the south offer Tamra, apart from a royal bride? He squirmed. He would have to do his duty to the Throne someday and present his parents with heirs. Even one of the Palace ladies like Lumi or a Silisean royal would be preferable to this spoilt and simpering Limarian Princess. Was that Mama's strategy, to corral him into committing himself to one of her other choices out of sheer relief at escaping this one?

' … and other riches too.' Dashon was saying, a spark in his basalt-blue eyes. 'Limar could offer you the best work in fine gold, exquisite pottery, other treasures, culture and history. It is to mutual advantage to recommence the trade between the two premier nations, not seen since the time that Princess Sheeva, daughter of the Sulkan, married Lokan Kapok over a hundred years ago.'

'Um, yes.' Mannok's brows wrinkled. At times like this, he wished he'd paid more attention to Ralton's interminable history lessons.

Dashon waved a pale hand. 'Of course, ancient history. But it would be … desirable, don't you think? Indeed, past time to reforge closer links between the two greatest countries of the Five Lands.' He turned, one hand gripping the saddle horns. 'It would be good to be brothers, no?'

No. Not. Ever. 'Are not all Filane, brothers and sisters? Children of the Five from across the Lapis Ocean?' Mannok flashed a smile and then focused on the steeper trail leading into the valley.

Once the trail levelled out, Mannok led the party to a shallow ford across the braided stream. Once on the other side, he urged Shadow into a slow trot toward a flat grassy area beneath the green shade of giant ceiba, red beech and mountain willows. Palace servants, sent ahead of the main party, busied themselves in spreading out woven cloths, rugs and cushions, and in laying out trays of food and drinks. A light mist from the falls cooled the air. Small birds flittered in the branches of the trees. The musical calls tinkled like bells above the muted roar of the nearby falls.

Mannok swung off Shadow and assisted Dashon in dismounting while a servant ran up to take the horses. Moments later, the rest of the party arrived and the bearers settled the palanquin in the middle of the glade. Garvin and the rest of his band dismounted and rushed to attend to the ladies.

'Have we arrived at last?' An imperious voice came from the curtained palanquin.

A pale hand covered in sparkling rings, then slim wrist swathed in bangles appeared and pulled aside the brocaded curtains. A gauzy scarf, sparkling with tiny seed pearls and crystals, circled the butter-yellow hair and swept across the Princess' face leaving bare, two sky-blue eyes staring at him with disdain.

Mama's instructions rushed to the surface of his mind. 'Mannok, whatever your personal feelings, don't neglect your duties as a Prince of Tamra, and future Kapok.' With a supressed sigh, he stepped toward the palanquin.

'May I?' He offered his arm.

Princess Kerri took it and leant her shapely form against him. A heavy cloud of perfume from some exotic flower caught his throat and his chest tightened.

Kerri stepped out of the palanquin into the glade. Rather than releasing his arm, she gripped tighter. 'Thank you, my dear gallant Prince. Where are these wonders, you wish to show me?'

'This way, Princess.' Matching his stride to her dainty steps, he led her through the overarching trees back along the valley, the sound of water rushing over the edge growing louder with each step. After one hundred tanis, they stepped into hazy sunlight.

White water fell in lacy sheets from above a high cliff into a rock-ringed pool. Iridescent ripples and creamy foam played across the tannin-dark surface. Spray drenched the ferns and rocks coated with lichen and emerald-green moss. Mountain lilies grew in profusion on the far bank beneath the trees. Trailing pink flowers attracted jewel-like hummingbirds and brilliant butterflies.

For a moment, Mannok stood still. In this hidden place, the world of the Palace with its intrigue and concealed threats seemed to fade. He'd praise it with lyrical words and fine phrases—if he'd inherited even a thread of Papa's skill with words.

'It's …,' Kerri tilted her petite head and smothered a yawn. '… quaint.'

Mannok clenched his jaw, surprised he didn't hear his teeth crack. If he heard that word one more time … He took a deep breath, then another.

'Isn't it glorious, Your Highnesses?' Lady Lumi strolled toward them.

Dressed in a deep blue tunic and cloak, edged with shells embroidered in gold thread, her silver eyes shimmered with amusement. His cousin Rizzi, Uncle Lukarn's eldest daughter, followed close behind, for once not bubbling over with enthusiasm.

'As you say, Lady Lumi. Bridal Veil Falls is reputed to be a place shrouded in legends.' Not that he could remember whether Namu and Solik or Tamrak and Ateva or some other couple met here. 'The name—'

'Yes, nice.' Kerri interrupted. 'Not far from Kuza, the Sulkan holds the festival of the Coming Rains at the Nine Tiers waterfall each year.' Kerri looked Lumi and Rizzi up and down and then glanced away as though dismissing the daughters of Markans and granddaughters of Tellek Kapok as having little importance. Instead, she stared into his eyes. 'I do hope you can see it someday. Kuza is three times the size of your walled city and Lake Tinaki is as wide as the sea. Such amazing things I could show you, Prince Mannok.'

'That would be … delightful, I'm sure.' Any boyhood desire to see the far-off wonders of Kuza scattered like cavies fleeing an eagle's hunting dive. 'Perhaps you would care to partake of refreshments, Your Highness?'

The Princess Kerri wrinkled her nose and pulled her gauzy overdress about her thin shoulders. 'Do you often eat outdoors like common folk?'

'It provides a welcome break from Palace routine, don't you think?' Garvin walked up to them, Hasuk, Trasin, Kimsak and Yalik not far behind, each escorting a Limarian maiden.

Kerri looked down her squib of a nose. 'And you are?'

Mannok frowned. 'Garvin is one of my age-mates, son of Kaptan Kaspin of the Yarma Clan.' Wasn't that the fifth time he'd reminded her? 'Yalik is son of Markan Amaruk and Princess Lakwi, Kimsak is Markan Lukarn's third son and Trasin, like Adjunct Puran, is the son of Lord Challak.'

'Oh, yes.' Her gaze flitted over each of the young warriors and rested on Estolik and Durrin, now chatting to Puran. Her eyes glazed over and she stifled another yawn. 'This would be so much pleasanter if it were a smaller, more intimate group like the dinner last night.' She stepped closer and walked her fingernails up Mannok's arm. He flushed as his body responded to her touch.

Her signalling was hardly subtle—giving the same message as her brother. The Limarians wanted Tamrin metals, and the Sulkan's daughter would offer her charms, such that they were, to sway him. Did she not feel reduced to common trade goods, like he sometimes did? A bargaining piece in the game of state? Despite her sophisticated airs, she looked about his own age, seventeen, maybe younger and maybe even a little scared beneath the haughty pride.

He disentangled himself from her clinging grip. Ista would never have degraded herself like this. Kerri might be a Sulkan's daughter, but he found her company tedious. He couldn't, wouldn't, marry her. Not now. Not next year. Not ever.

Chapter Eight: Nightfall

Lumi

Light bled from the purple-dark sky, taking the heat with it. Stars winked into existence and the silver moon, Argenti, rose plump and bright above the mountains in the east. A sudden brisk wind whipped down from the snowy peaks encircling the valley. Behind Lumi, a line of flaring torches curled across the valley. She shivered and pulled her cloak tighter. If the trip out had been slow, the return trip straggled along as sluggish as an ice-choked river. She didn't know how many more of these pleasure outings she could endure.

A couple of tanis ahead, the pale oval of Princess Kerri's face and her long slender pale arms flashed between the half-drawn curtains of the ridiculous palanquin. Mannok kept pace with her, sitting tall on his restive stallion, his head tilted toward her, as if to hear every single inane word from her painted mouth.

The Prince had a commanding physique and he moved with such grace and power. His wide shoulders, muscular build, trim waist set her pulse racing. The silent Limarian Prince riding on the other side of Mannok could not match him. Though of similar height and richer attire, the Limarian's slender build and foppish mien lacked appeal.

Lumi couldn't name the day when the transformation from annoying cousin to attractive and brooding young warrior occurred. Sometime after Rokkan Kapok rejected Father's proposal she marry the Kapok's only son to amalgamate the interests of the two great noble houses in Tamra. Lumi bit down on her lip till it hurt. What once would have been laughable, now seemed achingly desirable. Even if the Kapok's veto didn't block the way, Mannok accorded her only polite courtesy. As far as he was concerned, she might as well not exist.

She pulled her cloak over her head against the chilly edge of night and blinked moisture from her eyes. Leaning forward, she urged her mare, Caramel, into a fast walk and caught up with an unusually subdued Lady Rizanna riding on Snow Flake a few paces behind the Limarian palanquin.

'What a fun day it's been.' Lumi kept her voice low, to prevent her words carrying to the Limarian royalty in front of them, though she doubted either understood sarcasm.

Rizanna continued to stare at the Palace guard carrying a torch walking beside them.

'Rizzi,' she said a little louder. 'It's not like you to be so quiet. Are you well?'

Rizanna jolted, then turned and smiled. 'No, not at all. I mean yes, of course, I'm well, silly.' Rizzi's hazel eyes reflected back the twirling flames of a nearby torch. 'Watching that snake of a woman wrap herself around Mannu would make anyone feel sick.'

Lumi smothered a peal of laughter with her hand.

'It's not funny. She has no shame, clinging to him like an overgrown jungle vine,' Lady Rizanna hissed in Lumi's ear. 'Do you think they'll announce the marriage soon?'

'Not if Mannok has a say. He's being polite, but he likes her as much as we do.' Mannok's words and actions followed Palace protocol, without even a hint of his usual impish sense of humour, but the tension in every line of his body, the tight jaw and the tiny arrow-like crinkle between his eyebrows betrayed his true feelings.

Rizzi huffed out a sigh. 'Maybe, but if Uncle Rokkan insists, he won't have a choice.'

'The Kapok hasn't forced the issue so far. He wants Mannok to choose.'

'I know, but maybe he was waiting for an opportunity like this. I'll die if this Kerri becomes a Princess of Tamra, the next Kupanna. Can you imagine it?'

'I'd rather not.' Lumi's stomach twisted at the thought. The marriage of a Prince was a state issue of critical importance to the good of the realm. Father hammered that lesson into her at every opportunity. Nobles, particularly those of royal blood, married first and foremost to make suitable alliances for the good of the country and to strengthen the position and status of their family. It was a daughter—and a son's—duty to obey, whatever their personal wishes. Lumi swallowed hard. A bitter cup indeed, not only to lose Mannok to that woman, but to live with whatever alternative match her father planned for her. She feared he leaned toward that lout Durrin, to further strengthen the alliance with his odious father, Lord Durak, Markan of the Southern Marches.

They approached the city now, some seven hundred tanis away. The final embers of sunlight tinged the higher slopes of the Twin mountains. The horizon star shone like a beacon in the fading sky. Most of the city nestled in shadows, only the Palace and the watch fire on the apex of temple platform shone in the ocean of darkness.

Several moments later, shouts rang out from the city and torches bobbed along the city wall, indicating the presence of more than the usual guard. The city gates swung open and a party of warriors galloped towards them.

'Halt!' The Prince's commanding voice rang out.

His age-mates and Lutan Puran, of the Puma clan and in charge of the guards, urged their horses toward him, ready to defend their Prince.

Mannok turned on Shadow, his gaze sweeping the surroundings. 'Guards, close ranks. Don't leave the column unguarded. Lutan Puran, see if you can hurry up the stragglers.'

'Come on, Rizzi,' Lumi whispered. She urged Caramel to close the gap between them and Mannok. Rizanna shook her head, her bronzed face pale in the torchlight. She did not follow.

In front of Lumi, the palanquin lurched to an abrupt stop, swaying on the shoulders of the bearers. The Limarian Princess squealed and gripped corner posts.

'Are we under threat?' she demanded.

Prince Dashon dismounted, his retinue closing in around him and the palanquin, jostling against Lumi.

'What's going on? I demand answers.' Dashon said, his voice high-pitched. 'My father will not be pleased if we come to any harm on your lands.'

50

'Calm yourself, Your Highness,' Mannok replied. 'My warriors will counter any threat to you and your sister.'

Moments later, the horsemen from the city thundered up.

Kaptan Kaspin vaulted from his horse and knelt on the path before the Prince. 'Your Highness.'

'Kaspin, report.'

'The Kapok and Kupanna were concerned with your late arrival, Your Highness, especially following an incident in the Palace earlier today. I'm relieved to see you safe.'

'Yes, we're fine.' Mannok grimaced. 'The bearers found the slope into Veil Valley harder to transverse than we'd expected.' His eyes narrowed. 'What incident? Is the Kapok, my father, well? Has anyone been hurt?'

Kaptan Kaspin brought his fist to his chest. 'The two prisoners, Uson and Asik, were found dead in their cells not long after you left, Your Highness. When you hadn't returned by nightfall, His Majesty was concerned.'

Lumi leant forward and stroked Caramel's neck. All this fuss about two miscreants, though she could see why the Prince's late return could cause worry, though more likely Kupanna Marra raised the alarm than the Kapok.

Mannok frowned. 'Both dead, you say? How?'

'We are investigating. Though the Royal Physician assures us—'

'Dead? Are we safe? This is not acceptable,' Kerri shrilled.

Mannok's jaw tightened. He lifted his head a moment, then turned to the Limarian visitors. 'Your safety is assured. My father will have things under control.' He turned back. 'Kaptan, may I suggest we take our guests to the safety of the Palace at once.'

Garvin, cleared his throat. 'If speed is required, perhaps the Princess should transfer to a faster litter or go by horseback.'

'Imbecile, I cannot ride and my dignity and comfort ...'

'... are important, sister.' Dashon scanned the silent dark fields, with only the occasional light in a nearby village. 'But our safety is more so.'

Mannok ran a hand through his unruly hair. 'Princess, you would do me honour riding behind me on Shadow. The guards will ensure the rest of your retinue returns safely.'

The Princess quivered. 'Ride behind you? Do you mean to insult me?'

'Sister, I counsel you to accept the Prince of Tamra's offer.'

Lumi shook her head. It was Mannok who honoured the Princess, but of course the Limarians would not see it that way.

Kerri paled, if that was possible in a face already the colour of bone. Beneath the jewels and gold, the gauzy clothes and painted mouth, she looked suddenly young and out of her depth. Little more than sixteen, maybe even younger than she and Rizzi.

Lumi leant forward. 'The Prince will take care of you, Your Highness. You need not fear falling.'

Kerri nodded and swallowed. 'As you wish,' she whispered.

Her attendants helped her out of the palanquin and Mannok reached down, pulling her up behind him as though she weighed no more than one of her gauzy scarfs. With a squeal, she hugged his waist, her long dress flowing over Shadow's rump like a pale veil.

Heat surged to Lumi's cheeks and chest. If only she could enjoy such intimate closeness with the Prince.

The Prince's band and half Kaspin's guards formed around Mannok and Dashon.

'Lutan Puran, you are now in charge. Make sure the rest come back safely.' Mannok dug his heals in and Shadow shot forward. The group galloped off toward the Palace.

The dour northern lord, Puran, son of Challak rode to the front. 'Let's keep moving.'

Lumi urged Caramel into a walk. The clip-clop of Snow Flake came from behind her. 'What's the fuss about?' Rizzi asked, a quiver in her soft voice.

Lumi shrugged. 'We were late and some prisoners died. Usa and Sika, something like that.'

'Oh, you mean the war-orphans, Uson and Asik, that attempted to kill the Kapok?'

Lumi shivered. Yes, of course, that was their names. What horrid beasts. 'They were commoners, weren't they? I'm surprised they weren't already executed.'

'Uncle Rokkan accorded them the right of trial before the full Council at Festival of New Beginnings, as they were age-mates of the Prince.'

Lumi shook her head. The Kapok could be quite idealistic. Her father, Lord Haka, often railed against his penchant for elevating common people at the expense of noble families.

'I wonder how they died?'

Rizzi grunted. 'Does it matter? Mannok and Uncle Rokkan will surely be safer with them dead.'

What could she say to that? They rode the rest of the way to the city in silence.

Chapter Nine: Clues

Dinnis

Dinnis shifted his position on the desk in Kaptan Jakan's office and bit into a sunfruit, careful not to drip juice on his book. Beyond the ordered corridors of the command offices, the Palace hummed like a disturbed beehive. The flurry of indoor entertainments, banquets and often rain-drenched outings in honour of the southern guests continued unabated, despite Uson and Asik's murders nine days ago. Not that the lack of concern for the condemned prisoners surprised Dinnis. Guilty of attempted regicide, they had boasted few ties to the nobility or even clan connections to extended family. Most would argue that they deserved their fate, yet it troubled Dinnis that their lives counted for so little.

The clatter of footsteps in a familiar no-nonsense gait came from outside the office. Dinnis slipped off the desk, ducking his head to avoid the low-hanging lantern. He tucked the book under his arm just as the door of the office swung open.

Kaptan Jakan strode into the room, concern etched on his honest face. The Kaptan removed his headdress and threw it onto a bronze wall hook. He turned toward the desk.

'By the pit.' He jerked backwards, unsheathing his hunting knife. 'Dinnis!' His stance relaxed a hair's breadth. 'By the moons, lad, you're fortunate I didn't gut you. I thought you'd still be helping your Prince escort the Limarian guests.'

'Sir!' Dinnis assumed a more or less soldierly stance. 'The Kupanna arranged a boating party on the palace lake. No room for low-level underlings like me. Lutan Atorak said you wanted to see me.'

'Yes, I did, though I expected you later and I certainly didn't expect you to be standing in the middle of my office.' Jakan sheaved his broad-bladed knife, the frown not easing from his face.

A twinge of disquiet shifted in Dinnis' midriff. The last time Jakan wore that look was just before the attack on the Kapok. 'I can come back later, sir.'

'No, best to get this over with.'

That didn't sound good at all. 'As you wish, sir.'

The Kaptan threw his cloak on the hook next to the headdress. He walked past Dinnis and settled into the chair behind the old battle-scarred desk. A bronze ink pot, a stylus engraved with turquoise, a huge ledger and a box of parchments made an ordered geometric pattern on the otherwise cleared surface.

'Is that a book under your arm, Dinnis? What are you reading?' Jakan curled his fingers in a give-it-to-me gesture.

Dinnis hesitated only a second before handing it over. 'Kaisak's *The History of the War with Shanta*. Did you know there are some pages missing and sections that appear struck out?'

'That surprises me, given Ralton is more protective of his tomes than a jaguar of her cubs. The Shanti War, huh? Interesting topic.'

Jakan flipped through the pages for a moment or two before laying the book on the table. He leaned forward in the chair and tented his fingers. 'In the holding cells the other day, you mentioned striken as the possible cause of death.'

So that was what this was about. 'Yes. The signs left little doubt.' Dinnis tucked his hands in his tunic, his fingers itching to retrieve the book. If he didn't return it in one piece, Ralton would tear strips off his hide, maybe literally.

Jakan sat up straighter in the chair and cleared his throat. 'The Kapok gives the matter the utmost importance. We need to know who killed the lads and why. The garrison surgeon, Fulik, agreed striken may have caused the deaths, but Galen dismissed the idea. He believes it due to spoiled food or perhaps a miasma in the cells.

'What? That's rid—' Dinnis clamped down on his words. Criticising the judgement of the royal physician wasn't wise, even if he was a second-rate charlatan.

'The Kapok agrees with your assessment, Dinnis. No one else was affected, only those two and in suspicious circumstances.' The Kaptan fingered the carved leather cover of *The History*. 'The question is, why kill them? They were marked for death. Unless someone had a personal score to settle?'

'Who?' Dinnis caught the pointed look in Jakan's eyes. 'You don't mean me?' The twinge became a squirm. His stomach twisted. 'Am I being interrogated?'

For once, Jakan's face gave nothing away. 'It's my job to consider every possibility. For a companion of the Prince, you seemed to have detailed knowledge about the particular poisons used. Breathstill, wasn't it, and now striken?'

So, it was an interrogation. Dinnis kept his face void of expression. While he suspected Rokkan knew something, he needed to keep his arrangement with Anna and Laetil hidden in case Sparak saw his friends as a threat. Anyway, telling the truth might make him look more suspect not less.

'Answer the question, lad.'

Dinnis shrugged and fell back on a flippant response. 'That's not common knowledge?'

Jakan slammed the heel of his hand on the desk, making the book, ink jar and stylus jump. 'Dinnis, bury the manure and answer my question.'

'Yes, sir.' So, a partial truth. 'I've been collating a compendium on plants and their uses for Head Librarian Ralton. I'm interested in the medicinal and culinary properties of a range of plants.'

Jakan raised his eyebrows. 'Including their fatal effects. You have the knowledge and those two made your life difficult. Uson baited you every chance he had. As Atorak reminds me, you had reason to see them die.'

'Even if I wasted time yearning for revenge,' though he had for years following the Kapok's betrayal, 'I only needed to wait for the Palace to exact its punishment.'

'The Council hadn't delivered its verdict yet.'

'And you doubt what it would've been? Any physical attack on the Kapok warrants death under Tamrin law and custom. Even perceived dishonour or insult of our noble ruler could result in the living death of the lead mines, or a sanctioned walk off the edge of the Red Leap to ravine below.'

'By rule and custom, yes, but not one Rokkan Kapok has evoked since the end of the rebellion. Besides, when a grudge is personal, so too the need for revenge. Perhaps Palace justice was too slow for you.'

And he'd thought Jakan a friend. 'Uson is ... was ... a bully. I'm not going to pretend his imprisonment or even his impending sentence kept me awake at night, but I didn't wish him dead and I didn't kill him.' Dinnis dug the toes of his boots into the yarma-wool rug on the flagstone floor. 'Besides, Uson died some time before I found him.'

'So you claim. But, no one saw you arrive.'

'Because the guards weren't at their posts.' Dinnis raised an eyebrow. 'Lutan Atorak admits to hearing Uson's death throes over an hour before. Did he see anyone enter?'

'He was sorting in the records room and assumed one of the duty guards would deal with it.'

'And you were deep in the storerooms most of the morning. You didn't hear them?'

'No, Dinnis, the walls are thick down there and when we attempted to ascend, the door was jammed. Took us some time to free it.'

'Did the duty guards see anyone?'

'No. The duty guards left their posts at midday.'

Dinnis blinked. 'Over an hour early? How is that possible?' No wonder Jakan had a smouldering fire under him today. Adjunct Puran, as acting chief of the Kapok's security in Lukarn's and Waren's absence, would be steaming like a volcano at the rank incompetence or, worse, outright treason.

Jakan narrowed his eyes. He ran a hand through the thick mahogany-brown hair, silver threaded above his ears. 'The roster board marked the wrong finish time. Altered or wrongly set. And yes, they should have stayed no matter how late their replacements, but all four were newly-arrived, levied from the villages, green and tender as new bean shoots.'

'So, whoever did the roster ...'

'I did. Someone swapped out the more experienced guards I'd paired with the new arrivals. It seems we are looking for a person good at sneaking into places they shouldn't be. Someone good with a pen.' Jakan stood up and leaned forward on his hands. 'Any idea who that might be, Dinnis?'

Dinnis met the Kaptan's piercing gaze without flinching. 'Or maybe a duty officer with access to the rosters. I can't be the only literate person in the Palace.' Did the Kaptan really suspect him of arranging Uson and Asik's deaths. For revenge? Perhaps slipping into Jakan's office to wait hadn't been a smart idea. 'What about the maid who took the tray of food to the prisoners? Did she see anything?'

'The girl assigned to the duty found the tray gone and none of the other maids admit to taking it. Though, the guards in the breezeway noted a tallish girl coming from the kitchens bearing a laden tray just before midday. Do you know who she is, Dinnis?'

'No. Why would I?'

'I've been questioning a lot of the staff and the guards over the last few days. You've earned some popularity among the lower echelons of the Palace with your small herbal remedies and running of errands. Seems you're a lot more social than I gave you credit for.'

'My apologies, I didn't know making friends was a crime.'

'So, I ask again. Who is the girl?'

'I don't know. None of the kitchen maids I met could be called tall.'

'You have a motive and knowledge of the poison used. You could have altered the roster. You have friends among the kitchen staff. And you were discovered near Uson's body.' Jakan thrust out his jaw. 'So tell me, what were your exact movements that day? Can anyone confirm them?'

Dinnis folded his arms, pushing down the burning urge to shout. 'I broke fast early in the bachelor quarters, attended the Prince and other age-mates in the practice yards until an hour before midday, then ran an errand for you, returning a little late to deliver your parcel at the arranged time and place. Finding the duty room was unattended, I searched for you in the holding cells. I discovered Uson's corpse and called for help. That's when Lutan Atorak arrived, followed by you and the quartermaster shortly afterwards.'

'A simple errand that should have taken less than an hour, but you were absent for, what three hours? Why?'

This was the tricky bit. 'I had a few other errands that day from Ralton, the Head Cook and one from the Kennel Master. And since I was not required to attend the Prince, I ate the midday meal in the city before returning. The guards at the Palace gate can vouch for when I left and when I returned.' He'd taken a quick meal with

Anna, Tilli, and family, before accompanying Laetil on his rounds, but no need to tell Jakan that.

'Did you go into the kitchens to deliver the Head Cook's order? The Guards at the breezeway entrance said you entered that way.'

'Then, they would have told you I came from the practice yards, not the kitchens. I came direct from the goods gate to deliver your package first, before Ralton's inks. Sanak and Turuk didn't need their orders until later in the day. The guards at the goods gate will confirm when I returned.' Unless they were bribed to say otherwise.

Jakan tapped the desk with his fingers. He levered himself up and paced behind the desk. 'They agree that you returned to the Palace moments before the discovery of the body.'

Relief flooded through Dinnis.

'Which would be reassuring if you weren't so adept at sneaking in and out of the Palace. Dinnis, you're smart enough to make a covert entry, do the deed, sneak out and then be seen by the gate guards to prove your innocence.'

'Slide it, if that were the case, I would've gone somewhere else, like the library.' Dinnis took a deep breath and released the tension from his shoulders. He had to stay calm. 'Kaptan, I didn't kill those two, certainly not for revenge. If I poisoned everyone who insulted me or annoyed me, then half the people in the Palace might be dead by now.'

A choked-off laugh escaped Jakan. 'That is not a particularly reassuring thought.' He sat down and flipped the pages of *The History*. 'Both Uson and Asik claimed they were the sole instigators behind the attack on Rokkan Kapok, despite constant and close questioning for a full cycle of the golden moon.'

'It's unlike Uson not to find someone else to blame for his failures.'

Jakan raised an eyebrow. 'Indeed. Neither of those young blades seemed to realise the severity of their situation, whether through stupidity or some false hope of rescue or even reward. But that confidence wore thin as ten-days passed in the cells. In the days before their deaths, Uson hinted at a possible mastermind. Someone who wanted the Kapok dead.'

Dinnis ran a hand over his forehead and cropped hair. 'Why would I wish to kill the Kapok, my benefactor?' Slide it, he'd failed to keep a touch of irony out of his voice.

'You tell me, Dinnis. Why would you want the Kapok dead?'

'I don't. My loyalties and my allegiance remain with my ... His Majesty, the Kapok, and my Prince. You're looking in the wrong direction.'

'And what direction should we be looking in?' Jakan tilted his head.

Dinnis shrugged and stared at the angular patterns woven into the rustic rug at his feet. Was this interrogation at his father's instigation? Had he rescinded his promises of trust and friendship? Perhaps he should have taken up Rasel's offer to go with her Kin, all those years ago. 'Someone who wants the Kapok and his son dead?'

'Someone with the motive to kill them. You were at North Pass.'

'Yes, obviously.'

'Before the battle.'

Dinnis opened his mouth 'I ...'

'Remember, I was there. I saw you come from the postern gate, a skinny kid lost in the middle of the battle.'

'So, I thought my father had come to rescue me.' Had Rokkan told Jakan the full truth? He couldn't assume so. 'Akrad was holding us ... me hostage following his advance on Pylonis.'

Jakan's eyes widened and then narrowed. 'So you were at the Phoenix Nolmec court? Do you remember seeing the Kapok ... or the Prince Royal as he was then?'

'I was a small child and the only Tamrin that interested me was my father. If I'd suspected I'd end up in the heart of Tamra, I might have taken more notice of their names and ranks.' His mother had been the Kiprissa, with bloodline as noble and ancient as any Tamrin royalty. Not that that fact had ever worked in his favour.

'Are you working for the Nolmec, Dinnis?'

'No.' How could Jakan ask that after all these years? 'And I don't think the Phoenix Nolmec want Rokkan dead.'

'That is hardly reassuring. You claim your father was Tamrin.'

'Yes, a ... a warrior who came and went on his Kapok's interests. He died at ...'

'... the battle of North Pass. You were looking for him. I remember. You didn't mention he was dead then.'

'I ...' Dinnis took a deep breath and brushed his fingers over the wood of the desk. 'I thought he was still alive. The Kapok informed me of his death when I arrived at Tarka.'

'I don't remember you ever mentioning his name.'

The hair lifted at the back of Dinnis' neck. He looked down at his long grey-blue fingers and white half-moons at the base his fingernails. Fingers stained with ink and calloused by the bowstring. No one had asked that before.

Jakan raised his eyebrows. 'It's a simple question, Dinnis.'

He kept his tone casual. 'Trust me, sir, it's not. If you want to know more, you should ask the Kapok.' He met Jakan's gaze straight on. 'Though it might be better for your health if you didn't.'

Jakan held his gaze for a few minutes, understanding seeping into his eyes. He opened his mouth. Closed it. Swallowed. Gave a small nod. 'Right. I've sometimes wondered.' He seemed to collect his thoughts. 'The history of war, of conquest, a fascinating topic.'

'The fall of Shanta, like most wars, brought tragedy and pain.'

'Winners and losers, Dinnis. Have you ever dreamed of ruling? Maybe you could do it better than others, with your intelligence and passion.'

'Even if I had a valid claim to the Throne, one that the Tamrin would acknowledge, success would only be possible with the backing of powerful clan leaders.'

Jakan gave him a searching look. 'Stranger things have happened. Akrad ...'

'I am not Akrad.' Dinnis struggled to contain the sudden fire coursing through him. 'I saw enough death to last a lifetime at North Pass. I'd rather heal than kill.'

'Yes.' Jakan sat back in his chair, his green eyes clouding for a moment. 'You always miss the quarry in the hunt, even at point blank range.'

Dinnis hitched a shoulder. 'What can I say. I'm a terrible marksman.'

'And a good liar and too clever and secretive for your own good.'

'Instead of wasting your time on me, look to someone who wants to sit on the Throne.'

Jakan nodded. 'Right. With the exception of Prince Mannok, that would be most likely Haka and his heirs, and, at a long stretch, Amaruk or Lukarn. All of them were many lek away in their clan lands at the time of the murders.'

Dinnis sighed. 'A usurper would only need people to act for him, while he remains in the shadows.' Like Akrad used Tellek and Naetok.

Jakan gave a rueful laugh. 'I don't disagree. Either way, someone in the Palace killed the lads, either for their own reasons or as agent of another. If we find the accomplice, we're one step closer to discovering the mastermind.'

'And a noble or at least someone with an important position with a taste for chillied castana nuts.' Dinnis shrugged. 'Someone who maybe interrogated him, maybe stood there and watched Uson die.'

'And until we uncover who, the Kapok's life remains at risk. I intend to find him and smash the miscreant like a bug.'

'I hope you do, sir. I assure you, that person is not me.'

The Palace gong sounded the eighth hour.

'Have you finished turning me on the roasting spit? Do you mean to arrest me or can I leave?'

Jakan closed the book and handed it back to Dinnis. 'For now.'

'Kaptan.' Dinnis brought his fist to his chest with exaggerated flourish. He turned to go.

'Just a moment. You should know, the Kapok has curtailed all unnecessary outings from the Palace grounds. And,' Jakan puffed out his cheeks, 'he's given orders that the Silisean Palace be prepared to accommodate the Limarians, since they seem in no hurry to leave. Seems some of the trees along the wall need pruning back.'

Dinnis paused. 'What, am I on gardening duty now?' Slide it, that was his best unobserved way out of the Palace.

'You're hilarious.' Jakan stepped forward and gripped Dinnis' shoulder. 'I'm inclined to believe you, Dinnis. I'd even wager someone has tried hard to set you up. It's my job to protect the Kapok first and his family second. The stability of the realm depends on it. I can't afford to trust anyone, not you, not the Prince, not even myself.' He sighed. 'I had to ask. It was me or Sparak. I thought you might prefer me.'

Dinnis shivered. 'I'm surprised he didn't insist.'

'He did, but the Kapok intervened on your behalf. Just stay out of trouble.'

'I'll try to.' Maybe his father hadn't abandoned him again. Maybe his words were not empty promises.

'If you're at a loss for something to do, you could help Lutan Atorak in the armoury.'

Dinnis grimaced. 'Thanks, but I don't think the good Lutan likes me. Besides, Ralton is expecting me.'

Jakan waved him away 'There's not many who would willingly brave Ralton's acerbic tongue. Now, get out of here.' Jakan pulled a stack of parchment toward him and inked his stylus. 'And next time, wait for me outside like any normal person.'

'Yes, sir.' Dinnis exited the room. It seemed he'd be confined to the Palace grounds, at least during the investigation. If only he could remove himself from the stew of palace politics, once and for all.

Chapter Ten: Just a Dream

Dinnis

The crack of colliding spear shafts exploded across the practice range. Dinnis edged further back toward the looming three-storey wall of the Palace, one arm looped around his leather-bound book. The dazzling blue-white disc of the sun slipped from the top of the sky towards the mountains in the west, its light splintering off the shrinking puddles from the brief morning shower.

Dinnis grimaced. With this final bout between the two winners, the early afternoon sparring session edged closer to a welcome end. He'd been careful to be eliminated early on.

Estolik countered the Prince's sudden thrust with the padded practice spear. Mannok retaliated with a burst of powerful strikes. Forced backward toward the railing, Estolik sidestepped at the last moment and stumbled out of range.

'Go, Prince Mannok,' Garvin yelled from where he perched on the railings. Other age-mates joined in.

'Keep your guard up, Essu,' Durrin countered. 'You can take him.'

Dream on, Durrin. Mannok's technique was flawless, his focus sharp, his instincts impeccable. Odds were, he would win—and not just because it was considered discourteous to allow the heir to the Golden Throne to lose. An unspoken rule that Durrin and Estolik seemed determined to ignore and, to his credit, Mannok hated.

Dinnis stifled a yawn. He would have skipped weapons practice, but his alternatives were limited. True to Jakan's warning a couple of ten-days ago, Adjunct Puran clamped down on passes to the city, and worse, the Palace guards and Limarians swarmed the secondary palace, blocking his back-up escape route. The only way past the high red-painted walls of the Palace was in the company of the Prince. Anna would understand his continued absence, he only hoped Tilli and Laetil would too.

Dinnis adjusted his grip on the charcoal stick and sketched without thought. The clash of spears and the thud of feet a distant backdrop as the lines of a figure took shape.

Dogs yapped in the royal kennels and a horse whinnied from the Palace stables to his right. An answering whinny came from the entrance courtyard of the Palace, no doubt new arrivals. With the easing of the rains, a stream of nobles and clan hopefuls began arriving in the city for the Festival of New Beginnings. This year, Kimsak, Kontar and the other younger lads would undergo the Trial of Tears after the New Beginnings banquet in a few days. On the southern side of the practice yards, came the discordant music of pots clashing and cooks shouting, as they prepared for the Kupanna's afternoon entertainment.

A roar went up from the practice ground.

'Dolphin, Dolphin, Dolphin.'

'Jaguar, Jaguar, Jaguar.'

Estolik and Mannok circled each other, their sweat-slicked skin gleaming in the sunlight. Both working for breath, both tiring, but the strain more obvious on the stouter warrior. Mannok closed in.

Not long now then.

Maybe tomorrow, he should ask Ralton if he needed an extra scribe for library duties. Though the lower the profile he kept at the moment, the better. He'd heard nothing further regarding the murder investigation. Dinnis' jaw tensed and his skin dappled with sweat. For years afterwards, the visceral sights, sounds and smells of the battle at North Pass invaded his dreams. In recent days, these dreams had resurfaced mixed with the images and smells of Uson's tortured corpse.

His fingers flew across the page—quick, flowing strokes for the shape of her throat and face, the loose curls of her hair.

He had to let the past go. Focus on more positive things like the life he was building with Anna and Tilli. Whatever palace plot was underway, whoever was behind the duo's deaths and whatever their motives, it was not his concern. Let Puran and

65

Jakan find the culprits. And Lukarn, since he'd returned from Nakri a few days ago.

He feathered in the soft grey to blend the shadows and bring out the brilliance in her eyes.

Another loud thump, louder this time, and the ground vibrated beneath his thighs. Cheers and groans echoed across the practice yard.

Estolik sprawled in the dust. Mannok stood over him, the padded point of his practice spear touching Estolik's chest. 'Yield!'

Estolik took a whistling breath, his creamy brown face livid. 'I yield,' he rasped.

Mannok swung his spear up and held out a hand to his defeated opponent. 'Best of three, Essu?'

There was no love lost between those two, second cousins though they might be. Could Estolik be involved as accomplice to his father in the unsettling events of the last year, including the murders? Leave it be.

Dinnis' long fingers tightened on the charcoal. If only he could make a living as a healer. Share his life with Anna and Tilli and the others. Why shouldn't he have a family like anyone else? *Moros, because you're not just anyone else.*

He shaded in dark, luminous eyes, upturned nose and even features. Outstretched wings formed behind her, as though she could take flight at any moment. He frowned at the image of the mysterious lady from North Pass. Rasel. Memories stirred of her luminous smile, her kind words to a lost boy. As the nightmares faded over the years, she had remained his guiding star.

Dinnis' skin prickled as a shadow fell over the open pages. He lifted his head and met Estolik's cool grey-green eyes. Slide it, he should have been paying attention.

Estolik's lip curled. 'So, what did you think of the bout, Dinnu?' A heavy sheen of sweat covered the lad's creamy skin, a purple bruise beginning to flower just below his padded ribs. Dinnis glanced over to where the other young warriors clustered around Mannok some six or more tanis away. Garvin and the Prince fist punched. Hasuk slapped the royal shoulder and shouted his congratulations. No one was looking this way.

Dinnis returned his gaze to Haka's son. 'That I should offer you congratulations for lasting so long against our glorious Prince.'

Estolik's eyes hardened and the corners of his lips peeled back to show his teeth. 'Humph. You better not be mocking me. You couldn't fight your way out of a snowbank. You're the worst excuse for a warrior I've ever seen.'

'I may have a little skill, though nothing to compare to your mastery, Lord Estolik.'

Estolik looked at him askance. 'What have you there?' He lunged and snatched away the journal.

Dinnis shot up, his fingers brushing against the leather cover as Estolik danced away. Before Dinnis could follow, a meaty arm hooked him from behind, and jerked him backwards. Great, just great! So these two *mori* had decided to take up Uson's mantle, or was it payback for winning the Capture the Shield match a couple of *alume* ago?

Hot air tickled his cheek as Durrin panted in his ear. 'You need to practice harder, bluey.'

'Give my book back,' Dinnis gasped.

Durrin tightened his hold, his arm pressing down on Dinnis' windpipe. 'Or what?'

Black spots crowded around the edge of his vision.

Estolik's face split into a grin. He flicked through the pages until it fell open. Please, not the page with the drawing of Rasel. Estolik tilted his head. 'What's this? A girl? I didn't think you were interested.'

Heat flamed through Dinnis, a molten rage he normally kept dampened. He rammed his elbow backwards into Durrin's stomach and stamped down hard on his shins. Durrin grunted and doubled over. The tightness of his grip around Dinnis' throat loosened. Bending his knees, Dinnis pulled Durrin down with him until, unbalanced and gasping, the bully stumbled and fell sprawling in the dust of the practice yards.

Gulping down air, Dinnis rolled away and lunged towards a gaping Estolik.

A shadow fell over him.

'What's going on here?' Mannok stood beside them, a green cloak draped over his shoulder, his russet hair dripping with water. Jade-green eyes widened in mild curiosity. 'You know the rules, fighting should remain inside the practice field.'

Garvin and Trasin moved up behind the Prince. Durrin staggered to his feet, rage plastered over his blunt face.

Dinnis clenched his fists, his eyes fixed on the journal.

Sticking a manicured finger in the book, Estolik turned towards the Prince. 'You should look at this, Mannu. If you weren't about to marry Princess Kerri, you might consider this beauty.' He smirked.

'What?' Mannok's face tightened. His eyes narrowed. 'I'm not marrying the Princess.'

'Quite, though Princess Kerri doesn't seem to have gotten the message,' Estolik drawled. He opened the journal so all could see. 'Take a look at this.'

'Who is she?' Trasin asked. 'A lady of myth?'

'Maybe that's Dinnis' concern,' Garvin said.

Mannok's eyes flicked to the pages. His eyebrows arched.

Dinnis' heart pounded painfully against his ribs. 'She's no one. Just a dream.'

Mannok shook his head. 'She's not one of the court ladies or any of the nobles' daughters.'

'And you should know.' Estolik laughed though his lips turned down as if he'd bitten into an unripe inka berry. 'You've had the pick of every eligible woman from Nakri in the north to Kusa in the west, and Silisea and now Limar in the south. But it seems at last we can congratulate you, Mannok. The Princess said last night that she can't wait until the betrothal is ratified.'

Mannok made a sweeping motion with his hand. 'Yama droppings. She thinks we're all 'quaint' and backward.'

'With the exception of you, Your Highness. When can we expect the announcement? At your mother's soiree this afternoon or at the New Beginnings Banquet in a few days?'

'By the Maker's favour, neither!' The appalled look on Mannok's face would have been comical if Estolik didn't have Dinnis' journal in his thick, sweaty fingers.

'I wish you good fortune.' Estolik sneered, loosening his grip on the journal. 'You know, if you don't choose soon, your parents will decide for you, for the sake of the realm. To provide an heir to the Throne.'

Dinnis edged closer to Estolik.

'And for the sake of the rest of us,' Durrin grumbled. 'If you don't like the Princess, by the pit, choose someone else.'

'Is that so?' Mannok tilted his head, then waved his hand. 'Give the book back, Estolik. If you're sore at losing, we can always have a rematch. Don't take it out on Dinnis.' His slightly uneven teeth flashed in a grin. 'Besides, two against one? That hardly becomes you, as a noble warrior and great-grandson of a Kapok.'

Estolik lifted his chin. 'Your command is my wish, Your Highness.' He flung the journal in Dinnis' direction.

Dinnis caught it. He ran his hand over the cover, flipped through the pages before tucking it into his tunic. Estolik had left a couple of sweaty fingerprints on the covers, a few creases, but the drawings of people and plants— and of Rasel and his mother and Ista—remained unharmed. Some of the tension released in his shoulders. *Moros*, he should never have allowed Estolik to catch him by surprise.

'Thank you, Your Highness.' He dipped his head toward Mannok.

Mannok clapped him on a shoulder. 'You're a strange one, Dinnis.'

'In all honour, you should apologise, Estolik,' Garvin said, his brown eyes steady.

Estolik gave a stiff smile and a stiff bow. 'Of course, Your Highness. I do apologise, Dinnis.' Though all the while, he kept his gaze fixed on Mannok.

Mannok grabbed a long thick cloth from the railing and rubbed away the sweat. 'Let's go. We've a few hours before this afternoon's festivities.' Mannok's sober face lit up with sudden mischief and a certain recklessness. 'And I think I know the perfect gift for our Princess.'

Now what was Tamrin's favoured son up to? Dinnis let out a breath, glad the focus had moved from him and hopefully, his drawing of Rasel, his silver lady. This business with Uson and Asik had unsettled him more than he liked.

Garvin turned back and beckoned. 'Dinnis, are you coming?'

Dinnis nodded. He tucked his journal into his tunic and trailed behind the others into the Palace.

Chapter Eleven: Rivals

Lumi

Lady Lumi, Lord Haka's eldest daughter, took a silver beaker of guava juice and some honeyed yam bites from the tray offered by one of the Palace servants. All the nobles from across Tamra that mattered, and many that didn't, crowded the spacious reception room. Lords and ladies in feathered headdresses and sparkling robes mingled under tapestries of battles and hunts and state events. Others lounged on colourful sofas arranged around the room and framed by potted plants. High arched windows lining the north wall let in late afternoon sunlight. In front of golden entrance doors, a group of musicians played haunting traditional tunes with windpipes, shakers, sitars and drums.

'What a crush.' Lumi fanned herself.

She angled away from her father, speaking in low tones to Lord Durak, and towards where a welcome breeze filtered in from the archways leading to the main atrium. After a few steps squeezing through the press of people, someone with the delicate scent of mountain lilies and meadowsweet slipped an arm around her waist.

'Rizzi!' she squealed. Some of the tension eased at the presence of her best friend, Lady Rizanna, Lord Lukarn's daughter and first cousin to Prince Mannok. 'Why are you not attending the Kupanna?'

'My sweet mama, your mother and Princess Lakwi attend Her Majesty, so she sent me away to enjoy the party. I thought I'd never find you in this throng,' Rizanna raised her voice above the rumble of conversation and strains of music. She looked gorgeous, her chestnut hair caught up in a criss-crossed pattern. Dangling gold and ruby earrings matched her robe embroidered with stalking pumas. 'So many people!'

'Everyone who is someone has arrived in Tarka for the Festival of New Beginnings tomorrow and the Trial of Tears.'

'And to stare at our exotic visitors from faraway Limar.' Rizzi's hazel eyes sparkled, her more subdued mood in recent days replaced with a brittle exuberance.

Lumi pursed her lips. 'Or to be snubbed by them. Only the Prince and Their Majesties rate anything more than a sneer from our esteemed southern visitors.'

Rizzi giggled. 'Wicked, Lumi.'

'At least the rains are easing. Perhaps, they will take their boredom and slights with them back to that oh-so-much-bigger-and-better magical land of Limar.' Lumi smoothed her own marine-blue robe, embroidered with dolphins in silver thread. She and Rizanna looked good together, Rizzi's more golden looks complementing her own silvery shimmer.

Rizzi tittered and rested an elegant hand on her shapely neck. 'I wonder what they really want. Don't you think it strange that those two lads were murdered so soon after their arrival?'

A sudden chorus of laughter came from the arched colonnade that led out to the atrium balcony. One tenor laugh she'd recognise anywhere. Lumi's cheeks warmed and her heart missed a beat.

A band of young men entered the reception room from the atrium. Prince Mannok led the group, looking magnificent in a jade-green sleeveless tunic, darker green breeches and his cloak matching the nodding green and gold feather headdress. Gold arm bands and oval chest plate shone in the light streaming through the high windows. Now, what were they up to? She hadn't seen that look in Mannok's eyes since before that serving girl, Ista, disappeared.

'Maybe the Limarian's arranged it.' Rizzi shook her arm. 'Lumi!'

'What?" Lumi dragged her gaze from the Prince and raised her eyebrows. 'Oh, no, I hardly think so. Our royal visitors are much more interested in snaring our Prince. I'll be glad when they leave. No more select parties cheek-to-jowl with a stuffy Limarian Princess and her haughty self-absorbed brother.'

Rizzi deflated a little. 'At least we can keep our distance now, unless attending the Kupanna. Did Lady Yuta and Lord Haka settle in last night?'

'With the usual commotion.' She'd been delighted to talk to her mother after being separated for three alume, and her little brother and sister who had both grown taller since the Prince's birthday feast last year. Glad to see Father too, of course. Though, she found it hard to relax in his presence, never quite sure when he'd find fault with her or administer a stinging reprimand. 'And are Lord Lukarn and Lady Samarra settled in?'

Rizzi pealed with laughter. 'They have and my tribe of younger brothers and sisters, too. You know our suite here is like a second home. Though Papa is furious about the unannounced arrival of the Limarians, and the deaths of those boys. He went on a rampage, tearing strips off poor Puran, Sparak and Kaptan Jakan for lapses in security, especially after everything that happened last year. As usual, Uncle Rokkan told him not to worry, but I think Papa is right. Uncle Rokkan should take these threats to his and Mannok's safety more seriously.'

Lumi frowned. 'Oh, but weren't those two war orphans to blame for all the kerfuffle? And now they're dead, they can hardly do more harm.' She caught her bottom lip between her teeth. She'd heard whispers suggesting that Papa was behind these events because of the succession. He was ambitious, it was true, and expected her to report back any information she overhead in the Palace. Still, he was too intelligent to risk his position as the third most powerful man in all Tamra.

Rizzi's eyes flickered and she looked away for a second. 'Yes, yes, I'm sure you're right, dear Lumi.' She squeezed Lumi's arm and waved her beaker of juice. 'And the Limarians will soon realise that Mannok is never going to accept their ugly princess and will scamper back to the fabulous city that is so much better than ours. The sooner the better.'

'You've said it, sister.' They clinked beakers and laughed.

'There is one thing,' Rizzi lowered her voice. 'Waren plans to be wed this New Beginnings feast.'

Lumi squealed. 'What! Who? There hasn't been a noble marriage for an age.' Families were reluctant to betroth their daughters while the Prince remained unmarried and available.

Rizzi shrugged her shapely shoulders, 'Ah, well, some nobody from up north. Papa isn't too happy, but Mama—'

A shrill scream echoed off the lime-washed walls from the other end of the large reception room. Lumi startled, red guava juice slopping out of her ornate cup and over her hand.

Rizzi gripped her arm harder. 'What was that? Are we under attack?'.

Lumi's gaze swept the room. 'It sounds like the Limarian Princess.'

Another desperate scream followed the first. At the other end of the reception room, Princess Kerri slapped and tore at her robes in a frenzy to the discordant jangle of her numerous bangles. Long braids slipped from their complicated arrangement and trailed down her shoulder.

'Get it off, get it off, get it off.'

The Princess' attendants swirled around her like a nest of rainbow ants disturbed by a foraging anteater. Her duenna and other attendants reached towards her, but the Princess's frantic movements pushed them away.

Prince Dashon left his discussion with Estolik and strolled towards his sister, his hand on the jewelled hilt of his dagger.

'Keep still, Your Imperial Highness,' Kerri's old duenna huffed. 'Let me look.' Her voice slid upwards. 'Aargh! It's … it's a gigantic spider.'

Dashon's face paled and he took a step back. 'Is it poisonous? Will it bite?'

Kerri panted as she clutched her brother's arms, pulling him off balance. 'Please, get it off,' she screeched.

Rizzi tittered, and Lumi clamped down on the urge to laugh. The haughty Princess did look like a comic figure in pantomime. A spider seemed an unlikely assassination weapon, and its sudden appearance seemed all too familiar. A frog under the neatly arranged covers of a bed, a grasshopper landing on a well-coiffed head. Thank the Maker, more than a year had passed since one of the Prince's annoying pranks. Those days were over. Or were they?

A fit of coughing came from behind her. Lumi spun round. Some of the young warriors clustered around the Prince hid smirks behind their hands. Garvin sported a frown and that tall spindly Nolmec's blue face was as hard-to-read as ever.

Mannok stood in front with his arms folded, his jade-green eyes wide with innocence.

Lumi let out a pent-up breath and cooled her face with her fan. 'Another of Prince Mannok's wild pranks.' Who else would dare to play such a practical joke on visiting royalty at the Kupanna's soiree?

Garvin's brow creased and he whispered something into Mannok's ear.

The Prince shook his head, 'No, Garvin. Don't ...'

But the lad was already loping towards the Princess.

Palace guards poured into the Reception room from the main entrance doors and through the arched doorways leading to the Royal Atrium. The Kupanna, Lady Samara and some of the older matrons hurried towards the agitated Princess.

Rizanna sniffed. 'At least we are not the target this time.' Though she sounded a little miffed. 'Remember the snake in your bed?'

'Yes, a harmless tree snake. That was years ago.' When Mannok had seemed an annoying boy with grubby knees, not the attractive and accomplished young warrior.

Garvin got to the screaming Princess first. He pushed past Dashon, with an impatient 'Hold still, Your Highness!' He scooped up the spider in one light brown hand and caged it with the other.

Princess Kerri dashed the tears from her face, her chin raised, a rosy blush on her pale cheeks. The old duenna smoothed the Princess' hair and rearranged the folds of her gem-encrusted robe and gauzy veils while the other attendants huddled around murmuring consolations.

Prince Dashon waved a hand in Garvin's direction. 'Our thanks ... er ....'

Garvin's face tightened. 'Garvin, son of Kaptan Kaspin of the Yarma clan, Your Highness.' He bowed and sauntered back towards the Prince. He paused as he reached Lumi and Rizanna's position and stretched out his cupped hands.

'Want a look, ladies?'

Rizanna covered her mouth, her eyes rounding. 'Ugh, no Garo, take that horrid thing away. It could be poisonous.'

'Not poisonous and quite friendly.' Large, hairy black legs showed between Garvin's tan fingers. 'Are you timid too, Lady Lumi?' He smiled, a hint of mischief in his rich-brown eyes.

Lumi suppressed a small shudder. 'I'll take your word on that.'

She usually didn't take much notice of the Prince's loyal shadow. He was not unattractive, but as eldest daughter of Lord Haka and cousin of the Kapok, she expected to marry better than the second son of the Kaptan of the City Guard of an insignificant clan and some minor family.

'Where's it from?' Rizzi asked.

'A tarantula from the Mist Forests, in fact.' Mannok draped an arm around Garvin's shoulders, the corners of his mouth quirked up. 'Isn't she a beauty?'

Lumi's heart beat faster and her breath caught in her throat. 'That is a matter of opinion, Your Highness.'

Mannok nodded. He turned and gave Garvin a shake. 'Idiot, what did you do that for? Now everyone will guess I planted our little friend.'

'I felt sorry for the lass, Mannu. She was becoming quite hysterical. Really, if you are worried you should keep your distance and I'll take the blame.'

'What, I can't have that, Garo. But, my friend, it's always fatal to start sympathising with the enemy.'

'So Your Highness, is it just the Princess Kerri you consider 'the enemy' or are we all on your list?' Lumi's soft lips curved into an ironic smile.

Mannok turned towards her, his eyebrows raised.

Rizzi giggled. 'I wouldn't mind being taken captive.' She fluttered her dark eyelashes.

'Have you got something in your eye, Rizzi? Perhaps Garvin could help get it out for you. He is quite the champion today.'

'I believe his hands are rather full at the moment. Maybe you could help me, Your Highness?'

'Here, give me Flowerbud, Garvin, and help the beautiful lady.'

Garvin gave a wistful smile. 'I think she would rather the help of a gallant prince than my bumbling efforts.' He kept the spider firmly in his hold.

'Do you truly think I'm beautiful, Mannok?' Rizzi smiled demurely.

Lumi gritted her teeth. How could she flirt so shamelessly?

The Prince's jaw dropped a little and he took a step back. 'All noble ladies are beautiful are they not? I've never heard tell of one that wasn't, sweet cousin.'

Rizzi pursed her lips and frowned at him.

Lumi took the opportunity. 'And what of the beauty of our Limarian guest? Do you find her more beautiful than the ladies of Tamra?

'Not at all. Besides, she's so patronising. "My dearest Prince, the climate is so bracing here. How quaint your little palace is. Did you know the palace at Kuza is at least four times as big and made from pure gold? What droll customs you all have."' He mimicked the Princess' rather nasally voice.

A deep bass boomed behind them. 'Droll indeed, Prince Mannok. 'Tis not every nation that welcomes their honoured guests, royalty even, with a spider on the shoulder.' The Kapok's golden eyes narrowed and fixed upon his son and heir.

Lumi shivered at the hard edge not usually present in the Kapok's jocular tones. She bowed, as befitted the daughter of Lord Haka, Markan of the West. Rizanna and Garvin and the others followed suit.

Mannok grimaced and shifted his weight. 'Papa ... Your Majesty.'

'So, Garvin, is that the culprit?' The Kapok took the spider into his own large hands with surprising gentleness.

'Err... yes sir. I'm sorry he escaped. I ...'

'No need to apologise for my recalcitrant son's misdemeanours. Or can you truthfully tell me this was not his idea?'

Mannok folded his arms and lifted his chin, showing the slight cleft. 'Not only my idea but my own work.'

The lines between the Kapok's brows deepened and his expressive mouth pulled down at the corners. 'Garvin, take this beauty and find a safe place for her. Perhaps Ralton will be able to advise on the best option or Dinnis. As for you, Prince Mannok, go and wait for me in my study until I come. We need to talk.'

Before Mannok could reply, the Kapok spun on his heels and headed over to Kupanna Marra who was settling Princess Kerri on one of the divans. A servant brought her a drink on a golden tray and her ladies clustered about her. Kaptan Jakan directed guards back to their posts.

Mannok pressed his lips into a firm line. 'Can't anyone take a joke?' His face brightened with a swift grin. 'Though, I'm guessing there'll be no announcement tonight.'

Garvin puffed his cheeks out. 'You could've made your wishes clear to your mother.'

'Right! Have you tried that? She's not listening.' The Prince gave a crooked grin and inclined his head. 'Ladies.'

With a casual bow to Lumi and Rizanna and thump to Garvin's

shoulder, he strolled towards the grand double doors at the end of the long room.

Lumi followed his walk, his warrior's saunter, her pulse in tune with his stride. With the enmity between their fathers, most likely he could never be hers and she his.

Chapter Twelve: Consequences

Mannok

Mannok fought the urge to pace Papa's cramped office. Sunlight splintered through the latticework over the door, suspending dust motes in liquid amber and spilling down to pool across the small rectangle of floor. A massive wooden desk filled half the space and overstuffed bookcases lined the walls.

He sucked in a strangled breath, half-convinced the cluttered walls squeezed closer and closer. The sharp burr of singed candle wicks, old paper and polished wood mingled with the faintest hint of chilli. The familiar scents wrapped around him, both comforting and confronting. How many hours had he spent playing under Papa's desk as a child or trailing behind him around the Palace or on treasured expeditions to the kennels and the stables? Always anxious to measure up in his intelligent and powerful father's estimation, yes, but also deep-down certainty his father would protect and guide him. Yet, last year's events had shattered that trust.

Melted wax ran down the side of the single lit candle in one of the bronze candelabras along the wall, the slow drip by drip telling time like a waxen water clock. Mannok rubbed the contours of the jaguar embossed on the hilt of his hunting knife. Had he gone too far? Had he worn out Papa's patience? A shiver ran down his spine at the memory of the ice-hard glint in Papa's golden eyes. He squared his shoulders. Whatever the punishment for his break in protocol, even several alume worth of wall duty, would be worth it, if his actions banished the possibility of a match between him and the Limarian Princess.

The jumbled murmur of voices filtered along the corridors from the Great Hall, signalling the end of the afternoon's entertainment. Mannok swallowed down a growing queasiness. He wished Papa would hurry up and end the agony of waiting for the spear to strike.

The babble of voices and footsteps died away, replaced by the sounds of Palace staff clearing up. Light faded from the lattice and the candle burned brighter in the shadows of the room.

Mannok kicked the legs of the desk. By the moons, why should he stay? He was the heir to the Throne. He had better things to do than stand around here waiting to be upbraided like a common soldier.

Mannok stepped toward the door and grasped the bronze handle.

His father's quick decisive stride sounded in the small atrium outside the office. Too late.

He backed into the desk as the door swung open. Papa ducked his head under the lintel and surged into the cramped room. He brushed past Mannok and threw himself into the large wooden chair behind the desk.

Mannok's pulse thundered in his ears. Before he could lose his courage, he rushed in. 'Whatever you say, I'm not marrying her. She laughs like a sick yarma. She is totally stuck-up and ... and I'd rather marry a ... a sick dog.'

Papa arched his dark eyebrows. 'Your eloquence overwhelms me, Prince Mannok. After years of access to the education the Palace can provide, is that the best insult you can construct? Pompous arrogance, overweening pride, condescending self-importance or even small-minded haughtiness maybe ... but stuck-up?' The chair creaked as Papa leant back in the chair, stretching his long legs out on top of the desk.

Mannok blinked, opened his mouth then closed it. This was not how he imagined this interview would go. Papa leant forward, removed the lid of a small red and black pot with a deft twist and took a handful of chillied castana nuts.

'I am happy you don't like her. I don't like her. She'd make you miserable. More to the point, it would be a disaster to align ourselves with Limar.'

Mannok's jaw dropped. 'You don't approve the liaison?'

Papa flicked one of the nuts into his mouth and crunched down. His penetrating gaze fixed on Mannok. 'I don't. I'd rather keep the Limarians out of Tamrin affairs. The current Sulkan is rapacious and belligerent. Like ravenous piranhas, he and his father have devoured smaller groups such as the Parkuti and Favini to gain resources and increase their influence. While their first overtures promise friendship and peace, they are quick to find offense as an excuse to conquer and control. So, they grow in might and power, building on their Sulkan's empire.' Papa leaned forward, tenting his fingers. 'But Mannok, you would know this, if you paid any attention to the council briefings or Ralton's lessons in history and politics.'

Mannok squirmed. Perhaps history had a point after all. 'They haven't bothered us before, so why us? Why now?'

'Not since before Tellek Kapok's time. Their soldiers need the latest weapons. Those weapons of hardened bronze. That requires tin. Since their own mines are depleted, they hope a marriage deal would secure access to our tin mines and other mineral wealth.'

'So, a marriage alliance would be valuable?' Mannok scowled. 'And I'm the sweetener—'

'That's how alliances often work, Mannu. Perhaps, if they had something we wanted or if we could trust them. So far, our distance keeps us out of their orbit. It concerns me, that after many decades, they are beginning to look our way.'

Which wasn't his fault. He hadn't invited the Limarians to Tarka. 'So? Tamra leads the Five Lands. Our armies are stronger than theirs.'

'Not any more. Their larger agricultural base and absorption of the semi-settled tribes around them has expanded their borders and population. The Sulkan now commands a large standing army and can call on forced allies.'

'Size isn't everything. You defeated uncle Naetok and Akrad with their Nolmec allies when none thought it possible?'

'I won against the Naetok and Akrad, the Maker be thanked, yes. At a cost of lives lost, families and friendships torn apart. Mannok, you may have been a child, but you saw the devastation in the north after the war was won. We still suffer the effects. Meanwhile the Red Crane Nolmec hover north of our borders ready to exploit the first hint of weakness. Lord Haka and Durak's loyalties remain shaky at best. And with the assassination attempts ...'

'But the culprits were caught and punished.' Uson could have sabotaged the bridge.

Papa's flyaway eyebrows contracted into a wedge. 'Mannok, think about it. Someone had them killed!'

A new queasiness settled in Mannok's stomach like a weight stone. Whoever wanted them dead might still be free to cause mischief. He'd heard the rumours, the whispers. 'Who?'

Papa removed his headdress and placed it on the desk. He rubbed the grey hairs at his temples. 'I have my suspicions who might be behind it, but I need more proof before I move against him. In the meantime, we need—'

Heat rushed up Mannok's neck. '—to strengthen the succession. You want me to marry. Why didn't you and Mama have more children, if producing sanctioned heirs is so important?'

Papa ran a hand over his face. 'We would have, if the Maker had favoured us so. Your mother was fortunate to survive your birth and unable to bear more children. I was not inclined to put her aside or to take another wife.'

'Uncle Lukarn would not have liked that.'

'No, he wouldn't have, but for the sake of the Throne, he would have understood the necessity. But as callous and calculating as you and ...' he paused. 'As you may think me, there are some lines I will not cross. If we act as ruthlessly as our supposed enemies, what are we in fact protecting?'

'Oh, I don't know. Maybe ask Ista?' Mannok kicked the desk and winced.

'Maker give me patience. Ista has a new home and is happier for it. I've granted you the liberty to choose your own bride.'

'But now, you've changed your mind and you want me to marry Princess Kerri for the sake of peace.'

Papa clapped his hands with a resounding smack. 'Mannok, you are not listening. I want to keep the Limarians at a distance, not invite them into your bed.'

'Oh.'

'Which is why your prank is so reprehensible. If the Sulkan took this as an insult to his daughter and a pretext to set his own plans in motion ...'

Mannok's cheeks flushed. He looked down at his boots, feeling about five years old.

'But surely such a small prank ...' He looked up and caught the glint in his father the Kapok's eye. 'I'm sorry, Papa. I didn't think.'

'Exactly. You will be Kapok one day. You need to think of the Realm, not just of your own grievances or desires, however warranted they may be. Take out your ire on me, if you must, but don't put the safety of our realm in jeopardy. It's not good enough, Mannu.'

Anger boiled inside Mannok. What about Papa's own indiscretions, his liaisons with the Nolmec Kiprissa when he was betrothed to Mama. Didn't that put the realm in jeopardy? He swallowed it down. 'Yes, Papa.'

'I've made profuse apologies to the Princess and her outraged brother,' Papa continued, 'and I will send my apologies to her father and explain my son is too immature to choose a bride yet, along with generous gifts and platitudes.' Papa leant back in his chair. 'Dashon and Kerri both insist on leaving for Limar as soon as may be, but I believe I've averted total catastrophe.'

'They're leaving?'

'Yes.'

'And not coming back?'

'I doubt it.' Papa fixed Mannok with his eagle gaze. 'Is there not one suitable young woman in all the Five Lands that you'd consider marrying in a year or perhaps decade or so?'

'Right. Maybe a merchant's daughter or a farmer's? Or I know, we could always check out the Nolmec, Your Majesty,' he said, unable to keep the bitterness out of his voice.

Papa smiled, though it did not warm his eyes. 'Great idea, Mannu. I'll get Master Scout Sparak to start the negotiations. I believe General Nuktis has a couple of grandnieces that might fit the requirements.'

Mannok's eyes widened. 'You're bluffing.'

Papa's eyebrows shot up. 'Aren't you? All I ask for is a woman of noble birth of good character and reasonable ability and intelligence.'

'Well then I ... I'll think about it,' Mannok huffed. 'If you have finished lecturing me, perhaps you would be gracious enough to excuse me, your Majesty?'

'Not so fast, Prince.' Papa swung his legs off the desk. 'You acted without due consideration, insulted our guests, shamed me, the Throne and our realm, and put our people and lands at risk, and you still don't seem to appreciate the damage you have done. Do you think there will be no consequences?'

'Yes, I mean, no sir.' He stiffened his stance, waiting for the spear to fall.

'You will apologise to the Princess and her brother in the morning, on bended knee if necessary. You will apologise to your mother. And you will forgo your allowance for six turnings of the Golden Moon, the metal and goods going towards those in need.'

'Six alume? But ...'

'I haven't finished, Mannok. And you will serve a full term at the northern border under Waren's command, departing after the Fealty ceremony following the New Beginnings feast. While there, take the time to contemplate the consequences of hasty, ill-judged actions.'

Mannok's chin jerked up. Had he heard correctly? His chagrin evaporated like morning mist. Action at last, and no Palace full of potential brides to navigate. This last wasn't a punishment. Even a humiliating apology to Kerri would be worth an escape to the north. 'As you command, Your Majesty.' He bowed low to hide the smile he couldn't quench.

'Don't take my good will too lightly, Prince.' Papa's voice frosted over. 'I am your father. I am also Rokkan Kapok, son of Martal, the supreme ruler of Tamra. Heir or not, if you shame the Golden Throne of Tamra again, I will not be so lenient. Now get out of here.'

Mannok bowed lower and rushed from the room before Papa decided to revoke the border duty. Just wait until Garvin and the others heard the good news.

Chapter Thirteen: Loyalties

Lumi

Lumi rubbed eyes still drowsy with sleep and half-ran along the long atrium balcony towards the royal family's sleeping chambers. Pink and gold already smudged the rectangle of silver sky glowing through the open roof of the atrium. In the Palace grounds, tarrawongs greeted the rising sun with a joyous serenade, while mountain pigeons cooed under the eaves of the tiled palace roof. It was Lumi's turn to attend the Kupanna this morning and she was late.

She pushed the thought of her father's presence in the Palace out of her mind with an impatient shrug of her shoulders. She wasn't going to allow anything to spoil her golden mood this morning. Her mouth twitched up into a half-smile. Mannok had noticed her at the soiree yesterday. He had spoken to her and looked her in the eye. Maybe he wasn't as immune to feminine charms as he pretended. He might notice her again, even enjoy her company.

Like the Kapok, Mannok loved outdoor pursuits—dogs, horses, the hunt, wrestling—but, unlike the Kapok, he had little interest in books, poetry and history. Of all the cultured and well-born ladies welcomed to the Palace, only cold and remote Ista had attracted his attention. Until now. Well, at least a little. Perhaps the haughty Kerri's presence would work to her advantage, if it had brought her to the Prince's notice.

Ignoring the guards posted outside the embossed golden doors, Lumi walked through the spacious and richly-furnished antechamber and into the outer sitting-come-dressing room that granted access to the royal bed chambers.

Kupanna Marra's voice floated from the inner rooms. 'No! You can't send Mannok to fight on the border! You just can't. It's too dangerous, Rokkan.'

Lumi's heart cramped. Mannok to be sent to the border? Her hand fell from the door handle to her side. All the young warriors took a turn on the northern border, though there had been no Nolmec incursions for years. Still, it could be many alume before he returned to Tarka.

'He has overstepped the mark, Marra. A short stint of border patrol might help him realise that life is not a game for children.'

The Kupanna's footsteps came closer and then receded as though she walked up and down the large, richly appointed inner chamber, no doubt her back straight and her head held high. Should she announce her presence or should she go? Lumi took a step backwards and stopped. She had to find out more.

The Kupanna let out a puff of breath. 'That unfortunate prank ... I was mortified. I don't know what has got into him.' Her footsteps paused. 'Yes, I do. Ista, your ... your ... she's corrupted him. Mannok's been unmanageable ever since we put a stop to that unthinkable liaison. I'm not saying there shouldn't be consequences for upsetting the Limarian Princess, however provoking her haughtiness.'

'Indeed—'

'Confine him to the Palace or send him to the coast or the south to Silisea. But on the border with the Nolmec? Unthinkable. They burned whole villages, leaving no survivors. Killed our warriors without mercy.'

'The Red Crane Nolmec and close to fifteen years ago. The current situation ...'

'Those others, the Phoenix, sided with Naetok and Akrad.'

'Some did but—'

'I don't see the difference. Besides, it only takes one arrow.'

'We are not at war with the Nolmec. Besides, Marra, Mannok must learn to rule. He needs to face danger, to understand the risks, and to understand what he asks of his warriors, of his people. Better to do that when the danger is minimal, than in the middle of his first crisis. We can't keep him swaddled in the Palace with little to occupy his mind except games and pranks.'

'Mannok is our only son, your heir to the Throne. Or do you want your cousin Haka to inherit? Unless you're considering another as your successor?'

The Kupanna stopped pacing and Lumi heard a rustle as though the Kapok stood. Was he going to leave the chamber? Should she declare her presence? But, what did Marra mean by 'another'? The Kapok couldn't declare just anyone to succeed him. His eldest and only son would inherit, or her father, Lord Haka, if Mannok died without a son.

'I gave you my promise, Marra. I acknowledge Mannok as my only heir. But keeping him cooped up in the Palace when other young men his age do their duty makes him more reckless, not less. And if it reassures you, Lukarn and Waren will ensure his safety, maybe too well.'

'If he is injured … or … killed … I will never forgive you.'

Inside the bedchamber, a tense silence fell. Outside, the last carols of the morning birdsong yielded to the sounds of the palace stirring. In the distance a young girl sang, probably the child of one of the palace staff. The Palace seemed calm and ordered, but it could be a place of intrigue and sudden death.

Lumi shivered at the thought that the Prince's life might still be in danger. An unwelcome thought chilled her further. Who stood to gain the most by his death, if not Father? But he was not another Naetok. He fought on Rokkan Kapok's side in the rebellion and declared his loyalty to the Kapok each year in the ceremony the morning after New Beginnings Feast. And would, once again, in a few days, in fact.

'If Mannok had sons already, the danger would be less.' The Kupanna's worried voice interrupted her thoughts. The sound of her pacing stopped. 'I don't know what to do with him anymore. He has rejected the hand of every possible noble maiden from Nakri to Kuza. Who is left, unless you would reconsider young Lumi?'

Lumi caught her breath. Yes, it was exactly what she hoped for. If only Mannok would find her agreeable. She sighed and blinked back sudden tears.

'Hmm, well, I'm dead against Mannok making alliances with the Limarians. Let's keep them right out of Tamrin affairs. As for Mannok, give him time and space to do his own choosing, he's only seventeen. One of these days he will be swept off his feet.'

'Most likely by someone totally inappropriate.'

'Maybe that's better than no choice at all.'

Lumi shook her head vigorously. No, no, no. It wasn't acceptable.

In the other room, Marra snorted. 'Humph, just like you to say it or even think it. And where is that girl? How am I supposed to arrange my hair without help? I miss ...' her voice faded into silence.

'Here, let me. I used to help my mother.'

'Ridiculous. How many decades ago was that? And you can't have been more than eight before she died.'

'Seven. Hmm... hold still ... your hair is still as glorious as the day I married you.'

'Rokkan, that's not how you ... ohh...' Marra giggled. Lumi started at the girlish sound from the stately and proper Kupanna. 'I'm sure you didn't do that to your mother.'

'Last time I checked, you weren't my mother.'

'Well, yes but ... No, you shouldn't... oh ... besides I'm cross with you.'

'You always are ...'

'The girl might ...'

'Jaguar take the girl, my love, if she had any decency, she would make herself scarce for at least an hour or so.'

Lumi's cheeks seared with sudden heat. Did he know she was hovering outside the chamber door, listening in like a common maid? They said he had the acute hearing of a snowy owl, but she had hardly made a sound. She turned and stumbled into the antechamber, pulling the door to the sitting room shut behind her. Keeping her head down, she turned and smashed into the muscular chest of a young man.

Chapter Fourteen: Ultimatum

Dinnis

Dinnis held the satchel of herbs slung tight against his side and crouched lower on the smithy roof, waiting his opportunity. The message from Tilli tucked into his tunic, burned against his chest, the third similar missive she'd sent in recent days. Risky to slip away now, without a pass and against the express command of the Kapok, but he had to take it. He couldn't risk losing his connection with Anna and her family. At least, the chaos wrought by the sudden decision of the Limarians to leave as soon as practical and the resulting increased traffic at the goods gate worked in his favour.

A shrill whistle and warning shouts from the gate guards preceded the clank of the wheel and the gradual opening of the gate's bronze-studded wooden doors. A horse-drawn cart, towered high with provisions, stood in Little Royal Street outside the walls. Perfect.

'Bring the cart in slow,' a guard shouted.

'Hi-up,' the driver shook the reins and the vehicle lurched forward passing beneath the archway.

Dinnis had only a few minutes before guards ordered the vehicle to stop and searched its load. With a quick glance, Dinnis clutched his satchel of herbs and leapt down from the roof to the space shielded from the guards' sight between the cart and the gatehouse walls. He slithered beneath the cart and moved to the back, avoiding the slowly moving wheels. Catching his breath, he scanned the street running along the western wall of the Palace. Empty. He slipped out from beneath the tailgate, diving to the left, and flattened himself against the outer red wall.

'Halt for inspection,' the Lutan on gate duty yelled, in the Palace yard behind the wall.

The gates squeaked and shut behind the cart with a solid thud. Dinnis stilled a moment, the blood hammering in his ears and sweat slicking his underarms. He had to move fast, while the guards' attention remained focused on the cart. The morning sun gilded the painted mansions lining the adjoining Royal Parade and the sand-coloured stone of the royal buildings surrounding the Jaguar Plaza in front of the Palace. The serene snow-cloaked Twins shimmered above the triangular temple building and extensive gardens further to the north.

His path was in the other direction. Keeping close to the wall, he jogged halfway up the hill before crossing a paved road and turning west into a narrow dirt path tumbling downhill.

His long spindly shadow leapt away in front of him. Weeds skirted the shabby adobe buildings and ran up their blank peeling walls. Blue wrens and honey sippers flitted in the straggly bushes and long grass. And the occasional rat too. The path led out to Crooked Street where shops and two-storey adobe houses lined the stone-paved street.

Dinnis strode toward the haven of Anna's herbal shop, its newly painted shutters pulled down, not yet opened for the day. His stomach rumbled. If nothing else, Anna's family would have a pot of chilli bean stew bubbling away on the hearth. And with the Palace in such a turmoil of activity, he could risk staying out until nightfall.

Heat spread through his chest and warmed his chilled limbs. After sharing his morning meal with Tilli and her family, he'd offer to do any heavy work required in Anna's herb and food plots, help young Norak with his studies, work with Tilli in preparing potions and still have the whole afternoon to assist Laetil with the sick.

He slipped through the door, careful not to set the bell jangling, and stepped into the fragrant and heady dimness of the shop.

Tilli stood wreathed in shadows beneath the bundles of meadowsweet, bruiseleaf and guavamint hanging from the low ceiling, but she wasn't alone. His eyes narrowed. Not Anna's short, round form or the lithe forms of one of Anna's younger sisters or half-grown brother. Perhaps a customer in urgent need of a draught or potion for a fevered child, except that the figure stood facing her, their bodies a hand's breadth apart, heads bent toward each other.

A man, by bulk and shape. His blunt fingers played with the rough weave of her cloak. As Dinnis' eyes adjusted to the gloom, the intruder's features became clearer. Copper-skinned, a broad and crooked nose and large ears. Tujek, a worker at Hartil stables.

His face flushed. Time to go. He stepped back, felt the give under his feet, and groaned as the bell jangled, loud like a war horn.

Tilli and Tujek jumped apart, bumping into the hanging herb bundles and sending them swaying above their heads.

'Fine Morning,' Dinnis managed to say against the tightness in his throat. Heat flared from his neck to his hairline. 'Sorry to interrupt. I'll come back later.' Though when he couldn't say.

Tujek smirked. 'See you at sundown, Tilli.' He squeezed her hand and pushed past Dinnis and out into the street, setting the bell jangling once again.

Tilli cleared her throat. Her plump lips wavered into a half-smile. 'Dinnis, I ... I thought ...'

'What did that Tujek want?' Dinnis blurted out. He heard whispers about this young man, a wastrel and something of a bully.

'He was picking up a poultice for an injured horse at the stables. He works there.' A flicker crossed her hazel eyes, their normally sparking depths a murky brown in the half-light. She turned and, her back stiff, threw meadowsweet, briarweed and yuka root into a mortar. Picking up the pestle, she stabbed down, releasing the pungent aroma of newly bruised herbs.

Dinnis took a deep breath and released the painful emotions rioting inside. He liked Tilli. He liked her a lot and he'd thought she liked him, but the way she stood so close to Tujek ...

'Tilli, is there something you are not telling me?'

'You haven't been here to tell you anything.'

'I know, I'm sorry. The situation at the Palace with the arrival of the Limarians and the increased security since the murders ...'

She dropped the pestle and spun around. 'You abandoned us after you promised to come more often. Maybe you think you're too good for us, mister situation-at-the-Palace. Or maybe, one of those high-and-haughty Palace maids are more to your liking?'

'No, of course not! I came as soon as I could.'

'And when will that be different, Dinnis?' She dangled an orange ribbon between her strong fingers. 'See, Tujek has asked me to be his woman.'

An empty hollow exploded beneath his ribs. He'd thought Tilli might ... *moros*, of course love wasn't for him. 'Is that what you want? Where would you live?'

She stepped the distance between them and caught his hands in hers. 'He says he can find a place for us, but I haven't decided yet.' She was ninas away, her breath tickling his cheek, the sweet smell of meadowsweet intoxicating his senses.

He lifted her work-worn hands to his lips. 'I've been thinking.' He swallowed against the sudden dryness in his throat. 'Would you consider an offer from me.' He hadn't brought a ribbon, but he could get one.

Her lips parted and her stance softened. She brushed her fingers against his lips. 'We could be joined at the New Beginnings festival.'

'Two days away?' His breath quickened. Her body melted against his. 'Yes! No, my obligations to the Palace. In a few years, when I can set up as a healer.'

'Leave the Palace. Ma and me, we make enough with the herbal shop while you train with Laetil. You don't even like working for those nobs.'

'As a war orphan and companion to the Prince, I cannot walk away without permission.' And if only that was all, yet he couldn't explain, not fully. 'I'm bound to the Kapok.'

'Get permission. Please, Dinnis, I'm older than you, twenty-four and tired of waiting.'

She nestled her head against his chest. His heart strained against the cage of his ribs like a hummingbird desperate to escape. He inhaled her sweet breath and the taste of her lips.

'So, you agree,' she whispered.

'The New Beginnings Festival is too soon.'

'Then by New Growth Festival. That's six alume away. I can wait that long.' Her fingers intwined with his. 'Promise.'

Could he get permission to leave the Palace and the service of the Prince, by then, to marry? He stiffened, chilled by another thought. Would the Rokkan even approve of his marrying? Would Marra and Lukarn consider children, if he had them, a threat to Mannok's claim to the Throne?

Tilli pulled away from him, her eyes narrowed. 'I can't wait forever, Dinnis. If you want me, you will make our hand-joining happen and soon. Or I will consider Tujek's offer.'

He pulled away from her, took a step back bumping into one of the long trestles in the shop, setting the glass and pottery containers on it tinkling and chinking. Did she think him interchangeable with that lout, Tujek? He closed his eyes. But why not, what did he really have to offer, not even his own freedom.

'Dinnis.' She took a step closer, her voice uncertain.

'I have to go.'

He bowed with all the grace of the court, turned on his heel and rushed out of the shop, the bell clanging behind him.

'Dinnis, stop, aren't you staying for ...'

Closing his ears, he jogged towards Market Street, his blue cheeks burning. How had he been so foolish to think that he could have what others took for granted?

Chapter Fifteen: Family Reunion

Lumi

Lumi stumbled backwards and overbalanced. Strong hands caught her, stopping her fall. Hands warm on her arms, her face pressed against his chest. The faint scents of leather and chilli set her heart racing.

She whipped up her head and met Garvin's warm brown eyes. 'Watch where you're going!' she spluttered, her cheeks flaming.

'I beg your pardon, Lady Lumi.' Garvin dropped his hands and stood back, apology in every line of his open face.

Not much shorter than the Prince, but with a squarer build and plainer face. She rarely took much notice of the Prince's closest companion. Never went out of her way to speak to him. Never really understood the reason for the closeness, though rumours hinted that Garvin's mother, Lady Taraya, nursed the Prince along with her newborn son because the Kupanna hovered on the edge of death after the delivery. Garvin's family belonged to minor nobility of little renown from the insignificant Yarma Clan. Nothing special.

She clutched her upper arms, shielding her chest, and caught a ragged breath. 'What business have you here?' That came out harsher than she intended.

Garvin's eyes widened and his bronze cheeks darkened to a reddish brown. He straightened his shoulders. 'Mannok left his spare cloak and a few other things he needs in his old room. He asked me to fetch them because he's trying to keep out of his parents' way.'

He glanced at the closed door to the royal chambers and looked back at her. 'Have you finished waiting on the Kupanna already?'

Lumi smoothed down some creases in her long light-blue tunic. 'Kupanna Marra and the Kapok are … busy. I will come back a little later. Not that it's any of your business.'

'As you say. Oh, well hang on a minute. I'll grab the cloak.' He ducked into Mannok's old room, across the antechamber from the Kapok and Kupanna's chambers. The click of the door was soon followed by the sound of rummaging.

She stayed, rubbing her arms and studying the ornate fireplace, the divans covered in colourful satin, the tall potted plants, and the timbered walls adorned with tapestries of mountain birds and flowers. The Limarians were leaving, but so was Prince Mannok. How long would he be gone? She would miss his rambunctious presence, seeing him at formal meals, striding through the Palace or riding out with his age-mates.

Garvin reappeared, a light pack slung over his shoulder and a jaunty spring in his step. He'd recovered his sunny smile. 'Still here? I can escort you down to breakfast. Unless you're eating with your parents.'

'No need.'

His lips twitched into a straight line. He bowed. 'As you wish, my lady.'

She nodded to him, glanced at the guards at the entrance to the antechamber and walked along the upper balcony of the atrium towards the stairs to the Great Hall. A few moments later, Garvin's athletic footsteps tapped on the mosaic floor a few paces behind her.

He'd be meeting up with Mannok in the bachelor quarters.

She turned and inclined her head. 'So, you're heading north with the Prince?'

'Ah! I hadn't thought it general knowledge.' He gave her a penetrating look, then shrugged. 'Not that it's a secret. We're to leave after the Fealty Ceremony.' His eyes softened. 'I'll miss my brother's pathfinder ceremony, this year. And one of Waren's brothers' too, but duty calls, right?'

'Sileste to … er … to your brother.'

'Thank you, my lady.' He lengthened his stride and caught up with her. 'Are you joining your family in the Dolphin suite? I can see you to the door.'

'I ...' She paused, came to a stop. Papa would expect her, if she was free. 'Yes, my thanks for your offer, Garvin, but the Prince would be expecting you.'

He stopped too. His eyes crinkled in sympathy, as though he understood her apprehension. 'As you wish. Maker's favour.'

He moved past her, striding through the tall cavernous space. Soft pink light from the skylights in the high vaulted ceiling shimmered on his thick brown hair and two modest feathers of his headdress. With a final wave, he turned into the entrance to the bachelor quarters.

With a soft sigh, she turned toward the closer entrance leading to the Royal atrium at the ground level. A rectangular pool flush with the mosaic floor reflected the sky, bleached of dawn colours. The apartments for the four Markans were arranged around its perimeter.

Lumi paused outside the suite traditionally allotted to the Markan of the Western Marches and took several deep breaths to banish the flutter of moths in her stomach. Who knew what Papa's mood might be? Straightening her shoulders, she walked through the lapis-and-silver-embossed doors, along the corridor and into the common room of the Dolphin suite. Delicious smells drew her forward.

Her family clustered around a low table piled with roasted meats, pancakes, yarma cheese, various fruits, honeycomb, guava juice and maize beer. Father, as always, dominated the room, not least because of his unusual flame-red hair and startling silver eyes that some said had an uncanny resemblance to Akrad the Deceiver. Though not quite as tall and of slimmer build, he towered over most Tamrin. He wore the finest yarma wool tunic in russet, dark breeches and long grey cloak that didn't immediately draw attention, though made of rich and exquisitely crafted materials.

Estolik stood facing Father, a muscle in his cheek twitching. Of medium height, thickset and with mid-brown hair and green-grey eyes, he looked diminished beside Father.

Mother sat straight-backed and composed on a curved stool, as ever, immaculate in a rich gown and a few well-placed jewels. Her soft aquamarine tunic, embroidered with silver dolphins sporting in the waves at the cuffs and shoulders, was complemented by a necklace and earrings of gold, pearls and turquoise. Lumi's younger two siblings, twelve-year-old Tina and six-year-old Kanak, gave their full attention to the food.

'So, what of this Limarian princess, my boy? Has my estimable cousin Rokkan closed a marriage contract between her and the Prince yet?' Father's eyes bored into her brother. His fine lips pulled down. He wasn't happy about the prospect.

'Not if Mannok has any choice,' Estolik replied.

Father's nose wrinkled. 'His wishes are immaterial. A good son obeys his parents' requests regardless of his personal preferences. A Prince even more so. Rokkan spoils that boy as his father Martel spoiled Naetok. Still, the longer Mannok takes to settle down and produce an heir, the better.'

Lumi walked across the room. She bent forward and gave her mother a gentle hug. Mother looked up and smiled. The shimmer of a pearl-studded net over her intricately arranged hair stood in contrast to her wan face and tired eyes. No doubt she was still recovering from the long trip from Akra.

Father turned, his silver eyes cool and distant. 'What about you, daughter, can you better your brother's vague suppositions? Or have you been wasting your time by mooning after some lordling?'

Lumi dropped her eyes before her father's penetrating stare and flushed. Somehow, he had the knack of making her feel like a young girl in short tunics rather than a sophisticated young woman of the court, almost seventeen years old.

'Speak up girl.'

Her lower lip quivered. She had to say something and why not impress her father for once with what she'd heard this morning. The Kupanna would expect her to be discreet, but surely there was no harm in saying what would soon be general knowledge.

Pushing down a niggling sense of uneasiness, she took a deep breath. 'Prince Mannok despises Princess Kerri. We all do. Anyhow, the Kapok is strongly against any alliance with Limar. He wants to keep them completely out of Tamrin affairs.'

'Does he indeed?' Father's eyes narrowed. His foot tapped the curling waves patterned in lapis lazuli and shining quartz in the mosaic floor. 'Interesting. Though surely Rokkan didn't sanction that reckless prank against the Limarian princess?'

'I don't think so, Father. The Kapok has decided to send the Prince for a stretch at the northern border.'

'Yes, Mannok mentioned that last night.' Estolik's eyes gleamed, his face and manner coming to life. 'He's asked me to go with him. I can't wait to see some real action.'

'Foolish boy! You will decline the Prince's invitation.'

Estolik scowled. 'What excuse could I give this time? I am two years older than Mannok and as good a warrior. I don't want to be called a coward.'

Father's eyes narrowed and his lips thinned. 'I'd rather be called a coward, than a fool. Consider your loyalties, son. Rokkan has presented us with one ... no, two ... good opportunities to exploit. If an accident should befall the royal whelp as he and his friends patrol the northern borders, I don't want you in the vicinity.'

Estolik's jaw dropped. 'That ... that's treason! Look what happened to Prince Naetok.'

'Pshah, don't compare me with that idiot. Naetok lacked wit, subtlety, finesse. And his brother's brilliant grip on military strategy outclassed his petulant posturing.'

Lumi pressed her hand to her throat. Surely Father didn't plan to harm Mannok? Please, sweet Maker, don't let this be true. She would never forgive herself if information she had shared resulted in harm to the Prince.

Estolik and Mama stared at Father, eyes wide as startled owls. Even the children stopped eating, faces tense at the raised voices. At least there were no servants in the room to hear Father's seditious words.

'Are we not loyal subjects of the Kapok?' Estolik managed to say at last.

With a click of the tongue, Father seemed to notice the ten rounded eyes fixed on him. He shrugged and his pale lips bent up into a closed lip smile. 'Of course, of course, son. None could be more devoted to my cousin, the Kapok, than I. I never supported Naetok's attempts to steal his brother's throne. Nor do I wish to emulate that twerp. Yet accidents are prone to happen, especially on a contested border.'

'If such an accident did happen and I had excused myself from being present, then suspicion would fall on us, again. This is a repeat of the Trial of Tears last year when you insisted I refuse Mannok's invitation to join his band. To forgo that honour and then ... then the bridge was sabotaged. Father, I will have nothing to do with such–'

'Silence!' Father hissed. 'You are my son; you will do as I tell you or suffer the consequences.' He raised his hand, as though he'd strike Estolik, then after a moment, dropped it. 'Do not test me, son. You are not irreplaceable.' His gaze drifted to where little Kanak sat, open-jawed and looking like an agouti facing an eagle. Little Tina sniffled and buried her small head in the skirt of Mama's robe.

Estolik's nostrils flared. His mouth worked as though biting back words.

Lumi clenched her hands to stop their tremble. This time Father's anger was not directed at her. Still, even the smallest movement might attract his attention and his ire. She held her breath, pushing down the acid questions searing through her mind. Would he harm Mannok? Would he really disinherit Estolik, his oldest son? Would he discard her, leaving her nameless, homeless, clanless, if she failed to please him? She shuddered. He was bluffing, he had to be.

With a rustle of her cloak, Mother stood up from the couch, a pale ring around her lips, but otherwise outwardly calm. She glided to Father and placed a bejewelled hand on his arm.

'My Lord, our son is not questioning your authority. We are after all, as you say, loyal subjects and loyal to you.'

Father's smile showed his eye teeth. 'As you say, my wife.' Like a sudden change of wind in the middle of an ocean squall, the tension and fury leaked from his face. 'Though I would hear the boy say it to me.'

Lumi released her breath, her fingers tingling with relief. Everyone knew and feared Father's rages, at least everyone in Akra.

Estolik licked his lips and inclined his head. 'Of course, Father. I will be guided by your wisdom and ...,' a slight mulish tightening of his lips, '... obedient to your wishes.'

'Smart lad. Refuse the Prince's invitation tonight.'

'Yes, but he'll want to know why.'

Father clapped her brother on the back, causing him to stumble. 'We do need a good reason and I have a perfect one. A wedding.'

Estolik stared at Father and blinked. 'What wedding?'

'Yours, my son.'

Estolik opened his mouth, then closed it like a landed fish gasping for air.

Father smirked and turned to Lumi, his angular face relaxing into a satisfied smile. 'Excellent work, daughter. Be careful to remain in the Kupanna's good graces, and let me know if you hear anything else of interest. Now, I have plans to make.'

He strode out of the room without a further word.

Lumi's heartbeat ramped down. She exchanged looks with Estolik and Mama, both appearing as stunned as she. How often had she imagined her father praising her without the sharp sting of a snide comment or backhanded compliment? Yet now the moment had come, and she felt only fear and dismay.

Chapter Sixteen: Charge

Dinnis

Dinnis slammed his bound right fist into the padded target dummy and followed it up with his left. The stuffed leather body gave a satisfying thunk-thunk. He had the practice yards to himself, the sound of spear on spear or the thud of arrows absent. The Palace stables, workshops and garrison barracks that surrounded the yards drowsed in the heat as the workers took their meal and midday siestas. Even the Limarians seemed to have paused their frenetic preparations for departure. Only the guards stood straight and watchful at the entrance to the breezeway to the kitchen annex and the guard tower at the goods gate.

He wiped the sweat dripping into his eyes with the back of his arm. Prince Mannok and his close circle of age-mates were in the bachelor quarters, deep in planning and packing for their departure to the north early tomorrow morning after the Fealty ceremony. His few things were already packed, his counsel not needed. He'd requested leave, but Kaptan Jakan had insisted he go as part of the Prince's band, no matter how hard he pleaded. Six alume. If that included travel time, they might be back in time for the New Growth, if only just. How would Tilli take this, his longest absence yet? And Laetil would surely have no choice but to put Norak on as an apprentice in his place. All his plans were unravelling like a frayed tapestry, because of his half-brother's impetuous, foolish actions. Because Tilli could not, would not, wait.

Thunk, thunk. Thunk, thunk, thunk.

He aimed a flurry of high kicks at the target dummy, hammering the leather, expunging the image of Tujek standing so close to Tilli. He wanted what she wanted; a life together independent of the Palace. They would work well together, he a healer, she a herbalist. But getting permission from the Palace when the Kapok, or at least his minders, wanted to keep him close? That might never be possible, let alone by the New Growth festival. If he told her the truth, his connection to the Kapok, he'd put her and Anna's whole family in danger. Maybe already had by association. Perhaps he could talk to Rokkan, see if his father's promises meant more than a stinking pile of manure. Thunk, thunk. Thunk, thunk.

He fell back. Resting his hands on his thighs, he sucked in air. Who was he fooling? However remorseful Rokkan might be, however much he might ease Dinnis' situation, he wouldn't jeopardise Mannok's claim to the throne. Not by acknowledging Dinnis and Ista as his true-born children. And surely not by releasing him from the Palace or allowing him to marry, if it meant having children of his own.

The wind picked up, swirling dust into his face. He shivered as his sweaty skin cooled. What good was sowing seeds of love, as Rasel urged him all those years ago, if he couldn't let them grow? Would he never escape Akrad's curse, his blighted legacy?

A frustrated yell tore through his throat. He attacked the target with a frenzied combination of hands, feet, knees and elbows. One massive kick and the padded dummy shuddered, broke free of the pole and crashed to the ground. The leather split open, straw and padding spilling out like guts. He pulled up and rubbed his throbbing knuckles. Tears stung his eyes. His chest ached for air, for space and freedom.

'I think we can declare it's dead.' The deep voice bubbling with suppressed amusement came from behind him.

He swung around, his hands raised defensively and glared at the intruder.

Rokkan Kapok stood in front of him. Tall, broad-shouldered and powerful in plain cream tunic and orange cloak. He made the burly Lutan Atorak behind him look short and almost puny. It took all the self-control that Dinnis owned not to punch that smiling face with its majestic aquiline nose and amber eyes. Now, he shows himself, now after three alume of silence.

The Kapok raised his right eyebrow.

'Something troubles you?'

'And that matters to you because ...?'

'You might mistake me for a target?' Rokkan put his head to one side, then unfastening his cloak, he draped it over Dinnis' bare shoulders. 'It is unlike you, Dinnu, to let your feelings get the better of you.'

Dinnis looked down and took a deep breath searching for a nodule of calmness in the raging maelstrom. He grabbed the edge of the cloak to cast it off with a flourish. Yet its familiar smell of chilli and leather soothed without him wanting it to. He unclenched his fists, unclenched his jaw. Why speak to him now? What did Rokkan want? To bust him for leaving the Palace yesterday? To accuse him of Uson and Asik's murders? To charge him with treason?

'Lutan,' Rokkan's voice rumbled. 'Ask Wasuk to bring the young stallion, Blizzard, to the training yard. I'll join you in a short while.'

Dinnis looked up at the Kapok's face, as always, finding it hard to read the thoughts and emotions beneath the bland, smiling surface.

The Lutan fidgeted with his spear. He stared at Dinnis through slitted eyes. 'Your Majesty, pardon me for saying so, but is that wise?'

Rokkan lifted his chin and met the man's slate-brown gaze.

The warrior flinched and bowed, 'Your will, Your Majesty.' With a final scowl thrown in Dinnis' direction, the Lutan hurried away toward the stables.

Behind the high wall of the Palace grounds, misty clouds gathered around the snow-covered Twin Peaks. Dinnis pulled the warmth of the cloak around his body. It might shower later, the rains always reluctant to let go of the high mountain city.

Rokkan stepped to the bucket by the railing and dipped in the attached wooden cup. He thrust it, brimming with cool water, into Dinnis' hands. 'So, what's troubling you, lad?'

Dinnis stared at the circular ripples. Once, this man had been everything to him, but that had been someone else's life, another Dinnis. 'Nothing of importance, Your Majesty.' He lifted the wooden cup and gulped down the cool water.

'Hmmm ... well, keep your secrets for now. Dinnis, my offer, the one I made last year still stands.'

'Really? I might as well not exist for as much notice you've given me.'

'I can see why you might think that. I could help—'

Dinnis' heart thumped. This was it. His mouth went dry. 'Can you release me from the Palace and the Prince's band, if I promise to stay in Tarka, to remain loyal to the Throne?'

'No, I'm sorry. Not yet.'

Of course, why was he not surprised? He dropped the cup, water splashing over Rokkan's burnt-orange boots, and bowed low. 'Then, if you could excuse me, your Majesty? I have somewhere ...,' anywhere but here '... to be.'

Rokkan folded his arms. 'I haven't finished yet. Jakan informed me that you noticed something in Uson's cell, that you in fact found the body.'

Dinnis stilled. 'That was over an alume ago. Am I still a suspect?'

'No.' Rokkan gave him a measured look. 'You're a keen observer, Dinnis. Do you have any idea who might be behind this?'

'Someone in the guard, perhaps, or a noble serving the Palace.'

'A tool, most likely deceived or manipulated by someone with a great deal of patience and subtlety.'

'Lord Haka.' He bit his lip. He shouldn't have said that.

Rokkan tapped his strong chin with a finger. 'He does have the most to gain and we've been at odds these twenty years. This business with Estolik and the Limarian princess ...' He ran his hand through his dark unruly hair. 'He skates close to the line, but never over it, or at least, never with solid proof I could take to the Council.'

Dinnis shifted his stance.

'Unless you know something?' Rokkan's golden eyes were as compelling as Akrad's. And better to tell what he could.

'Last year, before the Trial of Tears, Haka offered me a position for ... services rendered.'

'For treason?'

Dinnis met Rokkan's steady gaze.

'Never in so many words, but that was the implication.'

Rokkan's face clouded. 'That is his style. Slippery as a fox, as patient as a vulture. But words said in private can be denied or explained away.'

'He gave me this token.'

Dinnis dug into the small pocket in his breeches and threw the small silver dolphin at the Kapok. Rokkan easily caught it. A quick look and he thrust it into a fold in his tunic.

'My thanks, Dinnis. We need to keep our eyes on Haka, while remaining open to other possibilities and motives.'

'Like ...?'

'Greed, fear, revenge.'

'Are you pointing your chin at me, Your Majesty?'

'You would have reason enough, Dinnu, yet when it comes to the point, you have always acted in our interests, to protect us. I do not forget I owe you my life.'

High above them a crested eagle keened as it soared on the high air currents. An uncomfortable silence settled between them.

'How can I help then?' Dinnis said at last. 'I told Jakan everything I knew.'

Rokkan paced the practice yard, his dark hair fluttering in the wind. 'If we find the man who killed Uson and Asik, we would be one step closer to our ... fox, whoever that might be. Jakan, Sparak and now Lukarn have questioned the guards, the Palace staff, anyone we think might be connected. We've found some irregularities, with the alteration of the roster, the maid who took the tray to the boys, but nothing to incriminate a specific individual.'

'Did you check who supplied the poison used?'

'Sparak canvassed all the dealers in herbs, all the healers. Striken is used by hunters.' Rokkan shrugged. 'Only one seemed suspicious. A cloaked and hooded man purchased striken from Unka's Apothecary. Unka could not identify the buyer. Above average height but not tall, clothes of fine yarma wool, a gold hilted hunting knife and yarma leather boots, but no jewellery, headdress or other marks of identity or rank.'

'Unka would've asked for a name.'

'He gave one. Nistar of the Agouti clan, staying at the hosthouse in Justice Street.'

'Nistar, "hidden one" in the old language. And there is no Agouti clan. No Justice Street.'

'A false name, yes.'

'But, a noble or at least someone with means and education.'

'Yes, and you found something else—fragments of chillied castana nuts near Uson's body. A rare item too expensive for all but the rich and noble. And not too many people's taste. Jakan is tracking down everyone known to like the treat and who were also present in Tamra at the time of the murders.'

'I can't afford such treats and wouldn't waste metal on them if I could.'

'You see things others don't. Anyone you know likes chilled castana nuts?'

'Both Haka and Estolik, though Haka wasn't in the city.'

'And the physical description of Nistar doesn't fit either of them.'

'Then, there's Waren.'

'Lukarn's Waren? I wasn't aware they were to his taste.'

'I have observed him buying them from time to time. Unless he was buying it as a gift for you?'

Rokkan shook his head, his eyes narrowed. 'He's my nephew, the son of my most loyal follower and closest friend. He has nothing to gain and would most likely lose out if I or Mannok were to die.'

'Then there is you.'

'Hmm, I think I'll absolve myself of my own attempted murder.'

Dinnis smiled at the joke. 'That's all I know. Is that it?'

'There is something. I want you to keep a watch for any threat to Mannok on the border.'

'Really? You want me to protect Prince Mannok?'

'Yes, Lukarn will keep him out of too much trouble, but he has a talent for finding it. Besides, Lord Haka informs me that Estolik will not be going with the Prince because he is negotiating a marriage agreement for his son, and needs him close by.'

'Oh, that's sudden. Who's the bride?'

Rokkan's mouth curved down. 'Princess Kerri of Limar. The fool. As I hadn't yet expressed my opposition to all such liaisons in the Council, I cannot accuse him of defying me.'

'You could forbid it.'

'Indeed, except to oppose it now would cause an even greater insult to the Sulkan. One which I've been at pains to avoid. Hard enough to smooth ruffled feathers after Mannu's little prank, as it is. I don't like the idea, but it's a worry for a future time. At present what concerns me most is that Haka is not keen to have his son beside mine in the North.'

'Like the Trial of Tears?'

'Exactly. That's why I want you to go with Mannok.'

Dinnis took a deep breath. 'Your Majesty, he'll have others to keep him safe, Lukarn, Waren, Garvin, Trasin, Hasuk. And I am … no warrior.'

'Right.' Rokkan looked pointedly at the vanquished dummy lying in the dust of the practice yard. 'I know you do not have the reputation. That is not quite the same thing. Besides, I'm relying on your sharp mind and instinct for danger.'

'I would be relieved not to go. I have ... other plans.'

'No doubt but I would find it very inconvenient to lose my heir to an assassin. I'm sorry Dinnu. In the circumstance it is unfair of me to ask this of you, but it would mean a lot to me. And it will give you more opportunity to uncover our nut fancier. I'll supply you with the chillied nuts.'

Dinnis stared at the rutted, strife-marked ground. 'Do I have a choice?' He looked his father in the eye.

Rokkan placed his hand on his chest. 'I have no natural right to ask. Your heart needs to be in it Dinnis, but I need you there. Mannok needs you.'

Dinnis shivered. What if his father was right? Could Mannok be in danger? Could he forgive himself if his irritating half-brother met a grisly end on the border? But what difference could he make? And if he left the city on palace business, his chances of winning over Tilli would fray like mist in the wind.

A whinny came from the horse training yards a few hundred tanis away. The head groom, Wasuk guided a three-year old colt on a long lead in one of the training yards. Lutan Atorak strode toward them, his eyes fixed on Dinnis.

'I should go,' Rokkan's large hand brushed Dinnis' shoulder then lifted, as though uncertain of his welcome. With a sharp nod, he vaulted the fence and strode toward the stable yards.

Dinnis stood still. 'Your cloak ...' But his father was already halfway to the stables, leaving a hard choice floating in his powerful wake. Or no choice at all. Perhaps, if he wrote to Tilli to explain, she'd understand his dilemma.

On the Royal Road, north of Tarka

Chapter Seventeen: Followed

Rasel

Rasel loped down the mountainside, enjoying the easy power in her jaguar muscles bunching beneath her powerful paws. She loved the freedom of flying in eagle-form, but the feeling of power when she took the jaguar form was bliss. A light rain beaded her fur and she tasted the heady aroma of water on soil, rock, pine and mountain ash. She painted the landscape and its denizens from the subtle mix of scent-trails lingering on the ground, leaves and air.

The sun slipped out from behind the clouds, transfiguring the slanting rain into lines of shining silver. A flock of mountain pigeons startled at her approach and scattered into the lucid air. Upwind, a family of peccaries rooted in the leaf litter.

With a swirl of leaves, the wind changed direction and another, more pungent smell hit her. She wrinkled her nose and sucked in air over her ridged palate, detecting the grass-sweet smell of horses mingled with the sweet-sharp-sour scents of oiled leather, smoke and human sweat. She moved her head from side to side, refining distance and direction and sifting through the subtle clues. The faint grassy smell of pack yarmas was absent. Not merchants or even a family group then, but Tamrin warriors on their way to the north, most likely to the border with the Nolmec.

The musical thud of horse hooves grew stronger, echoed in the soft vibration in the ground beneath her paws. She faded into the shadows. Her tail twitched and her rounded ears pricked forward.

A group of twenty or so riders rounded the bend at a comfortable trot. No sign of foot soldiers or baggage, apart from packs tied behind their saddles. Spears and shields hung in holsters on either side of the horses' flanks. The group moved in formation, so trained warriors from the Tarka or maybe under one of the clan lords, rather than the levy troops.

Something about the leader's wild russet curls, aquiline nose, wide-shouldered build and his air of easy command on a grey stallion seemed familiar. Ah, the princeling careening down the hill in Tarka, two alume past.

A solidly built young warrior on a roan mare followed close behind him. More horses and riders thundered past with a flash of feathered headdresses, painted shields and brightly woven cloaks. Towards the back of the group, Rasel glimpsed a grey-blue face and secretive oblique Nolmec eyes and cynical gaze combined with the prominent Tamrin nose. Another face she should know. She narrowed her eyes, pulling up memories from many solars ago. Could it be that young boy, Dinnis, all grown-up? The blue-skinned young warrior turned and stared straight at where she lay hidden in the grasses and undergrowth. She edged further back into the shadows.

When all of them had trotted past, the swish of horse tails disappearing around the next bend, she loped parallel to the group, keeping to the shadows and slinking behind rocks, fallen trunks and bushes for more than half a lek. The roar of white water rushing over rocks, combined with the aromas of alpine flowers and warm grass, signalled a ravine. The trail widened into an open area drenched by bright sunlight before connecting with one of the many vine-rope and plank bridges slung across a deep groove in the mountainside.

'I hope you're not thinking of following,' Semian's jaguar-voice growled from behind the tree trunk.

She whipped around, her muzzle wrinkled into a snarl. The clatter of horse hooves on the bridge planks echoed off the rocky faces of the ravine.

Semian, in his powerful jaguar form, crouched behind her, his long black-tipped tail lashed from side to side. 'You know the Kinleader's orders, youngest sister.'

'I do, but something is afoot, I feel it. Baba will want to know the details.'

'Tamrin Patrols go north to the Nolmec border all the time. It's nine years since they clashed, brother against brother, in active bloody warfare.'

'These are no ordinary soldiers. See there, that looks like Dinnis.'

Semian sat back on his haunches and yawned. 'Dinnis?'

'The boy who helped Da-baba escape at Akrad's tower, remember.'

'Hmm, yes, surly and cynical for one so young. I remember.' He narrowed his eyes.

'And the leader carries the golden jaguar emblem.'

'The baby prince. He has the look of young Rokkan about him, as does that Nolmec lad.'

'No longer a baby, it would seem.' Rasel smiled. 'You know the younger races mature much faster than we do.'

'Humph, barely out of the cradle and already on his way to war. Another blink of an eye, and he will be on his funeral bier, mourned by his children and grandchildren.'

'Anyone would think you were an ancient da-baba yourself,' she teased. Afterall, Semian was only twenty solars older than she was, the second youngest of her siblings. 'You haven't even chosen a mate yet.'

Semian's whiskers twitched. 'Ugh, not you too. Besides, who would keep you out of trouble if I had a bunch of younglings to shelter?'

She butted her head against his whiskered cheek. 'I can look after myself, sweet brother. But don't you agree, this is no ordinary patrol. We should follow them.'

'Does it matter, as long as they don't move any further into the Great Forest? Whatever secrets Akrad had, he took them to the grave.'

'So we leave the wide lands to them, hiding in shadows instead of making peace with them, as we once did?'

'We've been over this, Rasel. They hate us now and we can't trust them to remain true. The old days are gone and they're never coming back.'

Rasel growled low. Mistakes they may have made, but children of Tamrak weren't all bad, she knew this to be true.

'You weren't there, daughter of Jazadek.' Semian's eyes took on a haunted quality. He licked his shoulder, then shook his head. 'Come, let's rest and eat.'

'But ...'

He hooked a paw around her shoulders. 'And then we catch up on eagle form. Can't hurt to follow them to the border and check on the Nolmec too.'

A warmth swelled inside Rasel's chest, her jaguar heart beating strongly. Semian was the best of all her five brothers and the one least likely to treat her like a youngling. She licked the fur on his cheek. 'You won't regret this, elder brother, I promise.'

'By the Maker's grace, so I can only hope. And once you satisfy your curiosity, we'll return to the Great Forest and our Kin.'

'As you wish.' At least until the next time she scouted out the Wide Lands from the Lapis Sea in the west to the snow-capped mountains and the Great Forest in the east. For something kept calling her back, whatever the danger. However unwise.

Near the Nolmec Border

Chapter Eighteen: On the Border

Dinnis

'Steady, my beauty.'

Dinnis stroked Pumice's dappled grey neck with one hand and slipped the bridle over the greying nose with the other. Pumice blew hard through his nostrils, sending a puff of foggy breath into the chill morning air. A sharp bite of ice did not dampen the sour-sweet stable smell of hay, horses and manure of the castle stables. The rest of the Prince's band saddled their horses. Most smothered yawns, or rubbed night-crusted eyes, too sleepy to talk above the stamp of horses' hooves, the jingle of the tack, and the occasional whinny or nicker.

A band of silver light separated the black silhouette of Kaja's rooflines and surrounding mountains from the dark grey sky. Five alume, since the Prince's band had ridden north to this remote garrison town perched almost on the border. Dinnis let out a long, slow breath. Yet not a scent of danger, just interminable weapons practice, mindless guard duty, and routine patrols. And so far, only Garvin had displayed a taste for the chillied castana nuts the Kapok had sent him. No threat to Mannok, a dead end with the nuts, time lost on his apprenticeship, but at last Tilli had responded to the messages he sent. He patted the letter tucked away in his tunic. She looked forward to spending the New Growth with him. Those few sweet words carried hope for a future together. A rooster's raucous announcement of the coming dawn fractured the serene quiet of these remote mountains.

Garvin grinned at Dinnis. Nothing seemed to dint the lad's sunny temperament. 'You know, Dinnis, you've long outgrown old Pumice. Time you had a bigger and younger mount.'

'And how can I afford that?' Dinnis didn't want to part with Pumice. They'd been friends since he first came to Tarka as an eleven-year-old.

'Ask Mannok.' Garvin cracked his jaw in a wide yawn.

'Hmm.' And be even more beholden to the Prince? Not a pleasant prospect. Most of the others in the band had two or more mounts. He could cut into his repayments to Anna for his apprenticeship with Laetil, but he hoped this would be his first and last border patrol.

Dinnis fitted his spear and bow into the sheaths slung over Pumice's flanks.

Hasuk tightened the girth on his solid mount, Antler. 'Why does Commander Waren give us all the early patrols?'

'At least, we've been assigned some. The first three alume, he restricted us to training and doing manoeuvres,' Garvin said.

'Yeah, don't think I've seen a Nolmec yet, except Dinnis here.'

'I'm sure it's just a matter of time, Hasuk,' Trasin said.

Mannok's silver stallion, Shadow, arched his strong neck and whinnied, his feet moving in a constant dance. Mannok stroked his mount, the spirited horse calming under his touch.

He swung into the horned saddle. 'Stop your chatter and form up. A Nolmec patrol was sighted on or near the border to the east, near White Cliff. That's our rostered area.' Excitement bubbled in Mannok's voice.

Garvin and the others fist-bumped the air, teeth flashing in wide grins as they mounted.

So they might see some action after all, though most likely nothing would come of it. Dinnis nudged Pumice toward today's assigned place, behind Mannok.

A flash of movement from the castle caught his attention.

Lukarn's eldest son, Lord Waren, and two warriors approached the tacking area, the tall round towers of the keep, painted pink in the morning light behind them. Waren's cloak billowed, his stride determined, his face set.

Dinnis sucked in a breath. 'Incoming!'

Mannok turned Shadow in a half circle. 'Slide it!' He looked back toward the guarded gate like a songbird staring at an open cage door, then held up a hand. 'Whoa. Wait.'

Hasuk groaned. 'Now what?'

'Prince Mannok,' Waren called out. Lutan Atorak and another warrior followed a step behind him.

'Commander,' Mannok dipped his head. 'We're off to check White Cliff.'

'You've been reassigned to—'

'But we're ready.'

'Except that is not for you to decide, Mannok.' Waren folded his arms, legs spaced. 'I am the Commander of this garrison.'

'And I am your Prince.'

'I am aware of that, Mannu, but as novice warriors, it behoves you to submit to my command.'

'And so I have, but we have been in Kaja for close to five alume now. We are ready for this.'

'That is for me to decide. You will take the patrol route parallel to the western border past Pine Stand Gap.'

A series of groans erupted from the ranks.

Mannok's jaw twitched. He glared at Waren for a full minute before giving a curt nod.

'As you wish ... Commander.' Mannok raised his hand. 'Move out, Jaguars.'

Dinnis slowly let out his breath and urged Pumice into a walk. That was close. Waren had the right of it, but he was riding the Prince hard, an arrogance he might live to regret.

* * *

The pinks and peaches faded from the sky, replaced with pale greens and a deepening clear blue. The pale half-circle of the silver moon, Argenti, visible high above them. A breeze ruffled Pumice's mane, feathering Dinnis' face. He preferred this ride along the mountain paths to the endless drills and manoeuvres in the practice yards. The denser vegetation on the rugged slopes and warmer temperatures of the borderlands with the Nolmec reminded him of the terrain around Pylonis where he'd spent the happy years before Akrad had taken him and Ista to his tower at North Pass.

The sun climbed in the sky, burning away the mist in the hollows and warming up Dinnis' limbs. Once beyond Kaja's steep valley, the rough-paved roads wound across the rugged landscape with only an occasional village child herding yarmas to the tender shoots higher up the mountain or the whistling call of eagles floating on the air currents. They travelled a good five lek in silence. Mannok rode with Garvin at the head of the small patrol, with Dinnis and Hasuk behind them. Trasin and Mannok's young cousin, Yalik, son of Princess Lakwi, brought up the rear. Fourteen warriors of the Puma and Mountain Fox clans rode between the young nobles.

Mannok picked up the pace, urging Shadow into a trot, and Dinnis and the others followed. The path narrowed, with flinty sheer cliffs looming close on either side. Pumice twitched his ears and shook his black mane. He whinnied and Garvin's Glacier nickered back.

'Did last night's messenger bring any news from home, Mannok?' Garvin asked.

Mannok shrugged. 'Not much of interest. Except, ah, I almost forgot, it's confirmed that Estolik will marry Princess Kerri at the New Growth Festival.'

'What? I thought that was a crazy rumour. Weren't the Limarians leaving when we headed north?'

'Ah, so they were, but they only went as far as Lord Duran's lands and have been in negotiations with Lord Haka since.'

Garvin chuckled. 'So Estolik snatched the beautiful Princess Kerri from under your nose.'

'He is welcome to her. So, who's next. Garvin? Hasuk? Trasin, Durrin?'

'Mannok, maybe? What chance do any of us have when every young maiden the length of Tamra hopes to snare a prince,' Garvin said.

Mannok made a sour face. 'Our wise and wonderful leader, Commander Waren, found a bride—he's an old married man of five alume.'

'The daughter of a minor noble of an even smaller clan,' said Hasuk. 'Too love-sick to be discriminating, hey?'

'Jarrah is beautiful, sweet and very capable.' Garvin twisted around, his thick eyebrows nudging together in a frown. 'And hospitable to us since we arrived. Besides Hasuk, neither you nor I have much claim to high birth.'

Hasuk's tan cheeks darkened. He glared at Garvin's broad back. Garvin might be from the minor nobility, but they all knew Hasuk's father was a Kaptan of no known noble blood from the Deer clan. 'Maybe Dinnis could get himself a Nolmec bride since we're so close to the border.' Hasuk looked over at Dinnis with a lopsided grin.

Dinnis didn't bother replying.

'No problem slipping over the border,' Hasuk continued, not getting the hint. 'You would blend right in.'

'Do you even know what a Nolmec looks like?' Dinnis raised an eyebrow.

'I know they have blue skin and squinty eyes like you.'

'Well, I can tell you, there are not many with grey eyes or noses built like a mountain range. I wouldn't even pass as part Mokkan let alone as full Nolmec.'

'But don't you ever want to go home?' the idiot persisted.

Home? That was a joke. Dinnis sighed, ignoring the boy. He could pass as a Nolmec as easily as he could pass as a Tamrin. Which was not very well at all. That was one thing he loved about Tilli and her family. They no longer saw or picked at his different appearance.

A flurry of wind sent leaves rattling across the path. Dinnis' skin prickled with unease, as though someone watched them. He grimaced. This particular route was a good ten lek from the Nolmec's closest positions. They had traversed it on their regular patrol many times before without incident.

'Well?' Hasuk asked, jostling his horse up against Pumice.

'Give it a rest, Hasuk,' Mannok said. 'It's not that funny. Dinnis has proven his loyalty to Tamra and the Throne more than once.'

Up ahead, the path widened, though the steep cliff walls still pinned them in. On the left, large boulders edged along the cliff face from an old rock fall. On the right, the cliffs retreated a small way back, leaving room for a small stand of mountain pines and straggly bushes. No different from when they'd rode this way a five-day ago, except ... something seemed out of place. And the usual soft coo of wood pigeons was absent from among the pines. Pumice's flank muscles twitched, his ears angling forward. Glacier remained calm, but Shadow shied and kicked up his back hoofs. The wind dropped and tension thrummed in the still air.

Mannok slowed Shadow's pace and looked from left to right. He drew level with the first tall pine tree.

A soft guttural murmur, like a soughing wind, and a number of soft creaks came from the stand of trees.

Dinnis' neck hair lifted.

'*Shamar, shamar*, beware, beware, ambush!' he yelled.

Pushing Pumice into a gallop, he flanked the Prince and swung his shield up to cover them both. A chorus of twangs and arrows showered down on him like hail in a sudden storm. Pumice stumbled and collapsed to the ground. Dinnis jumped free to avoid being crushed, but his legs buckled under him as soon as his boots hit the dirt. Long shafts, fletched with black feathers, studded his faithful friend's grey body. Behind him was a confusion of yells and shouts.

'Take cover behind the boulders. Take cover.' Mannok's call came strong and decisive.

Dinnis pushed his legs under him to run. Excruciating pain shot through his right leg, which buckled under him again. A black-fletched arrow jutted out of his right thigh. Arrows whistled around him, striking the blood-soaked dirt. Keeping low, he scrabbled behind the bulk of his horse. More arrows slammed into the rocky path and the quivering flanks in front of him. The Prince and the rest of the band disappeared behind the cover provided by the boulders.

He stroked the graceful neck, the heaving sides. '*Dava aka*, don't ... don't be afraid. It will be alright, Pumice,' he whispered, not sure whether the words of comfort were for him or his dying friend. The gelding heaved a great shuddering sigh and laid still.

No time for tears, not now. Lying flat, he grabbed his bow from the saddle holster and notched an arrow to the string. Aiming at a blur of movement behind the tree trunks, he released the arrow. A muted cry told him he had hit his target. He fitted another arrow, pushing down the nausea welling up in his gut, the searing pain and weakness fogging his thinking. Wounded and with minimal cover, no doubt, he would soon follow his brave mount into the endless night. Perhaps there was some life beyond, a glimmer of hope that lay across the dark abyss.

Chapter Nineteen: Broken Arrow

Mannok

'Take cover behind the boulders. Take cover.'

Shadow responded to Mannok's nudge and galloped behind the large boulders against the far cliff face. Mannok checked down the column. Garvin on Glacier followed close behind him. The rest of his band scrambled for cover as best they could. Dinnis' warning had prevented the patrol from riding into the full assault of the deadly arrows. Especially since, at first, the enemy focused their fire on the front of the line leaving those behind untouched.

A second volley of arrows pinned them down, preventing a retreat to safety. Many of the smaller rocks provided minimal protection. Even the large boulder he and Garvin sheltered behind left little spare room.

He scanned the thicket of pine trees screening the ambushers. He tensed. Pumice lay motionless in the middle of the blood-soaked road, his flank bristling with arrows. Dinnis half-lay half-sat behind his fallen mount with a shaft protruding from his thigh. His discarded shield lay a short distance away studded with arrows. The fellow pushed himself, grabbed his bow and nocked an arrow. He pulled the string back and let fly, then ducked down as ten to twenty black-fletched arrows darkened the sky.

If his age-mate stayed where he was, pinned down and vulnerable, he would die. Mannok couldn't let that happen.

He wheeled Shadow around.

'Archers, lay down concerted fire,' he shouted.

The skilled archers in his patrol returned fire, and though their adversaries were concealed by the tree trunks, undergrowth and deep shadows, it distracted them enough.

'Dinnis. Get up.' Mannok galloped out from behind the boulder.

Dinnis glanced at him and nodded. Slinging his bow over his shoulder, he grabbed his spear and, using it as leverage, staggered upright.

Leaning along Shadow's flank, Mannok grabbed Dinnis' other arm and pulled him up behind him. With a tug of the reins, Shadow wheeled and raced back for the rock only a few tanis away. Another volley of arrows arched into the air and pelted down as they reached the boulders. Arrows slammed into the cliffside and sheltering rocks.

Catching his breath, Mannok slipped off his mount and eased Dinnis to the ground. His age-mate's breeches were soaked with blood, seeping up from around the arrow shaft. Kneeling, Mannok grasped the arrow shaft to pull it out.

Dinnis grabbed his wrist. 'Leave it. I could bleed out before we get back to Kaja if you remove it.'

Mannok nodded. Of course, how could he forget. Papa had said the same all those years ago when he had been attacked by uncle Naetok. He shivered at the baneful childhood memory. His father lying in a growing pool of blood, his own small three-year-old hands pressing down on the deep wound.

Dinnis grabbed his canteen and poured water over his thigh. His face paled beneath its smoky blue hue. A sheen of sweat popped out on the man's brow. He gritted his teeth and broke off the shaft with his hunting knife.

Mannok quickly grabbed his cloak. Tearing strips off, he used them to form a pad and applied pressure to the wound.

Dinnis lay back, resting on his elbows. 'I'll be okay, I'm going to be fine ... as long as I don't bleed to death ... or get a massive infection ... or develop gangrene or .... Slide it, maybe I should just shut up.'

Garvin barked a laugh. 'You are such a wit, Dinnis.' He slid off Glacier, crouched down and offered Dinnis his canteen.

Dinnis took a swig and gave it back. 'Thanks, Garvin. And my gratitude, Your Highness, I owe you my life.'

Mannok nodded acknowledgment. 'And I owe you mine.'

Mannok risked a glance at the pines and then scanned down the line. Behind the next boulder, Hasuk and Trasin shot arrows, as did others. How long would this stand off last?

'Fire at will but conserve your shots,' he ordered.

He glanced back at Dinnis, fingering his bow, then caught Garvin's eye. 'It looked like that first volley was aimed at me.' He frowned. 'And it's unlike the Nolmec to be this far across the border. The sighting was to the east not the west.'

'They are not Nolmec,' Dinnis said.

'Who else uses black-fletched arrows?'

Dinnis didn't respond. He slumped against the rock and closed his eyes. His face looked pinched and he flinched at the slightest movement. If he didn't get help soon, he could still die.

'We are pinned down here,' Garvin said. 'They can pick us off one by one.' He turned and gave Mannok a wavering smile.

Dinnis' eyes fluttered open and he sat straighter. 'I can still shoot. I'll give you cover while the others get you out, Your Highness.'

'I'm not leaving you behind. Besides you're not that good a shot.'

'Consider the bigger picture, Your Highness. I'm immobilised anyhow and your safety is paramount. I'm going to be really peeved if I took an arrow for you and lost my mount and you still get yourself killed.'

Mannok opened his mouth to reply, but Garvin cut in.

'I agree. I'll stay with Dinnis—you get out of here, Your Highness, and get help. We'll hold off as long as we can.'

Their attackers, now more sparing with their shots, sent arrows at the slightest hint of a visible target. His men returned fire, though the enemy were hard to see. It was a matter of attrition. Even if they took out the ambushers, it would take time and possibly lives. And Dinnis needed a healer sooner rather than later. He narrowed his eyes.

'We could attack ...'

'Too dangerous,' Garvin said. 'We can only guess the number of ambushers, but it has to be at least as many as the patrol.'

What they meant was, it was too dangerous for him, because he was the Prince Royal, heir to the throne. An attack would be risky and pinned down as they were, he couldn't send out scouts. Squaring his shoulder, he made his decision.

'Very well, but we'll need more cover.' He slithered to the other side of the rock and called across to the others, 'Dinnis, Garvin, Hasuk and Trasin lay down a withering fire on my command. Aim it high so you don't hit friends. Everyone else, mount up, and follow my lead.'

Ignoring the dryness in his mouth, his sweaty palms and fluttering in the pit of his stomach, he leapt onto Shadow. 'For Tamra and the Kapok.'

'For Tamra and the Prince,' roared two-tens of throats.

A volley of arrows sailed towards the enemy. Shadow sprung from behind the rock and galloped back along the road to Kaja. A feint, to confuse the enemy. After a few strides, he whooped and wheeled back toward the stand of pines. 'With me, Jaguars, with me.'

A few arrows whined by him. The yells of his warriors and the crash of galloping hooves followed behind. A wide grin curved up his face, the blood tingled through his limbs. He felt alive though his death could come at any moment.

He reached the deep shade of the trees. Startled faces, eyes wide and mouths open stared a moment before the blue shadowed figures scrambled and fled. He thrust his spear at a fleeing warrior.

The man collapsed to the ground, another grabbed the limp body and threw it over a horse. As quickly as snow melting before the midday sun, the attackers gathered their dead and wounded and fled along the road towards the northern border, leaving behind churned-up soil and broken arrows.

Mannok rode out into the sunlight. Garvin emerged from behind the boulders, supporting Dinnis. All his men still standing, though Trasin slumped from his horse, clutching his bleeding right arm, his face pale.

'Hasuk, attend to Trasin,' Mannok yelled, though the others were already rushing to help the lad.

It could have been worse. The last of the ambushers disappeared where the road curved around the flank of the mountain. And he'd counted less than twenty attackers, a number wounded or dead.

'Garvin, take Dinnis and Trasin back to Kaja with Yalik and two others. May the Maker give you speed. Hasuk and the rest of you, form up and let's stop these yellow-bellied crocodiles from escaping.'

Garvin frowned. 'Your Highness—'

'Get them to Kaja, Garo.' Mannok waved a hand and galloped down the road, the bulk of his patrol close behind. 'And send reinforcements. We've both got a job to do.'

* * *

Mannok leant forward in the saddle, the stone-paved road a blur beneath Shadow's hooves. His warriors stretched unevenly out behind him. After half an hour, they were gaining on the ambushers, but even his big-hearted stallion was flagging. A few minutes more and he would have them.

Another long curve in the road hid the ambushers from sight.

'Not long now, my beauty.' He urged Shadow on.

When he rounded the bend, the road was empty. Here the sheer cliffs broke and frayed into a jumble of boulders and bluffs, bare of vegetation. The Badlands. Fissures in the rock led into a maze of canyons and dead ends. He slowed Shadow to a walk, patting his mount's heaving side.

Hasuk caught up, his roan horse lathered in sweat. 'Which way, Your Highness?'

'Slide it, they could have taken any one of these openings.' The hard rocky road, now dried out under the midday sun, left few signs of the ambushers' passing.

'We could split up,' Kimsak suggested.

'Not a good idea this close to the border. The Nolmec could send reinforcements at any moment.'

Sooner or later, they would find evidence, a hoof print in soft dirt or a piece of torn clothing, but it could take hours, days perhaps, to track the band through the branching canyons. And the horses needed rest.

Mannok brushed his hair out of his eyes and sighed. 'We'll head back to Kaja and report to Commander Waren.'

Chapter Twenty: Hero

Mannok

Mannok glowered at his infuriating and oh-so-superior cousin. Waren glared back, his hazel eyes hard as flecked river stones.

'It was foolish to attack the tree line. And even more idiotic to chase after them. What were you thinking?'

Mannok seethed. Trasin was the only one who had been seriously hurt in the charge on the pines. He could just as easily have been injured in a dash to escape and others too, while the chances of survival for archers providing cover would've been minimal. Mannok's manoeuvre meant he'd left no one behind, even if the chase after the ambushers left them empty-handed.

Half-way back to Kaja, a tight-lipped Waren had met him with another patrol. His cousin had not stopped haranguing him during the ride back to base until now. At least if Papa or Uncle Lukarn decided to upbraid him, they did it in private. Waren had dishonoured and insulted him in front of his men and age-mates.

Thrusting out his jaw, Mannok stepped forward. Garvin caught his upper arm, holding him back. His friend was right. Getting into a fight with Waren wouldn't help.

'I regret my actions angered you, sir,' he conceded through tight lips.

Breathing heavily, he glanced around the small austere room, his eyes stopping at Dinnis. His age-mate lay stretched out on the wooden bench, his smoky blue face pale and mask-like, his eyes closed. Beside him the garrison surgeon, Valen, over-tunic stained with blood, washed his hands in a polished copper basin, having just come from treating Trasin's injuries.

'Are you listening, Mannok?' Waren said, his voice a little less heated. 'What would I have said to your father, had you been killed?'

'That I fought and thought like a warrior. Like he would have.'

'Taking the enemy by surprise after feinting an escape attempt is certainly worthy of Rokkan Kapok,' Dinnis said, his voice faint. 'It is not as if the Prince planned to ride into an ambush.'

Waren swung to face Dinnis. 'And what would you know about military strategy?'

The door creaked open and Lady Jarrah, Waren's wife, entered the room, her soft brown eyes lowered to the floor. With a quick bow to Mannok, she moved to stand beside the surgeon. Taking a knife, she cut through the cloth and blood-stained field dressings on Dinnis' thigh.

Valen straightened, his long face severe. 'Commander Waren, I would appreciate it if we could focus on the task at hand and leave the recriminations for later.'

Waren grunted, then nodded.

Valen offered Dinnis a wad of green leaves. 'Chew on this keka leaf. It will help with the pain.'

Dinnis hesitated and then took the wad and chewed as instructed. The surgeon ripped away the leg of Dinnis' breeches to expose angry and puckered flesh surrounding the broken-off shaft. Dark blood seeped at the edges of the wound.

Jarrah swabbed the area with hot water and maize spirits, while Valen laid out his instruments.

Mannok's stomach squirmed.

'Now my Lords, Your Highness, if one of you could hold your friend still there while we work?'

Mannok licked his dry lips and walked to the head of the bench. He looped his arms around Dinnis' narrow shoulders. Garvin moved to the other end to hold Dinnis' ankles.

Valen nodded and flashed a quick smile. 'Someone showed some sense in not pulling this thing out. Let's see how deep it is and whether it's lodged in the bone. Probe, Jarrah if you please.'

The surgeon prodded the wound and Dinnis stiffened, then his breathing became deep and steady. The sharp iron smell of blood and the pungent aromas of herbs filled Mannok's nostrils. He averted his eyes.

'Good, good, it moves freely, close to the bone but not in it.' The surgeon's tunic rustled and he leaned in closer. 'Hmm, the arrowhead almost made it out. I'll make an incision on the back of the thigh here and pull it through. Knife.'

'Here,' Jarrah said.

'This will hurt, lad. Hold him tight, Your Highness.'

Dinnis grunted and gripped Mannok's arm.

After a moment, Valen pulled out a dark, blood-stained arrowhead attached to a broken-off length of shaft and dropped it with a dull clang into a bronze bowl. 'There, that's it. Nothing broken off, no loose fragments in the wound. Best to let it drain, for now.'

Jarrah brought over a basin of water and washed the wound and then applied a thick fragrant salve.

'Briarweed, meadowsweet and honey,' Dinnis murmured, his eyes half-closed.

'So it is.' Valen raised his eyebrows and studied Dinnis. 'You've got fortitude, I'll give you that, lad. You can relax now. Do you mind bandaging, Jarrah?'

'Not at all, Dada,' Jarrah replied with a gentle smile. Mannok started. After five alume in Kaja, he hadn't realised that Jarrah was Valen's daughter. Minor nobility indeed, but he could see why Waren had fallen for her. Shy and pretty in a sweet sort of way, she showed herself capable and level-headed.

'Thank you, Your Highness. You can release him now,' she said.

Mannok stood up, his legs a little unsteady, his stomach unsettled. Jarrah wrapped the white cotton strips around Dinnis' thigh with a firm touch.

'My thanks, Surgeon Valen, Lady Jarrah,' Dinnis said in a threadbare tone. 'I appreciate someone who knows what they're doing.'

Valen washed his hands. 'You can repay us by getting well, lad.'

Mannok stretched his aching back. His limbs weighed heavy with fatigue, the early morning start, the hours in the saddle and the excitement of the skirmish catching up with him. Yet he couldn't leave until Waren, as commanding officer, dismissed him.

A loud booming voice came from the corridor. 'Stand aside, warrior.'

Uncle Lukarn burst into the room, looking wild, his bald dome glaring in the late afternoon sunlight filtering through the latticed window from the courtyard.

'Where is he, is he alright?'

'If we can keep the infection at bay, he'll be fine soon enough,' Valen said.

Dinnis propped himself up. 'Wrong patient, perhaps? You can find Trasin in the other room.'

'Indeed,' Valen confirmed. 'Trasin sustained serious damage to his left arm and shoulder, and a head injury, my Lord. By the Maker's favour, he will survive.'

Lukarn looked from the surgeon, to Dinnis and then to Mannok. He let out a long sigh and closed his eyes.

With a stride across the room, he pulled Mannok into a bear hug that crushed his ribs and stifled his breathing. 'Uncle,' he protested.

'Thank the Maker,' Uncle Lukarn breathed. 'On both counts. I just this minute rode in and when I heard my nephew was badly injured. I thought ... I'm glad you are unharmed, your Highness.'

'If I am, it's thanks to Dinnis, Uncle.'

'Probably saved more than a few lives today at the risk of his own.' Garvin moved away from the bench.

Lukarn's bushy eyebrows flew upwards. He glanced at Dinnis and shook his head in disbelief. 'The Prince's life was in danger.' He turned and glared at his son.

Waren swallowed and cleared his throat. 'We had no idea the Nolmec were in the area, Papa ... sir. A sighting was reported last night but in the opposite direction, at Whitecliff. We've never had any trouble at Pine Stand Gap before.'

'Humph, well it is strange.'

'They weren't Nolmec.' Dinnis' lips twisted as though he regretted speaking.

'Nonsense, the arrows were black-fletched,' Mannok said. 'And the warriors looked blue-skinned to me.'

'*Niktis ar thanis*,' Dinnis said, closing his eyes.

Mannok frowned. The words sounded Nolmec but they made no sense to him.

'Victory or death.' Uncle Lukarn rubbed the back of his neck. 'It is strange they did not stand and fight. Any Nolmec unit that deep into Tamrin territory would have been on a suicide mission. But if not Nolmec, who? And who else has motive to attack you?'

'They didn't fight like Nolmec soldiers. They used Tamrin formations.' Dinnis reached over and grabbed the blood-crusted arrowhead. He rubbed it between thumb and finger.

'Perhaps, they took the dead to prevent the discovery of their real identities,' Garvin said.

Mannok shifted his weight from one foot to the other. 'Come to think of it, they were too short and didn't ride like Nolmec.'

'And this is of Tamrin not Nolmec design.' Dinnis held up the arrowhead between finger and thumb. 'Look at the curve and the thickness and the quality of the bronze.'

'Piffle.' Uncle Lukarn snatched the arrowhead. 'Where did you get this?'

Mannok peered over his shoulder. 'Valen dug it out of Dinnis' thigh. Is that a clan mark on the blade?'

Uncle Lukarn grunted. 'It's been scratched to obscure it.' He rolled the blade to catch the light.

'A ...a seagull mark perhaps?'

'Could be dolphin or even puma. It's too abraded to be certain.'

'I think, my Lord, our patient needs to rest.' Jarrah's soft voice interrupted. 'Wouldn't you say so, Father?' she added. 'I'll bring some broth for Dinnis and then check on Trasin.'

Valen nodded. 'Indeed, war councils don't belong in the sick room.' And with that he ushered everyone except Lady Jarrah out of the room.

Nakri

Chapter Twenty-One: Amputation

Dinnis

Dinnis swam in hot lava, his flesh burning away. No, that wasn't right. But he was burning. Sweat dripped down his face. His tongue stuck to the roof of his mouth. He swallowed, his throat like dry Tamamak desert. His leg throbbed like a gong that warned of war.

He pushed against the weight of his eyelids and stared into flickering shadows. Curved stone walls wavered in and out, outlandish patterns of orange-red and black mottling his vision. A curl of dark smoke drifted in front of his eyes from a guttered torch. Weak silvery moonlight shone through the high glazed window cut into the thick, stone wall, glancing off the bronze brackets and metal bedframe. Carved deep into the heavy wooden door, a stalking puma stared at him with citrine eyes, its mouth wide in an angry snarl.

Where was he?

Memories filtered back in jagged bits. The ambush. The trip to Kaja. Lord Lukarn insisting he and Trasin be moved to Nakri as soon as they were stabilised. A feverish journey in horse-drawn frames over rough mountain roads. Arriving in the middle of the night to Nakri Castle, the seat of Lukarn son of Derik, Markan of the Northern Marches. The Puma's den. He looked around for Trasin, could see no one else in this cramped tower room.

The pain in his leg mushroomed. He bit into his fist, smothering a groan. According to Valen, the arrowhead had scraped his thigh bone, though not broken it. But infection was a worry. An expanding pain bored into him, sharp and insistent. He slowed his breathing, focusing his mind on happier memories, long ago, of Rasel meeting him on the northern road, of Anna's kitchen, with little Aska, Tilli's sister, serving rich aromatic stew on flat rounds of maize torkias. Nikki and Norak squabbling about whose turn it was to clean up while Tilli entwined her calloused and capable hands with his own.

Strident voices swirled outside the door, slowly solidifying into words.

'… a hard decision, my Lord, but a necessary one.'

The guttural brusque voice of Markan Lukarn's chief surgeon, Tamak, jarred him.

'Can't you save the limb? Lukarn's gruff voice.

'If I don't operate tonight, he will die. Even then, there are no guarantees.'

Ice lanced up Dinnis' spine. Whose limb? Did they mean his? Or Trasin's? He couldn't allow it to happen. What chance did he have as a cripple?

He swung his good leg out of the bed and pushed himself up. His bad leg twisted in a flash of blinding pain. He staggered, scrabbling to grab hold of the bedframe, missed, lurched forwards. The small table beside the bed and the tray resting on it crashed to the wooden floor. The room spun like a grinding stone and his world went black.

* * *

Dinnis thrashed his head from side to side, moaning. He opened his eyes as the last mists of stupor melted away in the recesses of his mind. Warm sunlight streamed through a window. The words of last night, if it was last night, echoed clearly in his mind 'Even if we take the limb tonight.' And now it was morning. Without a leg, what hope did he have? His breath caught as a shaft of agony shot through him. His thigh pulsated with pain. He laughed, raggedly, almost hysterically. Blessed pain. His leg was still there.

Digging his elbows into the straw mattress, he pulled himself up into a seating position. His fingers found his thickly bandaged thigh, still hot and tender and attached to his knee and lower leg. He rubbed tears away with the palm of his hands. A bad dream.

Moments later, the door swung open and Lady Samara, Lord Lukarn's gentle wife, entered, carrying a small tray with food, medicines and new bandages. Her husband and another man followed her into the small room.

'So you are awake,' Lady Samara said, setting the tray down on the table. 'The surgeon gave you a sedative after we found you collapsed on the floor. What were you thinking, getting out of bed?' Her kind smile took the sting out of the words.

'Tamak mentioned amputation last night,' he said, disgusted at how his voice shook.

Lady Samara's eyes glistened with tears, while Lukarn scowled, his face working to hold in his emotion.

'Rather cruel of you to gloat, slinky,' the other man said.

Dinnis' brow furrowed. Why would he be gloating? This young man seemed familiar. His dark brown eyes, strong nose and chin were not unlike Lord Lukarn's. Not as tall, yet strong, with a similar stocky build.

Dinnis looked again at the Markana's moist eyes, at her husband's pale face. Unless. He closed his eyes. Trasin!

'Tamak operated on Trasin last night. His arm turned gangrenous,' Samara said, confirming Dinnis' belated conclusion.

'I'm sad to hear that. How is he?'

'He came out from under the surgery, but it is still too early to tell whether he will recover.'

'I hope he does.' Trasin was a good man.

The stranger ... ah now he remembered ... Challak's eldest son and Trasin's brother, Adjunct Puran. He was in his mid-twenties, a couple of years too old to be included in the Prince's age-band.

Puran stepped up close to the bed, leaning over Dinnis with clenched fists.

'You are a right piece of work, faking concern. It's your fault Trasin was hurt. How did you know about the ambush?'

A livid scratch slashed across Puran's left cheekbone. Scabbed cuts crossed the back of his hands. Dinnis narrowed his eyes. Puran was appointed Commander of the region to the west of Kaja at the Festival of New Beginnings. If memory served, he'd been in Tarka at the time of the murders, standing in for Lukarn as the Kapok's security chief. Though, given his close ties with Lukarn, it seemed unlikely that he would act against the Kapok.

Lukarn gripped Puran's shoulder.

'Son, Dinnis saved the Prince's life by shielding him. I understand your anger but it is misplaced.'

'How can you trust a thieving Nolmec half-blood?'

'He has the Kapok's favour. And, at least in this instance, his actions speak for him.'

'Do not stress the lad, Puran.' Lady Samara's gentle face was creased into a frown. 'He is recovering from his injuries.'

Puran glared at Dinnis, his neck and jaw muscles bunched, a pulse throbbing in his terracotta cheeks. With a low growl, he headed out the room, slamming the heavy door behind him.

Dinnis eased back against the bolster, careful not to jolt his leg. 'I did not know, sir, that Commander Puran had seen action.'

'While on patrol a few lek west of Pine Stand Gap, he intercepted and engaged some of the stragglers from the ambush. The distance between the groups was too great and they escaped back to the border.'

'Then, you think it was the Nolmec?'

Lukarn ran his hand over his bald dome. 'No. I agree with your assessment. And that is what I've informed Rokkan.'

Dinnis blinked and gave a lop-sided smile.

'You agree ... with me? I must be dreaming.'

The Markan lifted his chin and folded his arms. 'Don't get used to it.'

Markana Samara clicked her tongue. 'Lukarn!' She handed Dinnis a herbal draught. 'Drink this.'

He gulped it down, making a face at its bitter taste. His eyelids grew heavy. A soporific then, probably sun poppy, purple pasak blossom and marosa tea by the taste.

Samara unwound the bandages on his thigh. Though her hands were gentle, he still inhaled sharply as she pulled at where the dressing stuck to the wound. She filled the basin with water from a jug on the table and washed his wound before wrapping it with clean bandages.

Lukarn stirred, bringing his eyes back to Dinnis. 'The question is, if not the Nolmec, then who?'

Golden Palace, Tarka

Chapter Twenty-Two: Messenger

Lumi

Lumi bent down to sniff the subtle scent of the mountain lily. The afternoon heat burned away all traces of the early morning chill, a reminder of the colder season long banished. A profusion of heady, floral scents hung in the sunlit air.

She selected a perfect bloom and placed the delicate flower in the flat basket held by Princess Lakwi's slim daughter, Lady Jati. Rizanna stood on the other side, her hazel eyes dreamy. Both friends shimmered like colourful blossoms in their long tunics and cloaks of fine yarma wool, a perfect match for her own grey tunic and indigo cloak edged in silver filigree.

She considered the heaped blossoms and foliage in the basket. 'Is that enough?'

Rizzi waved her garden shears. 'Without a doubt, Lumi darling. Isn't it your turn to attend the Kupanna? Jati and I can arrange the flowers in the smaller banqueting hall for the formal dinner tonight.'

Jati hugged the basket tight and spun in a circle. 'Do you think we could ride out to Jaguar rock early tomorrow morning, if the Kupanna can spare us?'

At fourteen, Princess Lakwi's daughter was newly appointed to the Kupanna's household, following the Red Flowers festival marking a young woman's entry to adulthood.

'Let's ask. A riding expedition would be a welcome change from embroidering cloaks and mending clothes.' Rizanna linked arms with

Lumi and Jati and together they strolled along the path towards the eastern side entrance to the Palace.

Lumi could only agree. Without Mannok and his band around to disrupt the normal routines, and most of the nobles that mattered returned to their clan lands, the Palace multiplied in dullness. 'Any recent news from the north, Rizzi?'

'Waren and Jarrah have settled in at Kaja. And just the normal shenanigans from my younger siblings.' She grimaced. 'Nothing about the border or our Prince.'

Jati hitched a slender shoulder. 'Nothing to report means no untoward events, right?'

Lumi swallowed her disappointment and nodded. Over five alume since the Prince had ridden north with his band. They hadn't returned for the Maize Harvest Festival during the cool season but, surely, he would return for the New Growth Feast in half an alume?

Small birds flittered in the branches studded with blossoms. Snow-capped mountains ringed the horizon, stark white against the ink-blue sky. The gardens at home were not nearly so intricate as these nooks, squares and oblong spaces connected by winding paths of the Palace precincts. Even so, she did miss the smell and roar of the ocean, the strident call of the seagulls and the dolphins riding the silver-crested waves out from the shore.

Rizanna bumped her shoulder. 'Lumi, I can take your duty with Kupanna this morning, if you wish to spend time with your family before they return to Akra.'

'A gracious offer, but I'm good.' She was in no hurry to face Father's critical gaze, Estolik's moody sulking and Princess Kerri's interminable whinging. Poor Mama, having to put up with it all.

Rizzi shook her arm playfully. 'Well, if there is any news about you know who, make sure you tell us every last delicious detail.'

'What's so interesting about border patrols?' Jati yawned and shook her head. 'Oh, I almost forgot. You will never guess, Rizzi. Head Librarian Ralton let me borrow an illustrated codex of the Lays of Namu, Lady of the Waterfall.' She gave a little dance, the flowers bouncing close to the edge of the basket.

Rizanna let go of Lumi's arm and clapped her hands. 'Oh, Jati, you must show me. Getting books past Ralton is like sneaking a cavy from the paws of a hungry puma.'

Lumi only half-listened to the other girls' chatter about the ancient legend and which version they liked the best, the ancient song of Namu and Solik or Melton's more recent lay.

Instead, other images filled her head, images of a mischievous young prince with russet hair, alluring green eyes and a playful grin, bending over her hand, helping her mount, riding to Bridal Veil Falls, or besting his age-mates in the practice yards.

They entered the side door between the military command offices on the eastern side of the Palace. Once they reached the Great Hall, Jati and Rizzi hurried to arrange the flowers in the lesser dining hall on the second floor. Lumi smoothed her hair and straightened her robe before hurrying up the great curve of grand stairs and along the third-floor balcony leading to the Royal suites. She nodded toward the guards before entering the antechamber to the royal sleeping rooms.

The Kapok, dressed in a plain tunic, sat on one of the sofas, one ankle resting on his knee. He glanced up from the sheath of important papers in front of him and smiled.

'Sweet Lumi, you are like a dazzle of sunlight at play amid the ocean waves.'

She blushed and bowed. 'Thank you, Your Majesty, though I've no idea what that means.'

'It means, my dear, that he will bedazzle you with words, smiles and deceitful charm, if you are not careful.'

Kupanna Marra entered the room to stand behind the Kapok. Her face softened into a fond smile, and she rested a hand on his shoulder. Her deep purple tunic embroidered in gold fruits and flowers and tied with a wide gold cloth belt matched the amethysts and gold dripping from her ears, neck and fingers.

'Ah, my sweet marosa, you wound me.' Rokkan Kapok slapped a hand to his chest and winked at Lumi, increasing her confusion.

Lumi was never sure what the Kapok would do next or when their banter might erupt into bickering.

She dropped her gaze to the floral patterns on the tiles and rugs on the floor. 'Kupanna Marra surely outshines me in beauty and wit.'

'A diplomatic answer.' A hint of a smile played at the corners of his generous mouth. He looked up at the Kupanna and the smile grew affectionate. 'My mountain beauty, my marosa, shines with the splendour of golden Alumi at the cusp of twilight. She still takes my breath away even twenty years on.'

'But not your golden tongue, it seems. Do you have to do your paperwork here, Rokkan? I was hoping Lumi could help me with the meal plans for the next week.' She turned to face Lumi. 'How long do you think your family will stay? They are welcome to, of course.'

'I ... I am not sure, your Majesty. Princess Kerri seems reluctant to go to Akra.' Despite Father's rapid announcement of Estolik's marriage agreement between Kerri and Estolik after the New Beginnings Banquet, the need to negotiate with the Sulkan in faraway Limar and the necessary exchange of gifts between the two parties meant the wedding would take place at the New Growth Festival. It would be an elaborate and sumptuous event, performed by Chief Priest Kaifak on the top of the Temple platform.

The Kapok grinned. 'Akra will be a big change for her, given she thinks the Golden Palace 'quaint' and 'rustic'. I wish your father the joy of his new daughter-in-law.' He placed the documents aside on a low table and leaned back against the sofa. 'Now my dear, don't hustle me out. I'll be finished in a minute. Then I'll take Blizzard out for a ride with my hounds.'

'Is that the young stallion Prince Tannik sent up from Silisea? Do be careful Rokkan, he's only newly trained.' The Kupanna picked up the papers and leafed through them. 'Why can't these minor nobles sort out their own inheritance squabbles without taking up your time?' She wrinkled her nose. 'Hmmm, well I wouldn't trust Lord Pirak with half a peck of chillies. He is obviously trying to cheat his cousin.'

'My thoughts, exactly, my dear. Maybe I should leave you to sort out this rowdy bunch of triers while I go riding with my dogs?'

'Oh, do stop teasing. Besides, you only have yourself to blame, Rokkan. You encourage them by holding court to all and sundry.'

'Just earning my keep.' The Kapok stopped and looked up towards the door, his eyes narrowing.

'What nonsense. You seem to forget you are the Kapok.' The Kupanna glanced at her husband. 'What is it?'

He grimaced. 'Someone is in a hurry.'

The doors swung open, banging against the wall, and a warrior, out of breath and in travelworn clothes, entered the room. He dropped to his knees and stretched out before the Kapok.

'Your Majesty.'

'Lutan Tavin? What is it?'

'A message from Markan Lukarn, Your Majesty,' the man said, raising to his knees and holding up a small leather pouch sealed with a leaping puma design.

An urgent message from the north! Lumi gripped her hands together. Mannok!

The Kapok took the pouch, broke the seal and extracted a parchment. 'Thank you, Lutan. Go and rest. I'll send for you if I have need.'

'Your will, Majesty.' The messenger bowed and backed out of the room, closing the door behind him.

'Is ... I told you I would not forgive you if ...' Marra hovered over the Kapok as he read the document.

'Hush, my dear. Don't buy trouble before its time.' Rokkan laid down the pouch on the table and took his wife's slim tan hands into his own large bronze ones.

'First, my marosa, be assured our son is well and unharmed. There was an incident ...'

Marra pulled in a sharp breath, her hands tightening in the Kapok's grip. Lumi slapped her hand to her mouth.

'... An ambush by an armed party, but Dinnis' warning ensured they found cover, and only Dinnis and Trasin received significant injuries.'

'Dinnis?' A crease deepened between the Kupanna's brows. She pulled her hand free and paced the room, her long robe whispering on the mosaic floor. 'Why would that ... Nolmec, why would he protect our son? Did he avert the ambush, or plan it?'

'Now, Marra—'

'Who does Lukarn think is responsible?'

Rokkan picked up the pouch. He pulled out part of a bedraggled and trimmed black feather and what looked like an arrowhead with a ruddy-brown substance embedded in the grooves.

'Lukarn thinks that while the black-shafted arrows might suggest the attackers were Nolmec ...'

Kupanna Marra threw up her arms. 'See, his existence threatens our son, our realm.'

'... the arrowhead points to another party, someone who wants us to believe the Nolmec are responsible.' The Kapok picked up the arrowhead and examined it. 'This was retrieved from the ambush.

It is Tamrin-made, though the clan markings are obscured.' He paused and looked straight at Lumi.

A chill ran from the nape of her neck to her tailbone. Did he suspect Father? She lowered her eyes and flushed. 'I am glad Prince Mannok is not hurt, Your Majesty,' she said, then as an afterthought, 'Are Dinnis and Trasin okay?'

The hardness in the Kapok's golden eyes softened. 'They should both survive, lass, all going well.'

Kupanna Marra sat down and touched the amethyst pendant. 'I think ... Lumi child, I think I'll postpone making the meal plans for now. If you would leave us, please.'

* * *

Lumi hurried from the royal apartments to her parents' guest suite. Her breaths came short and sharp, tightening her chest and causing her throat to burn. The more she thought about it, the surer she became that her own father had organised the ambush on Mannok. He had made sure that Estolik wouldn't be able to go north with the Prince. She had to find out what he intended, though even if she knew, what could she do to stop him?

Tell the Kapok. She shivered at the thought. No, she couldn't do that. She had no proof after all and if Father was found to be a traitor, the whole family would be ruined.

She burst into the Dolphin suite and her gaze bounced around the room. Light filtered in from the lattice above the entrance door, segmenting the space into golden squares. The candles remained unlit and the room stood empty of occupants. Of course, her younger siblings were playing with the children of some local nobility ... the ... the ... oh, she forgot which family it was. She shook her head impatiently.

Mama left early this morning with Estolik and Kerri to buy fabrics, perfumes, jewellery and some furnishings to take back with them to the coast. Akra was an important city and their home, a fortified mansion on the high sea cliffs. While substantial and well-appointed, the mansion could not compare with the comfort and riches of the Tarka and the Golden Palace, let alone, it seemed, the fabled Kusa and its golden-domed palace. It was a wonder poor Estolik bore it. Not that Father gave him a choice in the matter and he seemed to get on with Prince Dashon.

Perhaps she shouldn't speak to Father now, not when her emotions thrashed about like a storm-lashed ocean. She sank down on one of the divans and rubbed her aching forehead.

Moments later a too-familiar sardonic voice intruded. 'What are you doing here, daughter? I thought you would be with the Kupanna.'

Lumi jolted out of her reverie, her heart bounding like a startled yarma.

Father stood in the doorway, his face obscured by shadow as the light streamed in the windows from the atrium behind him.

'The Kupanna dismissed me. They ... The Kapok received some news from the north.'

A sudden gleam flashed in her father's silvery eyes. His pale lips parted in a predatory smile that disappeared as quickly as it appeared.

'Not bad news, I hope,' he said, stepping into the room, his tall figure towering over her like a shark barrelling down on a mackerel.

Her chest squeezed tight. She stared at him as though she saw him for the very first time. He was her father. All her life she had wanted his approval, longed for some sign of affection. She had always thought the fault was in her, that she was not pretty or good or clever enough, never realising how cold and calculating he was. She hadn't believed he'd do it, harm the Prince and spoil her small chance at happiness. Not really. But now, she could feel the dangerous power in him, the will to get what he wanted, whatever it took.

'The Prince is safe, I trust,' he added, false concern lacing his voice.

Sudden rage reared up past the fear. 'He is unharmed. Your plot was foiled and the Kapok knows it wasn't the Nolmec,' she spat.

The slap snapped her head back against the divan, jarring her head and sending her teeth into her tongue. She put her hand to her stinging cheek and swallowed the salty taste of blood. He'd never hit her before.

'Quiet, fool of a girl. You know nothing. You will say nothing.'

'I will not be part of any plot against Mannok!' she shouted.

He clamped his strong hands over her mouth and hissed in her ear. 'You will do as you are told, girl, or pay the price of a disobedient offspring.'

Her whole body vibrated. Hot tears tumbled down her face. 'Let me go!'

He shook her until her teeth chattered. 'Be quiet and do as you are told. Bah!' He flung her away and she crashed to the floor, her hip glancing off the wooden frame of another divan. With a low growl, he circled the room, hands clutching his red hair.

Big wrenching sobs racked her body. She flinched back as he stopped in front of her. His eyes were like glaciers slicing into her.

'Don't tell me you love that spoilt and preening princeling?'

She dropped her eyes, bitting down hard on her lips. She wouldn't put Mannok in any further danger, she just wouldn't, whatever her father did to her.

He stood staring at her for a long while, his long thin fingers stroking his chin. The purplish flush left his pale ivory face.

'I can't say much for your taste, daughter, but perhaps it could work in our favour … if you could snare His Highness' interest. Rokkan may not be so quick to reject a second offer from us, after his brat has refused every eligible in the Five Lands.' Bending forward he lifted her chin, his fingers burning like ice into her skin. 'Yes, when your eyes are not puffed and red and your nose is not streaming like a street urchin's, you could pass as a beauty, I can see that.'

'You … you would promise not to harm him, Father?' she said.

He smiled and stroked her hair. 'Of course, my sweet.' He lifted her onto the divan. Taking a cloth, he gently wiped away her tears with gentle hands. 'You must do your very best to win him, if you want him to be … happy.'

She nodded, not sure how to answer. A cold stone settled in the base of her stomach. Did Mannok's safety depend on her success? She would do it. She had to.

'Now, rest, my daughter. I will send a servant to attend to your comfort.'

With a smirk, he left the family room.

Should she warn the Kapok? What proof did she really have? Father had admitted nothing. In the days of Tellek Kapok, whole families died on the rocks below the Red Leap for the treachery of one. At the very least, their lands would be confiscated and their position and status stripped away. If she could convince Mannok to marry her, he need not be in danger.

She wrapped her arms around her legs and buried her head between her shaking knees. No matter how much she rocked, she couldn't stop shivering.

Nakri

Chapter Twenty-Three: Imitations

Dinnis

Dinnis' chest burned with the effort of descending three flights of stairs. Reaching the landing, he leant on the bloodwood cane and caught his breath. His legs wobbled and his thigh throbbed. It had been thirteen days since his arrival in Narkri and the night of Trasin's amputation. The rainbow hues on his thigh had faded along with most of the swelling, but it still hurt to walk, especially up and down stairs. Only the gnawing hunger in his gut sent him out of his cramped room, high up in the tower, in search of the kitchens and food.

Warm, delicious smells came from the room to his left, the solar or large reception room if the memory of his last visit to the castle nine years ago could be relied on. His leg trembled with fatigue and he wasn't sure he could go much further. He pushed open the doors and stepped into a largish chamber.

Golden sunlight streamed through the tall arched windows and splashed across the polished wooden floor. In the middle of the chamber, Trasin sat on a divan, hunched and forlorn, alone and wrapped in a colourful woven rug. A stack of books leaned precariously on a low table next to a tray scattered with honey, yarma cheese, an assortment of fresh-picked fruit and newly baked maize bread, most of it unsampled.

The fingers of Trasin's left hand fumbled with a small, lidded pot that repeatedly shifted in his grasp. 'Slide it! This is impossible!' he growled.

Dinnis limped toward the food. Despite the tap tap tap tap of the walking stick, Trasin stayed focused on the jar in his hand. He seemed younger than his sixteen years, shrunken somehow. His curved posture couldn't obscure the brute fact that his right arm ended in a heavily bandaged stump below his shoulder. According to the servants' gossip, Trasin had been gravely ill until a couple of days ago.

Compassion for the lad stirred in Dinnis' midriff. After all, it might have been him under Tamak's knife.

The lad's fingers fumbled on the lid and yet again the jar slipped from his grasp. Dinnis reached over, took the ceramic pot and twisted the lid. He placed the opened pot back on the tray.

Trasin let loose a string of curses. 'Idiot, I don't want your help! I asked to be left alone!'

Dinnis winced. 'My mistake.'

Trasin's head jerked up, his fawn-brown eyes widening, his face pale and drawn beneath the tan. 'You! What are you doing here? Get out!'

Dinnis' breath hitched. Had Puran's suspicions poisoned Trasin against him? He held up a placating hand and backed away.

'As you wish, though I need to catch my breath after walking down three flights of stairs.'

Trasin's eyes strayed to the cane, his brow crinkling. His left shoulder hitched up. 'If you must.'

Dinnis' stomach rumbled loud enough for the whole castle to hear. He hated the hollow, helpless feel of hunger. It reminded him too much of the years as Akrad's prisoner. Maybe he could palm a sunfruit or a couple of quail eggs from the tray. Though harder to do when he relied on the walking stick for balance.

He cleared his throat. 'Do you mind if I have some of the food, if you've finished with it?' he asked.

The lad growled, but didn't say no. Dinnis pocketed the sunfruit and quail eggs, then grabbed a slab of maize bread, slathered it with honey and wolfed it down.

'Don't they feed you?'

'Yes ... though it does seem to slip their memory as often as not, especially now my injuries need less care. And then, I'm not always sure I should eat what I'm given.'

He bit into a creamy wedge of yarma cheese, inhaling its tangy softness.

'What are you babbling on about?'

'The main attendant, the one whose nose droops down to almost meet his upper lip. He gives me the evil eye when he brings the food, and mutters curses under his breath.'

Trasin looked at him beneath his lowered brows, his single hand fiddling at the honeyed treats within the painted pot.

On a whim, Dinnis struck a pose, mimicking the old servitor's shuffling stoop, twisting his face into a sour expression. 'Blast and befuddle all filthy blueys. We ought ta be burying 'em not coddling 'em with treatments and victuals.' Dinnis pitched his voice high, with a northern twang, and added in a wheezy snuffle.

Trasin's lips twitched. 'You mean old Anton? He lost a wife and two of his sons to a Nolmec raid and three brothers in the rebellion.'

'Hmm, well, what if he decides to poison me?'

'He won't while you are under my uncle's protection.'

'Your uncle's protection? He likes me less than Anton does!'

Dinnis wrapped roasted cavy flesh, avocado and small tomatoes in a round of flat bread. This food was so much more appetizing than the half-congealed bean stew he'd been getting. Two bites, and he demolished the wrap, his stomach pleasantly tight. Leaning forward, he grabbed another couple of yellow sunfruit and shoved them into the folds of his tunic for later.

Trasin eyed him with a faint vee between his eyebrows.

Better not outstay his rather tenuous welcome. 'Sorry to intrude. Thanks for the food.' Gripping the stick, he turned to go.

'Dinnis, stay awhile.'

Dinnis met the lad's eyes. Somewhere outside the walls of the castle, an eagle screamed on the wind. The jingle of tack and the clash of spear on shield filtered up from the practice yards below the open window.

'Please.'

'As you will. Should I read to you?' Dinnis wiped his hands on a cloth and pointed with his chin at the pile books. History books, maybe. Or poetry. Sometimes the two were the same. And he hadn't laid his hands on a good book in far too long. Maybe a library hid somewhere in this antiquated pile of stone.

'Ugh, no. Talk to me. Have you heard any news from Prince Mannok?'

Dinnis perched on the edge of a facing divan and eased his injured leg at a good angle. 'No, just what I've overheard. No further attacks, it seems.'

'That's good.' Trasin rubbed his stump and winced. Then he smiled wanly. 'He said it's better to be alive with one arm than dead with two. I'm not so sure. I'll never ride with the Prince again.'

'Many warriors adapted to their injuries after the rebellion. Don't throw in the spear yet, Trasin.'

'Easy enough for you to say,' Trasin spat.

Dinnis held up both hands, his stick clattering to the floor. 'For a moment I thought Tamak would take my leg. Not an easy thought.'

'I ... I don't want to depend on others. A ... a useless burden.'

'We all depend on others. Who cooks your meals, makes your clothes, grows your food?'

'That's different.'

'Is it? You are capable, intelligent, and come from a noble family. You'll find something to do.'

'Ha!' Trasin slapped his thigh, sending the jar of sweet treats rolling across the floor. 'Do you know my father, Lord Challak, was once Markan of the North? This castle was ours.'

'Under Naetok.'

'Yes. My father's choice of loyalties lost us our position as head of the Puma clan.'

'That bothers you?'

'No, no, Rokkan Kapok allowed my father to redeem himself, and since Papa's death, Lukarn treats my brothers and I like nephews, like sons really. But some say the stain of treachery can never truly be washed out. I thought if I could serve my Prince with honour to prove otherwise ... but now ...' His voice faded.

Dinnis sighed. He got it. After all, he lived under an even greater fog of suspicion and distrust. The silver lady's sweet voice chimed in his memory, her words of hope. Dinnis leaned forward. 'Trasin, you can still serve your Prince. Find another way.'

Trasin shook his head, then gave a twisted smile. He looked down at where his hand should be and took a couple of deep breaths. The lad was close to tears. 'Who else can you mimic?'

Dinnis bit his lip. He shouldn't draw attention to himself. Too late for that. And besides, the lad needed cheer. One more impersonation couldn't hurt, could it?

He pushed himself up, pulling his shoulders back and standing squarely on his feet. Pain stabbed through his healing leg, but he ignored it. He jutted his head forward and creased his face into a fearsome scowl.

'Listen here, young scamp, who said it would be easy? You were raised to be a noble and a warrior, so quit skulking about and show them what you are made of.' He added a more subtle northern twang to his voice.

Trasin's head jerked up, startled. 'Uncle Lukarn,' he hooted. Tears of laughter streamed down his wan cheeks.

'This is a serious matter, son,' Dinnis continued. 'Are you a scion of the ancient and celebrated Puma clan or a chattering howler monkey? Stop associating with blue-skinned riff raff and accept the challenge in front of you.'

A slow hollow beat of one hand striking against another echoed from behind him. Dinnis swung round. Lord Lukarn stood squarely in the doorway, clapping. Slide it, he should have paid attention.

'Something of a performer, are we, mister riff raff?' Lukarn said as he stalked into the room.

He did not take his brown eyes off Dinnis. Trasin wiped the tears off his cheeks and clamped his hand over his mouth, though an occasional giggle still escaped him.

'My cue to exit.' Dinnis picked up his cane from the floor.

A familiar strong grip clamped down on his shoulder. 'Not so fast. What are you doing here? Lady Samara has had servants looking for you everywhere.'

'I grew tired of staring at the same four walls. Very dreary walls too. So I decided to look for breakfast instead.'

'Stop joshing me, Dinnis.' Lukarn's scowl deepened. 'It's late afternoon.'

'Ah yes, a very late breakfast then. I guess I'd better walk myself back up all thirty-six stairs.'

'Thirty-six ... by the moons, Tamak said you weren't supposed to walk up or down any just yet.'

'Can't he stay, Uncle? We could keep each other company.'

Lukarn's eyes narrowed. 'It is good seeing you smiling again, Trasin. If you want to, we could arrange to move the rascal to a chamber near yours. Though I'm more inclined to flog him. Puran will try to drop in as often as he can and Mannok and the rest of your friends should be here in less than a ten-day. The Prince will surely stay a few days at least before heading back to Tarka.'

'So, I can go too?' Trasin's eye's brightened and he sat up a bit taller.

'That will be up to Surgeon Tamak,' Lukarn said. 'But most likely, not.'

'I understand,' the lad said. 'I'll have to make the best of Dinnis' company while I can.'

His smile was wistful, but an echo of laughter still lurked in his brown eyes.

Dinnis stood straighter. He had to get back to Tarka as soon as he could. He missed Tilli and her family. More than that, he needed to get back by the New Growth festival. No way he was staying in the north once the Prince returned south.

Chapter Twenty-Four: Conquest and Nuts

Mannok

Mannok bounded up the spiral staircase, two and sometimes three steps at once. His duty stint on the border was over. Who would have imagined that he would be so anxious to return to Tarka? The ambush had been exciting, though the injuries to his two age-mates had taken the shine off that little adventure. And since then, Waren had made doubly sure that the Prince and his age-mates got the safest and most mind-numbing duties.

Still, he had learnt much by observing Waren and his officers. Now he was on his way home. Would it be impolite to leave Nakri at first light? Or should he stay a day or two? At the very least, he had to say goodbye to Trasin and Dinnis before heading off. His foot fumbled on the uneven step and he slowed down. Poor Trasin. Losing an arm. He swallowed. Somehow this visit was more nerve-racking than charging the ambushers at Pine Stand Gap.

He came out onto the landing. Behind him the racket of Waren, Puran and Garvin trying to keep up with him reverberated off the stone walls. He grinned and pushed through the metal-studded wooden doors into the chamber. It had a rustic sort of opulence, lacking the bountiful light and ventilation and the sophistication of the furnishings he was used to in the Golden Palace of Tarka. Yet it was well-appointed, with one large tapestry on the wall, puma skins spread in front of low tables, chunky divans and massive stone fireplace. In the middle of the room, Trasin and Dinnis sat opposite each other in curved stools, a Conquest board on the small, fluted marble table between them.

Trasin bent forward, his eyes fixed on the carved figures, his finger on a tall Markan piece. His right arm ended below the shoulder in a stump. Mannok swallowed hard and looked away. Dinnis sat straight, even thinner than usual if that were possible, his enigmatic grey eyes meeting his own gaze straight on. His age-mate nodded, gripped the cane leaning against his stool and began to stand. Trasin looked up and put his single hand on the table, pushing down in the effort to rise also.

'No need for formalities,' Mannok said. He covered the distance in a couple of strides and placed a restraining hand on Trasin's shoulder. 'How are you?'

Both young men sank back into the stools as the others came bursting into the room, their boots noisy on the wooden floor.

'I'm well, thank you, your Highness,' Trasin said, dropping his eyes. 'Or I would be if Dinnis didn't keep thrashing me at Conquest,' he added, his lips hitching up in a one-sided grin.

Dinnis smiled. Mannok glanced at the board then peered closer. He whistled.

'I can see he has you hedged in. You play as ruthlessly as my father, Dinnis. You could be a little kinder to the poor lad.'

Dinnis raised his eyebrows. 'He asked for a game and I'm giving him one.'

Trasin flushed. 'Really, I don't need coddling, like I'm a ... a cripple. I mean I know I am ...'

Dinnis leant forward. 'Trasin, can you pass me the jar?'

Puran rushed forward. 'My brother is not your lackey, Nolmec. Do you have ice water in your blue veins?' he snarled.

Mannok frowned. What was Dinnis up to? He wasn't usually this heartless.

'I'm happy to do it,' Trasin said with a lift of his chin.

Trasin picked up the small ceramic container. Wedging it up against a heavy dish he twisted off the lid and handed it to Dinnis with a broad smile.

A sudden grin flashed onto Dinnis' face. He took the jar and offered it to Mannok. 'Chillied castana nuts, Your Highness?'

Mannok shook his head. 'You know I can't stand them.'

Dinnis shrugged and offered the jar to Puran. 'My lord Puran?'

Puran grimaced. 'Imbecile. I don't like those foul-tasting extravagances. What fool can?'

'The Kapok?' Dinnis raised an eyebrow.

Puran growled deep in his throat and lunged at Dinnis.

'Commander Puran!' Mannok stepped forward and grabbed the burly commander by the shoulders and pulled him back.

Puran stood still, the back of his neck flushed. 'My apologies, Your Highness. I ... I should inform Lord Lukarn that you have arrived from Kaja.'

Mannok let him go. 'Perhaps, you should.' Dinnis snarky humour could be annoying, but didn't warrant Puran's over-the-top reaction.

Puran bowed low and left the room as though a swarm of bees followed close behind him.

With a half-shrug, Dinnis offered the nuts to Waren who shook his head.

'Not for me, Dinnis. What's with Puran?'

'He's been like a bear on an anthill lately,' Trasin said.

Dinnis popped a spicy nut into his mouth and placed the jar on the table. Garvin leaned forward and grabbed a handful. 'These would have cost an arm—'

Mannok frowned and jabbed his friend in the side. 'Err ... I mean ...' Garvin's voice trailed off and he flushed beneath his bronzed skin.

'An arm and a leg,' Trasin said. 'It's okay, you know. I don't mind you talking about it. If it wasn't for Dinnis, I think I would have gone mad. When anyone comes to see me, if they come at all, they all look like I've died or something. Most won't meet my eyes and then they whisper when they think I'm not listening. Puran is the worst really, he looks anywhere else than at me and he paces about raging at my misfortune. Then he keeps raving on about Dinnis.'

'Older brothers can be over-protective. Perhaps, that's why he feels guilty,' Dinnis said.

'Guilty? It's hardly his fault,' said Waren. 'He wasn't leading the patrol.'

He caught Mannok's eye and looked away. Mannok lifted his chin.

'I guess it's mine, if anyone's,' he said. Yet they were in a difficult situation. If he hadn't attacked and routed the ambushers, then Dinnis would have died, and most likely Garvin and Hasuk if they'd insisted on staying behind to provide cover for the escape.

'Or maybe it was the fault of the ambusher who let fly with the arrow,' Dinnis said.

Trasin grimaced. 'Or mine for being clumsy enough to get in the way of it.'

'Enough blame to spread around so none of us need miss out.' Garvin crunched down on the nuts, closed his eyes and smiled. 'I can never afford these, you know.'

'It is the two of us now since Papa died last year.' Trasin traced the chevron pattern on the divan. 'Though your parents are good to us, Waren, and even before then, when Papa was doing so poorly. He never really recovered from his wounds from the …' The lad stopped, bit his lip and looked down at the Conquest board.

'Naetok's Rebellion,' Mannok said. Lord Challak had been one of Uncle Naetok's biggest supporters. Naetok had appointed him Markan of the North. Yet Papa had given Challak and the other rebels complete amnesty in return for their sworn loyalty at the end of the war. Challak's decision to take the offer influenced the others to follow. 'I'm sorry, Trasin. Many were affected on both sides.'

Trasin nodded. 'I know.'

Mannok clapped the young lad on the shoulder, then wondered if he had been too rough.

Trasin grinned. 'I wish I was going back with you to Tarka.'

Leaning forward, Garvin replaced the lid on the jar and handed it to Dinnis. He gave an uneven smile. 'I'll eat the lot, if you're not careful, Dinnu.'

'I never knew you liked them until Kaja.' Dinnis gave Garvin a strange look, then shook his head.

'Garo is mad about them,' Mannok said. 'We used to sneak them from my father's desk when we were little. I ate a whole jar, and was up half the night with … well, you probably don't want to know what a full jar does on one's digestive system.' He laughed. 'Haven't been able to face them ever since.'

'They're so darn expensive,' said Garvin with a gusty sigh.

'I know, which is why I rarely indulge. So Waren gifts them to you?' A small frown formed on Dinnis' normally impassive face.

'No, Mannok or sometimes my grandma, but usually it's a treat I have to forgo.'

'Slide it, what does it matter anyway?' Waren folded his muscular arms across his chest.

Mannok frowned at his age-mate. 'Indeed, Dinnis, what's with the inquisition? A taste for chillied castana nuts is hardly important. We have more serious dangers to worry about.'

Like whether Mama would have another bride lined up for him when he reached Tarka. He'd rather face an ambush.

Way Station, On the Royal Road

Chapter Twenty-Five: Fire!

Mannok

Seven days later Mannok pulled his cloak in around him against the night chill and slipped out of the Way Station, careful not to wake the others. He was tired enough after several long days in the saddle riding south, but still couldn't sleep. He needed a snatch of fresh air.

In the end he'd stayed in Nakri two days and acquired two more companions. Dinnis insisted on coming with the band despite his healing leg and Uncle Lukarn insisted that Waren accompany Mannok on the Royal Road to Tarka. His cousin wasn't very happy about the separation from his young wife. Mannok wasn't happy about it either. He'd had enough of Waren's officiousness in Kaja. Uncle Lukarn sent Lutan Atorak ahead with a message to his parents of his coming and to check the Way Stations, traditionally provided and provisioned by the Kapok and the custodian villages for those travelling the Royal Way. The saddest thing was Trasin's forlorn look as they left, but Surgeon Tamak insisted he needed further care.

Though it was a few hours before dawn, the light of golden Alumi lit up the night, reflecting off the snow on the serried mountain tops. The stars, still brilliant in the west, seemed close enough to touch. Mist curled around his feet, rolled over the rocky outcrop and sank over the edge into the deep gorge. A sudden wind buffeted Mannok, rustling the tops of the mountain pines behind him and sending his cloak swirling, then dropped as suddenly as it had come.

A branch snapped closer to the Way Station. Someone else must be finding it hard to sleep tonight. He should go back and attempt a few hours more sleep.

A flurry of soft wings sounded on the wind and a large snowy owl flew straight at him. He ducked and covered his eyes. It swooped past within ninas of his head, the backdraft of its wings ruffling his hair. He took a step back from the sheer drop in front of him, his heart pounding. He turned and examined the shadows under the trees. The owl had disappeared.

From the Way Station came the sound of furtive footsteps and a crackling noise. A sooty acrid smell assaulted his nostrils. Closer, a woman in a strange long white tunic, ghostly in the light of the moon, ran towards him. Her skin looked like silvery Argenti, skin like Ista's. As tall as Ista too, though her curves were unlike his half-sister's slim, boyish figure. Her dark hair streamed behind her in long curls. He had seen her face before, but where? Maybe, he was caught in a dream?

She waved her hands and shouted. 'Fire, man of Tamra, fire.'

Then it hit him. Smoke. He could smell smoke. And not just from a hearth fire.

He looked past the woman. His gut twisted. Rosy light flickered from the shuttered windows of the large stone building. From inside, a muffled uproar, urgent, fearful shouts. A few tanis away, the horses neighed and circled on their tethers. Why was no one escaping?

He sprinted towards the door.

The flames were licking along the eaves and into the thatched roof. A pall of smoke drifted his way, it's sooty opaqueness mixing with the mountain mist. It stung his eyes and obscured his vision.

Coughing, he put out his arms to feel his way and crashed into something. Large dark shadows jutted out where they shouldn't be. Boulders, branches and debris had been wedged against the door. There was a hammering on the other side. His friends were trapped in there.

He had to free them. He pulled away what he could. The woman in white joined him, helping him shove away the heavier obstructions with a surprising strength. She was taller than any woman he'd known, even Ista. The smell of pine and flowers for a moment overcame the stench of burning wood.

As together they pulled the largest boulder to one side, the door edged open. Thick smoke tinged with orange light streamed up and out. He levered the door open, as shadowy others pushed from inside. Once it was half open, the young men and the attendants clutching bundles and gasping for fresh air, squeezed through and staggered outside. Mannok counted each one and came up two short.

With a groan, he dived through the door. Dense grey smoke filled the common chamber, while flames twisted through the thatch, like ribbons in a girl's hair, sending burning fronds twirling down to the floor. He put his cloak over his face. His eyes were streaming, his lungs burning. There. He saw a tall, thin figure creeping towards him, limping and dazed. Orange-red lights reflected off a smoky-blue face and almond eyes. Dinnis!

Mannok darted further in, grabbed Dinnis' elbow and half pulled, half carried him to the door and safety. At the door, hands reached in and pulled them both out.

'Mannok, you should have stayed outside.'

It was Waren. Who else would be scolding him at a time like this? The roof groaned.

'We need to move away,' Mannok croaked, falling to his knees.

A roar and the roof collapsed. A cloud of sparks swirled upwards. Flames, orange red and hungry, leapt into the smoky night air.

'Someone is still inside,' he said. Another death on his conscience.

'I was the last out,' Dinnis gasped. Tears streamed down his ash-coated face. He sat on the ground, clutching his leather satchel and pulling in huge drafts of air. Waren stood behind, his face unreadable in the shadowed night. Had he miscounted or was the missing person the nightwalker already outside, either unable to sleep or, perish the thought, setting the fire?

'Mannu, thank the Maker.' Garvin rushed up with only minimal smudges of ash on his face and clothing. He handed Mannok a skin full of water. 'We couldn't find you. I ... I was worried you were still in there.'

'Mannok, where were you?' Waren said. 'The door was stuck.'

'Outside. I couldn't sleep. The door wasn't just stuck. Someone blocked it from outside.' Mannok lifted the waterskin and the cool stream flowed into him, cooling his burning throat and slaking his thirst.

'What? You mean the fire was deliberate?'

Mannok nodded. What other conclusion was there? He handed it to Dinnis, who nodded mute thanks.

Someone had meant for them to die. Was this another attack aimed at him, like the ambush and the cut bridge rope at the Trial of Tears? Another failed attempt. The arsonists would have thought him asleep in the private chamber at the back of the building trapped inside with his companions. If he hadn't been outside, if the owl hadn't caught his attention and if the woman hadn't helped free his friends, the results would have been tragic.

Mannok stood up and looked around at the ash-covered figures, garish in the light of the leaping flames, huddled at a safe distance from the blazing structure. The silver lady was nowhere to be seen. Who was she? A peasant from the nearby village? Or a spirit of the mountains or the pine trees?

* * *

Mannok urged his tired stallion into a canter along the road tracking round the eastern base of the Elder Twin. The late afternoon sun played hide and seek with the mountain peaks, the burnished disc sometimes slanting beams into his eyes and throwing off a long shadow behind him, sometimes slipping behind the shadowed heights and leaving a chill in its wake. Garvin and Waren rode behind him, with Hasuk, Dinnis and Yalik further back. A small contingent of warriors followed some lek back at a slower pace with his camp master, Palarn, other attendants and what was left of the baggage. The fire delayed them a couple of days as they regrouped, and it weighed on the party's spirits for the rest of the journey despite the breathtaking views and generous hospitality.

Mannok's heart quickened, as it always did, riding up the long slope of this particular ridge in the road. As he crested the hill, the great walled city of Tarka glimmered like a jewel between the Twin Peaks, its tiered heights gilded by the sun. Stretched out in front of the city were fertile fields of maize, beans and red flowering chinwa, punctuated with an ancient stand of pine trees and circled on the far side by sharp-edged cliffs. At this fading remnant of the day, the roads criss-crossing in front of the wall were less crowded and the hawkers were beginning to pack up their stalls.

A rider galloped toward them on a young silver stallion. Mannok narrowed his eyes. The man was tall, his brown cloak twisting and billowing out behind him. He wore no obvious insignia, no headdress or finery. A couple of lean hunting dogs loped behind the horse. Surely not ... was that Papa on Blizzard with Tracer and Lead? He pulled Shadow to a stop as the rider drew alongside them. The horse reared and sidestepped, blowing air through his nose.

'Mannok, good to see that you made it home in time for dinner, if not for the New Growth Festival.'

It was Papa, his golden eyes laughing, a huge grin curving up his strong face. He leant forward, soothing the skittish stallion with soft whispers and gentle strokes on its arched neck.

'Papa! Your Majesty! Should you be riding alone?'

'Alone? I had a brace of guards tailing me.' Papa raised an eyebrow, then turned Blizzard in a tight circle, looking down the road. 'Hmm, I seem to have lost them. Must have been the jump across the gully. It wasn't that difficult, surely.'

Mannok suppressed a smile. Mama would often complain that Papa was the most reckless rider in all of Tamra. Certainly, there were few if any that could match his riding prowess.

Two galloping horses appeared from the crossroads that wound up the flank of the snow-capped Elder Twin. The plumes, tassels and bronze regalia of the royal guard adorning both the mounts and the riders caught the last rays of the blood-red sun.

'Here they come now,' Papa said.

'Your Majesty, forgive me, but if we had been assassins ...' Waren's forehead was rutted into a frown.

Papa gazed with mock seriousness at the bunch of young nobles. 'Are you assassins, lads?'

'But sir this is serious.'

'Hmm, Commander, you are beginning to sound like your father. I tolerate such liberties from the Markan of the North and my Commander of the Horse,' Papa leaned forward, his hands resting on Blizzard's withers, 'but not from a young whelp who hasn't finished cutting his wisdom teeth.'

Waren opened his mouth but closed it again as Papa raised an eyebrow. Mannok bit down on his lip in an effort to suppress his smile.

Papa turned back to him. 'I'm happy to see you have returned unharmed from your adventures.'

'Just two to speak of,' Mannok said. 'Though we didn't come out quite unscathed.'

'Two? Lukarn informed us of the ambush, but the second incident?' Papa's eyes bored into him and Mannok squirmed.

'I would have sent a messenger, but we were three days out and I thought it best not to worry Mama. Someone set fire to the Way Station at Bent River Village while we were in it.'

'Anyone hurt?'

'Minor burns and most of our personal baggage is gone. It's why we were delayed,' Mannok replied. Shadow snorted and moved restlessly beneath him.

Papa sat back on Blizzard, eyes narrowed. 'Our friend's been busy, then. The Maker be praised you are unharmed. How was young Trasin when you left him?'

'Recovering and in good spirits, considering. And Dinnis here is definitely on the mend.'

'So I see. First thing in the morning, I want each of you to come to my office to debrief.'

'As you wish, Papa.' Mannok lowered his head and grimaced. Great, not another interview. No doubt it would be a repeat of Waren's trenchant criticisms of his behaviour and competency.

'And Mannok.'

'Sir?'

Papa slapped him on the back, almost unseating him.

'It's good to see you can keep your head in a crisis. You and your age-mates showed courage, teamwork and resourcefulness. Well done all of you!'

Mannok blinked. There was no hint of sarcasm in his father's face. Easing his grip on the reins, he sat back and lifted his chin, waiting for the sting in the tail. Papa's eyes crinkled and the corners of his mouth twitched. Here it comes.

'There is one more thing.'

'Yes, Papa.'

His shoulders tensed. Come on, get on with it.

'See that outcrop?' Papa pointed with his chin at a distinctive reddish rock still visible in the gloaming a few hundred tanis down the road. 'I warrant Blizzard can beat Shadow to it without even trying.'

Without another word, he dug his heels into his restive horse and was off down the road at a headlong gallop. Mannok grinned, leant forward and urged Shadow after him, ignoring Waren's strangled protests.

Tarka, royal city of Tamra

Chapter Twenty-Six: Hunted

Lumi

Lumi nudged her mare, Caramel, along the path that wound its way up through an ancient stand of ornamental trees in an old quarry below the Palace. Rizzi and Jati hadn't needed much persuasion to come with her. The early morning sun filtered through the heart-shaped leaves and pendulous yellow blossoms, falling on Caramel's flank and the dirt track in flickering splotches. This was a tame ride compared to the wild rides along the edge of the sea cliffs back home, with the white-water foaming against the rocks far below and a wild wind whipping her hair. Yet her heart had fluttered in excitement.

Mannok arrived back from the north a ten-day ago, just days after the New Growth ceremony, and since then she'd made use of every opportunity to discreetly find herself in his company and capture his attention. A plan that was working slowly but surely without Ista or the newly married Kerri to distract him. True, this morning's plan to encounter the Prince's riding party, seemingly by chance, had failed, but few wars were won by one skirmish and Mannok was not a man to rush.

'I love the lengthening days after the New Growth festival,' Rizzi said, riding beside her on gentle Snowflake. 'Full of the heart's scent of flowers, the busy bustle of bees and sweet bird melodies.'

'You could be a poet, Rizzi,' Jati rode behind the two older girls on a dappled grey pony. A couple of guards followed them at a discreet distance.

On a small rock to the side, a black and white tarrawong let out a riff of ascending and descending notes.

'Even the birds agree,' Jati said.

Lumi let out a bubble of laughter, the other two girls joining in.

'It's the kind of thing the Kapok would say.' Lumi shook her head. 'Sometimes I have no idea what he is talking about. He said the other day that I looked like "a dazzle of sunlight at play amid the ocean waves."'

'I like it,' Jati said, clapping her hands. 'Uncle Rokkan wrote poetry as a young man.'

'You know, I can imagine Uncle as a dashing prince dazzling all the young ladies and breaking their hearts,' Rizzi said. 'It's much harder to imagine Aunt Marra as a young woman.'

'Mannok is not poetic, but just as much a heartbreaker.' Lumi sighed.

'Well, Mannok's not breaking my heart,' Jati said.

They came out of the wood into the bright sunlight and trotted up Straight Street. The high red Palace wall ran down one side, and three-storeyed tiled houses lined the other side.

Rizzi giggled. 'Do you have some other young noble in mind, little cousin? Please do tell.'

Jati lifted her chin. 'I'm not in any hurry to be bound to hearth and home. I want to have fun while I can.'

'I'd do anything to win Mannok's favour,' Lumi said, then clamped down on her bottom lip. She hadn't meant to say that out aloud and the other girls hadn't seemed to hear. She leant forward and stroked Caramel's soft neck. She had made progress, she was sure of it. Mannok now greeted her more often than not at various informal occasions and they'd found a common interest in horses. She'd smiled while he talked of being on border patrol and the exploits of his dogs. He'd even promised her a puppy from his dog Ripple's next litter and to Jati and Rizzi too, but that did not matter.

They turned west onto Royal Parade, with the red wall of the Palace on one side and the military barracks, municipal buildings and host houses clumped around Jaguar Plaza on the other.

Rizzi pulled Snowflake up close, her legs brushing up against Lumi. Caramel sidestepped, pushing air through her long nose in protest.

'I would too,' Rizzi said in a hushed voice. She looked up at Lumi, her hazel eyes like deep tree-shadowed pools and her mouth twitched up at the corners as if testing a smile. Rizzi leant forward and placed her brown hand on Lumi's lighter one. 'Whatever happens, Lumi, let's still be friends.'

Lumi frowned as she met her best friend's eyes. 'Yes, of course.'

Better her friend than one of the other girls though, except her failure to win his love could endanger Mannok's life. It didn't help that she could feel her father's penetrating eyes boring into her, watching to see if she could succeed. Not that she could say that to Rizzi. Caramel flicked her tail and increased her pace, no doubt eager for a rub down and feed in her stall.

Rizzi leant in closer, her face taut. 'Lumi, have you ever done something you're ashamed of?'

Well, she had eavesdropped on the Kupanna, informing her father and possibly putting Mannok at risk. Though he would have learnt about the trip up north eventually, wouldn't he? She hadn't actually done anything wrong. Papa denied having anything to do with the fire at the Way Station after he'd promised to do ... what exactly? Give her time to win him.

'No, not really,' she said. 'Why do you ask?'

They reached the Palace's main gates. Lumi brought Caramel to a stop, waiting for the guards to grant them access.

Rizzi shrugged. 'Oh, no reason. Only I'm—'

The drumming crescendo of horse hooves drummed on the cobblestones behind them. In a flash, a band of riders surrounded Lumi and her friends. Two clear long notes denoting the arrival of the Prince Royal sounded from the gate tower. The large golden gates glided open. Whatever Rizzi was about to say was drowned out in the noise and confusion.

'Good morning, lovely ladies,' the Prince said, giving a half bow as he rode past. 'It's a grand day for a ride.'

The other young blades followed behind him.

'Mannu,' Jati squealed. She dug her knees into her pony's round flanks, urging him into a trot and caught up with Mannok and Garvin even as the group poured into the large Royal Forecourt.

Both Lumi and Rizzi urged their horses forward, the young men letting them through. Estolik nodded as she passed him. From beside her brother, Durrin smirked at her. Lumi looked the other way and snagged the oblique eyes of the aloof blue-skinned Dinnis. Shivers ran down her spine. Her father would often question why

Rokkan Kapok had included a cold-blooded Nolmec into the Prince's own age-band.

Rather than wait for the attendants to take the horses, the Prince directed his stallion towards the stable area.

Jati kept up with him on her small pony. 'Where were you? We went to the Pine Grove but did not see you.'

'We went in the opposite direction, little cousin, to the Temple Peak to visit the House of the Maker.'

Jati wrinkled her pert nose. 'Oh, why go to the Temple? It's not a special feast or holy day is it?'

'No. We went to make an offering of thanks to the Maker for Trasin's recovery and our escape from the fire,' Garvin said.

Mannok dismounted and helped Jati down with an easy gallantry. Lumi would have been jealous except that she could see the amusement crinkling the corners of his jade-green eyes. He tousled Jati's flyaway hair and she grinned back at him.

This was her chance. Lumi phrased the words in her mind. An invitation to a boat party on the lake perhaps or—

Next to her, Rizzi squealed. Her friend's normally placid mare snorted and sprung into a headlong gallop, heading straight for Mannok. Lumi's eyes widened and then narrowed. What was Rizzi thinking?

Frantic attendants ran towards the spooked horse. The one in the lead grabbed the bridle to bring it under control. As the mare brushed past the Prince, Rizzi slipped sideways and fell in a slump at his feet. The Prince took a step back and caught his balance, then just as quickly, knelt beside Rizzi, crumpled in the churned-up mud of the yard. Yet Lumi was sure he had rolled his eyes first.

'Well, if she thinks that will work, she is not as smart as I thought,' a pleasant baritone voice sounded beside her.

Lumi turned with a start. Garvin stood beside the shoulder of her horse. He grinned up at her, taking hold of the reins and offering a strong sturdy hand to help her dismount.

She ignored it, instead looking into his brown eyes and open face. 'What woman has the slimmest chance to win the Prince's affections?' she said before she thought about it, then blushed.

He shrugged his solid shoulders, wry amusement flitting across his face.

'I've only known one to manage it and she wasn't in the habit of fluttering her eyelashes or falling in a heap at his feet.'

Did he mean her? Lumi's heart fluttered. 'Who?' she asked.

'An aloof, stately beauty with silver skin, a tongue as sharp as a hunting knife and a mind like a trap. Not my idea of womanly perfection.'

'But who ... Oh, you don't mean Ista?'

He nodded.

'No wonder she was sent away. A common serving wench aspiring to entangle a prince.'

'There was nothing common about Ista.'

Lumi snorted.

Garvin cleared his throat. 'You know, my lady, I am beginning to look remarkably silly standing here with my hand outstretched.'

Lumi glanced about her. Everyone else had dismounted. Rizzi slumped against Mannok for support. Jati stood with hands on her girlish hips, a look of disgust in her grass-green eyes. Most of the young warriors clustered close to their Prince, hiding smiles or grimaces behind hands or tied-down lips. Was it this silly caper that Rizzi meant in her cryptic comments earlier?

'Of course, I'm not a handsome prince,' Garvin said, his lips twisting. 'A little common even.' He began to lower his hand.

Lumi caught it and allowed him to help her off Caramel.

'Thank you, Garvin,' she said. 'You should not belittle yourself. You are from a noble Tamrin family.'

'No need to humour me, my lady. I know who I am and where I stand.'

She blinked her eyes. All at once, she wanted to cry. She lowered her head and pulled her fine woollen cloak around her. If only Mannok could look at her as his friend Garvin did.

'Ever the gallant, Garvin.' Mannok's voice sounded next to her.

Her heart gave a sudden lurch as she looked up. His hand resting on his friend's shoulder, a sardonic smile playing at the corners of his mouth. She shivered at the hardness in his eyes that she had never seen before.

'So, Lady Lumi, you missed a golden opportunity, or do you still have a trick or two hidden beneath your magnificent cloak?'

His tone was brittle.

She took a deep breath and lifted her chin. 'Isn't playing tricks your speciality?' she asked with as much dignity as she could find. 'Is Rizzi okay?'

His face softened a fraction. 'A sprained ankle and some grazes is all. Waren's taking her to the Palace where a medic will look at her injuries. She is fortunate. That was a downright dangerous stunt.'

She nodded. What could she say? He had a point and probably a fright with a runaway horse heading straight for him. She took a deep breath.

'I'm sorry, Your Highness. Snowflake is usually quiet, but even the most placid horse can spook.'

'Maybe.' His eyes softened. 'Forgive me for being churlish.'

'Nothing to forgive, Your Highness.' She bowed. 'If you would excuse me. I would not be late in attending the Kupanna.'

'Of course, please do not let me detain you, Lumi. I know how strict she can be.' He smiled and this time it reached his eyes.

Jati joined her and took her arm as she turned to go. They picked their way through the muddy horse yards, holding up the hems of their long tunics, and headed towards the Palace Forecourt. And after all that, she'd forgotten to invite him to an outing on the lake. Though maybe not the best timing.

Behind them, came Mannok's jocular voice. Lumi slowed her pace, ignoring Jati's impatient tug. Best to catch as much of the conversation as possible.

'So, Garvin, I 'm thinking we should head to our favourite Hunting Lodge.'

'Isn't it early in the season for a hunting expedition, Your Highness? Besides, having just returned from the north, we could spend more time in Tarka.' Garvin's voice sounded wistful.

'Better to be the hunter than the prey, I think.'

'It's a long way to travel to the southern wilderness, Mannok,' came Estolik's strident voice.

'Then the sooner we leave the better,' Mannok said, his voice now barely audible. 'Besides, Essu, you needn't come if you prefer to accompany your bride to Akra.'

Lumi let the skirt of her long tunic drop as they reached the well-attended paving stones of the Courtyard. He had smiled at her. Even if he did go south now, he would have to come back to Tarka in time for his birthday feast. And perhaps, just perhaps, she could win a reluctant Prince's heart.

Chapter Twenty-Seven: Leftovers

Dinnis

Dinnis leaned against a post and studied Anna's shop squatting with the other establishments in the mid-afternoon sunlight like yarmas huddled in a crooked line. The herbal shop seemed unchanged from when he had left Tarka half a year ago. He and Tilli's little brother Norak had repainted the large swinging sign, *Anna and Family – Herbalists*, only last Growing season, but the ramshackle adobe and stick structure and shutters could do with more attention.

Hopefully, Tilli would be there. He had to talk to her. Arriving back in Tarka after the long trip from the north, he had found it difficult to get away from the Palace until this afternoon and now he would be leaving tomorrow with the Prince to the southern Hunting Lodge. Another separation until at least the Prince's Birthday feast in a couple of alume. And he'd missed the Autumn Feast deadline. He straightened his shoulders and limped towards the shop.

Dinnis slipped through the door, avoiding ringing the warning bell. In the welcome and fragrant dimness of the big front room, Old Anna bent over the main bench. A little more stooped than he remembered and even in the dim light he could see her hair was almost all grey. She fumbled and knocked over a jar, her fingers groping to find it. He breathed in sharply. She was using her touch as much as her eyes to complete the task. She turned her head towards him.

'Who's that?' She grabbed her stick and squinted at him. 'Dinnis? Be that you? Surely there be only one person in Tarka stretched out like a bean pole.'

He laughed over the lump in his throat. 'The Kapok is as tall, if not taller than me.'

'As if his almighty Majesty would come sneaking into my shop. Besides, he be a lot wider. Where have you been, boy?'

Taking a couple of steps forwards, he engulfed her in a hug. She rested her head against his chest before pulling back and feeling his face. He could see the milky fuzziness of the cataracts growing in her eyes. Why had he not noticed them before? Had he been away that long?

'You know, you should get more light in here, maybe widen a window or put glazing in.'

'And where would I get the metal for that?'

'Here maybe.'

He swung the satchel off his shoulder and spread out the contents of the herbs he had gathered on one of the benches. 'Not as much as I'd hoped and a bit smoky, but I gathered a good deal of northern snow balm, as well as spear leaf, mountain sage and ice berry. It should cover the metal you advanced for my apprenticeship. I have some hot spur for Laetil also.'

She patted his cheek, her work-worn hands rough and calloused against his skin. 'You be a good lad, Dinnis. Who'd have thought all those years ago that an annoying young scamp hanging about my shop like a bad smell would be like my own son?'

'I did.' He grinned. Anna had done just about everything she could to get rid of him, including setting the city guards on him. Yet, the Herbal shop called him and he'd somehow known that the old woman had a warm heart under her crusty exterior. And so it had proved to be.

She laughed, slapping her sides, though there was a hesitation beneath the hilarity. Something was not quite right. He took a deep breath.

'Where's Tilli, Mater?'

His chest tightened when she did not answer at once. She gripped his hand. 'She be at the food markets.' Even as he let out his breath, she added. 'I be a sorrowing, son. She hitched herself to that ne'er do well from Hartil's Stables at the New Growth Festival. The bludger moved in here the next day, more's the pity.'

178

His heart dropped away, leaving his chest hollow. He leaned back against the bench.

'To think a daughter of mine be so daft. I tried to tell her but would she listen to her old ma? Of course not. There be tears over this for sure.' Anna's voice came to him as if muffled by water.

Dinnis pushed himself off the bench and strode towards the door, his leg catching and slowing him. Anna darted after him, showing a sprightliness he had not thought her capable of. She grabbed his arm, her knobbly fingers digging into muscle.

'Don't run off. 'Tis too long since we saw you.'

'I ... I need to think. I'm not ready to face her.'

'I know that, lad. I don't want us to be strangers. 'T'would break my heart, it would.'

He stood still, staring at the green flaking paint on the back of the door, resisting the urge to run through it. If he hadn't gone north ... Yet if he hadn't, would Mannok be alive? Did he care? Yes, the problem was that he did. He cared even though he had tried so hard not to and sometimes he still raged at the unfairness of it all. And he cared for Tilli and her family too. Why couldn't she understand? Why couldn't she have waited? He was caught between the life he hadn't asked for and the one he couldn't have.

'Maybe, it's for the best. I ... I don't think I'll ever be able to free myself from the Palace. There are ties I can't speak about. It's perilous ...'

'I know, lad.'

He turned to face her, looking down into her face full of ... what? Pity? Understanding? His hands clenched and unclenched.

'You can't know. No one does except ...'

'Did I tell you that I worked up at the Palace as a slip of a girl, when I be about Aska's age?'

She poked him in the ribs with her stick. He pushed it away, half-annoyed, half-reassured by her familiar gesture.

'No, what has that got to do with it?'

'It were afore my elder sister, Nerra, decided she didn't want the herbal shop 'cos she caught the eye of Sarak, the Spice merchant. I started as a nursery maid for the Kupanna, not this Marra but her aunt Saraya. Prince Naetok was a babe in arms then. I stayed at the Palace until Bambik and me had enough to set up a herbal shop on our own. Then my ma died, and Da needed me to take over the shop and look after the little ones. Prince Rokkan, as he be then, many a day he popped into the nursery. He was a right favourite with his half-brother and sister, well with us all.'

Dinnis frowned. 'That's interesting, Mater, but ...'

'You're very like your father, lad.'

'I look nothing like hi—' His eyes opened wide. A shiver ran through him. How did she know who his father was? She couldn't, nobody did.

'Looks, yes, you have something of his looks, but there be a lot more to it than the shape of an ear or a nose.'

His mouth was dry. He swallowed a couple of times before he could speak. 'Who else knows? Is ... is this common knowledge?'

'Na, 'tis not many know the both of you like I do.'

'It's just that, if what you say were true and it were generally known, you could be in danger. My life could be forfeit. It's the succession ... Lord Lukarn, the Kupanna, Sparak.' He swallowed hard against the lump in his throat. 'If you can discover it, then others ...'

'Listen, lad, there may be many who know you, but I reckon there be not one of them that sees you. They see a mixed blood, a Nolmec, a warrior perhaps or a medic—they don't see you, really sees you like I do.'

He stood still as if frozen in time. She was right of course. In part, for the reasons she mentioned, but also because he took care to stay unnoticed, unrecognised. He'd lived in the shadows for so long now, since his father rode away from him and his little sister, Ista, that one last time never really to return. Papa had left and when he came back, he was a stranger, the supreme ruler of Tamra, Rokkan Kapok. Perhaps, he had always lived in the shadows, his whole life a lie. Yet he had started to build a life of his making here in this place, with Tilli, yes, but also with Anna and her other children, competent Nikki, shy Aska and roguish Norak. Was that all to end now, like this?

'There was another who saw me once. The silver lady,' he said.

She would counsel him to not throw away the love of good friends, yet all his instincts to his very marrow said flee. He wanted to retreat, like he always did, to heal his wounds and stay safe in the shadows.

Anna remained silent, her rich chocolate eyes with their milky centres, fixed on his face.

Would not staying put those he claimed to love in danger? He breathed in, the air hissing through his Tamrin nose, and gently removed Anna's old hands off his arm.

'I don't think ...'

Running footsteps drew closer to the shop and the door flew open, within ninas of hitting him in the face. A young lad came hurtling through the entrance, the bell jangling loudly. He stopped, whooped and leapt at Dinnis, almost barrelling him over.

'Have a care, Norak,' Anna barked. 'Feckless boy.'

'Whoa, there scamp,' Dinnis gripped the bench as his injured leg threatened to collapse under the impact. Young arms encircled his waist and squeezed him tight.

'Dinnis, you're back.'

'That I am.' He eased his leg into a more comfortable position and ruffled the boy's hair.

The boy stood back, his brow wrinkled. 'Is there something wrong with your leg?'

'I used it to stop an arrow is all.'

'Wow, you actually were in a battle? Exo! Were you scared?'

'A skirmish more like. Even so, terrified.'

'Bet you weren't,' Norak said, 'Bet you were braver than half-a-ten of nobs. Bet you were as brave as my da was.'

He executed a flurry of imaginary spear thrusts.

'Boy, stop babbling. Dinnis, you better let me look at that leg.'

'It's healing well, Mater. I just have to get some of the stiffness out of it and build back the strength.'

Norak paused in his imaginary manoeuvres. He thrust out his chest. 'Cousin Laetil swears by kapsika liniment to heal muscle ailments. See, I am learning, Ma.'

'Laetil is teaching you?' Dinnis asked, his stomach sinking. Not that surprising really, that the physician had acquired another apprentice. He was gone so often and this had been the longest. Anna reached up and patted his shoulder.

'I did a deal with Laetil. Norak stands in for you when you're off on Palace business. Then when you finish in a year or two, he can take on the full apprenticeship. I figured you wouldn't mind.'

'No, it's a good idea. I'm off again tomorrow for an alume or two.'

'You only just got here. It's not fair,' Norak said.

'At least come in and spend time with us before you be running off again,' the old Anna said. 'I reckon Nikki can find some tasty leftovers to fill those hollow legs. One thing be sure, they didn't feed you up north. You're as thin as a whip.'

Dinnis hesitated, looked through the shutters into the sun-drenched street, then hitched his shoulders. Who was he to resist Nikki's leftovers?

West of the White Mountains

Chapter Twenty-Eight: Under My Command

Dinnis

Three days later, Dinnis shifted in the saddle to ease the ache in his thigh. He missed Pumice's steady gait and quiet affection yet he was beginning to bond to Chasm, an unexpected and generous gift from Mannok. The fierce noonday sun splintered off the rocky cliff and battered against his face. He squinted down the rough track, so narrow it forced the Prince's entourage to ride in single file.

Whirr. Whirr. Whirr. A flock of pigeons rose in a flurry of wings and feathers from among the tussocks of grass lining the mountain trail. His young mount, Chasm, shied.

'Whoa, boy.' Dinnis stroked the soft dark neck, soothing the gelding.

Mannok kept up a fast pace, clearly in a hurry to get to the Hunting Lodge. With every young lady at court vying for the Prince's attention, it seemed he couldn't get away from Tarka fast enough. Dinnis was just as happy to be many hundreds of lek away from Tarka. Anna was right. He didn't need to break with her and the rest of the family, but he didn't want to run into Tilli or Tujik just yet. His lips tightened and a tense knot lodged somewhere between his third and fourth rib. Best not think about Tilli.

Brushing a persistent fly away from his face, he studied the trail winding down the steep incline. A maze of ridges and steep tree-lined valleys rolled out to the horizon. The impressive snow-covered peaks of the White Mountains loomed behind them.

'Are you sure this short cut will take us to the Western Road, Mannok?' Estolik called out.

Mannok turned back in his saddle, a small furrow creasing his brow. 'Yes, Essu. I came this way with Papa some years ago. He likes to explore the weirdest paths sometimes.'

'Weird is right.' Waren shifted on his big chestnut horse immediately behind Mannok and clicked his tongue.

'Are you sure it's quicker?' said Estolik.

'That's the idea,' said Garvin, looking over his shoulder. A smile lit up his amiable face. 'Don't worry. Mannok knows where he's going.'

'Where will we spend the night?' Durrin rode immediately in front of Dinnis. 'Won't be a Way Station on this abandoned track.'

'Come on, it's just for a couple of nights. Can't be any worse than the Trial of Tears,' Garvin said.

'Or the five-day we spent camping at the Yapa outpost,' Hasuk added.

The others, all except Estolik and Durrin, groaned.

Yapa was a beacon site, perched high up Mount Serran. Waren must have decided to keep Mannok as far away from harm as he could after the ambush. Dinnis shook his head. His leg had healed enough to be back on active duty. Unlike poor Trasin adjusting to life without his spear arm. Worry for his young cousin, as well as separation from Jarrah no doubt explained Waren's morose mood. Concern for Trasin most likely explained Puran's erratic behaviour at Narki too.

Dinnis rubbed his aching thigh. He hadn't been too surprised when Puran rejected the chillied nuts, but Waren's dislike for the treats and Garvin's passion for them had been unexpected. Why did Waren buy them if he didn't like them? And Garvin—the idea of Mannok's most loyal friend as Uson's killer and potential assassin of the Kapok was laughable. What motive could he have? All three young men had similar builds to the mysterious Nistar of the Agouti clan, well-built and of medium height. All had been in Tarka at the time of the murders, but none, for various reasons, fitted all the criteria. So far, he'd discovered no one else with a preference for the incriminating nuts and nor had Jakan. This mystery resisted solving.

* * *

Hours later, the terrain looked as rugged and remote as ever. The sun neared the western horizon and a hint of the night-time chill kissed the air. Emerald-green and fire-red birds flashed overhead, accompanied by raucous calls of a family of woodland parrots. Somewhere down the trail, the sound of water rushing over rocks teased Dinnis' dry throat. He took a swig of his canteen.

The riders in front of him disappeared one by one as the trail bent in a sharp corner to the left. The quarrelsome roar of the nearby water drowned out the sounds of hooves and the jingle of tack. Chasm's nostrils quivered and his ears perked forwards. He picked up his pace unbidden.

As he rounded the corner, Dinnis saw the front riders—Mannok, Waren, Garvin, Estolik and Durrin—bunched up along the side of a fast stream hurtling across the track. White water foamed over grey rocks, swirling in eddies and racing down the hill.

He pulled Chasm to a stop.

'What is it?' Yalik asked as he jostled up behind and attempted to peer over Dinnis' shoulder. The riders behind stopped down the line.

'Dead end,' Waren said with a sour smile. 'Looks like we'll have to turn back.'

Estolik groaned. 'It'll take us all of another day to get back to the main route. That will be at least two days of travel wasted.'

Mannok scanned the area, his eyes narrowed, his face sombre.

'We could cross it. There is a track on the other side,' Garvin said, though even he looked doubtful.

Another group of parrots flashed overhead in noisy derision. Dinnis pulled his cloak tight against the deepening evening chill. The sun neared the jagged horizon. He nudged Chasm forward to get a better look. The stream was a couple of tanis across, swift and strewn with sharp and mostly submerged rocks. The ford, if there had ever been one, was washed out.

'It would be madness to try, Mannok,' Waren said.

'We can't be that far from the Western Road.' Mannok looked back at Dinnis. 'You're the expert with maps, what do you think?'

'Doesn't matter how far we are, if we can't get over the stream.' Waren pulled on his reins. His stallion moved restlessly beneath him, swinging a little to the left to face back towards the way they had come. 'Though there is not much flat ground, there is water. We could camp here for the night and head back to the Royal Road tomorrow.'

Mannok continued to look at Dinnis, his green eyes intense. 'Dinnis?'

Dinnis sat back in the saddle and visualised the maps kept in the library. Maps he used to pore over for hours as a child; inhaling their fusty scent, imagining where the roads and rivers might lead, considering escape routes back to Pylonis. In the end, he had stayed in Tarka, mostly because of his sister Ista, Anna and ... and Tilli. Well, if he was honest, also because he didn't know where he could go or who would accept him. His uncle Timon hadn't wanted him without Ista. He looked again at the hills on the right and turning in his saddle, he tipped his head back to catch the outline of the white mountain peaks floating serenely above the serried hills to the left. Yes, that was Mount Pele, then Hammerhead and next to them Mount Kocha.

'This is pointless, Mannok,' Waren said.

Mannok waved his cousin to be silent, not shifting his gaze from Dinnis.

He shrugged. 'It's hard to say, Your Highness, but not that far as the parrot flies.' He pointed his chin at the turbulent white water. 'This is most likely Heartbreak Creek which feeds into the Sha River maybe ten or so lek to the southeast.'

'Heartbreak?' Mannok's lips twisted into a smile. 'Fitting enough.' He rubbed his chin. 'If we follow it, we could cross further down.'

'Quite likely.'

'And the Sha would eventually lead us to the Western Road.'

'If we find a suitable place to cross,' Dinnis nodded his head, 'then yes, it would.'

'And if Dinnis is wrong? Or we can't cross? We could lose days in this trackless wilderness,' Waren said, his eyes narrowed.

Mannok met his cousin's gaze. The Prince was sitting erect and relaxed on Shadow's powerful back, the low rays of the sun burnishing his russet hair. Mannok lifted his chin.

'True, Lord Waren, we might. Yet, we will undoubtedly lose time if we turn back. I like your suggestion of camping here, but I am not ready to give up finding our way yet. In the morning we will follow Heartbreak in pursuit of our goal.'

'Don't be stupid, Mannok. Why not admit you have already led us astray and follow wiser heads?'

Silence fell over the group, the mumble of conversation cut off as with a knife, rigid and still in their saddles, all eyes on

Waren and Mannok. Dinnis tensed. Would Mannok let such an insult slide?

Mannok sucked in a breath. Shadow sidled and snorted, his ears twitching. The Prince's hunting dogs which had flopped down close to Shadow, sat up, fur ruffled.

'I hear what you are saying, cousin. I say we continue our course. Should I remind you, we are not at the border now.'

'Right. And sometimes it is wise to retreat. As I believe it to be in this case.'

Mannok's jaw clenched and unclenched. His nostrils pinched.

Dinnis looked down at Chasm's sleek mane. Maybe Waren should heed his own advice and shut up. Though it was probably too late for that.

When the Prince did speak, his voice was quiet and difficult to hear above the noise of the torrent but ice hard. 'Indeed, Commander Waren. As you say, you will go back. You can choose two or three companions to accompany you. And when you arrive in Tarka, present yourself without delay to Kaptan Kaspin for two full alume of double duty at the city walls.'

Waren's eyes widened, his broad cheeks darkened. He pressed his lips together. The two young men locked eyes.

The older lad looked away first. His mouth stretched in a flat smile. He bowed. 'As Your Highness commands.'

Swinging his horse around to face the trail, he raised his fist in salute, then urged the stallion into a walk, pushing past the wide-eyed riders lining the trail.

Chapter Twenty-Nine: Capitulation

Mannok

Mannok watched his cousin push past the other riders, stopping only to ask two of the older lads to accompany him back to Tarka. Waren's back was stiff, his head held high. He could have camped with them for the night but he was probably too offended for that. The sun would soon be below the horizon.

Mannok shifted his weight in the saddle and soothed Shadow. He could not allow his command to be continually challenged and keep the respect of his age-mates. He ground his teeth. His cousin still treated him like the tussled-haired boy who used to follow him around, begging to be included in the older boys' games. The stint up on the northern border had not helped. But they weren't at the northern border now. When his cousin disappeared around the switchback, Mannok pushed up against the saddle horns, holding Shadow still.

'Would anyone else like to join Lord Waren?'

He looked directly at Estolik, who dropped his gaze. He then looked in the eyes each of his age-mates now clustered at the small clearing beside Heartbreak Creek. Most saluted or looked away. Dinnis, as usual the odd man out, raised an eyebrow, but didn't say anything. No one else challenged him.

Suppressing the urge to run his fingers through his hair, he raised his voice so all could hear.

'As Lord Waren suggested, we will camp here for the night. Tomorrow we will find a crossing over Heartbreak Creek or maybe even the Sha and make our way to the Western Road.'

Hopefully, Dinnis' knowledge of maps could be relied on and they'd discover a feasible crossing tomorrow or he'd look a right fool.

* * *

It had been an uncomfortable night. Stones, sticks and small grass clumps littered the rough ground and gave little room to pitch the tents or even find a flat spot to sleep. His slumber had been broken and his dreams haunted by an elusive figure, the mysterious silver lady who had disappeared into the smoke and mist the night of the fire. Mannok rolled over and stretched his cramped limbs.

The curve of the sliver moon peered at him through the lattice of thin canoe-shaped leaves. All but a handful of stars had faded and a strip of light pushed up the dark cloud-wreathed sky from the silhouette of the mountains. About him the parrots, tarrawongs and ground birds made more racket than courtiers at a New Beginnings banquet. He pulled in a huge lungful of cool fresh air and smiled. He loved the southern wilderness and didn't really mind getting lost in it. Once it had been a kingdom of its own, one of the Five Lands. But some generations ago, cultured Shanta had been defeated by Tamra and Silisea and most of its people taken away. That much he knew from his history lessons as a child. For some reason, the land had remained mostly unpopulated, except along the coast and the seaward banks of the Sha, and made an ideal area for hunting despite its distance from Tarka. Too far for the ladies of the court to follow him.

A wadded cloak softly hit him in the face. 'You getting up, Mannu? Or are you planning on sleeping the day away?'

He bounded up and tackled Garvin to the ground.

'Peace, Mannu.' Garvin laughed.

They scrambled up and wolfed down the cold breakfast handed around by one of the servants.

* * *

Following Heartbreak Creek was not easy, as the track running beside it became almost too narrow for even a single file at some points. At other places they needed to clear rockslides or fallen branches. The creek itself remained uncrossable, sometimes running swift over sharp rocks, or strong and deep as it cut through ridges and snaked around outcrops of grey jagged rock formations.

As the day advanced, Estolik and some of the others were becoming increasingly restless. At first, gusty sighs, then muted conversations that fell silent when Mannok turned around to look at them. The longer they travelled, the further they'd need to return, but the crossing could be around the next bend, for all he knew.

The path widened, the dense forest falling back and revealing the tantalisingly close but so far unreachable lowlands of the steep ridges of the Blue Mountains. White fluffy clouds were building up on the horizon, reaching into the sapphire sky like towers and walls of a long-lost city. Behind him, the majestic, serried towers of the White Mountains, so painstakingly descended yesterday, floated serene and untouchable.

Garvin urged Glacier forward, to ride beside Mannok, taking advantage of the extra room. 'What do you think, Your Highness?'

Mannok's chest tightened. Was even his most loyal friend going to question him? Perhaps he would have to admit defeat and turn back soon. The sun was a fingerbreadth off midday. He would give it another hour, then they could get back to last night's campsite, with only three days of travel wasted.

'About what?' he snapped.

'About that cloud—don't you think it looks like a koraktil?'

'What?'

'See there's the long tail, there's the rampant wings and there's its snout spewing fire.'

Mannok scrunched his eyes and shook his head. Though now that he looked at the long cloud formation, he could see the legendary animal glaring back at him, at least before the wind began to fray its snout and spread out the wings. And that cloud could be a lady with a bird flying over her shoulder. Slide it, now Garo had him playing this child's game.

'That one's a beautiful lady ... see they are even chasing you down here.' In the uncanny way they had since they played together as infants, Garvin echoed his thoughts.

'You're an idiot.'

'At your service.' Garvin bowed with a flourish, his affable face split by a big grin.

Mannok's irritation frayed away like the ephemeral clouds. He grinned back. Then he sighed as the memory of Rizzi careening towards him on Snowflake sent a shiver up his spine. When assassins weren't attacking him, court ladies hounded him instead, and he didn't know which was worse. His cousin, generally such a sensible girl, had caught the madness. Since the Limarian Princess, they'd all gone crazy.

Except ... perhaps, Lumi. He saw again the proud flash in her silver eyes when he had accused her of having some trick hidden in her cloak. Eyes stunning in their silvery brilliance and sweeping, dark lashes. Something stirred at the thought of her soft curves, flawless amber skin, and long dark hair. Many of the young and not so young nobles admired her beauty. And she could ride and converse intelligently too. Pity her father was Lord Haka.

'Well, you should at least be safe for now,' Garvin said, breaking into his thoughts.

Mannok's shoulders slumped. And when they got back? Would the Kupanna have another foreign bride lined up for him? Would he continue to stumble over a bevy of beauties every time he turned a corner? Waren was right, sometimes retreat was the best strategic manoeuvre as a means to regroup. He could not hold on to his disappointment about Ista forever.

He stared at the horizon. Maybe it was time to make a tactical choice. 'Marriage can't be all that bad can it?'

Garvin blinked then cocked his head on one side and tapped his ear.

'Sorry, what did you say?'

'Yes, marriage, I can't put it off forever. Though what if she is a nag? Slide it, I don't think I'll get a moment's peace until I do marry and I probably won't get much peace afterwards.'

'There are some perks, you know.' Garvin raised his eyebrows. 'So, who did you have in mind?'

'I might have said Rizzi once, but she's become a bit erratic this last year. Jati's sweet but she's a bit young. Maybe Lady Tika of Silisea?'

'Didn't she marry Prince Tolteal's younger brother recently?'

'Oh, yes.' He frowned. Tolteal, Crown Prince of Silisea, betrothed Ista only last year too. He still wasn't sure if he liked the idea or not. Tolteal was a quiet, scholarly fellow, though a fantastic rider. Ista had seemed interested in the fellow on his last visit to Tarka and he would probably make his half-sister a good husband. He let out his breath in a long sigh.

'What about Durrin's younger sister, Lady Illari, or Lady Lantu of the Horse Clan or Lady Suzi of the Otter Clan?' Garvin said.

'This is depressing.' Mannok leaned forward and patted Shadow's noble neck. They were pretty enough, but mostly insipid. What did he really know about them anyhow? Only one stood out from the rest. And maybe marriage could heal the rivalry between their houses. 'I know ... maybe Lady Lumi of the Dolphin Clan.'

Garvin's eyebrows drew together and he looked away.

'Don't you like the idea? I know she's Haka's daughter, but she has many good qualities.'

'Perhaps. You'd have Haka for a father-in-law and ...' he paused, shrugged, 'she is forceful.'

'Our marriage might mend the breach between our families. She knows her own mind. She keeps her head in a crisis. Mama is fond of her. I think I could live with that.'

Behind them, one of the riders urged his mount into a canter, catching up to them. Mannok turned and saw Estolik, his pouty lips pinched together. 'Your Highness, how far do you intend to search for this crossing?' he asked.

The sun was at its zenith, the time he had appointed to turn around. The stream had widened and was shallower but the sharp rocks and strong current made it still too dangerous to cross even with the horses. Time to admit he was wrong.

Yet something about the insincere smile plastered on Estolik's plump face made him hesitate. He wouldn't announce it yet. He sat back in the saddle, pulled gently on the reins, and held up his hand to signal the group to stop.

'Time for a midday meal and siesta, I'd say. How about you let the others know, Essu.'

Estolik's grey-green eyes narrowed, then he shrugged. 'Your wish, Your Highness.'

Pulling down hard on the reins, he wheeled his red roan stallion around and trotted down the line with the message.

'And Estolik would be your brother-in-law,' whispered Garvin.

Mannok laughed. 'Essu's not that bad, though he does lack subtlety sometimes. I think I've decided on Lumi unless you've got any real objections.'

194

Garvin's smile wavered then broadened.

'No, she'd be happy to have you, I'm sure, but then they all would.'

'Happy to have a throne you mean.'

* * *

Mannok stirred and half-opened his eyes at the muffled sound. The embers of a small campfire glowed in a circle of stones beside him. His stomach felt pleasantly full after maize bread and potatoes baked in the ashes. Now everyone sprawled out along the sandy stretch beside the fast-flowing stream except those he'd assigned as guards.

He probably should get everyone up, eat humble stew, and start back up the mountain. Three days wasted plus the extra three they would have saved if the bridge hadn't been washed out. Six less days to hunt, but they had time. The muffled sound came closer—soft footsteps in the sand. Ripple and Singer stirred but didn't bark. Mannok sat up, his hand on his hunting knife, and scanned the area.

Dinnis appeared from around the bend in the river. He had his satchel slung over his shoulder and the bottom of his breeches were wet. He looked up and brought his fist to his chest in salute. Jumping over a medium-sized rock, he loped towards them.

Estolik rolled over, rubbing sleep from his eyes. Garvin yawned and stretched.

Dinnis knelt before Mannok. 'Your Highness—'

'You shouldn't wander off, you might get lost,' Estolik said with a yawn. He brushed the crumbs from his fine tunic.

The expression on Dinnis' face did not change.

'What is it, Dinnis?'

'I found a ford about a couple hundred tanis downstream. It's a bit tricky but I think we can cross it.'

A slow smile spread across Mannok's face. Jumping up, he punched the air, then pulling Dinnis up, he clapped the fellow on the shoulder.

'Capital. Come on, you sleepy heads. Time to get up and get going. We have a Hunting Lodge to get to. We should be there before nightfall tomorrow.'

A day later, they rode up to the Hunting Lodge in the Shanti woodlands. Now Mannok had decided about marrying Lumi, he felt lighter, more at peace. And long days of hunting in the wilderness with his companions and without Waren's constant corrections stretched ahead of him. Long days of freedom before he needed to return to the expectations, strictures and dangers of the court.

Southern Wilderness

Chapter Thirty: That Boy

Dinnis

Dinnis bent forward to take a closer look at the faint carvings in the stone block. He savoured the sounds of the forest about him—the bustling calls of birds about their daily business, the soft rustle of the wind in long grass and in the spindly leaves of the tall trees that encircled the site of this ruined city. After two alume of hunting with the Prince and his band most days, and sometimes at night, he was glad to slip away when he could.

He ran his fingers along the edges of the block and traced the shallow lines, trying to decipher the figures etched in stone. He could make out the shape of a crouching jaguar and perhaps a tall man looking into the distance.

The large stone blocks were scattered across this area as though thrown by a giant, with barely one left on top of another. The broken and hidden foundations, the scorched stones and old grey compacted ash, even the odd half-buried broken spear or shattered shield, all told of a tumultuous tragedy played out in the not-so-distant past. This was a place where men had fallen in fierce affray, women and children had been cruelly bereaved and hopes and dreams had sunk away in the blood-soaked earth. If he remembered the maps right, this was likely the capital of Shanta, destroyed by Tellek Kapok and King Jehotil of Silesia ages past.

A tremor passed through his lean frame as the traces evoked a more recent bloody battle in his own childhood at North Pass, the sickening sounds of metal on hardened leather shields and muscular flesh and bone, the fierce battle cries, the shrieks of agony and the acrid smells. He pressed his forehead against the cool grey stone block, slowing his breathing and holding himself still, sinking into calm as he banished the memories. His heart slowed to its normal steady rhythm.

The fluted susurration of strong wings sounded behind him. The sound also tugged at the edges of his buried memories. Turning, he saw a tall woman standing in the afternoon shadows a few tanis in front of him. Long black curls flowing over the woman's shoulders, framing an open face with expressive coal-black eyes looking deep into his without hesitation or coyness, the slender, upturned nose and the generous mouth now formed in a small questioning smile. He blinked. It was her, the silver lady, Rasel.

The years had left no imprint on her. Her skin, the colour of the silver moon, Argenti, glowed as smooth and white as it had been the day his world had changed so radically at North Pass over nine years ago. He stood still, his treacherous heart hammering against his ribs.

'You are that boy,' she said at last with the same musical lilt he remembered. 'I wasn't sure at first, as you have grown so tall. By the Maker's favour, you are taller than me now,' she added when he did not answer. 'Though just as tongue-tied as the last time we met.' Her eyes lit up with amusement.

He closed his eyes then opened them again. She was still there looking at him with her head slightly tilted to the right. She was dressed in a simple draped tunic that reached past her knees and left her long pale arms bare. A forest-green sash circled round her right shoulder to below her waist. She raised her shapely eyebrows and waited.

'My name is Dinnis, if you remember,' he said at last finding his voice, 'and I am not a boy anymore.'

She smiled. 'Dinnis, that's right. A Nolmec name.'

He frowned and looked down. For all he loved his mother, it was not a heritage he was especially proud of these days.

'I'm sorry,' she said taking a step closer, 'I did not mean to offend you.'

'It's true enough,' he said unable to keep the bitterness from his voice. 'You are far from your home, my lady,' he added, hoping to change the subject.

'As are you,' she said.

He lifted his shoulders.

'What brings you here alone among these sad echoes of Shanta's past glory?' she asked.

'I was looking for herbs. Bruiseleaf grows well in this area. Besides, the carvings on the stones intrigue me.'

'Herbs? What interest do you have in herbs?' She studied him, a slight frown creasing her smooth brow.

'I am apprenticed to a physician and before that I was apprenticed to a herbalist. I like collecting my own herbs when I can.'

'A physician? I like that,' she said, her whole face lighting up in a brilliant smile that stopped his heart.

He smiled and eased off the tight hold on his feelings. She was like the sun's warmth on a winter's day or a rainbow of hope adorning a rain-washed sky. She had lit up his life for a brief moment that fateful day at North Pass and he had not forgotten her in the long years since. Her small kindness towards him had been like a guiding star pointing him away from the dark fires of anger and revenge. Perhaps with her, he did not have to hide.

'I am glad you do not follow in the ways of Akrad the Betrayer,' she said.

He stiffened, the lightness of heart fraying. 'Do you think me capable of that?'

She looked into his eyes with a grave concentration that unsettled him. 'You are a child of Akrad, Dinnis of the North, and you shut your thoughts and feelings up behind strong walls hard to penetrate. Yet, you are right. Your past action of mercy should speak for you. It was your interest in herbs that made me wonder if you followed the sorcerer's path.'

'I know nothing of that practice.' Unlike his sister, Ista, Akrad's training had never interested him. 'You do not look any older than when I last saw you. You were surely at least eighteen then.'

'And how old are you?' Her laugh was as light as thistledown, her dark eyes merry.

'Twenty-one.'

'And grown so tall and serious.' Her eyebrows pulled together. 'Did you find your father? Did he come for you?'

'No, he didn't come for me. He died.' That mistruth did not roll so easily off his tongue as it once did. Not with her.

Her face clouded. 'I'm saddened to hear that. My da-baba died that day.'

It did not surprise him. The man had been gravely wounded.

'I grieve your loss,' he said. 'He was a brave man.'

'Yes, he was and a good one. We mourn and miss him still. But what of you ... you have found a home? You have been cared for?'

'I was taken to Tarka with the other war orphans. I still have obligations with the Palace though I hope one day to set up as healer in my own right.'

'Then Tarka is your home though you are as far south of that city now as you were north of it then.'

He nodded. 'I have been staying at one of the Hunting Lodges with the Prince's band. In a few more days we should be heading back.'

He drank in her beauty as he would the grandeur of a sunset or of a waterfall. He longed to reach out and touch her, to catch hold of her hand and kiss it, but he stood still as the stone block behind him. A cloud passed over the intense afternoon sun, throwing them both in deeper shadow. Nearby, a half-grown tarrawong chick strutted through the yellow grass squawking its hunger.

'Well, I am glad you have a place ...' She stopped speaking and turned her head to her left.

He followed the direction of her eyes to where the sole remaining wall stood sentinel beneath the dappled shadows of a large ironwood tree. Beyond the wall stretched the open forest that he had negotiated on his way to the ruins earlier in the day.

He stiffened, becoming aware of the subtle stilling of the birdsong around them, the slight swish of movement through the long grass, a jingle of metal riding tack. He felt rather than saw her take a step back into the shadows. Behind him, Chasm, tied up to a nearby tree nickered a soft welcome which was echoed soon after by another.

One of the others from the hunting party must be searching for him. Garvin, most likely. The sun emerged from behind the clouds dazzling his eyes and lighting up the rider appearing from behind the wall. Dinnis' grey eyes widened as he recognized the erect poise, powerful build and aquiline gaze of Prince Mannok astride Shadow. Mannok brought his stallion to a stop.

'Dinnis, there you are.' His gaze fixed on him, then moved to take in Rasel standing beneath the swaying branches of the ghostbark tree.

Jade green eyes locked with coal black.

Dinnis felt himself fade into insignificance as Mannok and Rasel connected in a single charged moment.

Chapter Thirty-One: Mannok

Mannok

Mannok gazed at the strange woman standing beneath the grey-barked tree. The skin of her flawless face and slender arms was silvery white, like Ista's, and seemed to radiate with its own light. Her dark eyes were large and wide. She was tall, taller than he was, with a shapely figure. She gazed back at him without any trace of fear or flattery. It was as if she could peer deep into his spirit, sifting his merit. A shiver ran from the nape of his neck to the base of his spine. Would she find him worthy?

Her black wavy hair lifted in the wind and she pulled a dark green sash over her slender shoulders. Her eyes stayed fixed on his, her face serene, even a little expectant. She was as ethereal as the owl-lady at the fire. Was she the same woman? Surely not. How could she be hundreds of lek from her home?

He took hold of himself and looked back at Dinnis standing beside one of the large monumental blocks of stone. Urging Shadow forward a short distance, he swung himself to the ground and hitched the reins over a branch beside Chasm.

'So, this is where you hide yourself,' he said.

The young man's smoky grey eyes met his before sliding away to the long grass at his feet.

'So it seems, Your Highness,' he said, with a small bow.

Mannok inclined his head and turned back to the woman who was watching them both. 'Who is your friend, Dinnis?' he asked, 'Would you be so good as to introduce her to me?'

Dinnis turned to the woman. 'My lady, may I introduce you to Mannok of Tarka, Prince Royal of Tamra, Lord of the Southern Fief, Champion of the Rokkan Kapok, Pathfinder, best and bravest of all his age-mates.'

Mannok grimaced as his full rank and titles rolled off his age-mate's acerbic tongue. Could he detect a hint of sarcasm? And just like Dinnis to wilfully misunderstand him and introduce him rather than the woman.

She stepped forward out of the shadows and arched a slender dark eyebrow.

'Mannok of Tarka, son of Tamrak, what a great many titles you have.'

Her dark eyes danced with laughter and her voice was like liquid silver, like the mysterious woman at the fire. He bowed in return, though he suspected she had no rank. How else would she be alone in the wilderness without a mount or companions? Yet she thrilled him in a way no other woman had ever done before, not even Ista. A deep passion for life lay in her dark gaze, a recklessness of spirit that quickened his pulse and called to him, yet at the same time she had a natural dignity, a sure calm. Looking sideways, he caught Dinnis' appraising look before his age-mate dropped his gaze.

'Your Highness, Prince Mannok, this is Rasel of the Forest Folk.'

'Rasel!' The name lingered like the echo of a tinkling bell. He bowed low. 'A beautiful name with as little need of affected titles as its owner is in need of flashy decoration. For how can perfection be enhanced or bettered?'

Her pearl-like teeth flashed in a quick smile and her black eyes crinkled with amusement. 'Prince of Tamra, you do have a golden tongue. Do you seek to flatter me?'

'My lady, I do not think it possible to flatter you. Not only is my poor tongue incapable of giving you sufficient praise but you are surely too astute to be swayed by the prattling of a fool.'

'A clever and eloquent fool then. In the very course of declaring it impossible, you flatter me a second time. Surely you charm all the young ladies of Tarka with dashing ease.'

'Whatever success I may or may not have had among the ladies of the court, it seems I have failed to impress the one lady that I would most like to.'

'You do not need cleverly-fashioned compliments to impress me, Prince of Tamra.' Her eyes looking directly into his. 'I can see who you are as a man—strong, intelligent, honourable and brave.'

'Ah, now you mock me.' He dropped his eyes and frowned. 'You miss the mark for I am not known for my intellect or for fair speech. As no doubt Dinnis here would be only too glad to confirm.'

Dinnis snorted. 'There is a difference between having wits and using them.'

Mannok narrowed his eyes and glared at his age-mate. He'd laid himself open for that jibe. He swallowed back his anger. So much for impressing this Rasel. Now he felt doubly foolish.

He took a deep breath and gazed at her without flinching. 'Be that as it may, my lady, I beg your pardon if my clumsy—perhaps witless—attempts to express my admiration sound trite and insincere.'

'No, not witless, not trite or insincere—just extravagant,' she replied. Her laugh rippled with merriment. 'If you asked my brother, Semian, or any of my Kin, they'd assure you that I'm far from a paragon of perfection. But why do you doubt yourself? Why shower me with fulsome compliments yet refuse to accept my simple ones? I only speak what I can see, man of Tamra.'

'Your imperfections must be minor, for I cannot perceive them … but before you chide me again for flattering you, I will accept your good opinion with as much dignity as I can. I will admit to some repute in the hunt, some skill with horse and spear.'

'Is that so Prince of Tamra?'

'Ah now, you have reduced me to a braggart.' He shook his head. He took a step towards her and blurted out. 'Yet, I would protect you with my life, if you would let me.'

He stopped, his hands and body trembling. What had he just promised to this mysterious woman? He didn't even know who she was. His parents would be horrified. He took a deep breath. His body strummed like a taut bowstring. He was as alive as in the closing moments of the hunt, as he came face to face with a magnificent quarry—a jaguar or stag—or in the midst of battle. He took another step forward.

Her carmine lips slightly parted. Her eyes, at first luminous, clouded over. She bowed her head and took a step back.

'What do you know of me, Prince of Tamra, son of the Kapok? You do not … cannot realise what you ask of me.'

He stood stone-still, slowing his breathing, mastering his urge to sweep her off her feet and ride away with her. She was on the verge of taking flight, he was sure of it. A cold shiver coursed through him.

If she left now, he might never see her again.

Chapter Thirty-Two: Rasel

Rasel

Rasel stood still, her chest rising and falling, fighting for breath. The Tamrin prince's aquiline stare locked onto hers. She could feel his quickened pulse in her own, his eager ardour that he was holding in check with a visible effort. An answering exhilaration surged inside her, tingling her skin and limbs, threatening to pull her towards him. He was young, at the threshold of manhood with the alert agile stance of a hunter. Despite his diffidence, the hidden power coiled within him, ready to spring out at need. His bronzed face with its strong curved nose and slightly crooked teeth, was open, guileless. Set deep beneath his straight brows, his eyes were rimmed in a dark opaque jade, the centres a translucent golden green flecked with brown. They reflected a great capacity to love, yet a shadow harboured within them. He was a warrior, a man of violence, a man of Tamra, a prince.

She should not stay. She should leave before she was lost. She tensed her muscles to turn and run, to fly away high on the air currents. The wind picked up, flattening the grass. It whipped her hair about her face and cooled her heated cheeks. The tree branches swayed with abandon, rustling and whispering their secrets.

'Don't go.' He took a slow step back, arms spread wide and low, palms out, as though gentling a wild horse. 'Forgive me, my lady, if I have distressed you with my excessive and untoward fervour.'

She inclined her head. 'It is of no consequence. I should go.' She did not move.

'Indeed, your companions must be concerned that you are separated from them. Are you lost? Where did you last see them? I could help find them for you.'

He was concerned, protective even, and eager to help, as though she could not look after herself. How amusing.

'Companions? I am travelling across the Wide Lands alone, though no doubt my brother will soon catch up with me. I saw Friend Dinnis here and stopped to greet him.'

The Prince's brows drew together, his eyes darkening. 'Then you know each other well?'

'We met before. Brief encounters,' she said.

'Only the once,' the boy—no, the young man now—spoke, his quiet contained voice overlapping hers.

Her eyes met his grey oblique ones and she smiled. His thin lips twitched upwards a fraction in response. Such a stark contrast, these two young men, one standing so still in the bluish afternoon shadows she could forget his presence; the other poised and standing astride in the golden sunlight so none could fail to see him. Yet there was a similari-ty about them too, something that she could not quite yet discern.

The Prince's tenor voice broke into her thoughts. 'Surely, my lady Rasel, you cannot be travelling alone? Even in more settled lands such a course would be unwise for a young woman of delicacy, but here in this wilderness, it would be madness. There are no villages for many lek around these ruins. The peasants will not settle here. They think the place haunted. Superstitious nonsense, of course, but wild animals are com-mon and bandits do camp here from time to time.'

'I am well able to take care of myself.'

Doubt clouded his eyes. She lifted her chin, stood a touch straighter and stared back at him. He returned her gaze without wavering.

'Then my lady, let me ... us,' he gave a quick glance at his silent compatriot, '... ac-company you back to your village. You could ride behind me and we would have you back to your family in far less than it would take to walk.' He smiled. 'I would be hon-oured to meet your parents, to assure them of your safety.'

She laughed. No doubt he was sincere in offering to help her, yet how eager he was to find out where she lived, to stay longer in her company. While he had backed off from his impetuous declaration, his eyes still darkened with longing.

And her own treacherous body thrilled in turn. Like him, she did not want this mo-ment to end. She wanted to prolong it, to make sure that she would see him again. But she dared not, lest she fall for him.

For all his fiery spirit, the goodness in him, he was a man of the Five Lands. How could she love a man from Tarka, the scion of the house of the Kapok? Though perhaps such a union could heal the past? No, it was impossible, unthinkable, unwise. But a friendship might heal the grievous breach between their peoples.

'Prince of Tamra, my home is many days journey from here. I would not trouble you by taking you so far out of your way.'

'But ...' He cast his eyes around the clearing, looked closely at her again. 'Forgive me, but you appear to have no more than the scant clothes you are wearing. You have no mount, no pack, and no companions. How can you be so ill-equipped and so far from those who should be protecting you? Even a peasant family would not be so care-less of their daughter's safety.'

'I like to travel light. It is faster that way, easier ...' to shapeshift. She frowned at him. Was what Semian said true, that the Tamrin hated her Kin for who they were, for what they could do? More reason to leave. She was glad to know that the boy, Dinnis, had found his way, that should be enough for her.

'My lady Rasel, the Prince is right,' Dinnis said. His hand rested lightly on the stal-lion's powerful neck as it calmly pulled at the long grass and flicked its tail. 'It is not safe for anyone to travel alone in these parts.'

'Yet I found you here amongst the ruins and so absorbed in cold stone that anyone or anything could have crept up behind and ambushed you.'

'As indeed you did, my lady.' A hesitant smile tugged at the corners of his mouth.

Mannok laughed. 'Rasel has got you there, my friend. I can't for the life of me work out what you have been doing, sneaking off by yourself these last several days. Though ...' He turned back to Rasel.

She smiled. 'I am no expert on royal protocols, but I would have thought a prince, indeed the heir to the Golden Throne, would be more likely to attract ambushes than I would and would be well-advised not to travel alone.' She arched a brow. 'Perhaps I should escort both of you back to the safety of your companions.'

'She does have a point, Your Highness,' Dinnis said.

The Prince glowered for a moment. 'I do not need a nursemaid.' Then he threw back his head and laughed, his eyes lighting up. 'But brilliant idea, my lady. The sun will set in a few hours. Since your home is so far away, let us bring you back to our lodgings for this night at least. Then, in the morning, I can arrange an escort to bring you safely back to your family, if you agree ... or not, if that is what you wish.'

He took two rapid strides till he was standing in front of her, his green eyes glowing, his face made handsome by a wide friendly smile. 'It would be my honour to accompany you.' He caught up her hand and brushed the back of her hand with his lips.

A shock went through her at his feather touch. Her breath caught. 'I could not, I should do that. I ... it would not be safe,' she whispered.

His strong fingers curled around hers, his grip tightening. 'I would not harm you,' he said. He dropped to his knees, both tan hands holding her silvery white one. 'Rasel, on my honour, I would not hurt you for anything. I would protect you with my life's blood. Come with me, come and be my princess.'

Chapter Thirty-Three: Hunting Lodge

Rasel

A lightning bolt shot through Rasel to her very core. As ridiculous as it seemed, his words felt so right. It was often so with her Kin, that strong, near instant connection with a mate. And yet, he was not of the Forest Folk, not Kin, but a man of Tamra many years younger than she. To bind with such a one would be foolishness. She should go. Yet, she could not move, could not speak, could not shift her gaze from his, could not still the rapid rush of her feckless heart.

Dinnis stirred, took a step forward, a look of anguish melting through his outward mask of indifference. 'Your Highness, Mannok, do not make rash promises you cannot keep. Even if you mean this honourably, your royal parents would never permit it!' With his sudden fierceness and strong Tamrin nose, he was like a young hawk ready to dive for the kill.

Mannok frowned, but did not turn to look at his compatriot. Instead, he kept his eager eyes fastened on her face. 'I want you at my side, Rasel. Surely, they will grant me this happiness.'

'If you think that, you are a bigger fool than I thought.' Dinnis growled. 'The marriage of the Prince Royal is a state matter of great importance not to be decided on a whim.'

The Prince's face became more determined, more certain. 'Not a whim. My parents wish me to marry, to choose a woman worthy of a prince. Until this day, this very moment, I had not found her. And I would not lose her now.'

'Prince of Tamra, I cannot—'

He held up a hand. 'Hush, sweet Rasel, Lady of the Forest. I do not ask you to choose now, but I can't leave you alone in the wilderness at the mercy of wild beasts and bandits. Let us escort you to the Lodge for this one night at least. On my shield of honour, you will not be harmed.'

Could she trust him? She searched his face, the clear open wells of his eyes, and felt assured of the sincerity of his words. Besides, how could he, warrior that he might be, hurt her, the daughter of Jazadek and Rutiah, Pathfinder of her people? If she left now, this moment would not come again. If she stayed, even only a night, she could learn more of these children of Tamrak than she might in years of observation from afar. This attraction she felt, a whirlpool that sought to sweep her away, was not beyond her control. She could leave at any time if she felt endangered.

Not a few paces from them, a black and white tarrawong burst into a long carolling call. Deep within, she found a swelling joy answering the bird's melodious song.

'I will stay a night to ease your concerns, Prince of Tamra.'

'Rasel, this is madness.' Dinnis' wild cry startled her. 'Would you stake your happiness and safety on rash promises? Though his intentions are honourable, it is doubtful he can bring them to pass. And what then is to become of you?'

Mannok leapt to his feet. He whipped around, his eyes narrowed to slits. 'You forget yourself, Dinnis.' His right hand hovered over the hilt of his hunting knife. 'You insult me. What do you mean by this disloyalty?'

The man of the north stood completely still. He did not drop his gaze but continued to glare at the Prince with a ferocious intensity. Rasel could feel the tension crackle between them.

The wind dropped for a moment then roared back into life. A hawk negotiating the air currents with some difficulty far above them gave a long high-pitched whistle.

She took a step forward, placing a hand on the Prince's shoulder, 'Mannok, son of Rokkan ... don't do anything rash.' Her hand slid down his arm and caught up his strong brown hand into her own.

Dinnis stirred at her voice, his mouth twisting into a bitter smile. He hesitated then bit his lip and dropped his eyes. He sank to his knees. 'My Lord Prince, I mean no disloyalty. Who else is here to speak on Rasel's behalf? But do with me whatever you wish.'

Mannok gave a derisive snort, waved him away with his free hand and turned towards her. His serious eyes searched her face. Her lips wavered into a half-smile.

'I would never dishonour you, sweet Rasel. I give you my word as a prince that you will be treated with modesty and courtesy. And, if ... if you decide to come with me to Tarka, I will do all in my power to protect you and give you your due, so I promise on my heart's breath.' He turned and clapped his companion on the shoulder. 'Dinnis will be your protector, champion and chaperon. He will be my conscience.'

Tarka! Her heart thrilled at the thought of that fabled city. Yet it was a temptation she must resist. For she suspected that the longer she spent in the Prince's company, the harder it would be to resist her heart's song and to leave, as she must.

She smiled and nodded at Dinnis to reassure him. He'd again submerged the flame that smouldered within him behind his mask of indifference. A mask even she found hard to penetrate, but clearly, he cared for her.

He swallowed and lifted his sharp chin. 'As you wish, Your Majesty.' He bowed. 'Lady Rasel.'

'Capital.' A fierce grin curved up Prince Mannok's face. 'Let's go then.'

He whistled and the stallion shook his head, dislodging the reins, and trotted over. Mannok swung up into the saddle and held out his arm to assist her in mounting up behind him, which was cute and endearing. Without another glance, he urged the stallion back the way he had come, heading to the Lodge in the west.

* * *

Rasel sat behind the Prince on his powerful stallion. Dinnis rode a black gelding behind them, keeping his thoughts to himself. A burnished blood-red sun hovered above the horizon, its disc striped by tree trunks and obscured by undergrowth. The strong wind tossed the tall forest canopy in wild abandon. The tree trunks creaked and moaned, the upper branches rustling with an eerie high-pitched song. On the forest floor, sheltered as they were, stray gusts of wind caught at Rasel's long hair and whipped the ends of her green sash about her, leaving her limbs chilled.

They rode for an hour with the darkness of the night settling all around them. Night time creatures rustled in the undergrowth. The soft hush of wings and a pale shadow swooped over their heads. Not Semian or any of her Kin, a regular owl. She was not afraid of moving through the wilderness on her own even at night. The Filane presented far greater dangers than the largest and most ferocious predatory beast. The soft breeze shifted and the acrid smell of humans, of sweat, horses, dogs and smoke, and the sound of anxious voices filtered into the night.

'Not long now. Look, you can see the night lights in the Lodge up ahead.' Mannok's pleasant tenor voice broke through the gloom.

'Something seems to have stirred them up.' Dinnis spoke from behind, his tone muted, flat.

Tongues of orange flames flickered from between the ghostly grey trunks, bobbing about in random directions. Torches, most like, held by perhaps twenty people spread out in a rough ever-moving circle. Dark figures stood out against the warm light glowing from the low windows of a stone building perhaps thirty tanis away. The babble of shouts grew louder. Horses whinnied and dogs barked warnings. The pungent smells of scorched torch oil, maize and peccary flesh, chilli and sweat grew stronger.

The Prince urged the stallion into a fast walk. The hairs of her arms prickled. Someone or something was close by in the gloom.

Two warriors in feathered headdress, loomed up in the path in front of them, barring their way with their spears and shields. 'Stop! Declare yourselves!' a burly warrior shouted.

The stallion reared, sharp hooves pawing the air. Rasel's thighs gripped the horse's flanks to stop slipping backwards. She tensed, taut and ready to shapeshift, to distract or protect, as the situation warranted.

The Prince remained calm; his body relaxed against hers. He soothed the horse, 'Peace, Shadow.' He laughed. 'Would you bar my way, Garvin? Best be prepared to defend against my spear.'

'Prince Mannok.'

'Your Highness.'

Both men lowered their spears, dropped to their knees and brought fists to their chest.

'Up, up, no need for formality.' The Prince of Tamra dismounted and touched each man on the shoulder.

The one named Garvin stood and bowed before the Prince. 'Your Highness! May the Maker be praised! We were about to send out a search party.'

'Indeed, Mannok,' the well-padded man agreed. 'You have no idea of the panic you caused when we realised you weren't with any of the other hunting parties and no one had a clue to where you had gone. Your disappearance is not something we would care to explain to His Majesty, the Kapok!'

The Prince chuckled. 'I would imagine not, Estolik, but there was no need to worry. I had Dinnis to protect me.'

He gestured back down the path. The man of the north swung off his horse and stood beside Rasel. His dour facial expression almost invisible in the dense night shadows.

She leant forward and stroked the velvet neck of the stallion, Shadow. The wind dropped and the soft vibrations of the night crickets filled the air overlaid with the more chaotic shouts coming from outside the Hunting Lodge.

The one called Estolik shook with laughter. He gasped for breath. 'Had we known, we would have been doubly worried, Your Highness.'

Rasel frowned at the mockery in the young man's tone. She bent down and touched Dinnis of the north's shoulder. He shot her the briefest of looks, and she felt, rather than saw, his slight shrug.

'Perhaps, our friend has more ability than we give him credit. I did not notice any lack of military skills in the ambush on the border, Essu. Though, of course, you were too busy getting married to be there. Besides, he found me, not you,' the Prince of Tamra said.

'The other way round, Your Highness, for you found me,' Dinnis replied.

'I am beholden to Friend Dinnis, for without him, I would not have met you, my Prince,' Rasel said.

Both Garvin and Estolik jumped as though they just now saw her.

'By the moons, a woman,' the padded one, Estolik said, clutching his chest. Semian had mentioned that name before. A son of the Dolphin Lord, Haka. A man to watch.

Mannok threw his head back and slapped his sides. 'Estolik, your powers of observation are non-existent. You too Garvin. What has happened to those famous sharp eyes of yours?'

'It is almost pitch black ...' the son of Haka fired up. Then a hood slid over his indignation. 'My mistake, Your Highness.' Even in the darkness, she could sense the split in this man's being, the conflict in loyalties simmering below the surface.

'Keep your excuses for later, my friend,' the Prince said between chuckles.

He offered Rasel a hand. She took it and swung down from the horse.

'But I am remiss. My lady Rasel, let me introduce you to my second cousin, Lord Estolik, eldest son of Lord Haka, Markan of the Western Marches. Estolik, my lady Rasel of Shanta.'

'My lady,' Estolik cast her a surly glance and a token bow.

'And this is Garvin, second son of Kaptan Kaspin of the Tarkan City Guard.' Mannok clapped a hand on the man's burly shoulder.

'My lady Rasel, a pleasant surprise to meet such a charming guest in these wilds.' An open welcome radiated out from this companion of the Prince, though he hid something that troubled him. A grief, a disappointment perhaps.

'Opportune, indeed,' agreed Mannok. 'I have promised the Lady Rasel safe passage to Tarka.' His voice held a hint of warning, as though he expected objections.

The rush of footsteps on the path and a short, balding man in a simple woollen tunic came running up with a flaming torch. 'My Lord Prince,' he gasped. 'Thank the Maker, you are here.'

Passing the torch to the one called Garvin, the man dropped to the ground and stretched out at Mannok's feet.

'Ah, Palarn, good man. Take the horses to their stables if you will. They will need a rub down and tonight I'd like to settle our guest,' the Prince said.

The old one rose to his feet and took the reins of both horses. He bowed low to Mannok once again and then led his equine charges back down the path towards the Lodge.

'Garvin, my friend, call off the search party before they set off into the wilderness.'

The Prince's friend bowed, handed the torch to the son of Haka. He hurried toward the milling shadows outside the Lodge. The Prince of Tamra looked toward the silent man standing behind her.

'Dinnis, the lady should have my room to ensure her privacy. Be so kind as to remove my things and make it comfortable for her.'

217

'As you wish, Your Highness.' Dinnis bowed to Rasel, then gave a smaller bow to Mannok before strolling after Garvin.

'That man is incorrigible,' the son of Haka growled.

The Prince snorted. 'He wouldn't be the only one. Now, Essu, I hope you haven't eaten all the food because I find myself famished. And I would be embarrassed not to set a decent meal before our fair guest.' His strong teeth flashed in the dark. He offered her his arm, and when she took it, tucked it into his own.

Estolik bowed. 'I am sure the kitchen staff will be able to rustle up something worthy for the both of you.'

'Good, good.' Mannok drew Rasel closer to his side.

Brilliant stars peeped between the swaying canopy of leaves above their heads. Together, arm in arm, they walked toward the sprawling stone building situated so close to the sad ruins of doomed Shanta and within a few lek of the arbitrary border between Tamra and Silisea. Close to the place her matu birthed her during the height of the years of the Betrayal. She shivered and drew closer to Mannok's fierce warmth. She stepped through the open door and into the jaguar's lair.

On the Royal Road, south of Tarka

Chapter Thirty-Four: Falling

Dinnis

Dinnis mopped up the amber sweetness oozing out of the honeycomb with the last fragment of maize bread. He slipped an avocado and sunfruit into the folds of his tunic for later before leaning back against the cushions. Soft morning light filtered through the shuttered windows, gilding dust motes and spilling over onto the flagstone floor cluttered with boots, bows and hunting trophies. The twenty or so lads of the Prince's hunting band lounged about the long low wooden table set in the centre of the large common room. Most were trying not to stare at Rasel sitting beside Prince Mannok, her bright eyes taking in everything around her. She was a vision of loveliness totally out of place in the disorderly, musty domain.

Mannok sat up straighter and rapped the rough wood with a silver spoon, drawing all eyes to him. 'Once finished our morning meal, we'll pack up. We will leave for Tarka by midday.'

The whisper of smothered protests, suppressed sighs and shuffling rippled around the room at the sudden change of plan. Dinnis tilted his head. However disappointed the others might be, he at least, was ready to leave. He had collected all the herbs he needed and missed his training sessions with Laetil and Anna. But surely, Rasel, his silver lady, always so elusive, didn't intend to accompany the Prince to Tarka.

Garvin looked startled. 'What now? Don't we have another two days before ...' He met Mannok's eyes, then flicked a glance at Rasel, his mouth settling into a flat line. 'As you wish, Your Highness.'

'Midday?' Hasuk asked. 'But what about our spoils?'

'Camp Master Palarn and his crew will follow with anything you can't fit in your saddle packs.'

Estolik and Durrin leaned toward each other, whispering behind their hands. Mannok swung round to look at them, his eyebrows raised.

Estolik placed a half-chewed peccary leg on his plate. 'What of the white stag the scouts saw to the west yesterday?'

'I would not be late for the birthday banquet. The Kupanna will have extended a great deal of trouble to arrange it.'

Dinnis' lips twitched. Mannok said this with a straight face although all present, except Rasel, knew of his inventive efforts the past several years to avoid this very event.

'Yes, but it only takes seven days to travel to Tarka from here,' Estolik huffed. 'One more day won't make much difference.'

'Indeed, cousin, if all goes well. I would not like to risk any delays on the road as has happened in past years. You can stay and hunt it, if you so please.'

Estolik darted a look at Durrin before holding up both hands. 'Your Highness, it would be our pleasure to accompany you.' He didn't quite keep the sullen tones out of his voice.

Mannok folded his arms and looked at each young warrior in turn. 'Would anyone else like to speak to our departure?'

'Your command, Your Highness,' the others returned as one.

'I am glad we are all agreed then.' Mannok's hand covered Rasel's slender one and a wide smile lit up his eyes. 'And will you join us, my lady?'

She hesitated a moment, then she smiled. A smile that dazzled the room. 'I have always wanted to see the city of the Kapoks, son of Tamrak.'

Dinnis' heart sank. He clenched his fist, a new determination stirring. Yesterday afternoon, Mannok appointed him Rasel's protector, and whether the Prince had done so in jest or not, Dinnis would fulfill that role. He would protect Rasel, the silver lady of North Pass, to the utmost of his ability, for as long as she needed him.

* * *

Apart from his gathered herbs, Dinnis had little to pack. The rest of the Prince's hunting party didn't take much longer and they set out on the road north to the capital well before noon. This time, Mannok elected to take the more normal route. They crossed the lowland dry forests via the Western Road, camping under the stars at night. On the second day, they joined the Royal Road winding from the north of old Mokka to the southern reaches of Silisea along the mountain ridges, over passes and across plateaus. Now they stayed in the Way Stations built centuries ago by the Kapoks for the use of all travellers.

On the eighth day, Dinnis rode behind Prince Mannok and Rasel. Garvin rode next to Dinnis, uncharacteristically morose. The rest of the band strung out behind them. They made good progress despite the steady rain over the last few days.

Now the sun hammered down once more, the heat shimmering off the cliff face and sucking up the moisture from yesterday's relentless downpour. Sweat beaded on Chasm's dark coat and dripped between his shoulder blades.

Garvin flicked his hair out of his eyes and muttered, 'Who is she?'

'A friend.' Dinnis bristled, ready to defend Rasel from insult. At least Estolik and Durrin, the biggest sources of the snide whispers, rode several paces back, bringing up the rear.

Garvin flashed Dinnis a look. A smile wavered on his blunt face. 'You too, Dinnis?' Then he shrugged. 'I can see the attraction. She is captivating. I've never known anyone like her, but who is she? Who are her parents, her clan?'

Dinnis tilted his head. 'I've not known you to be concerned about status before.' He kept his voice low, though Mannok and Rasel seemed absorbed in their own intimate discussion, heads bending toward the other, voices soft.

'I'm not. How could I be? But the court will be, the Council will be, the Kapok and Kupanna will be. It's as though she's enchanted him.'

'Or he, her.' Dinnis sighed, stroking Chasm's velvet neck.

He was not quite sure what to think. Mannok and Rasel's sudden passion burned with unwavering flame. Their hands brushed against each other at mealtimes or as they rode together, Rasel on the old mare Mannok leant her. Their eyes strayed to each other like moths to the moon or sparks from a fire to the sky.

Yet Mannok had kept his word. He gave up his own royal accommodations and bunked in with the rest of the hunting band at the Way Stations, so that Rasel could sleep in privacy. He treated her with all the courtesy and ceremony due to a lady of highest rank. Could he really be planning to present her as his bride on arrival at Tarka? Dinnis' stomach squirmed at the thought of the Kupanna and the Kapok's response. What would happen to Rasel, caught in the crossfire? Should he warn her of the danger?

He looked up and met Garvin's thoughtful brown eyes and lifted a shoulder.

Garvin smiled and stared toward misty peaks on the horizon. 'Love can be like that, vaulting over reason, taking you where you know you shouldn't go. But you're a good judge of character, Dinnis. If you trust our mysterious new friend, then so will I.'

A loud resounding crash, followed by long grinding sounds, echoed from the road ahead, bouncing off the mountainside in a series of diminishing percussions.

'Sounds like a landslide,' Yalik muttered from behind them.

'Could be.' Mannok held up his hand, slowing the horses' pace from a steady trot to a walk.

The jarring sounds grew softer and petered out, to be replaced by shouts and cries of many people. They passed terraced fields and a small village perched on the edge of the steep ravine with no sign of catastrophe.

They rode around one more sharp bend in the road.

'Slide it,' Mannok growled. He and Rasel pulled their mounts to an abrupt stop.

Dinnis shortened Chasm's reins and stared at the scene before them. A raw scar of exposed rock and dirt gouged out the steep cliffside above and spilled out over the paved road in a jumbled tangle of smashed trees, boulders and rubble.

A group of elders were huddled to the side of the landslide, overseeing the men, women and children already clearing the debris and shoring up the side of the road crumbling into the precipitous ravine.

The others jostled behind them, horses restive and snorting.

'At least, this wasn't aimed at Mannok,' Garvin muttered, leaning forward over Glacier's neck.

224

Mannok urged Shadow forward, moving to a portly man with white hair, his face wrinkled with age. He wore a single gold-brown feather and a fine cloak, most likely signifying him as the headman.

Garvin and Estolik followed. Dinnis stayed with Rasel. Mannok had, after all, named him her protector.

'My man, how long before the road can be cleared?' Mannok called.

The villagers turned their heads toward him, eyes popping. As one, they prostrated themselves on the torn-up road.

'Your Royal Highness,' the white-haired man said. 'We beg your forgiveness.'

Mannok sighed. 'Please, raise yourselves. This,' he waved his arm at the rockslide, 'is hardly your fault, but of the unseasonable weather and the will of the Maker. And you are?'

The old man levered himself to his feet, his villagers following his lead. He bowed deeply. 'Headman Saluruk, Your Highness.'

'And how long before the road is cleared, Headman Saluruk?'

The headman swallowed, his voice nub bobbing. 'Six days or more.'

Mannok's hands tightened.

'We'll not get to Tarka in time for the Feast then,' Garvin said.

'So, we could've stayed and hunted the stag after all,' Estolik muttered.

'I don't have a seeing bowl, Essu!' Mannok growled. He glanced at Rasel.

She tilted her head and looked at the sky. 'What other paths can you take, Prince of Tamra?'

Mannok's face brightened. 'Headman Saluruk, can we detour around the spill?'

Headman Saluruk shook his head. 'If Your Highness backtracked to Three Rock Village, there's a bridge across the Sha River that would take you to Knifeedge Pass and to the plateau. Then at Crystal lake, the Five Chasms path will bring you back to the Royal Road.'

Mannok frowned. 'That would add at least four days to our journey.' He looked at Dinnis and raised an eyebrow. 'Any other suggestions?'

Dinnis scanned his memory of the maps of the area and shook his head. 'None that I remember.'

'Why the hurry to get to the feast, Mannu?' Estolik asked. 'It wouldn't be the first year that the guest of honour failed to attend.'

Mannok pressed his lips together, then sighed. 'What most seem to forget is the feast celebrates my father's ascension to the Throne, as much, or surely more than the circumstance of my birth. So I would hardly think I'm the guest of honour.' He looked across the deep valley beside the road to the ridges and hills undulating toward the distant flatlands, his fingers tapping the horn of his saddle.

'So what do we do now? The nearest Way Station lies north, past the rockslide and the one to the south at Eleven Terraces village, means backtracking more than half a day's travel,' Garvin said.

Saluruk cleared his throat. 'Your Highness, Mist Falls Village may be small, but we would be honoured to give you lodgings as best we can. You and your close companions can stay in my home and we will find places for the others.'

Mannok looked back at him and smiled. 'We would be honoured to accept your gracious offer, and I will ensure you will be recompensed for your trouble.'

'No need for recompense, Your Highness. It will be our honour.'

'Do not dispute this with me, good Saluruk. I will accept no other terms.'

The headman bowed. 'Your will, Your Highness.' He waved to a small stand of avocado trees a little further back on the road. 'Please, make yourself comfortable in the shade. My people will bring food and drink for you and your horses while your places are prepared.'

* * *

Dinnis woke in the dim pre-dawn light, with the vanishing shreds of a dark dream and a crushing weight lodged in his chest, the air stale and choking. The headman had moved his family out, despite Mannok's protests. Mannok then insisted the headman's bedchamber be given to Rasel. He took a smaller second room while Dinnis, the three Markan's sons, and Hasuk found places to bunk in the open family room.

Dinnis stepped his way around his sleeping companions. He lifted the bar on the door and walked out into the open air and along the packed-dirt streets of the village. The sun, invisible behind the mountains in the east, painted the sky in soft reds and yellows. Fires, already lit, glowed from the shuttered windows of thatched adobe homes. Terraced fields grew thick with green, broad-leafed maize, edged with hoary avocado trees and trellises of beans. Young children with sticks released yarmas from stone-walled pens and guided their charges up to higher pastures.

Dinnis pulled his cloak tighter and hugged himself for warmth in the icy dawn. A path led along a rushing stream away from the village. He followed it, munching on a few pieces of cold peccary he'd salvaged from last night's meal. Not that he felt hungry.

The weightstone in his chest made it hard to breath, to swallow, to eat. Everything he touched fell apart. Tilli married to Tujik these two alume or more. His dreams of life apart from the Palace put in storage, maybe for ever. Who was he kidding? One skinny half-Nolmec war orphan pitting himself against the might and will of the Palace? And now Rasel, his silver lady, each day growing closer to the Prince, rushing on without thought into disaster.

The path dipped down as the stream cascaded over the edge fifty tanis into a translucent pool of water in the valley below, before bubbling over grey moss-cloaked rocks and splashing away down the mountainside. He scrambled down the path, his injured thigh only pulling at the more strenuous stretches.

The thunderous, numbing roar of the water engulfed him. Rasel had been his guiding star, pure, bright, a paragon far beyond his reach. More a dream and a memory than a woman of flesh and blood. Even now, he could not imagine that one such as him would be her equal. Yet he wanted her to see him as she had when he was a child at North Pass. Now she saw only the Prince of Tamra.

Spray caressed his skin. Milky water beaded his cloak, ran down his face. He blinked, taking a hold of his tumultuous feelings, his dark thoughts. As though caught between grinding stones, his heart squeezed. Here she was, like any of the young ladies of the Palace, like his sister Ista, giddy with love or passion or whatever it was, for his privileged younger half-brother. His lips turned down at the corners. Which, of course, all made a perfect kind of ironic sense. Tangling with a Prince of Tamra hadn't worked for fabled Namu, maybe not even for his mother, though she was Kiprissa of the Nolmec, granddaughter to the Sunburst Queen. Yet Rasel didn't belong to him. She could choose her destiny. If she found joy with Mannok, he shouldn't begrudge her that, or Mannok for that matter. Even though it hurt.

He should head back, find out what the Prince planned to do, whether to wait for the road to be cleared or to gain maybe a couple of days following the roundabout route. Knowing Mannok, he wouldn't sit still, he'd have to be on the move.

Another time, sitting alone in the depths of the night on the road to Tarka, she had come to him there, a vision or dream or maybe, like now, as flesh and blood. Her words then had pulled him back from the brink of despair. Replace the negative with a positive. Sow seeds of love. Find another path. He lifted his head. No one could take away what he felt for her. But no matter what happened, he would be her protector, her champion and, by the Maker she extolled, that would be enough.

The sun caught the curtain of water, turning it to liquid fire. Dinnis stepped back from the spray and worked his way along the edges of the mountain pool. Rare bladeleaf, good for the lungs and the blood, grew among the silverfern, moss and rocks. He paused a few more moments to gather some before climbing up the path. By the time he reached the edge of the village, the sun stood well above the horizon. Hopefully, Mannok hadn't left him behind in his hurry to return to Tarka.

Chapter Thirty-Five: Road Ahead

Mannok

Mannok glared at the pile of boulders blocking the road. In the deep shadow of the mountain, two or three-ten of villagers swarmed over the muddle with shovels, mattocks and liftbars, ropes and buckets. More than half were women or children or old men. Even if he decided to take the detour, they'd still be a day or two late for the festival. The irony was, if he'd returned by the short-cut, they'd have bypassed this blockage. His hunting band lined the road behind him, their voices in muted conversation, no doubt wondering what decision he'd make or why he was in such a hurry to get to Tarka.

He kicked a boulder and regretted the sudden burst of pain that shot up his leg through his bruised toes. Rasel moved beside him, her hair falling in waves about her heart-shaped face, the clean scent of meadowsweet and pine filling his senses.

She placed her hand on his arm. 'Prince of Tamra, what troubles you? Why fret when landslides were part of the mountains' life song. Beauty abounds here and, as the Maker wills, a small delay will not change things, surely.'

He looked into her laughing, carefree eyes and felt some of his tension ease. 'The Feast is in four days. Already, the clan leaders and nobles will be gathering in Tarka.'

How could he explain to her why this was so important to him when he found it hard to explain it to himself? Hard to know how his parents would react to Rasel, but they'd surely be more open to his explanations if he arrived before the banquet rather than late. Besides, he couldn't dislodge the feeling Rasel might leave any moment, for she'd agreed to accompany him to Tarka and no more. And if she left, he might never see her again. He felt hollow at the thought. Whatever else happened, he wanted her to stay.

She squeezed his hand. 'If it is so important to you, then it is for me. Let's help these good mountain people to clear the way.' She took a liftbar from a startled youth walking past them with a bunch of tools.

'Oh no, you can't ... we can't.'

'Why not?'

He stared at her. 'Because ...' because protocol forbad it. The Prince Royal of Tamra clearing the road. Ludicrous. He glanced at his band—two-tens of strong young men, with nodding headdresses, cloaks and spears, standing by with nothing to do but wait. Two-tens that would effectively double the workforce and halve the time it took to clear the road. Yet he couldn't ask the sons of Markans and clan leaders to grub in the dirt like common folk, could he? Papa wouldn't mind getting his hands muddy, a small inner voice said. Mama, the daughter of a noble from a lesser house, was the one to stand on ceremony.

Mannok couldn't break with tradition and ask his age-mates to help without risking insulting them and their houses. But he could help. Far better than killing time while others did the work.

He took the liftbar from her. With a nod, he stripped off his cloak and accoutrements, and walked to the huge boulder perched near the edge of the ravine.

The headman rushed over, his face aghast.

'Your Highness, you shouldn't demean yourself.'

'Nothing demeaning about honest work, good Saluruk.' Mannok placed the liftbar beneath the boulder and heaved.

Garvin, Estolik and the others rushed over.

'Mannok, what are you doing?' Estolik shouted, shock written over his face.

'What does it look like, Essu? Clearing the road so we can arrive in Tarka before the feast.'

'But ...'

Mannok waved him away. 'I don't have time to debate this. If you're not helping then go find something else to do.'

'I can help too.' Rasel beamed at him, making his heart sing.

Estolik's plump lips curled in derision. Durrin smirked, arms folded.

He believed her, and he almost said yes, but if she worked alongside the villagers like a peasant now, who among his age-band would believe she was worthy of a prince.

'No, sweet Rasel.' He met her gaze, willing her to understand. 'My lady, I must insist you refrain from such a mucky job. Please make yourself comfortable.'

She looked at him, silvery white forehead crinkled and then nodded. 'Then I'll fetch some water. You may need a drink in a while.'

Mannok's shoulders relaxed. He beckoned over a young village girl, maybe eleven or twelve years. 'Keep the Lady Rasel company.'

He returned his focus to the boulder, repositioning the liftbar, applying his full strength to it. The boulder shifted a fraction, then settled back onto the road.

'Let me help.' Garvin was beside him, stripped to his undertunic and breeches. Hasuk came in on the other side. Together they heaved and the boulder shuddered and dislodged. It rolled over the edge to crash into the ravine below.

'Seleste,' he shouted and he fist bumped with Garvin and Hasuk.

One down, a few hundred more to go.

He stretched his back and scanned for the next huge boulder. Along the road the rest of the young nobles joined in, working beside villagers.

Mannok grinned. They could do this.

* * *

Every muscle ached, even some he hadn't realised existed. In the west, the sun slid down the red-gold sky. Alumi, in a shaved circle, peeped above the mountain peaks to the east. He rubbed his face, brushing away dirt and grit that had snuck into every crease and crevice of his skin. Mannok sighed. He moved closer to Rasel and focused on Saluruk's words. Their shadows stretched across the road and onto the mountainside, smoke-blue in the honeyed light.

'Please, Your Highness, accept our thanks. But I beg you, on the morrow, allow us to finish the task.'

Mannok glanced back at the road. They'd made a big dent, yes, but much remained to do. 'I must insist, Saluruk.'

'But, sir, if your royal father were to hear of this ...'

'He'd most likely applaud my willingness to help.'

'And what will people say of our village?' Saluruk wrung his hands.

'That they served their Prince. Headman Saluruk, I must reach Tarka by the Feast and if lending a hand is what it takes, then that is what must happen. Perhaps tomorrow we could use the baggage horses to make faster progress.'

The glum lines on Sulurak's face etched deeper, but he brought both fists to his chest and bowed. 'Your will, Prince Mannok.'

Mannok pulled a jaguar token from his tunic and handed it to the headman. 'I will not forget the favour. If ever you or your village need a favour from me, you need only to ask. Now, I need to bathe, eat and sleep.'

He turned his steps back towards the village. Rasel slipped an arm around his waist, sending his heart racing despite his bone tiredness.

He pulled away. 'Sweet Rasel, I'm filthy.'

She tightened her embrace. 'The dirt will wash out, Man of Tamra, and was it not well earned? Though, you should have let me help too.'

He shook his head, too exhausted to argue.

'Maybe tomorrow I can help with the horses, then,' she continued. 'Waiting around with nothing to do but carry water is tiring.'

The horizon star stood out like a beacon in purpling sky. Below them, the golden glow of cooking fires winked from windows and the enticing smells of woodsmoke and cooking food drew them toward the village.

She lifted her head. 'It would take but ten hours from here to Tarka as the koraktil flies.'

'Koraktil?' Mannok choked off a laugh, his stomach muscles protesting. 'Ah, and if only such fantastical beasts existed.'

He blinked as he felt a sense of sadness wash over him. Rasel snuggled in closer. 'I wept when the last one died in the Valley of a Thousand Winds,' she said. 'But who knows, perhaps they still glide across the heights of the vast sky in the lands across the Lapis Sea.'

'You speak as though legends are true.'

'Because they are, man full of doubt.'

Mannok shook his head. Many villagers believed them to be true, but not educated people. Such an enigma, his Rasel, with the poise, intelligence and beauty of a noblewoman yet simply dressed, travelling without retinue, and so naïve.

Up ahead in the gloaming, a small knot of his age-mates huddled on the path outside the headman's house, partially obscured by inka berry bushes. Their weary voices echoed in the stillness of evening.

'... horrid suspicion we'll be at it again tomorrow and every other day until that malodorous landslide is cleared,' came Yalik's piping tenor voice.

A bulky figure leaned over a long thin shadow. 'So, you lazy fellow, you won't be able to escape working tomorrow.' Durrin's gravelly voice.

'Dinnis worked as hard as anyone,' Garvin's voice protested.

'Not at first.'

'Soon enough.'

Dinnis stood still and silent, making no effort to defend himself. Another enigma, Mannok found hard to unlock, as though he were missing a vital piece.

'Why do they pick on him, like a mob of crows attacking an injured bird?' Rasel whispered in his ear.

Because he's irritating, Mannok opened his mouth to say, then closed it. Dinnis did have a cutting wit, an annoying manner, but that wasn't the reason bullies like Durrin and even Estolik, like Uson and Asik, picked on him. Maybe not even because of his Nolmec blood. Rather, because he was different and alone, without clan or kin to defend him.

Estolik's mutinous voice broke the silence. 'If you ask me, the last several days are beyond belief. First, he brings a common peasant girl out of the wilderness and treats her like a princess. Then he cuts short the hunt on a whim. Now he expects us to work like peasants to clear the blasted road. I'm all for getting to the banquet on time, but this is too much. We are the sons of nobles or at least most of us are. We are warriors not serfs!'

Estolik paused and glared at his silent companions. When no one ventured to voice an opinion, the Markan's son continued. 'If you ask me, I think he has gone clean out of his senses.'

Blood rushed to Mannok's face. His fists tightened. Estolik's words were not just an insult to him, the Prince of Tamra, but to Rasel. He pulled from her hold and quickened his pace to close the distance between them, rounding the corner in a couple of strides.

'What's that, cousin? Who has gone out of his senses?' he growled.

233

Five startled and stricken faces turned toward him. Well, four, Dinnis held on to his normal guarded expression.

Rasel caught up with him and brushed his shoulder. 'Go gently, my Prince. Do not be insulted on my account,' she breathed.

He lifted his chin. People had been lashed for less, yet perhaps Rasel spoke true. He took a steadying breath. 'What are you doing here, chattering away like a bunch of tarrawongs. I thought you would be in the bathhouse by now fighting over the water.'

Estolik snapped his mouth shut and swallowed hard. He bowed deeper than he ever had before.

'Your Highness, we … that is, I mean …,' he cleared his throat. 'I was referring to Dinnis here wandering off on his own again. Who knows what dangers lurk on the mountain slopes? This morning, a villager reported that a puma has been sighted.'

With a small sigh Dinnis folded his arms and looked at the path.

'Son of the west, you surprise me. You mentioned peasants and nobles, warriors and serfs, not pumas. Did I mishear you?'

Estolik startled at the sound of Rasel's lilting voice. 'Yes, well.' He shifted his feet, tugged at his tunic. 'As I said, the serf spoke to me of the puma. Of course, such a beast would not be dangerous to a noble warrior but … err a peasant or … err a … hem a blunderer… like Dinnis would be endangered.'

Rasel's frown deepened. She turned to Mannok. 'Why is he lying?'

'Because it's considered suicidal to call your prince crazy to his face,' Mannok breathed back. And after he'd sent Waren back to Tarka, even Estolik might fear the same fate.

Perhaps it would be better to ignore an outburst not meant for his ears, intemperate words spoken after his band had worked so hard at an uncommon task and against custom all for his sake.

He turned to Dinnis. 'It would be a shame if you were eaten by a puma, my friend.'

Both Dinnis' eyebrows shot up. 'Really, I am sur … touched by your concern, Your Highness,' he said with a bow. 'Indeed, by yours too, my Lord Estolik. This has indeed been a day of wonders.'

'Well, pray do tell, what wonders are those?' Mannok crossed his arms.

'No pumas, to be sure, my Lord Prince. Not even a whisker or a paw print. Although, I did discover a waterfall half a lek from the village.' He pointed vaguely to the southeast.

Mannok snorted. 'Now that is a wonder indeed, to discover a waterfall in the high mountains.'

Dinnis shrugged. 'And also the sight of a score of young courtiers covered in mud from a hard day of honest labour. I would have never imagined I'd encounter such a thing as I lived.' Hard to see, a small smile tugged at the corners of his mouth.

'Maybe that won't be such a long time,' Durrin took a step closer to Dinnis.

Mannok stepped forward, between them. 'Come, let's not allow our tempers to fray. We are all tired and hungry. My thanks to all of you for your help today. The foreman assures me that with another day or two of concerted effort, the road should be cleared.'

A chorus of groans came from the young men.

'Two days,' Estolik spluttered.

'Why don't you take tomorrow off Estolik ... and anyone else that has found today's labours too arduous? Now, I for one am definitely going to avail myself of the bathhouse before the water cools and then devour a solid meal.'

He slipped Rasel's arm into his own and strode off to the headsman's house, his tired and dirty age-mates falling in behind him.

Chapter Thirty-Six: Conversations

Rasel

A cool wind blew off the mountain slopes, catching Rasel's hair and flattening her tari against her legs. She took a firmer hold of the pack horse's halter. Debris half-filled the sledge made of supple saplings and attached to the mare by leather straps. It had taken all her persuasive abilities for Mannok to accept this small participation.

Over the last two days, they'd shifted the bulk of the landslide with only a few drifts of smaller rocks and gravel scattered across the road. Mannok along with Dinnis and the other young men and the villagers shovelled the rubble into large grass-woven baskets and wooden buckets. Others tipped them onto the sledges attached to the pack horses. The one called Durrin, with the loud brash voice, stayed in the village and refused to help after the first day. But he was the only one, for even the sulky son of Haka worked alongside Tamra's Prince.

The sun slipped down the sky, lengthening the shadows and warming the rocks. One by one the piles diminished. Dinnis backed the other pack horse with its fully loaded sledge to the edge of the ravine, and a group of villagers emptied the load into its maw.

The low mournful whistle echoed off the cliff side. A crested eagle battled with the turbulent air currents. She caught her breath and then released it. An ordinary eagle, not one of her Kin, not Semian or Baba, as she half expected. Most times her nearest brother caught up with her if he thought she'd been absent too long. He would try to argue her out of accompanying the Prince of Tamra to Tarka, that she knew. If only he could see the bright flame amongst the shadows in Mannok's eyes. The ways of the children of Tamrak were not those of the Kin, yet were they not also from the Maker's heart and hand?

Mannok and Garvin carried the heavy basket weighed down with rocks towards her position. With a grunt, they emptied the contents into the sledge.

Mannok checked the harness, tightening the straps. 'That's the last basket. Ready to empty the sledge?'

'As ever, Prince of Tamra. This way, daughter of the wind.' Rasel coaxed the mare toward the dumping point at the edge of the road.

The mare shook her mane and whinnied. At the right point, Rasel brought her parallel to the edge and then turned her forward so the sledge pivoted into position. Mannok and Garvin walked to the back of the sledge.

The sudden gust picked up the dust and small gravel, flinging it at them and stinging Rasel's eyes and exposed skin. The mare's ears flicked backward, her eyes showing white. Her coat rippled. She flicked her tail and reared, her hocks hitting the front of the sledge. It tilted and slid a few ninas over the edge, a scatter of rocks rolling off the top of the load.

'*Dava aka*, don't be afraid,' Rasel soothed.

'Hold her firm,' Mannok called. He and Garvin strained against the weight. Dinnis and Asik and a few villagers ran up to Mannok and Garvin and helped stabilise the sled.

Rasel tightened her hold on the halter and stroked the mare's neck. She sang soft words to her. 'Daughter of the wind, be still, for you will come to no harm.'

The horse quietened, responding to her heart-words.

Rasel placed her hand over the mare's eyes and she walked her forward a couple of steps. The others tilted the sledge and the debris tumbled and bounded off the cliff side.

'That's it! The last one.' Mannok fistbumped the air, his green eyes sparkling in a dust-rimmed face.

'Seleste,' Garvin hooted.

'Thank the moons for that,' muttered the son of Haka.

The Prince of Tamra did not appear to hear. 'Three hours until sunset. We could reach the Sweetwater Way Station if we left at once.'

The son of Haka groaned. He opened his mouth, closed it, then spoke. 'Is that your wish, Mannok?'

Rasel stroked the mare's face. In koraktil form, she could reach the city of Kapoks by the next day if she flew through the night, especially with a favourable wind. But she could only carry three of the sons of Tamrak. Would the Prince accept her offer?

'Prin—'

'Argh, I don't know about you, Your Highness, but I'm ready to drop.' Garvin stretched his arms over his head and cracked his neck.

Mannok let out a long, deep sigh. 'You all deserve a rest, at least for tonight. We leave at dawn on the morrow.'

On second thoughts, perhaps arriving in koraktil form might give the Tamrin the wrong idea, if the children of Tamrak feared the Kin.

The Prince of Tamra tucked her arm in his.

'My thanks, sweet Rasel.'

She smiled at him. 'Everyone helped, Prince of Tamra.'

'Yes, and your brilliant idea to do so. With no further mishaps, we should make it back in time for the banquet.'

Together they walked the path back to the village. The muddy bunch of young nobles turned and stumbled wearily behind them.

* * *

Rasel tucked her legs under her and selected roast vegetables and greens from the platter offered to her by the headman's daughter.

'Would you like some meat, my lady?' the young girl said.

Rasel shook her head. She took a wedge of the creamy yarma cheese, a round of maize bread, both of which she'd sampled and enjoyed before, and added a selection of inka berries, blueberries, avocado, sunfruit, and guava.

Mannok sat cross-legged beside her, dressed in clean tunic and breeches, skin scrubbed clean and his shoulders slumped in weariness. He'd worked harder than any of the labourers over the last three days. And apart from the silent Dinnis, he was the one to complain the least of aches and pains or blisters, though she knew he had just about worn the skin off both his hands. The Prince's close companions lounged against cushions around the low serving table, their faces part in shadow and part gilded by the flickering light of the candles and the small hearth fire.

'Maize beer? Birch wine, Rasel?' Mannok offered to fill her cup.

She returned his smile and pointed at her beaker half filled with cool mountain water. She had sampled the other drinks the first night at the Hunting Lodge and found she disliked the bitter taste of the first. While the second was sweet, it clouded her mind.

Relaxing back against the cushions and rugs, she tuned out the loud voices and laughter, and strained to hear the soft night noises outside the adobe walls of the headman's house; the bleating of the yarmas in their night pen, the rustle of the wind in the wide leaves of the avocado trees surrounding the village and the mournful hoot of a mountain owl.

The son of Haka's loud voice snapped her back to the crowded, stifling room.

'… a monstrous big cat with fangs a couple of ninas long. I struck him straight through the heart with my spear. His momentum carried him a little further till he fell dead at my feet.' Estolik's expansive gestures knocked over a bowl of stew in front of him.

'Bravo!' The son of Durak cheered, clapping his friend's back. 'A feat hard to top.'

'Oh, I've seen better.' Garvin waved a hand, a slow smile spreading across his open face.

'Nonsense,' Durrin said, his speech slurred.

The son of Haka sat up straighter. 'Don't tell me you've done better, Garvin?'

'No, not me. Prince Mannok.' Garvin took a slow sip from his beaker.

Mannok stirred at the mention of his name. He raised his eyebrow. 'What are you prattling on about?'

'That jaguar that you took out with your hunting knife, Mannu.' The stocky lad's smile widened into a grin.

'Oh, by the moons, don't remind me.' The Prince grimaced, then chuckled. 'Though I can still see the expression on your face, Garo. You looked like you had seen the ghost of Akrad.'

'I was terrified it was your ghost I'd be seeing.'

'With a hunting knife. Ridiculous!' A frown creased Estolik's soft forehead.

'With a hunting knife,' repeated Garvin firmly. 'Do you call me a liar?'

'Those cats can crush a skull with one bite of their jaws.'

'Dinnis was there too. And Hasuk. They can confirm it, if you doubt my word.' Garvin leant forward, his brown eyes narrowed.

'Steady, there friends,' said Mannok. 'It is hard to believe but there it is.'

'If the Prince says it ... of course I believe it.' The son of Haka darted a look at Durrin and smirked. 'Do tell us about it, Mannok.'

Rasel shivered at the undercurrent of aggression and the talk of blood sports. This is what Semian meant, this drive to kill, not for the necessity but as a competition, a show of prowess, the glory of war.

'Hmm, not much of a story really.' Mannok squeezed Rasel's hand. 'And I would not distress Lady Rasel with it.'

'Do not refrain on my behalf,' she said.

He studied her a moment, as though sensing her unease, then nodded. 'We were following the track of a peccary boar. When we passed a small hill, steep with boulders and thick brush on top, a jaguar leapt out at me. She must have been hardly a tanis away to start with and before I knew it, she bowled me over. My spear arm was pinned by one of her paws, nor did I have any room to use it, but I could draw my knife with my left hand. A thrust beneath her ribcage ended her life. Next thing I knew, I was flat out on my back and pinned down by the weight of a dead jaguar.'

'Aye, we all stood and gaped like stunned fish certain the Prince was dead, till Dinnis leapt forward and pulled the cat off. That was almost worse, for Mannok was covered head to toe in blood,' Garvin said.

'Most of the blood was the jaguar's rather than the Prince's,' Dinnis said drily.

'Yes, only a few scratches which Dinnis bandaged quite handily,' Mannok said.

Rasel glanced at Dinnis, remembering he'd mentioned training to be a healer as the reason for his interest in herbs. A wave of sadness swept over her at this simple story about the death of a daughter of the shadows. Rasel pushed away her plate, no longer hungry.

'Were you not reading the signs, that you stumbled close to her?' Would they have still killed the jaguar if they'd known she was there?

'She was well-hidden and also downwind of us so the dogs didn't catch her scent,' Garvin said.

The son of Haka tented his fingers. 'Good save then, Mannok.'

The Prince of Tamra gave a dismissive wave. 'As I said, not much of a story.'

The son of Haka and the other young men moved on to another tale of the hunt.

Rasel fiddled with the gold brooch that fastened the long white folds of her tari. They spoke of killing and death with such ease, even her Prince.

Mannok moved closer, his scent tingling her senses. 'What troubles you, sweet Rasel?'

'Do you often hunt jaguar for no other reason than the thrill of it?'

He gave her a startled look. 'Only if a rogue cat is terrorising a village, but, as a rule, no, I don't hunt a noble beast, the emblem of our clan after all. We hunt mostly peccary, deer, tapir and sometimes bear, for the meat and hides.' He gave her a searching look. 'The hunt is thrilling, but we would only take game where there is need. Our kills are not wasted. Do not your own people hunt?'

She shook her head. How to explain? The forest folk avoided eating the beasts whose forms they could assume. 'We do not kill or eat larger animals.' Tears misted her eyes, suddenly overwhelmed by the noise, the smells, the closed-in feel of this mud and stick hut, suddenly missing the Great Forest and her Kin.

He brushed her cheek, wiping away an escaped tear. 'Are you crying Rasel? What would you have done if a jaguar attacked you? Let it eat you?'

She hiccoughed a laugh. 'No, but I would not have allowed myself to be taken unawares. And if I had, I would have told the daughter of shadows that I intended her no harm.'

Mannok's eyebrows shot up. 'And if that didn't work?'

She would've shifted to bird-form. 'I'm of the Kin, the Forest Folk. I would've taken to the air and flown out of harm's way.'

He blinked, then his smile widened. 'You do say the strangest things, sweet Rasel.'

He twirled one long curl of her hair and leaned closer, his warm breath tickling her skin. A strange fluttery feeling of anticipation and possibility surged through her. She held her breath.

After a heartbeat, he glanced down the table at his age-mates and he moved back. She sighed, disappointed, though she wasn't sure what she'd expected him to do.

She could read his scepticism swirling with his longing for her. He didn't believe she could do the things she said. Didn't understand who she was, what she was, even though she'd told him in plain Filane. But maybe she didn't need to explain unless she decided to stay.

Chapter Thirty-Seven: Waterfall

Mannok

Mannok fingered the rough carving on the wooden beaker. Even though their shoulders did not touch, his right side tingled as though brushed by the charged air of a thunderstorm. Rasel's sweet forest scent, her melodious voice, her quick smiles and quicksilver moods, her every breath and movement seared itself into his awareness. Her response to the jaguar kill and stories of the hunt took him by surprise. The ladies of the court, like Lumi and Rizzi, would have exclaimed more, maybe even declared themselves shocked, but nevertheless been impressed by such tales of physical exploits. Rasel's responses sung through him like a cleansing wind blowing away the fog and mist of drenching rain. Unpredictable, maybe even disruptive, but exhilarating.

The dinner conversation swirled around them. The candle wicks flickered in growing pools of melted wax. He should bring the evening to a close. They were all tired and in need of sleep's healing balm. Yet the thought of speaking, of getting up and preparing to retire felt like too much effort. Besides, it would mean parting from Rasel, even if for the short night hours.

Durrin made a sudden retching noise. He stood up quickly, knocking over dishes of food. He rushed outside, leaving the wooden door gaping.

Mannok frowned. Durrin had taken him at his word and spent the last couple of days lolling around in the village while the rest of his band, even Estolik, worked at clearing the road.

'Someone should go after our friend to make sure he gets back inside alright. Perhaps we should turn in for the night.'

'I'll go.' Garvin pushed himself up and beckoned to Hasuk. The two of them set out after Durrin.

Mannok smiled. He could always count on Garo. He turned to Rasel. 'My sweet Rasel, would you like to retire for the night?'

She stifled a yawn. 'Sleep sounds enticing, but I would love to breathe some fresh mountain air first.'

How could he deny her? He stood. 'Then stroll we shall.'

Estolik, lounging back against the cushions, winked at him. No doubt the son of Haka would assume the worst if he walked with Rasel alone. Two days out from Tarka was not the time to relax the protections he'd put in place, no matter how much he longed to spend time alone with his love.

He tapped Dinnis on the shoulder. 'Come and show us the waterfall you discovered. Bring your spear in case we run into that puma.'

'Why bother,' Estolik grinned. 'The lady could ask the cat to leave.'

'As you wish, Your Highness.' Dinnis bowed without the slightest hint of sarcasm. He shot Estolik a pointed look. 'An assassin dogging our prince's steps might be less obliging.'

Estolik smirked. 'The Prince armed only with his hunting knife would be a more formidable foe than any weapon you carry, Nol ... Dinnis.'

Heat rushed up Mannok's neck. 'You weren't at Pine Stand Gap, Estolik, were you? Dinnis saved my life there. I think I know who I can trust to have my back.'

Estolik's jaw fell open and his face paled. 'I didn't mean ...'

Mannok turned his back and offered his hand to Rasel. 'Let's go.'

They left Estolik still protesting.

* * *

Mannok walked side by side with Rasel through the hushed fields in the light of the moons. Dinnis trailed a few steps behind, holding the spear as though it might bite him.

'I hope your thoughts are pleasant,' Rasel's melodious voice broke Mannok's exhausted haze.

'Enjoying the moment.' He took her arm and patted her hand. 'We will be in Tarka in a couple of days.'

'And that troubles you?' she asked, with a perceptive look in her wide dark eyes.

'No.' He frowned. 'Well maybe a little. I want to welcome you to my city, to show you its wonders, but my parents may not understand, not at first.' Maybe not ever. Look how they'd treated Ista. So close to arriving, he felt his confidence ebbing. Maybe it was the exhaustion speaking. He had to succeed.

She let out a soft sigh. 'I understand. My family, my parents, my brothers and sisters, my Kin would not want me to step foot within the grey stone walls of the city of Kapoks.'

He felt a small jolt of surprise. 'Is that so?'

She dipped her head down and frowned at him, then laughed. He smiled, loving the way that her lively emotions played across her face like moonlight across the surface of a tranquil lake. Her openness contrasted to the polite masks and affected manners of the ladies of the court and Ista's more serious mien.

'Yes, Prince of Tamra,' she said, her tone mock-severe, 'My Kin distrust the people of Tarka and especially their leaders after what happened between our peoples many solars hence.'

Who were her kin, these Forest Folk? Who was she? Maybe, a daughter of one of the fallen Shanti noble houses. That would explain her apparent poverty and her noble manner. With her silvery-white skin so like Ista's, and not unlike Haka's pale skin, she could have descended from the daughter of Sil and Akrad. Though he'd been taught that none of the Shanti nobility survived Tellek's war. If they had, what would that mean for Tamra?

'You are from Shanta?'

'I am of the Forest Folk though my mother fled its ruin while I was a babe in arms.'

'That's not possible, sweet Rasel, for that happened over fifty years ago.' He laughed and shook his head. 'And your parents, who are they? Would they not be concerned about your absence?'

'I am a Pathfinder for my people, capable of defending myself.'

'Really? Alone in the wilderness.'

'Yes, truly! Besides if I'm gone too long my brother, Semian, comes looking for me. You know what older brothers are like.'

'No, for I have no brothers whether younger or older.'

Something he regretted though Garvin was closer than a brother, like a twin. He slowed his steps, tilted his head towards hers and inhaled her fragrance, the aroma of the wild and freedom sending his senses reeling.

Dinnis cleared his throat and Mannok jumped, having all but forgotten the presence of his brooding age-mate lagging a few tanis behind them.

'Your Highness.'

'Yes?' Mannok snapped.

'If you wish to see the waterfall from below, the path goes down here. Not that I'd recommend it in this uncertain light.' Dinnis pointed down a steep trail clinging to the mountainside.

Close by, the stream roared over the edge and fell into deep shadow. Clouds of spray shone like spun gold and silver in the double moonlight.

Rasel clapped her hands. 'Oh, yes, let's do it.'

He felt her excitement frizzing in his own veins.

'Take it slow then.' He slipped his arm out of hers and took hold of her slender hand. Her grip was firm, confident, her skin supple and cool.

Together, they picked their way down to the bottom of the path, stepping with extra care on the spray-slicked stones. Dinnis followed behind.

From below, the full length of the waterfall gleamed in the moonlight, falling in a wide pool edged with glimmering foam.

'Magnificent.' Spray dewed his face and beaded on his yarma-wool cloak.

A step ahead, Rasel stood on the very rim of the pool, her green mantle wrapped around her head and shoulders, her head tipped back and eyes staring at the milky feathers of water falling endlessly into the dark pool, the moonlight creating faint rainbows in the spray. Her skin shone like Argenti in the darkness.

'Glorious.' Mannok's spirits lifted. Perhaps he had been worrying unnecessarily about his parents' reactions to Rasel. Surely, they would see how wonderful she was. And Mama and even Papa should be happy he'd finally chosen a bride, that is, if Rasel would have him.

Rasel turned to him and let go of his hand. 'Race you to the middle.'

'Wait.'

Before he could stop her, she leapt onto a large flat stone, a pale streak level with the rippling water. Without stopping, she leapt from wet stone to wet stone towards the curtain of roaring water.

In his hurry to follow her, his boot slid on the second stone and he caught his balance in time, his heart pounding hard against his ribs. Taking a deep breath, he ignored the currents swirling around the rocks, and focused on jumping.

She stood on a large spray-drenched slab ninas away from the lacey tapestry of falling water, her eyes closed, her face lifted up as if to receive the spray's benison. She sang with clear soprano notes rising above the roar of the water, her voice seeming to blend with the spray and moonlight.

He made the last jump, landing beside her. She wrapped her moonlit arms around him. She was only a ninas or two taller than him. Her hair, beaded with spray, seemed to float around him like its own dark waterfall.

'Why ... you're shaking.'

'I can't swim,' he said.

Her dark eyes widened. 'Mannok, you should have stayed on the riverbank. What if you had slipped and fallen in? You really don't know how to swim?'

'I'm mountain bred,' he laughed. 'So, I do have experience in rock hopping.' He drew her close against his chest, the vibration of her heart against his. She melted into his arms, her sweet breath tickling his cheek.

He turned his head, their lips met.

The sky and waters swirled around him and he floated. He wanted to never let her go, wanted this moment never to end. He wanted her, all of her.

He pressed his body against hers and brought a hand up her smooth arm, glimmering white in the dark night, and found the brooch on the shoulder of her tunic.

Something sharp jabbed him in the small of the back. He jerked away and spun around.

Dinnis stood, balancing on a smaller rock with the spear in his right hand.

Mannok bunched his fists. 'By the pit, what do you think you are doing?' he roared, ready to jump at the fellow.

'What you told me to do.'

'What! Stick me with a spear? You're an idiot!'

'Protect the honour and reputation of the lady.'

If Dinnis had given the slightest hint of a smile, he might still have thrashed him, but the fellow's face was impassive, inscrutable.

'Enjoying yourself?' he spat, instead.

Dinnis grunted. 'What do you think? I'm over here balancing on a tiny rock with a rather sharp spear being glared at by an angry prince while you are over there with the beautiful Rasel in your arms. We could always swap places if you truly think you've got the sharp end of the stick.'

Mannok narrowed his eyes and then, suddenly seeing the humour of the situation, threw back his head and snorted laughter.

Rasel looked from one to the other, uncertainty in her eyes. She touched his arm. 'I should go?'

Had he offended her? Scared her off? His cheeks flamed. Dinnis was right. 'My lady, you must not think that I ...' He stopped, sucked in a breath, dropped to his knees and took her hand. 'Rasel, I meant what I said. I want you to wed me so we can live life together, side by side. We belong to each other.'

The cold wet stone dug into his knees. Spray flattened his curls and dripped down his neck. And all around, the shock and roar of water.

Rasel looked over his head and into the distance as the moments dripped by. Would she reject him? Would she leave? He would be bereft forever.

He bit down on more words, words threatening to tumble out in a riotous effort to convince her.

She pulled him to his feet with surprising strength and smiled sweetly. 'I too wish for life together with you, man of the mountains. Whether we grow old together or not, I cannot deny the truth any longer. Like the ocean and the wave, we belong together, heart of my heart. And while we have each other, that will always be enough.'

Caressed by the spray and illuminated by the light of the moons, Mannok embraced her. 'I will never betray you, my love.'

Tarka, royal city of Tamra

Chapter Thirty-Eight: Tarka

Rasel

Rasel opened her eyes and stretched like a languid jaguar. She covered a wide yawn with her hand and sat up on the overly soft straw mattress. Pearly light filtered through the single shuttered window, sending shadows across the stone walls of the Way Station at Sweetwater village. Beyond the rough wooden door came the groans of the young men being roused from sleep by the Prince's commands, the clatter of ceramic platters and the general hustle and bustle of packing up.

She hugged the woven cover to her chest. She would wed the Prince of Tamra, her brave Mannok. She smiled at the thought of being swept away by spray, moonlight and Mannok's embrace two nights ago, his scent, the feel of his arms, the beat of his heart against hers. She loved his heady mix of volatile power and witty diplomacy, of slow measured responses and quick intelligence, of gentle courtesy and headstrong passion. His was surely the jaguar's song. If Dinnis was like the dark pool full of hidden depths, invisible currents and surprising phosphorescent highlights, Mannok was like the roar and plume of the powerful waterfall. At any other time, she would have been tempted to unravel the mysteries concealed behind the son of the north's impassive face. But it was the son of Rokkan and Marra, the Prince of Tamra, that captured her thoughts and heart.

A soft knock sounded on the door. Rasel jumped up, ran over and opened it. Mannok stood in the doorway, dressed in a sleeveless cream tunic, tan breeches and a fine jade green cloak. On his head was a modest gold band adorned with an arc of gold and green feathers. A crescent shaped gold plate, engraved and studded with jade, rested on his chest. Both upper arms sported engraved gold rings. A gem-encrusted woven belt encircled his waist. He gave a whisper of a kiss on her forehead.

'Breakfast is ready, my love. I am keen to get away as soon as possible.' He smiled into her eyes.

She smiled back at him. 'Blessings on your birthday. You look very fine this morning,' she teased.

'Thank you. Tonight, we shall arrive in Tarka. Time to play the part of a Prince. I only wish I had means with me to dress you with the finery fit for a princess.'

'I am content to appear as I am,' she said

'If it was just up to me ... but it is the court we have to impress.'

'Are you worried that I won't?'

'My love, you are wonderful, enchanting, angelic ... the court ... my parents, the Kapok and Kupanna, put weight on birth, position and wealth. And how they perceive you at first can make all the difference. If they see what I see in you, in time, they will accept our love.' A nervous energy leaked from him, but an underlying confidence too.

'I am sure you are right, my love.' She ran her hand over his muscular arm. 'I have something to celebrate your birth remembrance day.'

'Sweet Rasel, no need.'

She put a finger on his lips and placed a belt woven from dried grasses into his hands. 'I made it for you over the last ten-day with love and song. The pattern of gold and black jaguars against a green background match the fastener for your cloak.'

'Beautiful.' He ran his fingers over the weave and shook his head. 'When did you have time?'

'In the alone times at night. You like it? It's a simple gift for a prince.'

'I love it.' And he meant it, she could tell. He took off the ornate belt he was wearing and replaced it with the one she had given him. 'I will treasure it as I will always treasure you, my love.'

He took his golden jaguar brooch, placed it in her palm, folded her fingers over it and placed his other hand over hers. 'My father gave me this, and his father before him. This is my pledge we belong together, always.'

* * *

They left the Way Station with the sun barely visible above the jagged mountain skyline to the east. The Prince of Tamra set a fast pace, with brief stops to rest the horses and refresh along the way. The further north they rode, the more travellers they passed and the closer together the small mountain villages perched amidst terraced fields of maize. This crawling along the surface of the land was a slow way to travel. Yet perched on the back of the daughter of the wind, Rasel could see things through new eyes. Perhaps, this too was a form she could learn in time.

The sun was halfway down the western sky when they passed through the largest village yet.

'South Ridge village,' Mannok grinned and his eyes sparkled. 'Were the horses fresh, we could be in Tarka in half an hour.'

The villagers working in the maize fields near the road greeted them cheerfully. Young children with bright eyes drove their herds of white, cream and tan yarmas to the side to allow them to pass. Farmers with produce, merchants with yarmas laden down with wares and even the occasional contingents of spear-carrying warriors all made way before them, bowing or saluting as they passed.

They rode past the last house in the village and down the path over a ridge. Across the green valley was a patchwork of fields and orchards and one solitary stand of ancient pine trees, the Twins silhouetted against the stark blue sky. Mannok brought Shadow to a stand and Rasel urged the daughter of the wind to stand beside him.

'And there she is; Tarka, city of legend, called blessed and built by my ancestors.'

The Prince of Tamra pointed out the great grey walls and the grey and adobe terraced buildings, piled on top of each other beneath the serene snow-covered twin peaks.

This city, which her Kin abhorred, a city of blood and terror. This strange, threatening place which haunted the songs of her people with its savagery and treachery. The pyramid shape of the Great Temple stood at its apex, with plazas and a road joining it to the Palace below. Despite the warmth of the sun on her skin, she shivered.

253

What had seemed so intriguing from air currents high in the sky many alume ago, now felt menacing. What had seemed so exciting in the forests of Shanta now seemed foolhardy. What had seemed so certain cocooned in the spray of the waterfall, now seemed risky. Would she die in that city, like so many of her Kin had done on the day of Betrayal? She fingered Mannok's jaguar broach, now fastened to her tari.

The Prince of Tamra nudged Shadow closer. 'Is something wrong, my love?'

She met the warm concern in his marvellous jade-green eyes, so like the reflections playing across a forest pool. She inhaled his scent, his warmth, listened again to his song. The Maker alone knew the future, but whatever happened, her love was worth the danger.

'No, nothing, Prince of Tamra,' she said. 'Lead on.'

He nodded, and with a squeeze of his knees, urged Shadow into a trot, and she rode beside him. His band of young warriors followed, the Prince's banners streaming behind them.

Two hours later, they approached the walled city. People jostled along the roads, moving aside and prostrating themselves on the road as the Prince and his party rode by. The great height of the stone wall loomed over Rasel. The loud insistent shouts of hustlers, the laughter of children, the bleats, squeals and neighs of the animals swirled around her in chaotic confusion. Her nostrils were assaulted by the smell of rancid meats, rotten fruit, sour milk, unusual spices, animal droppings and human sweat. She had never seen so many people and animals crammed together before, or at least not at ground level. She felt hemmed in on all sides with no pathway of escape. She moved her mount closer to her love.

As they reached the gates, the clarion sound of trumpets erupted from the top of the wall above them. A contingent of six warriors rode out, led by a white-haired man with a family likeness to Garvin. The man dismounted, bowed low and fell to his knees before the Prince.

'Your Highness, Maker be praised. The Kupanna will be happy to know you have arrived.'

The Prince of Tamra, her Mannok, waved him up. 'Ah, Kaptan Kaspin, it is good to be home.'

With a salute, the Prince urged his horse through the massive gates and headed through the congested plaza and along the wide street running up the hill. The horses' hooves clattered on the

254

cobblestoned roads, but once they left the environs of the walls and the lower market streets, the way was less crowded and the air fresher. Rasel began to breathe easier. The tall houses displayed shuttered windows and balconies with flowering plants and vines entwining the balustrades and flowing down the stone walls. Many were adorned with carvings of birds and forest animals. She welcomed the splashes of vivid colour and the sweet smell of red pasak flowers and chalice vine that relieved the cold expanses of grey stone surrounding them.

At the top of the crest, they turned into another wide road, with the red Palace wall on one side, and buildings and a plaza on the other. Intricate stone carvings of jaguars, boas, eagles and flame-breathing koraktil ran along the wall until they reached a large gate flanked by narrow towers. Two sustained notes of a horn sounded and the gates swung open into a walled area.

At the other end of the stone-paved space, a huge building like a cliff with tall windows high up the wall and a roof of golden tiles reared up. Seen from the air, the Palace of Tamra looked like an ornament; viewed from the back of the daughter of the wind, it intimidated.

'The Golden Palace of Tarka,' Mannok said.

He dismounted and helped her down, though she could easily have done it herself. She smiled. He treated her like a fragile flower or perhaps it was an excuse to hold her.

People rushed up toward them, bowing and taking away the horses. A short man, dressed in a long flowing tunic with a golden shoulder sash, rushed towards them. He knelt before the Prince of Tamra, bowing low to the ground.

'Your Highness.'

'Bitjarnan, good to see you.' The Prince waved the man to his feet.

'My lord Prince, you have arrived just in time. Well, a little late but still, in time for a Prince,' the little man babbled, his worried hazel eyes seeming not to settle on anything in particular but to take in the Prince's hunting band in a most haphazard manner. Finally, his gaze rested on Rasel and he jumped. His grey-threaded eyebrows shot up.

'Your Highness, ah, should I arrange for the young woman to be shown to your quarters, I mean I don't think ...' His voice trailed off.

Mannok scowled at the little man. 'The Lady Rasel is my guest and will be sitting by my side at the banquet tonight.'

The little man's mouth rounded like a gasping fish. 'Yes, yes, Your Highness. Though Her Majesty, the Kupanna made no mention—' Mannok raised an eyebrow and folded his arms. The little man deflated. 'Your wish is my command.'

'You said that proceedings have already started, Bitjarnan?' The Prince looked towards the west where the sun still hovered a hand breadth above the horizon. 'But surely the banquet is not for a few hours.'

'Yes, Your Highness, but you remember of course, the ... ahem ... the reception of the attending dignitaries in the Throne Room beforehand?'

'Ah, yes, the reception. There's always a reception.' The Prince sighed.

'One the Prince doesn't often attend,' the son of Durak muttered from behind them.

'Hush,' the son of Haka hissed.

The little man darted a look at Rasel and shuffled his feet. 'Your Highness may wish to freshen up. I could have hot water sent to the bachelor quarters. And the lady ... ahem ... I am not sure, would she go with you to your ... or perhaps ...'

Rasel covered her mouth with her hand. The one called Bitjarnan radiated confusion and embarrassment because of her arrival, though why was harder to read. She wouldn't normally laugh at another's distress, but his antics were comical.

Mannok clearly was not amused. 'Madomo, the sooner we make the Lady Rasel's position clear to everyone as my honoured and esteemed guest, the better.'

'Yes, Your Highness.'

'So, stop fluffing about and announce us.'

The little man bowed lowed. 'As you command, Your Highness. Are you sure you don't want to freshen up first?'

Mannok's brow furrowed. 'Get on with it, madomo.'

'This way, Your Highness. My ... Lady ... Rasel.'

The little round man turned, almost tripping over his small feet, and led them up the flight of wide semicircular grey stone stairs, through the massive front doorway into a large rectangular atrium, ringed on three sides with three tiers of balconies.

Rasel crossed over the threshold into the Palace of the Kapoks. The high peaked ceiling above was inserted with a number of thick opaque glass panels, allowing the golden light to stream down into the room. Large golden candelabras, their tall candles already lit, stood against the walls. At the far end of the entry room were two large doorways, the one to the left was open while the right one was closed. Beyond the open doorway was a broad hallway, with smaller doors off the left side and large, gold inlaid doors at the end. Spear-wielding guards stood to attention at each of the major doorways.

Escape would be difficult from such a place, even on the wing. The air, thick with candle smoke, the smells of roasting meat, yarma wool and people, so many people, stifled her. Each step became harder than the last. She looked sideways at Mannok, his strong face and aquiline noise. With his feather headdress and sombre face, he seemed a stranger, not the flame-bright young Tarmrin who had captured her heart.

He turned towards her and smiled as though she were the only person in this great pile of stone. Bending his head towards hers, he whispered, 'Nervous?'

'I am, Prince of Tamra.'

'I'd rather be facing a pack of furious mother jaguars or twenty Nolmec patrols right now.'

Rasel smiled and squeezed his hand. 'It can't be that bad,' she whispered back.

He stopped, turned and looked at her, his eyes grey in the strange light. 'It could very well be a lot worse. Are you sure you want to do this, Rasel?'

'Are you?' She noted his slightly flared nostrils and dilated pupils. The vibration of his heartbeat against her fingers keeping beat with her own.

'Yes!' His steady gaze did not waiver.

'Then so am I, heart of my heart.'

His mouth curved up into a ferocious grin. 'Good, let's do this then, my love. Victory or death.'

He turned and walked towards the fidgeting madomo waiting outside the golden doors on the left. Behind them followed, four abreast, the two-tens of young warriors with Dinnis somewhere at the back.

The guards pushed open the doors and the little man stepped through. She went to follow him, but Mannok nudged her to stand in the doorway.

A flood of bright candlelight, the babble of a hundred voices, loud music, the heat and the smells hit Rasel like a wave. Multi-layered candelabras circled a large rectangular room with tiered wooden seating on the two sides. A multitude of people dressed in a rainbow of colours crammed into the large space; most of them standing about in small clusters and eddies with a few older people sitting on the lowest tier of wooden seats. Some less gaudily dressed people circulated through the throng with plates of tiny food and containers of drink. A small group of musicians played plaintive tunes of heartbreak, sorrow and loss. At the front of the room, four great casement windows separated five large tapestries depicting scenes from battles.

'Your Royal Majesties, lords, warriors and ladies,' the madomo announced in a surprising booming voice. 'I give you, the Prince Royal of Tamra, Lord of the Southern Fief, Champion of the Great Kapok, best and bravest of all his age companions, Prince Mannok, with his valiant band and the ... the lady, Rasel.'

Mannok and Rasel stepped through the doors. The room hushed and all eyes turned towards them. A rustle of sound swelled among the children of Tamrak, starting soft as a breeze and growing in volume like a wind through the trees.

Rasel walked arm in arm with the Prince toward the central tapestry. The crowd opened, forming a path and revealing two large golden chairs, one larger than the other, with high backs and solid armrests set against the wall. Four smaller wooden chairs flanked on either side.

A tall broad-chested man with dark hair greying at the temples, golden eagle eyes, and aquiline nose sat in the biggest chair. His headdress of yellow and orange feathers was larger and more elaborate than anyone else's in the room. His likeness to her Prince of Tamra, declared him to be the Kapok, Rokkan son of Martal and Tula, grandson of Tellek and Innis, the rulers of Tamra. His piercing gaze homed in on Rasel, stealing her breath. She pushed down the sudden niggle of fear. Was she not of the Kin, and he a short-lived Filane? But also, a child of Akrad, and not just in name, for she could sense the Betrayer's power in him as she had

258

in no other. Maker preserve and guide her. With him, she needed to take care.

A stately woman sat with back straight and chin raised in the golden chair on the son of Martal's left. Her rich dark brown hair showed a single silver streak. Her rich ruby tunic and chocolate-coloured cloak were flecked with gold thread and sparkling gems; gold and jewels encircled her forehead, arms, waist and dropped from her ears. She darted a look from the Prince of Tamra to Rasel and back again, and her brow creased.

Of eight wooden chairs on either side of the Kapok and his Kupanna, six were occupied. Of them all, a tall thin man with blood-red hair and an intense, hungry expression caught her eye. She drew in a sharp breath at his striking resemblance to Akrad the Betrayer. Another of the Westerners spawn though his was the lesser power.

She walked by the side of her love, Mannok, Prince of Tamra, each step taking her further into the enclosed hand-built stone cavern toward the daunting array of the highest powers of this land.

When they came within a couple of tanis of the thrones, Mannok stopped and sank into a kneeling position, bowing his head. Rasel followed his insistent tug and imitated his movements. Behind them, Mannok's young men knelt also.

Nobody moved.

Small sounds—a smoothed cough, the sibilant stir of cloaks, the muted clash of metal bangles—nibbled at the silence. Her heart tapped a warning rhythm, her breath whispered in and out. The cold stone floor pressed hard against her knees. Moments slid by and it took all her courage to remain in the vulnerable and unfamiliar position, surrounded by so many past enemies of the Kin with their spears and knives ... to remain under the penetrating, questioning stare of Akrad and Tellek's heir, Rokkan Kapok of Tamra.

Chapter Thirty-Nine: My Bride

Mannok

Mannok knelt on the cool, stone-hard floor. He resisted the urge to glance up at Papa and Mama or look sideways at his lovely Rasel. The next move was his father's. His confidence seeped out of his pores with each tense moment in the crowded Throne Room. This was a mistake, a disaster in the making. He should have sought a private interview, given his parents time to adjust and respond.

'Good of you to grace us with your presence, Prince Mannok,' Papa's sardonic voice cut through the silence. 'You may rise.'

Mannok stood, tugging Rasel up with him. He bowed to his parents. 'Your Majesties, please accept my apologies for my tardiness. A rockslide near Mist Falls village delayed us.'

'Indeed, Prince Mannok. I'm constantly surprised at how nature and misfortune seem to conspire against your timely arrival to the banquet each year. If anything, you appear to be early.'

'Yes, sir.'

Lifting his chin, he glanced at his mother for some encouraging sign. A deep furrow ran between her brows, her lips pursed instead of the full smile she would normally bestow on him on being reunited.

Rasel's hand slipped into his own and she gave it a gentle squeeze.

Mama's frown deepened. 'You have acquired a companion in your travels, Prince.' Her voice, usually so warm when she spoke to him, splintered with icy disapproval.

He looked at the angry brown eyes of his mother to the cynicism in his father's golden stare. Sometimes the only way out of danger was to keep going.

Taking a deep breath, he said, 'Yes, Ma ... Your Majesties. May I present Lady Rasel of the southern forests?' He turned to his love. 'Sweet Rasel, I present my father, Rokkan Kapok and my mother, Kupanna Marra of Tamra.'

'How dare you bring some low-born courtesan and present her as a lady!' his mother hissed.

Warmth mantled his neck and cheeks. With a great effort he kept his own voice calm.

'Your Majesty ... Mama ... she is not as you judge her. I have offered the lady safe passage to Tarka so she might join the banquet tonight.'

'You bring some nobody into the Throne Room and invite her to the banquet without asking me? She should leave, now.'

Heat seared through him. She didn't ask him about inviting the Limarians to the court. He didn't ask her to send Ista either. Mama would not take his sweet Rasel from him. 'She is not a nobody, I lov—'

'Mannok, be quiet.' Papa's warning voice cut through his like a lash. 'Marra, we will discuss this later.'

'My love,' Rasel said, her voice for his ears only. 'Would it be better to wait?'

He shook his head. He knew how that worked. The discussions behind closed doors, the pressure for him to go back on his promises. 'Rasel and I are betrothed to be married,' he bellowed.

Startled gasps and exclamations of astonishment rippled through the room.

Mama stood up, her body rigid. 'That cannot be!'

Mannok glared at his mother. 'I have given her my promise, on my honour as a prince.'

'Somewhat rash,' said Papa, his eyebrows raised. 'Brave, perhaps. Definitely foolhardy.'

There was not a hint of a smile in Papa's face or voice. Mannok's heart gave a painful thud. A chill settled deep into his bones. This was not how he imagined it would be.

He put his arm around Rasel's waist and drew her closer to him. 'That may be, but it is what we intend to do.' He faced his mother. 'Mama, you want me to marry, pressing me at every turn to make a choice. Rasel is my choice. I understand that this is not exactly what you had in mind but I wish that you could still be happy for us.'

'She is an unacceptable choice.' Mama sat down, her back straight, her head held high.

His father sat back in the throne, his long fingers tapped the armrest, his face as inscrutable as Dinnis'. Mannok struggled to breathe in air heavy with the scents of candle wax, pastries and perfumed clothing of the Throne Room. Rasel turned her head, her hair releasing her distinctive floral and pine scents. Her shapely hip rested under his hand, her rapid breathing and her sweet warmth pressed against his chest. Had he placed his love in irretrievable danger? Dinnis had warned him and he had not listened, sure he could persuade his parents given time and the right circumstances.

'What does the young woman have to say? Are you in agreement with this reckless proposal, Rasel of the southern wilderness?' Papa asked.

Rasel looked straight at him, seemingly undaunted by his fierce gaze. 'Great Kapok of Tamra,' she said, her clear voice ringing out in the hushed room, 'I regret my presence here in your great stone halls brings such consternation. However, what the Prince of Tamra says is true enough. We love each other and wish to marry.'

'I see. Which of the great houses do you belong to? I'm not aware of any in the southern forests.'

She lifted her chin a fraction. 'I am not from any house of Tamra, great or small. Perhaps, you would regard my family as simple folk. We may not be great builders or bloodthirsty warriors, but we are an ancient and proud people.'

'And what wealth or resources is your family likely to offer as a dowry? What connections or alliances will our two families secure as a result of your union to my son?'

'Son of Martal, our people's wealth is in our children. We do not accumulate piles of stones and gold or weigh ourselves down with fripperies. That is not our way. And while in centuries past we had alliances with all the peoples of the Five Lands, to our great sorrow we have been isolated in recent years.'

'So what you are saying is that you have no birth, no position, no wealth and no influential connections,' Mama said.

'Perhaps, it would appear so in your eyes,' Rasel said, meeting Mama's scornful gaze.

Papa leant forward and tented his big hands. 'And, Rasel, how long has my son been courting you? A little over an alume or two?'

'Twelve days,' she replied. Then she turned to Mannok and her face lit up with one of her stunning smiles that set his heart racing. 'Twelve glorious, marvellous, wonderful days,' she said.

He could not help letting out a wild grin.

His father's jaw slackened, then tightened. His amber eyes skewered him.

'So, after twelve days dalliance, you march into my presence before the assembled nobles and Markans of Tamra and demand to be married?' he asked, his voice close to a whisper.

Mannok's stomach hollowed, his legs turned to warmed honey. 'Yes, sir.'

Papa turned back to Rasel.

'Well, Rasel,' he said, his voice laced with sweetness, 'What can I offer you? How much gold and jewellery, how many fine clothes or horses, maybe even houses and lands—what will entice you to release my foolish son from his promise?'

Rasel hissed in a breath. 'There is only one thing from your realm that I desire,' she said.

A shiver ran down Mannok's spine. He glanced at her before looking straight ahead, the palms of his hand slick with sweat.

His father's face relaxed into a predaceous smile. 'And what may that be?'

She raised her chin, her eyes flashing. 'The one thing you cannot grant me. The love of the Prince of Tamra. For that is only his to give.'

Mannok released his caged breath and clamped down on the urge to laugh. She was magnificent, courageous and truly terrifying. Never before had he seen his father bested in a battle of wits. Yet, this was a dangerous game.

Papa nodded his head as though acknowledging the score of a worthy opponent. He crossed his arms across his deep chest and studied Rasel as he would a game of Conquest.

'So, there we have it,' he said. 'The Prince is free to give his heart with whatever reckless abandon he so chooses. However,' Papa leaned forward, his voice strong and threatening, 'he is not free to march into my halls in defiance of all decorum and honour and to issue me, Rokkan Kapok son of Martel Kapok, son of Tellek Kapok, Lord of Tamra and Shanta, Overlord of Tarka, Great Warrior of the North,

Protector of widows and orphans, to issue me ultimatums on matters of state importance. No one is, not even the Prince of Tamra.'

Mannok had never seen his father so angry, so like Martal Kapok in one of his cold rages. Whatever happened, he, Mannok, should take the brunt of that anger, not Rasel.

Letting go of her hand, Mannok took two strides and dropped to his knees at his father's feet, lowered his face to the floor, his headdress brushing up against the Kapok's burnt-orange boots.

'Forgive me, I mean no disrespect, Your Majesty.'

After a moment, his father's hand lightly brushed over Mannok's hair. 'Then give up this nonsense. Send the girl away and we will speak of it no more.'

Mannok closed his eyes. 'I cannot do that, Papa. Without her my life will be dust and ashes.'

'Better than no life at all. Do you think I can ignore such a flagrant and public challenge to my authority?' he said so low that only Mannok and perhaps his mother could hear him.

His mother sucked in a breath. 'Rokkan. Don't do or say anything rash. We should at least talk about this in private.'

'As I suggested, Marra. It is too late for that.'

'Mannok, please,' Mama said. 'Let Bitjarnan take the girl to one of the guest suites. She won't be harmed. Tomorrow, after the banquet, we can explore possibilities.'

She wanted to separate them, but it gave them time, time for his parents to see what he saw in Rasel. At the very least, he could ensure her safety.

With his forehead pressed to the stone floor, a flicker of movement caught the corner of Mannok's eye. Four pairs of boots stalking toward Rasel. His heart squeezed. Even as Mama made promises, they sent in the guards. He leapt to his feet, jumped backwards and pulled Rasel towards him.

He spun around to the right, kicking the closest guard hard in the abdomen, sending him flying backwards into the ring of startled courtiers. The other three froze where they stood. He turned and glared at his father, the Kapok, the schemer.

'Mannok, do not defy me.' The Kapok moved forward on the Throne, his hands rigid on the carved jaguar heads.

Markan Amaruk, Princess Lakwi and even Markana Yuta looked on aghast, but Markan Haka smirked, hardly hiding his glee.

What was he doing, playing into Haka's schemes? But what choice did he have? He could not abandon Rasel to fiasco. Not when he'd promised her safety, promised her his love.

He surveyed the room, looking for escape routes. More guards were streaming in through the golden doors from the Great Hall and the military offices.

'What do you want to do now, my love?' asked Rasel. She stood as straight as a pine tree, her bright eyes fastened on him, ready for anything.

'Perhaps, my love, it is time for us to find your family.'

The crowd was thinner and the guards less numerous near the door leading to the banqueting hall. If they made it that far and they were fast enough, they could disappear into the secret passages Papa had shown him as a child. Whatever he did, he needed to act now.

'Rasel,' the Kapok's voice boomed out, 'I cannot overlook the Prince's flagrant insubordination. However, I am prepared to guarantee you safe passage back to your family.'

Rasel turned to the Kapok, her eyes hard as obsidian. 'Even if I trusted the word of a Kapok, an unnatural father and the son of a House with hands covered in innocent blood, I could not accept such a cowardly offer. My fate is now linked to that of my Prince.'

'Is not my son heir of the same house and line you spurn? Heed your own words and go home to your people while you can.'

At that moment, two contingents of Palace guards came bursting into the room, one through the door to the hallway from the atrium behind them, the other through the double doors to the banqueting hall on the right. Their arrival cut off any hope of escape.

Mannok's throat burned. He brought her hands to his lips. 'Perhaps you should consider the Kapok's offer, my love. I would not bring disaster on you.'

She held his gaze with her glorious midnight eyes. 'Would you send me away? You promised me a place at your side.'

'I promised to protect you and to make you my wife. It seems my promises are worth naught.'

'I told you I don't need your protection.' She bent forward and brushed his lips with her own.

He pulled her towards him and kissed her back. A guard moved in from the left.

'Duck,' he cried, and slammed his fist into the man's face over the top of her head.

The guard crumpled into a heap at their feet. Pushing him away with his boot, Mannok rubbed his stinging knuckles on his tunic. With at least one eye on the guards, he began to slowly circle on the spot holding his love close.

'Two promises you can keep,' she said, matching his lead. 'A place by your side.'

He laughed at that. 'Very well, if that is what you still wish.'

She thrust out her foot and tripped the third guard that had made a sudden rush towards them. They both jumped out of the way as the man sprawled to the floor.

'And the second?'

'Marry me.'

'I would, my love but how?'

He twisted to the side and brought his knee up into the solar plexus of the last of the original guards lurching for them. The man staggered backwards and collapsed to one knee with a sick groan. Mannok sucked in air, his heart galloping faster than Shadow.

'By the customs of my people. All we need is the presence of witnesses,' she said.

'We have enough witnesses.'

She nodded. 'The willing consent of both betrothed.'

'I am willing, are you?'

With a grunt, he planted a solid kick between the shoulder blades on the second guard as he began to struggle to his feet, winding him. He could see the newly-arrived warriors pushing through the crowd. Without his asking, his own band had formed a protective semi-circle around Rasel and him.

'Yes, I am willing. We need a long cloth like this ...' She took her broad dark green sash and ripped off a long narrow strip. 'Which we should wrap around our right hands to show that our lives are now bound together.'

Catching his breath Mannok stretched out his hand, his eyes on hers, as she wound the cloth around their wrists in a simple pattern. He stooped to grab the spear of the winded guard and threw it with his left hand so that it pinned the cloak of the fourth guard to the ground, before he could complete his rise from his slumped position.

'What next?'

'The words of commitment.'

'Which are?'

'I, Rasel daughter of Jazadek and Rutiah of the Forest Folk promise to hold fast to Mannok, son of Rokkan and Marra of the Mountains of Tamra in love and partnership as long as we shall live.'

'I Mannok, son of Rokkan and Marra of the Mountains of Tamra promise to hold fast to Rasel daughter of Jazadek and Rutiah of the Forest in love and partnership as long as we shall live.'

Rasel frowned, looking concerned for the first time. 'Do you have some food? We need to share a meal together.'

He shook his head,

'Prince Mannok, catch,' Dinnis shouted from the back of the band. He lobbed an object at them, a flash of orange yellow.

Mannok stretched out his left hand and his fingers curled around the sunfruit. Taking a bite, he passed it to Rasel, who bit deeply into it.

'Now we need to exchange some token, a ring, pendant or bracelet.'

She took an agate pendant shaped into an eagle from her own slender neck and hung it around his. He removed the signet ring from his finger and slipped it onto her third finger, a difficult task with only his left hand free. The guards moved towards the double ring of age-mates shielding them.

'And then someone should say the blessing and it is done. Usually, a parent or uncle or aunt would say it, but I don't think it matters if I do. "May the Maker of all bless Rasel and Mannok with long life, plenty to eat, many children and love that lasts. May songs be sung about their great love by their children, their children's children, and their children's children's children and so on throughout the ages." Then the Kin group usually sings while the new couple kiss.'

He did not need another invitation. Standing still, he leant forward and kissed her. A few minutes later, he heard the scrape of boots on the mosaic floor on his right.

He snapped open his eyes, moved his torso back, and sent his fist toward the face of the approaching assailant.

The golden and orange feathers, the eagle eyes and strong nose, the imposing build. Just in time Mannok stopped his thrust within ninas of his father's face.

Papa folded his arms across his massive chest and pinned him with a fiery gaze.

Everything he'd done so far was bad enough, but to strike his father, Rokkan Kapok, his liege lord and the supreme ruler of Tamra and Shanta, could never be forgiven. His life would be forfeit and Rasel's with it.

Mannok dropped his arm to his side and drank in the dark beauty of his bride. He felt no fear, he was past that, only saddened by what would come next. Rasel smiled back at him, her eyes expectant and ready for anything. Not shadowed by doubt or regret.

He turned back to his father, side by side with Rasel, their hands bound together, and waited for the spear to seal their fate.

Chapter Forty: Reverberations

Lumi

Lumi gripped Rizzi's arm and pressed up against her friend for support. She blinked hard, sure she'd soon awake from this bizarre nightmare. None of it made sense. The Prince, who'd rejected every proposal or suggestion of marriage, now presents some unknown woman as his bride, in open defiance of his father Rokkan Kapok and in front of all the nobles of Tamra. She pressed her hands to her side to still their shaking, but could not stop her knees, her whole body, from trembling. Please don't kill him.

The Kapok stared at his son, his normally mobile face an inscrutable mask.

'Prince Mannok, it seems I have been wasting my metal on entertainers when I could have had my idiot son perform. Do you really think that little farce you enacted means anything?'

The strange tall women with the silvery white skin stirred. 'It means something to me and my people.'

The Kapok ignored her, his eyes drilling into Mannok.

The Prince looked into the dark eyes of the woman. 'It means something to me too, sweet Rasel.' He squeezed her hand and looked back at the Kapok.

The Kapok scanned the four groaning guards sprawled out on the mosaic floor, the semi-circle of nervous young men still holding their position around Mannok, the agitated courtiers and the two units of royal guards under the command of Kaptan Jakan.

He returned his bronze-hard gaze to the couple standing before him. 'And what do you think you've achieved with this grievous insult to the Throne of Tamra?'

'My Lord Rokkan,' Kupanna Marra stood and placed a shaking hand on the Kapok's arm, her stately face grey beneath its normally rich golden-brown tones. 'Your Majesty, I beg you to forgive the Prince's unruly behaviour.'

The Kapok did not turn his head. 'What have you to say for yourself, Prince?'

Mannok moistened his lips. 'Sir, Your Majesty, I apologise for the disruption and I deeply regret any offense my behaviour has caused you. I mean no disrespect, but I cannot regret my love for Rasel. Perhaps, you have forgotten the power of love.'

The Kupanna stretched out her hands. 'Mannok.'

'What indeed would I know about love?' the Kapok said with a twist of his lips.

'That is not what I mean, Papa.'

'Are you determined to hold to this woman though she lacks noble birth. What do you really know of her? She could be a spy or an assassin.'

'I am, as I gave her my promise, and she is not our enemy.'

'Even taking into account your mother's plea on your behalf, your obstinate refusal to give up the young woman limits my options. You will be punished.'

'Rokkan, please,' the Kupanna sank to her knees, desperate eyes fastened to the Kapok's face.

Lumi twisted her hands together. Please, please, not the Red Leap, even prison or exile would be better for either might be reversed.

The Kapok's lips tightened. 'First, Prince Mannok, you will apologise personally to each of the guards for any injuries you have wilfully and wantonly caused them, ensuring they receive full care and pay while they recover.'

Mannok nodded. 'It shall be done.'

Relief flooded through Lumi. But what came next? Was this the prelude to a more severe punishment?

'So like Uncle Rokkan to worry about the guards,' Rizzi whispered in Lumi's ear.

'Second, for your grievous disrespect to the Throne and the people of Tamra ...' The Kapok paused and a stillness settled in the Throne Room as though the whole nation held its collective breath. Lumi clung tighter to Rizzi. 'You will present yourself to Kaptan Jakan for ten stripes of the lash.'

The strange woman shivered and her lips twitched as if she'd say something until Mannok brushed his free hand across her arm.

He bowed his head. 'As you command, Your Majesty.'

Lumi held her breath. Was that it or was there more to come?

'Third, present yourself to Kaptan Kaspin for double duty on the wall for a full Argen while you contemplate the duties of a Prince of Tamra. And five days later, at the Welcome to Land Feast ...' The Kapok paused again and tilted his head.

By the Maker's mercy, don't let him die. Don't let him die. Don't let him die.

'You will marry this woman, Rasel of the southern wilderness, and may you have the joy of it.'

'What?' Both the Prince and his mother spoke in unison.

'What?' echoed Lumi. Marry her? She rubbed her ears, sure she'd misheard.

'Rokkan, you can't be serious. You can't possibly accept this ... this girl as a suitable wife for the Prince Royal of Tamra,' Kupanna Marra's voice shrilled.

Father jumped up from the Markan's chair, the smirk wiped from his face, his silver eyes blazing. 'Rokkan, this is madness.'

The Kapok faced her father, his eyebrows arching. 'Are you contradicting your Kapok, Lord Haka?'

Father's face slackened. He stepped back and held up open palms. 'No, no, Your Majesty, just ... a Prince of Tamra's marriage is of state importance. It is customary to present it to the Council. Ah, ... ' His voice faded as the Kapok stared him down.

'A custom, yes, but the decision was and is mine to make.' Rokkan Kapok turned to his wife and pulled her to her feet. 'My dear Kupanna,' he said, his face impenetrable, 'I agree with you, she is a dubious choice.' His lips thinned in a grim smile. 'However, we did give the Prince the freedom to choose. Of the numerous suitable young women presented to him over the years, she is the first one he has found acceptable. Of course, we could renege on our promises and insist he give her up or face more deadly punishment. Is that your wish?'

The Kupanna Marra's hand flew to her mouth. She swallowed. 'No, Your Majesty.'

'And do you object, Mannok?'

'I ... no, not at all.' Mannok bowed low. 'My eternal thanks, Your Majesty.'

'Humph. We shall see how well that wears after two ten-days of tramping up and down the wall for sixteen hours a day. Make sure she is accommodated appropriately for the night. Tomorrow, she can move into the guest palace. In the meantime, we have, I believe, a banquet to attend and I intend to freshen up first. This has been quite the drama.'

With that, Rokkan Kapok took the Kupanna's arm and stalked out of the room, the Markans, their wives and royal guard falling in behind him.

The room erupted into a tumultuous babble of voices. Nothing like this had occurred in living memory, unless one counted the assassination attempt of the Rokkan Kapok's younger half-brother which sparked the civil war. Three-year-old Mannok had been the only witness to that.

Lumi eased her grip on Rizzi's arm, her eyes still fixed on the Prince. Her erratic breathing and pulse eased back into a normal rhythm.

Prince Mannok hadn't moved, the strange woman pressed against him in scandalous intimacy and his age-mates surrounding him. Though Estolik peeled off soon after and headed towards Princess Kerri sitting with a stony face in the front tier of seats.

The courtiers delayed, as protocol demanded, to see if the Prince would follow his father. When he didn't move, first the clan leaders and heads of noble houses, the brigans, commanders and all the fine ladies, bowed in the direction of the Prince and trickled out of the room.

'I can't believe what just happened!' said Rizzi.

Lumi gulped and nodded. 'I thought his life was forfeit.'

'How can Mannok spurn us all for the sake of that upstart peasant woman? How could Uncle Rokkan accept this farcical marriage? She's a nobody. She must be a sorceress to entangle him so,' Rizzi spluttered.

'It does beggar belief!' Lumi wrung her hands. For all the punishments, the Prince had escaped lightly, but it was still a disaster. She had no hope of winning him now. What would Father do next?

Someone tapped her on the shoulder and she spun around. Estolik stood behind her with Kerri in tow. The Limarian Princess nodded at Lumi and Rizzi and then studied her painted nails, boredom written across her pale pointy face.

Lumi swallowed a snarky remark and turned to her brother. 'Estolik, how did you let this happen?'

He pursed his lips. 'You know Mannok. Once he's made up his mind, there's no stopping him. Besides, I didn't think he'd really do it.'

Was that a hint of admiration in her brother's voice? She shook her head. Surely one of those young men could have talked the Prince out of such a preposterous proposal. Not that it mattered now.

She sighed. 'Father will want to see us.'

'Yes. We might as well get it over with.' Estolik grimaced as though tasting a sour inka berry. 'Rizzi, can you keep Princess Kerri company until the banquet?'

Kerri darted Estolik a scorching look. 'Back for less than an hour after two alume, my husband, and already you leave me to the care of others.'

Estolik held up his hands. 'We will have time together later tonight, I promise.'

Kerri sniffed. 'Come then.' She grabbed poor Rizzi's arm and dragged her out of the Throne Room.

Estolik's shoulders slumped and his breath whooshed out. He ran a hand over his face. 'Maker preserve me. She is like a swooping tarrawong in nesting season.'

At any other time, Lumi might have laughed at his woebegone face. 'What do you expect, running off with the Prince barely a ten-day after the wedding? And you at least have been spared your wife's sweet company these last alume.'

'Can you blame me for trying?' Estolik straightened. 'Come, better not keep Father waiting.'

* * *

Lumi eased open the door of the family room of the Dolphin guest suite. Father paced in front of the empty fireplace, his hands clasped behind his back and a thunderous look on his long thin face. Mother and the younger children were absent, perhaps resting in their private rooms before the banquet tonight. Lumi felt the urge to turn around and flee into the garden and hide up a tree as she had often done as a child.

Too late, her father looked up and speared them with his silver gaze. He strode across the room and slapped Estolik's face with a loud thwack.

'Foolish boy. How did you allow this to happen?'

Estolik rocked backwards, blinked and rubbed his cheek. 'Father, I ... didn't think he was serious. And even if he was, who could imagine that the Kapok would accept such a mismatched union.'

'I think he almost didn't,' stammered Lumi.

Father growled, his normally pale face livid. 'Uncle Martal would never have tolerated such defiance, at least not from his heir. Rokkan has always indulged his cub. But this? It's a travesty, an insult to our family, to our realm.'

'Father, be careful,' Lumi hissed. 'Someone might hear you.'

'Don't worry, we can speak freely here.' Father ran a hand through his blood-red curls. 'You're right, girl, Rokkan didn't like it, but he has only the one son. He's a sentimental fool. He should have put Marra aside years ago or at the very least taken a second wife to produce more heirs.' Father tapped his chin. 'Rokkan's acceptance of the wench could be a delaying tactic. Gives him time to ween the Prince off this sudden and unwise infatuation.'

Hope sparked inside Lumi's chest. She lifted her head. 'Do you think so, Father?'

'Maybe. We need information. Quick, go attend the Kupanna. Find out what you can.'

'What, now? I haven't been called.' His nostrils flared, and she hastened to add, 'Of course, Father, if that is what you wish.'

'Yes, yes, don't stand there gaping, girl.' He grabbed her by the shoulders and pushed her out the door. 'Report back as soon as you can.'

* * *

'Rokkan, you can't be serious. This is unacceptable. I just won't have it, I won't.'

The Kupanna's voice had been audible from the atrium corridor. Lumi took a deep breath. Her legs trembled as she pushed through the golden doors into the Royal antechamber.

The Kupanna paced up and down the room, wringing her hands, strands of hair fallen from her intricate hairstyle and floating over her stately shoulders. Rokkan stared into the empty fireplace, one boot on the stone ledge and a hand resting on the carved arch above it. He turned as soon as she entered the room, one eyebrow angling up.

'Lumi! And to what do we owe the pleasure of your company?' His voice was light, but his eyes were as hard as metal.

'I …' She cleared her throat, 'Your Majesty, I … I thought the Kupanna might need some help with her attire … before … before the banquet.'

The Kapok studied her with a flat smile. Her cheeks flamed. By rights, it was Jati's turn to serve, though the young lass wasn't present, probably already dismissed. She looked down and inspected the patterns of flowers and birds in the woven rugs on the floor. The Kupanna turned around and pressed a shaking hand to her throat. She looked past Lumi, not seeming to see her, and fixed her eyes on the Kapok.

'This is intolerable, Rokkan.'

'So you keep saying, my dear. What do you suggest? My decisions were made before the gathered nobles of Tamra. To retract now would dishonour the Throne.'

The Kupanna's chest heaved. Her lips pressed together and her nostrils flared.

'How could you agree to that … that … We should have withdrawn to a more private setting. We could have persuaded Mannok from this madness.'

The door pushed open and a tall, willowy lady in richly embroidered robe and sash sallied into the room, pausing only to bow before the Kapok. He brought his boot to the floor and stood back.

'Princess Lakwi—did I somehow indicate I'd be holding court this evening? Who else has decided to intrude on our privacy?'

'Just me, dearest brother. You do know, don't you, that you and that mischievous son of yours has set the whole place in an uproar. The Maker knows, it's Mannok's duty to give you an heir, but agreeing to a union with a total unknown … she could be anyone, anything. Eleven days he's known her!'

'Indeed!' Rokkan's lips stretched into a small, flat smile.

'How could you give way so easily?' In a daze, the Kupanna dropped onto one of the divans and buried her face in her hands. 'I don't understand.'

The Kapok let out a frustrated breath. 'Lumi, if you must be here, at least make yourself useful, and get the Kupanna some sweet birch wine or some chinkona tea. Perhaps a cold compress as well.'

Lumi hastened to a small low table against the wall. Her hands shook as she poured the clear pink liquid from the decanter into a cup. Even as she set up a small tray and offered it to the Kupanna, the conversation continued around her.

'And if I had forbidden the marriage,' the Kapok said, folding his arms across his chest, 'would Mannok have accepted that decision?'

No one answered. Lakwi's fine forehead creased while the Kupanna shuddered.

'The truth is, he's been challenging my authority ever since Ista went to Silisea. Her recent betrothal to young Tolteal hasn't helped matters.'

'At least Ista is Akrad's granddaughter,' Lakwi said slowly. 'A nobility of sorts.'

'There is no way that girl would have been suitable. She's ...' Kupanna Marra glanced at Lumi and pressed her lips together.

'Yes, but this Rasel—' Princess Lakwi threw up her arms.

The Kapok waved a hand. 'This Rasel has captured his attention. He believes he is in love with her. The more we oppose him, the more convinced he becomes. What's more, he has made his determination public. His rebellious display today was teetering on treason.'

'Maybe not such a good idea to send in the guards.'

The Kapok grimaced. 'As became evident, the moment I gave the order. A tactical mistake which meant giving up more ground than I liked. Indicating my acceptance of the marriage gives us the breathing space you rightly suggested as desirable, Marra.'

'Better an injudiciously married heir than a dead one?' Lakwi sighed. 'I'll have some of that birch wine too, if you don't mind, Lumi.'

'Something like that. A lot can happen in an alume.'

'Oh?' Lakwi's face perked up. 'I guess it might give enough time for your spies to find out if she is a little chancer thus opening Mannu's eyes to the foolishness of his actions.'

'I will send Sparak and his best scouts south to find out who she is. Besides, once he sees this low-born woman in the context of Palace life, he may find she is not the paragon he thinks her. Especially as double wall duty will give them little time together. Like a blue-skied rain shower in the mountains, infatuations can blow away as fast as they form.'

'And if the Prince himself decides to break off the relationship ...'

'Exactly.'

Lakwi smiled broadly. She patted Rokkan's arm. 'You haven't lost your touch, brother.'

So Father was right. For the first time since the Prince had walked into the Throne Room with that woman on his arm, Lumi breathed easier. If he tired of the upstart, he could still be hers and Father wouldn't pursue his ... other more drastic plans. She handed a cold compress to the Kupanna.

Marra pressed it against her temple and closed her eyes. 'What if he still wants to marry her at the end of the alume?' she asked.

'If his attachment is that strong, my dear, I will have no choice but to honour our agreement. The girl does have spunk, I'll give her that.'

A tense silence settled on the room. Outside, the mournful call of a mountain owl sounded from the gardens. In the other direction, a distant babble of voices marked the arrival of the notable citizens and minor nobles waiting in the Great Hall for the doors to the Banqueting Hall to be opened.

'Could we at least cancel the banquet, Rokkan,' the Kupanna asked.

Rokkan let out a long breath. 'Would that we could, my dear, but all the notables of our land are already assembling into our halls.'

'Then, I need a moment to myself.' The Kupanna staggered up, walked towards the Royal chambers and shut the door firmly behind her.

'I must admit, they were magnificent—like the romantic tales you used to tell when I was a child, Rokkan,' Lakwi said with a whimsical smile. 'Though quite unsuitable as most of those romantic tales are. I should get ready also, if you will excuse me, Your Majesty?' She leant forward, kissed him on the cheek, and swept out of the room.

As the Kapok watched her go, he breathed out some words as if to himself.

> 'Love against all power and might,
> In secret tryst and illicit kiss
> Dares shine forth its honeyed light,
> And thus entwined cares not
> What fate it finds.'

Lumi gasped. Rokkan looked up, his eyes meeting hers.

'Still here? Well, if you could stay while I rustle up my Master of Scouts, in case the Kupanna needs you? Then you can report

... I mean join ... your estimable father and reassure him of the realm's stability.'

Her cheeks began a slow burn. She bowed her head. 'As you wish, your Majesty. I ...I ...'

'It's okay, Lumi, we both know how things stand, I think.'

She lifted her head. 'Your Majesty, I will keep what has been said here to myself.'

His face relaxed and he surprised her with a chuckle. 'Don't worry, lass. I would have thrown you before this, if I wanted to keep our discussion from your father. Tell him what you will, but Lumi ...'

'Sir?'

'Remember the price of disloyalty to the Throne.'

She bowed low. 'I would never harm the Prince or yourself, I am loyal to ... to you.'

'That, we shall see.'

With a nod, he strode out of the room.

Chapter Forty-One: Rasel's Song

Rasel

Rasel watched the Kapok and his retinue leave the Throne Room. He was both all that she had expected and yet somehow not like it at all. He had seemed immovable right up to the last moment when he surrendered all of a sudden. Yet he did not carry himself like one defeated. There was a small bounce in his step, a smugness in his glance that niggled her. While the emotions and thoughts of the majority of these Tamrin played over their faces as clear as sunbeams on a mountain stream, this Rokkan was deeper, more difficult to read.

The vast room emptied rapidly, though most of Mannok's age-mates clustered around him, knocking fists, slapping him on the back and laughing.

The one called Garvin clapped him on the shoulder. 'By the Moons, Mannok, I didn't think you'd get out of that skirmish alive.'

'Nor I, Garo, nor I.' Mannok turned to her and raised their bound hands. 'How long do we remain hand-tied, sweet Rasel?'

'Forever,' she said, dimpling. 'But we can take the cloth off now, if you like.'

She helped him tease the knots, both of them with only one hand to deploy. As the last ties slackened, she looked about her.

Dinnis was hiding at the back of the band, sending covert glances towards the door. He seemed set to slip away. She walked towards the tall lad, Mannok close behind her.

'Friend Dinnis.' She flashed a friendly smile.

'My lady,' he replied with a bow to her and the Prince.

'Thank you for your timely help. Throwing that sunfruit was surely inspired.'

He lifted his shoulders a fraction. 'Luck, no doubt, my lady.'

'I am not sure I believe in luck.' She studied his impassive face. Here was another one hard to read. Why did he hide his abilities as though they were shameful? He was as big an enigma as Rokkan. But with his heartfelt confession at the Shanti ruins and his actions at North Pass, Dinnis had proved himself her friend.

Prince Mannok laughed. 'Then maybe the Maker was looking after us. Dinnis is about the only warrior I know who has a talent for missing his target.'

'Unlike the Prince who always hits his. It was certainly an inspired catch,' Dinnis said.

The Prince's eyes narrowed beneath his furrowed brow.

'What is it, Prince of Tamra?' Rasel asked.

'Humph. I was trying to work out where the insult is hidden.'

'My love, it was a compliment.'

'Exactly! Dinnis never gives out accolades. There has to be an insult in there somewhere.'

Dinnis looked down at the colourful mosaic floor, the smallest twitch of his lips giving away his amusement. Suddenly tempted to ruffle his complacency, Rasel took hold of the half-eaten fruit she had stowed in her robes during the ceremony and sent it hurtling at his head. With a start, he reached out and caught the missile before it smashed into his face. Looking from the sunfruit back to her, he raised his eyebrows.

'I beg your forgiveness, my lady. Did I do something to offend?'

'No, man of the north, but it would seem there is nothing wrong with either your reflexes or your catching skills.'

He lifted his chin and looked at her. She met his stare without blinking. What went on beneath those smoky grey eyes?

Dinnis shrugged. 'A lucky catch. On any other day, I'm sure I would have dropped it.'

'I'm sure you would have, too, if you'd had time to think about it.'

He gave a small nod, not unlike Rokkan acknowledging her wit earlier that evening.

By now the hall was empty except for the men and women cleaning up and those preparing the banqueting hall next door. Of the Prince's band, only Garvin, the Prince's loyal shadow, stood waiting nearby.

'The banquet will be starting soon, Mannu,' Garvin said.

Mannok's fingers tightened on her arm. He sighed. 'We had best be on time, my love. The bachelor quarters is hardly appropriate for you, but we can freshen up in the guest chambers.' He looked at Dinnis with a tight smile. 'How about you make yourself useful and see about some suitable accommodation for Rasel in the guest quarters tonight? Let me know at the banquet once it's organised. And see about getting the Silesian Palace if you can.'

'Could we not arrange this ourselves, my love?' Rasel asked.

'If we arrive late for this cursed banquet, everyone including my parents—especially my parents—will know. If Dinnis is late,' he shrugged, 'no one will notice. I don't want to aggravate my father more than necessary.'

'Forgive me, my love, but your parents seem so cold and demanding.'

'Well, you have met them on a bad day. Give them time. But we really must hurry.'

He slipped his arm in hers and they strode towards the Great Hall, Garvin trailing behind.

* * *

An hour later, Rasel stood beside the Prince of Tamra on the threshold of the Banquet Hall. A crowd of people milled about the huge stone-walled room, high and big like a cavern of the mountain Darane. The people jostled for position, moving towards long low tables lined up in serried ranks along the length of the Hall. A raised dais stood beneath the casement windows and tapestries on the far wall. On the dais, stood three large tables draped in cloth of gold and arranged in a square, with the near side left open.

'Prince Mannok of Tamra and the Lady Rasel,' the small round man, Bitjarnan, announced in his booming voice. 'Noble Garvin, son of Kaspin, Kaptan of the City Guard,' he added almost as an afterthought.

The room pulsed with candlelight, body heat and noise. Rasel held on tighter to Mannok's arm. She had welcomed the calm of the small guest sitting room where she, Mannok and Garvin spent a few quiet moments preparing for this evening's entertainment. Now it was back into the tumult of people, more people than at the big Kin gatherings such as the castana nut harvest or the Jubilee festival, maybe more than she had ever thought existed in the world.

At least the press of people melted before them as Mannok led her towards the dais. The Markans and the Markanas, as well as Estolik, Yalik and Durran, stood in a small knot of people in front of the raised platform. Standing with them was another weary-looking young man, with some resemblance to Mannok though shorter, and a few young women dressed in colourful and ornate clothing and whom she didn't recognise.

'Prince Mannok.' The one Rokkan named Lord Haka stepped towards them and dipped his head. Though close to Rokkan's height, the fine yarma cloak and majestic Tamrin headdress of blue and silver feathers gave him an imposing presence. Yet it was his uncanny resemblance to Akrad, with his narrow build, pale skin, red hair, silver-grey eyes and an indefinable something in his stance, that sent warning signals fizzing through her body. His fulsome smile did not reach his glacier eyes.

'Lord Haka.' Mannok returned the smile, though his arm tensed beneath her fingers.

'Your Highness, I'm glad to see you returned safely from the southern wilderness with no mishaps. We must congratulate you on your success at hunting, though your choice of fair game seems ... unusual.'

Mannok's neck flushed and his hand tightened on her arm, but his smile did not waver. Rasel pressed her lips together. The man meant to insult her beneath his smooth double-intended words.

Mannok's faithful shadow, Garvin, stepped forward. 'The Prince always bags the jaguar's share of game, my Lord.'

A crinkle appeared on Haka's sculpted brows, but before he could answer, one long note of a horn sounded and the room stilled like the forest before the storm. The assembled nobles and dignitaries turned as one towards the big double doors and bowed like trees before the wind as Kapok Rokkan and Kupanna Marra swept into the room.

Only when the royal couple sat in the two high-backed chairs at the centre of the high table on the dais, did the others find their places around the tables and sit down.

'This way Lady Rasel.' One of the young women with silver eyes like Haka and dolphins embroidered on her cobalt-blue robe guided Rasel to a seat beside the Kapok.

Her own love disappeared from her sight. She fought for air in the stifling atmosphere, feeling alone and abandoned in this throng of strangers.

Leaning forward, she caught Mannok's eyes where he sat on the other side of his unyielding parents. The son of Martal's eyebrow ticked up, his full lips stretching into a sardonic knowing smile. Blushing, she shifted in the half-backed chair and fingered the little jaguar brooch Mannok had given her at the Way Station only this morning. And now she wore his ring and he wore her pendant. If she could face down jaguars, crocodiles and wild tribes in the Great Forest, she could endure these haughty children of Tamrak for the sake of her love.

With a signal of the Kapok's hand, a gong was sounded and men and women laden down with trays of food streamed into the room. Whole roasted peccaries, roasted duck and other birds, even a deer still with antlered horns, large tureens filled with soups and stews, jellied meats, fresh and dried fish were placed first on the high table and then on the tables around the room to the gasps and appreciative sighs of those present. The meats were supplemented with trays of breads of all kinds, roasted vegetables, cooked beans, cheeses, greens and sauces. Other servitors poured wine, maize beer or juices in the mugs and cups provided. The savoury smells, both tantalising and overly rich, besieged her senses. The amounts seemed excessive. Surely even this big crowd could not consume such a huge quantity of food?

Even as the tables were filled, the man with snow-white hair, sitting on the other side of Mannok, stood up and offered a long-winded thanksgiving for the food. As his loud sonorous voice faded and he finally sat down, the Kapok leant forward and picked up a duck leg.

'The Maker be praised,' he murmured though whether he was delighted with the quality of the food, supplementing the man's prayers or just pleased that they had finally ended, Rasel couldn't determine.

In front of her, a peccary with glassy eyes stared at her. She averted her gaze and looked about for something more appetising.

She found some baked fish in a chilli sauce and added gem potatoes, beans and steamed emerald chaya leaves to her plate. Around her, the Tamrin piled their plates and consumed the food with noisy enjoyment. She sighed. This was going to be a long night.

'So ... Lady ... Rasel, would you like some venison? Your plate is empty.' The honeyed voice came from the facing table.

Rasel looked up and encountered the silver eyes of the girl who had directed her to her seat. Her resemblance to both Haka and Estolik suggested a close relative, perhaps Estolik's sister or cousin.

'I have sufficient for my needs, thank you, Lady ...'

'Lady Lumi. And this is Lady Rizanna, daughter of Lukarn Markan of the Northern Marches. And here, my father, Lord Haka, Markan of the West. Estolik, you know, and his wife Princess Kerri of Limar, Princess Lakwi ...' Lumi introduced her to the other glittering nobles at the raised tables.

'I imagine this is your first visit to Tarka,' the Lady Rizanna said after a short pause.

'Yes. My family have not been to the City of the Kapoks in over seven decades. It ... it is as beautiful as the songs say.' And as perilous.

'It is a long journey for peasa... for any who must come on foot from the Shanti wilds,' the daughter of Haka said. 'I must say, Rasel, your attire, such simplicity is quite unique.'

Princess Kerri, sitting between Haka and Estolik sniggered, then said in a high voice, 'Oh yes, so droll to wear such rustic clothes.'

'No doubt you had no time to change into your other gowns, my lady,' continued Lumi, her pretend smile not wavering.

'I have no other gowns.' Rasel looked down at her fine cotton tari and forest-green mantle. The whole hall was a riot of colour, with glittering tunics, feathered headdresses, golden accoutrements and flashing gems, none more splendid and preposterous than Estolik's new wife, Princess Kerri. 'This tari is all I need. Besides I only like to take with me what I can carry.'

'Carry?' Lumi blinked, a spoonful of soup paused halfway to her mouth.

'Yes, an excess of belongings weighs one down, don't you think? Though I suppose if you live in a big palace like this one you might feel the need to cram it full of ... of stuff, but then it must be a major effort to go anywhere.'

284

Lumi stared at her, then hitched an elegant shoulder. 'That's what servants are for.'

'Servants? Oh, well my Kin are a simple folk. We don't have servants.' Rasel looked again at the men and women in plainer clothes flitting around the tables, refilling cups, carving the meat and serving. Of course, there had been some servants in Mannok's retinue too though nowhere near as many as this small army of retainers.

'That the Prince is well endowed with riches can only enhance his other attractions.' The icy red-headed man, grandson of Tellek, leaned forward, the whites of his eyes and his teeth flashing in the candlelight.

She wiped her hands on the provided napkin. 'Not at all, Lord Haka. If anything, I would say the opposite.'

He narrowed his eyes. 'Surely you do not expect us to believe that the Prince's wealth and position is of no interest to you?'

'You are welcome to believe whatever you wish, man of the west, but it seems to me and to my Kin that family is more important than accumulating possessions. We don't like being tied to one spot. As Suza says:

Long-necked yarmas groan beneath heavy burdens of gold
Sluggish hoof steps on the trail nearing the mountain hold.
Warriors rub their weary eyes, standing before the door,
As bandits creep upon them to attack with murderous roar.
Above them in sapphire sky, the crested hawk soars and wheels
Floating like gossamer on high winds, no worldly concerns it feels.

Haka's cold eyes widened, then he smiled. 'Humph, strange you know Suza. She is often obtuse and not so popular these days. I much prefer Vagnak. You have heard of Vagnak, I presume.'

Mannok's father, speaking to Princess Lakwi, a tall willowy woman with green eyes sitting on the other side of Mannok, stopped in midsentence. He turned and studied Rasel.

She turned a shoulder to his scrutiny. 'Oh, yes, Vagnak. My least favourite and the most bloodthirsty of the Tamrin poets and sages.' Then she turned back to the son of Martal who still studied her, his thoughts hard to fathom. With a tilt of her head, she added, 'No doubt, Ruler of Tamra and Shanta, Vagnak is your favourite poet also?'

The conversations hushed around them and the eyes of all at the raised table were riveted on her. Mannok, hidden by his father's

285

bulk, shuffled in his seat. Had she been too direct? These Tamrin were very touchy about status, especially the Kapok's it seemed.

A small smile played at the corners of Rokkan's mouth. 'You mean the most likely choice for a bloodthirsty warrior and son of a House dripping in innocent blood?' His words caused a hush to spread to the surrounding tables and throughout the Banqueting Hall.

A chill crept down the back of her neck. He was baiting her, trapping her with her own words spoken in the heat of the moment and enticing her into further indiscretions. Why? She could see the tip of Mannok's green feathers hidden by the bulk of his parents. She took a deep breath and looked around her at the stormy eyes of Lumi, the scornful glances of Kerri and Rizanna, Haka's sardonic smile echoed by his wife and by Durrin's parents. On the other side, the green-eyed Lakwi looked inquisitive while the others were blank or hostile. In the sea of faces, only nervous Garvin, showed any sign of friendliness, until she caught sight of Dinnis taking a seat amongst a group of his age-mates on one of the lower tables.

She returned her gaze to the Kapok and waved a hand at the tapestries on the walls. 'Forgive me, son of Martal, am I mistaken? But as with Vagnak, the most exquisite weavings crowding your walls celebrate the great battles of the Kapoks – the Battle of Red Lake, the Battle of Kaja, the Fall of Mokka, the Fall of Shanta and in the Throne Room, the Battle of Mid Pass, the Siege of Nakri, the Battle of North Pass.'

He tipped his head and surveyed the walls, his eyes wide and innocent, surely an act. 'As it happens, daughter of Jazadek and Rutiah, you are mistaken. My favourite poet is Meltan not Vagnak. Though Suza has her charms, she is often too fanciful for me.'

'Fanciful?'

'Mythical creatures— the first ones, the Adelphi, shapeshifters, the shadows and the like.'

'Mythical?' Rasel smoothed the tablecloth. 'Interesting.' Had the children of Tamrak such short memories or was it guilt of their blood-stained deeds that led them to confine her people to legend and myth, even when she'd told them who she was?

'Simple folk like peasants still accept their existence,' Haka said. 'They frightened their children into obedience with tales of the evil shapeshifting Adelphi. But such creatures are indeed the stuff of legends.'

Princess Lakwi pushed her plate away. 'How much have you read of our poets, Rasel? You must know that Meltan, Suza and indeed minor poets such as Elluk and Kolrik speak of love as much as war.'

'Yes, wonderful tales—of Prince Solik and beautiful Namu of the Waterfall, of brave Tetzel and sweet Sil—but Tamrin love stories always seem to end in tragedy.'

'Martal Kapok's love for Suraya is as beautiful and romantic as the old tales and it did not end in tragedy,' the Kupanna said.

Lakwi let out a soft breath. 'I guess that depends on how you define tragedy. My mother still mourns my father's death at the hands of my brother Naetok.' The sparkle in her merry eyes faded for a few minutes, then brightened again. 'You seem well-educated in the poets and the histories, my dear. No doubt you are the best scholar in your village.'

Rasel laughed. 'Not at all. I lack the concentration and discipline to be a good student. My sister Rebekka and brother Levian are the most knowledgeable in the Filane classics though my father's brothers love to debate the merits of Sokan and Meltan, along with Masu. Baba, that is, my father, claims that trying to teach me has given him his grey hairs.'

'Your slackness appears more fruitful than the diligence of some young princes I know.' The son of Martal tapped a rhythm on the table with his finger. 'I haven't heard of Masu, and Sokan is not much in favour these days.'

'We all have different strengths and weaknesses. I know my Prince excels in other things. I do love Suza and wish I could have met her.'

The son of Martal raised his eyebrows. 'Born a bit late for that, lass. She died in the time of my grandfather, Tellek Kapok. So what do you excel at, apart from turning your father's hair grey?'

Rasel laughed again. Maybe he was a tyrant, but he did have a sense of humour. 'I'm a terrible worry to my family. I often resolve to be more circumspect, but I can't help it. The song of the forests, the mountains, the plains and, yes, the song of the sea and the sky call to me. Among my family I am considered both an excellent pathfinder and a gifted singer. Yet that could be said of many of my Kin.'

The servants began clearing the tables and placed big platters of fruit and sweetmeats, along with cups of steaming koka, before them.

Rasel closed her eyes and heard in memory the pure, melodious voices of her people intermingling and soaring into the night sky as sparks from the campfires spiralled upwards to find the stars. She missed their voices, missed the easy camaraderie, the teasing and the love of her family. Starting low and soft, she sang the song of the jaguar—the song of her love—and the songs of her Kin.

When she opened her eyes, she found the hall hushed and silent with every eye upon her. She bit her lip and looked to the Kapok. He had a strange expression on his face, not exactly displeased but incredulous and pondering.

'That ... that was exquisite, my dear,' he said.

'But totally inappropriate,' Mannok's mother said, 'We generally leave the entertainment to the entertainers. Please remember that in future.'

Rasel looked down at her empty plate as at the other side of the room, seven quill-flute players sent breathy and plaintive notes swirling through the renewed murmur of the conversing multitude. If only Mannok was sitting right beside her rather than on the other side of his parents. If it wasn't for him, she would have followed the songlines home by now, most likely with a scolding Semian for company. But for all the strangeness and hostility she'd received, she didn't regret binding herself to her love, the Prince of Tamra.

Chapter Forty-Two: Love and Marriage

Mannok

Mannok woke with warm sunlight striping across his face. Snores and heavy breathing came from the other sleeping rooms overlaying the normal morning noises of the busy Palace. Apart from a thin layer of dust, his room in the bachelor quarters looked unchanged from the last time he'd slept there. Had he dreamt his clash with Papa in the Throne Room yesterday, the last few alume? His pulse ratchetted up. Would Papa change his mind or try to spirit Rasel away? He needed to find her.

He leapt off the bunk, splashed his face with water from the ceramic basin, and threw on the first clothes he could grab.

He paused outside Garvin's door and then dropped his hand. No, he had no time for explanations and delays. He strode along the corridors and headed down the stairs to the lowest floor of the guest quarters, to the room Dinnis had arranged for Rasel. The room where he'd left her last night.

She sat on a bench beside the atrium pool, a tray of cornbread, fruit, a pot of honey, and a round of yarma cheese beside her. She looked as fresh and awake and delectable, her skin luminous in the shade.

'Mannok!' A sunny smile lit up her face. She jumped up and wrapped her slender arms around him.

He buried his face in her hair. 'Sweet Rasel. Did you sleep well?'

'Yes, come eat.' She pulled him down to the bench and piled a plate for him. He didn't need to be asked twice. Together, they ate in companionable silence.

He finished mopping up the last of the honey with a hunk of maize bread and popped it into his mouth. 'Would you like a tour of the Palace, my love?'

She clapped her hands. 'Yes, and the gardens. Did I see some trees when we rode past the wall yesterday?'

'Yes, the orchards and there's a grotto, a look out, and a lake—'

At the sound of boots on the stone floor, he looked up.

A guard strode through the entrance and dropped on his knee. 'Your Highness, His Majesty, the Kapok, requires your presence in the Throne Room.'

The Throne Room, not one of the smaller reception rooms. Papa hadn't forgiven him, yet. 'Tell my father, we'll be there shortly.'

Several moments later, they strode past the guards at the door in the huge echoing vault of the Throne Room. Papa sat on the Golden Throne, one leg tucked over the other, the only adornment on his attire, his smaller everyday headdress and the golden brooch on his shoulder. His mother's chair was empty and Madomo Bitjarnan and a few other palace staff stood at the other side of the room, out of earshot, but close enough to respond to his father's signals.

'Good of you to grace us with your presence, Prince.'

'Your Majesty.' Mannok bowed low, and Rasel followed his lead. 'Will Mama be joining us?'

His father gave a thin-lipped smile. 'The Kupanna retired with a headache last night.'

'I regret if I have distressed her.'

'Indeed.' Papa turned to Rasel standing tall beside him and gave her a long, appraising look.

'Well, Rasel, daughter of Jazadek and Rutiah, who are you I wonder? Are you related to any of the houses in the south, even the minor ones?'

She shook her head. 'No, Ruler of Tamra, just as I said yesterday.'

'Ah yes, all you want is my son's heart? Such a small thing to ask for, yet by winning his heart you win a realm.' He sighed and turned back to Mannok. 'And you, Prince, you insist on marrying this woman?'

Weren't they already married, at least by the customs of Rasel's people? Yet, wiser not to remind his father of that fact. He lifted his chin. 'Yes, Papa.'

His father rubbed his jaw. 'You have known each other for the briefest time. Does it occur to you this might be a fleeting infatuation?'

'Papa, you agreed.'

'Yes, I did, a concession we may all regret.' He looked at Rasel, his eagle eyes hooded. 'She has a quick tongue, intelligence and courage, at least, and knowledge of our literature and history, if not our customs. Still, you may change your mind.'

'I doubt it, sir.'

'Ha, well young love surges ahead blind to the snags and submerged rocks before it.'

'Better the risks of love than never to have loved at all,' Rasel said.

Papa sat back on the throne, one eyebrow cocked. 'So says a girl who is ... what, not yet eighteen? What do you know of love? Marriage is not dolls' play or a piece of romantic make-believe, my dear. It is a solemn business and, in this case, a matter of state importance.'

'I am older than I look, man of Tarka. Is that what guided your own choice of a partner? Matters of state?'

'Your Majesty, will suffice, my dear. As to my marriage to the Kupanna, it was arranged when I had barely lost my first baby teeth and she just weaned.'

'How cruel to fetter the future of young children so.'

'Cruel is a harsh word indeed, young lady. I didn't impose an arranged marriage on my son and look at the chaos that's brought my realm. To my mind, cruel is civil war ripping life and limb from young warriors, ripping apart families and sending violence, starvation and pestilence stalking across the land.'

'War is terrible, I agree, yet the foundations of your realm can't be strong if love of a single couple tips the balance into chaos. If you knew love as we do—'

'You think I don't?' Papa leant forward on the throne with a sudden flare of emotion. His hands gripped the armrests. 'Impudent girl. You know nothing.'

Rasel met the Kapok's blazing gaze without flinching, her head tilted a fraction. Mannok stepped closer to her, to protect her if necessary. His father had fallen in love and secretly married a Kiprissa of the Nolmec, Akrad's granddaughter and Ista's mother. But, because that union had not worked, didn't mean that he and Rasel could not find happiness together.

'You do not love my mother.' The bitter words burst from his mouth before he knew he would say them.

Papa sat back, the full force of his attention now on him. 'You think I do not love her?'

'You begged your father not to marry her. And ...' Since Papa defeated Akrad and returned from the war, he and Mama had sparred together as constantly as sunshine and rain. Though, maybe Papa bringing Ista to the Palace after North Pass had something to do with that.

Papa's eyelids fluttered and he ran a large hand over his face. Grief for the woman he loved so fiercely and buried as a young man?

'That was close to twenty years ago. Ancient history.' His lips twisted. 'Still, you are wrong to think I don't love your mother. Mind you, I'm not her favourite person at the moment. She thinks this fiasco is all my fault and no doubt she is right.'

Mannok didn't know what to say.

Rasel squeezed his hand, her face thoughtful. She took a step forward and bowed. 'I have been presumptuous, man ... Your Majesty. I apologise.'

'So the young firebrand can back down. I should warn you, Rasel, that constantly challenging your Kapok is not considered acceptable or safe.'

'I thank you for the warning, man of ... Your Majesty. My people are known for their frankness.'

'So I have noticed. But the morning grows long and we have business to attend to.'

'Business?' Mannok and Rasel asked together.

Papa waved a hand. 'We would normally negotiate the marriage settlement with your parents, Rasel. If you could tell me which village they come from, I can send for them.'

'My people are of the Forest Folk. They move often and you would not find them.'

Papa raised his eyebrows. 'Then who will speak for you? Do you have relatives nearby?'

'I can speak for myself.'

Papa's eyes narrowed. 'No doubt. And your dowry?'

'I doubt we have anything to offer that your people would value. I am sorry—our wealth is in the memories of our ancestors, the future of our children, the songlines of the Maker and our loyalty to each other. It is a long time since the children of Tamrak have valued such things.'

'Some would say that such things are invaluable, but it is hard to use them as barter. A princess should have a dowry. If your parents can't provide a tangible one, then I guess the Throne will have to. And we will determine titles and prerogatives following the happy event. Is that acceptable to you, Rasel of the Forest Folk?'

'It is more than I expected.'

'Is it, indeed? We will settle a fitting endowment on you and any future children if ... forgive me ... when you marry your prince.'

'You are gracious, son of M.... Your Majesty.'

Papa grunted. 'So you do have some manners. Which reminds me. Mannu, in all the commotion, I believe we forgot to wish you birthday felicitations last night.'

Mannok flushed. 'Understandable in the circumstances, sir.'

'Quite. I've set aside the Silisean Palace for the use of your betrothed, and for you both after the wedding. And I will increase your allowance to be more commensurate to your married state.'

'My thanks, Papa.' A pinprick of nerves mantled his skin at how reasonable Papa was being. 'Is that all?'

'No of course not.' Papa's eyes bored into him. 'You have not forgotten the other conditions, I trust.'

'No, Papa. When—'

Papa smiled thinly. 'I've asked Kaptan Jakan to draw up the cost of reparations to the guards. As for the other matters, present yourself to the good Kaptan tomorrow morning and for wall-duty five days after later.'

So he had a day to spend with Rasel before that unpleasant business of the lash. 'Then by your leave, sir?'

Papa chuckled. 'Not so fast.' He beckoned Bitjarnan over. 'Send for a couple of chairs for the Prince and the Lady. And we will need some scribes to record agreements. This may take a while.'

Great, just what he needed on his last free day, paperwork.

Chapter Forty-Three: Encounters

Lumi

Lumi stepped out of the large emporium. The gilded writing on the sign read, 'Sarak Spice Merchant: best quality spices and herbs.' So why didn't it have the herbs they needed. Around her, merchants set up stalls and hawkers spruiked their wares. A soft mist dewed the canopies and covers with tiny pearls. A hint of pink blushed the purple-grey clouds shrouding the snow-covered twin peaks.

'That was a waste of time,' she said. 'Where next?' They'd tried all the herbal suppliers along Upper Market Street.

Lady Rizanna shrugged her shoulders. 'What about Crooked Street?'

Lumi frowned. Crooked Street bisected the lower west district, a poorer part of the city. Yet the Kupanna needed the herbal concoctions to relieve her pain and nausea.

When Lumi had arrived to attend her first thing this morning, Kupanna Marra lay in bed, pale and limp and distressed with a sick headache. The Kapok wasted no time in sending Lumi to replenish Marra's medicinal herbs and she couldn't return without them. Not only was the Kupanna relying on her, she had to stay in the good graces of the Prince's parents if she was to have any hope of winning the Prince. She placed a hand over her mouth to stifle a yawn. Restless dreams of losing Mannok forever had disrupted the little sleep she'd managed to secure last night.

Rizanna grabbed her arm. 'Is that Waren?'

Diagonally across from them, two warriors stood at the entrance of a smaller shop bearing the sign 'Tuson's Tasty Treats', facing the other way. One had a rich chocolate brown cloak edged with the insignia of the Puma clan, the other's blue cloak looked more threadbare with a faded yarma insignia. Both stood at about the same height and build, with similar colouring, but with different bearings and ranks. The sign obscured the number and nature of feathers of their headdresses.

'Yes!' Rizzi clapped her hands. 'I'd recognise my brother's wide stance anywhere. And I think that's Garo with him. Maybe Mannok's ducked into Tuson's. Let's check it out.'

Before Lumi could reply, Rizzi darted across the stone-flagged road towards her brother, dashing out of the way of a cart loaded with potatoes of different shapes, sizes and hues.

Lumi picked up the long skirt of her tunic and followed her friend, avoiding the worst of the puddles. Would that woman be inside with the Prince, or would he be alone? How could she wean Mannok off that wild beauty and win him over?

'Waren,' Rizzi called. 'Is the Prince with you?'

Waren turned and smiled broadly. 'Rizzi, what are you doing here?'

'We're looking for some chinkona bark and Wiri root for the Kupanna. Sarak's doesn't have it.' Lumi said.

'You could try Zusak's or Anna's in Crooked Street.' Waren shifted his long spear in the crook of his elbow and bowed, stiff and formal as Lumi reached them. 'Lady Lumi.'

She inclined her head. 'Is there nowhere closer, Lord Waren?'

Garvin spun round, his eyes meeting hers then dropping away. He nodded a silent greeting.

Waren shrugged. 'I would accompany you but I'm due at the wall. It's a rough area.' He clapped his companion on the shoulder. 'Garo, you can escort the ladies along Crooked Street.'

'It would be my honour,' Garvin responded, his genial face unusually solemn.

Rizzi frowned. 'Then, Mannok is not with you?'

'No,' Garvin said. 'Haven't seen the Prince at all this morning, but I believe he and Lady Rasel are in meetings with the Kapok.'

Lumi raised her eyebrows. 'What are you doing on wall duty, Lord Waren?'

'I had a run-in with a certain Prince who needs to grow up. The spiders and interminable practical jokes are bad enough, but with his rash attack at Pine Stand Gap and now this.'

Lumi bristled at the unfair criticism of Mannok. Last year, Mannok's pranks had driven her crazy, but apart from the spider episode with Kerri, he'd not pulled a stunt like that since Ista left. Waren made him sound spoilt and feckless.

Garvin shifted his feet and cleared his throat. 'With respect, my Lord, he is Prince Royal. To persist in contradicting him was unwise. And he had the right of it. We found the shortcut he'd promised the day after you left and reached the Lodge three days early.'

'Humph.'

'Besides,' Lumi lifted her chin, 'The Kapok commended him for his fast thinking and bravery at Pine Stand Gap.'

'I wonder what Trasin thinks about that?'

'You can't blame Mannu for the Nolmec ambush, Waren.' Rizzi shivered. 'He could have been killed.'

'You weren't there, Waren.' Garvin nodded. 'We're all sorry about Trasin's injury, but we would have sustained many more losses if we had stayed pinned down as we were.'

'Perhaps. But what about demanding to marry a woman he barely knows in front of the Kapok and the nobles of Tamra—is that a mature act?'

'That's not Mannok,' Rizzi said with a sharp nod. 'She's enchanted him.'

Lumi shivered and pulled her cloak tighter. Did Rizzi have the right of it? There was something different about this woman, Rasel. Her skin, so like Ista's or Akrad's for one thing. Or her father's, an inner voice suggested. But there was something uncanny about Rasel. And the way Mannok looked at her, as though she were life itself.

'What does he see in her? A peasant.'

Waren tugged his chin. 'I can see why Mannok is taken with her. And she isn't uneducated. And I've never heard anyone sing as beautifully as she did last night.'

'Mannok thinks she may be a survivor of the Shanti Royal House, perhaps a great-granddaughter of Sil,' Garvin said.

'That could explain her skin and her knowledge of the classics,' Waren said. 'But even so, to present her as his betrothed without permission or discussion with his father. And before the gathered nobles of Tamra. What was he thinking?'

'And what if she is Shanti?' Rizzi threw up her arms. 'If so, she could be plotting revenge. Did not Tellek Kapok massacre her family for their treachery against the Throne of Tamra?'

'No, I don't think she would,' Garvin said.

'It doesn't seem likely.' Waren spoke at the same time.

'See what I mean? She has enchanted you too, Waren.' Lumi shook her head. Even sensible Waren and loyal Garvin were taken in by Rasel's wild, dark looks. What hope did her Mannok have? If only the Kapok was right and the interloper would be shown up for what she really was, a low-born chancer.

Waren chuckled. 'I'm a happily married man, Lumi. But I will tell Uncle Rokkan your theories, girls. I better go—I don't want to be penalised with more of this cursed wall duty for being late!' Balancing his spear, he bowed and headed back towards Royal Parade.

He had only gone a few paces when he turned back. 'Oh, by the way sis, I forgot.' He pulled a small parcel out of his tunic and threw it to Rizzi. 'Happy birthday.'

With a wave, he sprinted down the street and disappeared around the corner, towards the wall and the main gate.

'Let's get these herbal compounds for the Kupanna then, Lady Lumi, Lady Rizanna,' Garvin said as he headed up the hill.

* * *

Garvin was a reliable and courteous guide, leading them straight to Zusak's Herbarium and escorting them back to the Palace. The mist lifted from the mountains and the clouds parted, revealing glimpses of washed-out blue sky as they entered the forecourt.

Garvin bowed. 'Excuse me, ladies. I better see if Mannok needs me today.'

'I was surprised to see you without him, Garo. You and Mannok are inseparable,' Rizzi said.

His mouth twisted a second before wavering into a smile. He shrugged. 'Mannu has other priorities now.'

Garvin looked like a lost puppy and Lumi resisted the urge to hug him. She touched his arm with her fingertips. 'He will soon remember his friends.' Or so she hoped.

A smile warmed his face, a flash of the old Garvin. He bowed low and sprinted toward the entrance of the Palace.

Lumi and Rizzi, arm in arm, followed at a slower pace.

The sun slipped out from behind a bank of clouds, warming their cheeks and evaporating the milky beads of moisture on their cloaks. A dog barked in the Royal kennels, the clang of metal on metal came from the smithy near the stables and a tarrawong trilled in the gardens on the other side.

'... a different priority now.' Lumi stiffened at the sound of Father's cutting voice. He didn't sound happy.

He stood in the shadow of the Palace, a stocky young noble of the Puma clan standing close to him. Father lowered his voice, continuing to make his point with his hands. Who was Father talking to? He looked familiar, not unlike Waren in build and face. Rizzi would know.

Father looked up, frowned, then beckoned her to join him.

She touched Rizzi's arm. 'It's Father. He wants me.'

'Is that Adjunct Puran with him?'

'Puran ... oh, he's Trasin's older brother and your cousin, isn't he?'

'Yes.' Rizzi stopped and pulled her arm free. 'Give me the box of herbs. I'll take it to Aunt Marra.'

'Lumi!' Father strode toward them, Adjunct Puran trailing behind.

'Lord Haka, Puran, we ... I have an urgent errand for the Kupanna.' Rizzi thrust out her hands. Lumi pulled the package from her robes and gave it to her friend.

'Wait, Lady Rizanna. Adjunct Puran would be delighted to escort you on your errand of mercy,' Father said.

Rizzi licked her lips and, after a slight hesitation, nodded. 'As you say, Lord Haka.'

Puran swept his arm in an expansive gesture. 'Lead the way, Rizanna.'

The man's face looked sullen, no doubt because of the tongue lashing from her father. Though for what reason, Lumi wasn't sure. Maybe some council business? With Lukarn still in the north and Waren on wall duty, Puran might stand in for the Markan of the Northern Marches.

Rizanna and her noble cousin soon disappeared through the Palace doors. Lumi clutched her hands together, stilling their slight tremble. What did Father want with her now?

'The Kupanna not well?'

298

'No, Father. She has a headache.'

'Hmmm. Not surprising given her darling son's recent antics. So, what is that sly jaguar up to? Did you find out?'

'If ... if you mean—' She stopped. If someone overheard Father's disrespectful words of the Kapok ... She no longer trusted what he would do with her information. Yet the Kapok had said she could tell him.

'Get it out, girl.'

She cleared her throat, her chest tight. 'He's hoping Mannok will get over the infatuation.'

Father snorted. 'Ever the optimist, but I'm not so sure after her performance at the banquet last night.' He raised his sculpted eyebrows. 'She outshone every woman there and she showed you up, Lumi.'

Lumi looked down at the cobblestones of the courtyard. Not just me, you too Father. Not that she would dare say the words.

'It doesn't suit our purposes if he marries her and starts having children by the ten, as likely as not with a peasant girl.'

Lumi lifted her head. 'Father, you are not planning to do anything rash.'

'Don't be silly. Surely, no one could doubt my loyalty to the throne. But you need to try harder and smarter, girl, for the sake your precious Prince.' He gave a lean, hungry smile. Guiding her by the shoulders, he led her into the Palace.

Chapter Forty-Four: Job offers

Dinnis

Honeyed afternoon light burnished the glass of the mullioned windows and gilded the spray of the fountain in the centre of the courtyard outside. Dinnis walked through fragrant courtyards and the spacious rooms of the Silesian Palace with a critical eye. Everything seemed in order, nothing out of place. Divans draped with woven throws, large floor cushions, potted plants and low ebony tables dotted the main reception room. Tapestries of waterfalls, woodland scenes and birds adorned the walls. The son of the second cook lit the long candles in the candelabras, while his cousin Leesa, a young girl of fourteen, arranged a display of flowers. Appetising smells wafted from the kitchen, accompanied by the noisy clatter of cooking.

Dinnis scrubbed his face and yawned so wide his jaw cracked. He'd started on preparing the rooms for Rasel before sunrise, making arrangements, seeing to repairs, assigning staff, checking furnishings and fittings, stocking the kitchen, bringing across tapestries, linen and more from the main palace, ensuring that the Silesian quarters were habitable, indeed pleasant and comfortable.

Now Anna's herbal shop called to him like the promise of a heated meal after a three-day tramp in the wilderness. Hard to know where he stood with Laetil, who could have given up on an apprentice who was absent far more than he was present for most of this year, but Anna and the rest of the family would welcome him. A decision for another day. Tonight, he needed to sleep and tomorrow he'd visit Anna, if he didn't get lumbered with another job first.

'Petrak.'

'Yes, sir.' The young man lit the last candle and blew out the long wooden sliver.

'Send someone to the Prince to inform him the rooms are prepared for Lady Rasel.'

'Yes, sir.'

Dinnis slung his satchel over his shoulder and headed for the entrance.

Rasel's silvery laugh came from the large front courtyard outside.

Dinnis stood still. Had he imagined it?

Wind rustled through the branches in the orchards surrounding this secondary palace. And, yes, the smack of fast footsteps and the hum of Mannok's tenor voice outside, then louder in the entrance hall.

Dinnis let out his breath. 'Never mind. I'll tell him myself.'

The door of the front reception room swung open and Mannok swept in with Rasel on his arm. His face lit up with an infectious laughter, reflected in Rasel's starlit eyes.

After a few strides, Mannok stopped and turned in a slow circle, surveying the room. His eyes snagged on Dinnis.

Dinnis bowed. 'Your Highness.'

'By the moons, this is not what I expected.'

Dinnis frowned. 'It does not meet your approval?' What had he missed?

'But it's beautiful.' Rasel twirled around, hands crossed over her chest. 'I could imagine I'm not contained by walls and I am so glad the tapestries celebrate natural beauty and simple themes rather than battle scenes.'

'So it is, Rasel. Exquisite and finished, when I expected to find chests half unpacked, walls still bare. It's a marvel you managed all this in a day. Show us around, my friend.'

Dinnis led them through the reception rooms, a dining room, kitchens and the vegetable gardens in an enclosed courtyard, offices and separate accommodation for staff, and then eventually the private rooms including a spacious bedchamber with a small courtyard beyond tall, shuttered doors.

The tour ended in the small dining room adjacent to the bedchamber. Rasel snuggled close to the Prince's side, her dark eyes sparkling with delight.

'You have worked hard,' Mannok said. 'Well done.'

Dinnis shrugged, uncomfortable at his half-brother's praise. 'All the major renovations and repairs were done when the Limarians moved in earlier in the year. And I found most of the furnishings and tapestries in the Palace.'

Mannok raised his eyebrows. 'Still, to bring it all together. To choose the pieces. You reveal another hidden talent, my friend.' He closed his eyes and sniffed the air. 'And something smells delicious.'

'Your camp master, Palarn, agreed to act as chief cook until you can make other arrangements. He is preparing the evening meal.'

Mannok clapped Dinnis on the shoulder. 'You think of everything. We will eat as soon as the food is ready.'

'A wonderful idea, Prince of Tamra. Even though we have done nothing all day but peruse and sign bits of paper covered with fancy words and columns of figures, I am famished.'

'Then, I will take my leave, Your Highness, Lady Rasel.'

'Oh, but you should join us, friend Dinnis.' Rasel took his hands and squeezed them. 'Enjoy the fruits of your hard labour.'

Dinnis' hands tingled at her touch.

Mannok folded his arms and his face remembered how to scowl.

Dinnis freed his hands and stepped backwards banging against the wall. 'Thank you, my lady, you are very gracious, but I would not wish to intrude.'

'It would not be an intrusion, would it Mannok?'

Mannok creased his nose. 'Yes, right. Do join us, Dinnis.'

He should have refused again, but he didn't. Soon they were seated on the scattered cushions, Mannok and Rasel on one side of the low table, Dinnis opposite. Palarn, with the help of Pedrak and Leesa, served platters of seasonal fruit, nuts, yarma cheese, cold meats, cornbread and potato cakes, fruit juices and spiced birch wine. An awkward silence ensued while they passed each other dishes of food and Dinnis poured the drinks.

'How did my lady enjoy the banquet last night?' Dinnis finally said to break the tension.

Rasel looked up from her plate, once again laden with fruit and vegetables and a little cheese, but no meat. 'It felt overwhelming after a long, event-filled day. I am not used to crowds and I'm still adjusting to your customs.'

Mannok stroked her shoulder. 'I must admit, I find the endless formality of such affairs rather trying. Though at least this year the speeches were omitted.'

'Speeches, my love?'

'In the Prince's honour. Celebrating his great talents and accomplishments,' Dinnis said.

Mannok grimaced, but Rasel smiled.

'I am sure you have a great many, my love. Though, I do find the Tamrin custom of heaping out extravagant praise with sometimes bald-faced insincerity strange. The Lady Lumi for instance showered me with pleasing words, yet she clearly despises me.'

Mannok stirred beside her. 'Despise is too strong a word, my love.'

Dinnis snorted. 'Painted smiles, false friends and intrigue, it's the way of court. It took me time to adjust to it after I arrived at the Palace.' In some ways the duplicity was worse than Arkon Akrad's unchecked spite. 'Lady Lumi is jealous, as no doubt is every other eligible young lady of the court.'

'Jealous?' Rasel laughed. 'Whatever for?'

'For winning the love of the Prince, thus dashing fondest hopes.'

Rasel looked thoughtful. 'Perhaps you are right.'

'You exaggerate, my friend.' Mannok gave Dinnis a hard look as he sipped his birch wine. 'Our table companions were less than kind, sweet Rasel. But you dazzled them with your knowledge of the classics and divine singing, and in time, most of them will appreciate you as much as I do.'

Leesa entered the room and removed the empty platters.

'Wait awhile,' Dinnis pushed back his plate and stood up. 'My lady Rasel, this is Leesa. She is helping Petrak serve. I've taken the liberty of engaging her as your personal maid.'

'What would she do?' Rasel asked.

'Assist with your dressing, do any errands you require, anything you want really.'

'I can do those things myself.'

The young girl bit her lip, a sheen forming over soft brown eyes.

Rasel looked distressed. 'Why is she crying?'

Dinnis shrugged. 'She is afraid that if you have found her deficient it might reflect badly on her and shame her family.' He'd reassure the lass before she left tonight.

Mannok shifted against the cushions and took Rasel's hand.

'My love, I know this is new to you, but it would be a good idea to take on a maid.'

'Just think of her as a younger sister,' Dinnis said. The Prince gave him an incredulous look, but he continued nevertheless. 'She knows palace protocol and is honest, hardworking, discreet and good natured.'

Rasel smiled. 'I've always wanted a younger sister. It is so trying being the youngest of nine. Everyone is forever telling you what to do or acting as if you don't know anything.'

Mannok blinked. 'Nine? I often wished my parents had other children.' He paused a moment, no doubt, thinking that he did have a half-sister, Ista, the one sibling he knew about. 'Nine does seem a lot.' He smiled, entwining his fingers with Rasel's.

Rasel smiled back at him, her face radiant. 'I hope we have many children.' She raised their joined hands and kissed them. 'If you think it wise, then I will accept young Leesa's assistance.'

Leesa sank to her knees. 'Thank you, my lady.'

'That will be all, lass,' Dinnis said.

Leesa dipped her head and backed out of the room, balancing the empty platters. Maybe it was time to take his leave. Surely the servants could act as chaperones to this besotted pair.

Rasel turned and looked straight at him. 'Whatever happened to your sister, man of the north?'

Mannok startled. 'Sister? I didn't know you had any family, Dinnu? You are an orphan, are you not?'

'Yes, my mother died when I was three and my father at the battle of North Pass.' Slide it, this was awkward. If Rasel blurted out that Ista was his sister, then Mannok would know the whole truth of it. Not that he minded, but he didn't know how the Palace would react or Mannok, for that matter.

'But you have a sister?'

'We were separated after the battle at North Pass and grew apart. Anyway, she has done well for herself and would not wish to be reminded that she had a brother.'

'She must have done very well for herself indeed if she would disdain one of my age-mates.'

Dinnis shrugged and looked down. 'I'm not exactly the pick of the bunch nor do I have any prospects she would recognise.'

'Hmm, well, speaking of prospects, would you like to be my madomo? You've shown a flair for organising a household.'

'Maybe you should at least wait till you see how much metal and goods I've outlaid on your behalf,' Dinnis said, his lips twitching. Then he shook his head, 'You should offer Palarn the job. He has served you loyally as your camp master and would make a competent madomo.'

'Well,' Mannok hesitated. 'My Master of the House, then. It's an honourable position.'

'Yes, indeed, far too honourable for me, Your Highness.'

Mannok's green eyes hardened. 'You refuse me a second time? Why? I could hardly offer you higher.'

Dinnis hesitated, choosing his words carefully and keeping his voice even. 'The Prince's Master of the House will in time be one of the future Kapok's right-hand men. Such a position is too important to be offered on a whim.'

'This is no whim. By the pit, man, you have shown yourself to be loyal, resourceful, competent and courageous. I wish to thank and reward you.'

Rasel leaned forward, her gaze intense. 'My love is right, at the ruins, at the waterfall, in the Throne Room and now here, you have done more than duty alone requires, man of the north.'

Mannok nodded. 'I've owed you my life on more than one occasion.' He hesitated then, lifting his head, added, '... and my father's life too, though I did not appreciate it at the time.'

'I owe my life to you also, Your Highness.' Dinnis traced the raised patterns on the small pot of chillied castana nuts. Mannok's mood floated high on love like flood-drift during the Heavy Rains, yet how long would that last? Even if he wanted it, he could not accept such an elevated position in the Prince's household without stirring up Lukarn and Sparak and Marra's suspicions of his intentions.

'More reason to accept.' The Prince folded his arms across his chest and glared. 'It is not customary to refuse a Prince's request to serve.'

Dinnis stilled. 'I mean no disrespect, my Lord Prince. I am honoured by your generous offer. Yet, if my opinion is of any value, I would suggest that you appoint your cousin Waren as your Master of Horse and ...' He hesitated, glanced at the pot of chillied nuts. He'd stake his life on Garvin's loyalty. 'And Garvin as your Master of House.'

'Garvin would be an excellent choice. But Waren? You are ribbing me, aren't you?'

'No, Your Highness.'

Mannok shook his head, jumped up and strode around the room. 'Waren? My cousin shows me no respect, second guesses my every decision, acts like he knows everything because he is a few years older and, unlike Estolik, doesn't know when to stop talking. Why would I make him my Master of Horse? The man is insufferable.'

Dinnis swallowed, then shrugged. Might as well fall the whole distance. 'Why? Because Waren isn't afraid to speak his mind, does not hide his opinion behind duplicity, and is in fact intelligent and knowledgeable if a little overbearing with it.'

The Prince narrowed his eyes, 'Humph, on those criteria you would be a perfect candidate for the job.'

'But I am not deemed much of a warrior or counted highly among the nobility. Besides, Waren has this advantage over me. However much he may infuriate you, the Prince would need a solid reason to harm his cousin and the eldest son of the fourth most powerful man in the land. I have no such protection and I am strangely fond of living.' And your parents would never agree to the appointment.

Rasel stirred. 'Dinnis, Mannok would never harm you.'

'If you say so, my lady.'

Mannok closed his eyes and took a deep breath. 'Just for the record, I have not killed any of my age-mates, however tempted to do so I may be.' He opened his eyes and glared at Dinnis. 'I will admit to having a temper, but the fact that you are still breathing is surely evidence that it is not ungovernable.'

Fair point. A bubble of laughter escaped Dinnis and, for once, he went with it, his eyes watering.

Mannok's scowl deepened, then vanished as his lips twitched into a reluctant smile.

'Alright, alright. I will think on your suggestions, but what position should I give you? Court jester may be tempting but not appropriate at conveying my level of gratitude for your loyalty.' He threw out his arms. 'Kaptan of the Prince's security? Keeper of the Records?' He stopped, raised an eyebrow. 'My Head of Scouts? Name it, what position do you want?'

'You know, my love, you could set him free.'

Dinnis' heart lurched. If only that could be.

'What? Why would I do that? And what would he do? The Palace provides for him, is his only family.'

'But Dinnis is apprenticed to a healer,' Rasel said. 'Could he not use his knowledge of healing herbs to help others?'

Dinnis flinched and waited for the hammer to fall.

Mannok's eyes widened. 'What are you talking about Rasel? He can't be apprenticed to a healer. He is a member of my band, a warrior and my sworn liegeman.'

'That is what he told me.'

'One of his teases then. Isn't that right, Dinnu?'

Dinnis looked up for a moment through the window at the Alumi rising in the western sky. He could not lie, not to Rasel. 'The lady tells the truth.'

'What?'

Dinnis swallowed. 'I am apprenticed to a healer, to Laetil from Greyhaven Street. I have been these four years. Soon I can set up in my own right.'

For a moment nobody spoke. The sough of the wind in the trees and the chuckle of the fountains an ironic contrast to the crackling tension in the room. Dinnis gripped the side of the table, waiting for the Prince's anger, for the consequences, whatever they might be.

'Dinnis, you're speaking a load of yarma droppings. If you had been apprenticed outside the palace, Markan Lukarn, Kaptan Jakan or even my father would have had the courtesy to inform me,' the Prince said stiffly.

'They did not make the arrangements. I did.'

'How could you possibly pay the apprenticeship fee? When would you have time to do your duties? This is nonsense, man.'

Dinnis lifted his chin and met Mannok's troubled gaze. 'Mostly I skipped the midday meal and afternoon weapons practice. I made myself available in the early morning. I paid the fee from metal I earned selling herbs and doing errands about the city. I have no wish to spend my life as a washed-up warrior in the city or the Palace Guard. Besides, it's what I want to do, have always wanted to do.'

'By the moons, I've never heard of such a thing.' Mannok shook his head, his frown deepening. He dropped down beside Rasel and drummed his fingers on the table. He gave a short laugh. 'I don't know whether I should be impressed at your ingenuity or insulted that you find being in my service of such little value.'

'Your Highness, it's not that—'

Mannok held up a hand. 'I know what my lady would wish. Very well, I release you from your daily duties as part of my band, but not from my service. You will attend me, should I wish it, and I'll appoint you as my physician.'

Dinnis' eyes widened, his eyebrows shooting up, 'You will release me?'

'That is what I said. I want you in the groom's party at the wedding. I will take your other suggestions under advisement.'

Dinnis let out a long slow breath. His dream made actual. He should grab it with two hands before the Prince had second thoughts.

But how could he abandon Rasel to the Palace? True, Rasel and Mannok only had eyes for each other. True, the Prince had made good on his promises. And true, Rasel proved to be different from the perfect, ethereal paragon he'd imagined over the last nine years. Yet she was still the first person to believe in him, to not betray him, and he doubted very much that as innocent and goodhearted as she was, Rasel knew the strains and dangers she'd face living in the Palace. She would need a friend and protector in the days to come.

'Isn't that what you wanted, friend Dinnis?' Rasel asked.

'Yes, I'm trying to work out what the catch is.'

Rasel laughed merrily. 'Sometimes, I think you two are as alike as two river stones in the stream. The Prince cannot accept a simple compliment and you can't accept a gift freely given.'

Dinnis and Mannok looked at each other and grinned.

Rasel leant forward and touched his hand. 'You should accept, man of the north. Don't be concerned for me.'

Dinnis startled. Could she read his thoughts? A burr of joy tickled his ribs. As Mannok and presumably Rasel's physician, he could look out for her. 'You will need to square it with your father, the Kapok.'

'I will. So, do you accept?'

'Yes. A multitude of thanks Your Highness, I will not forget this.'

The Prince smiled back. 'Everyone in Tamra is trying to get a Palace position. You must be the only one fighting to get out of one. And I think I like you the better for it. Now, maybe you have some other business to attend to?'

'Yes, Your Highness.' Forget sleep, he'd head to Anna's tonight and tell her the good news.

Chapter Forty-Five: Reckoning

Rasel

Rasel sat cross-legged on a woven rug on the floor opposite her Prince, with the remnants of their shared breakfast on the platters between them. Morning light streamed through the large windows and doors in the airy eating room, illuminating the tapestries and colourful mosaic floor. Sunbirds, flycatchers and mountain finches flitted in the foliage and flowers in the adjoining walled courtyard. With the soothing tinkling of falling water and the song of wind in the trees, she could imagine herself resting in the woodland forests in the foothills of the White Mountains.

'I'm pleased you could join me for the morning meal again, my love.'

Mannok nodded without looking at her. He traced the black and red pattern in the glaze of the empty clay dish with his fingers. Callouses from wielding a spear and half-healed blisters from shifting rocks at Mist Falls village covered his strong hands. Today he donned a plain tunic, breeches and green cloak, his reddish-brown hair windblown from his walk from the bachelor quarters to join her before sunrise. Yet he'd said few words during the meal and yesterday's bright humour had subsided into a more pensive mood. Was he having second thoughts about her? She wouldn't believe it.

'Why so thoughtful, my love?'

He looked up and met her gaze. He smiled and his green eyes lit up like fireflies on a dark night. 'Sorry. I'm poor company this morning.'

'Something you want to talk about?'

'Yesterday, we worked out the reparations to the guards with Kaptan Jakan.'

She nodded. That seemed only fair, given the men acted out of loyalty to their Kinleader, their Kapok. 'And?'

'So this morning, I have the appointment in the discipline room. And the sooner that unpleasant business is over, the better.'

A cold icicle lodged at the base of her spine. 'I don't understand. If your father has agreed to our marriage, why insist on further punishments? And why do they fall on you, but not on me?'

'The punishment is not for wanting to marry you, sweet Rasel, but for publicly defying my father. The Kapok cannot disregard such a flagrant undermining of his authority and retain the respect of the clans.'

'But surely respect should be built on loyalty and love, not fear. And enforced by such a barbaric physical punishment. I understand increasing your duty shifts, but this? He is your father.'

'Should there be one rule for me and another for everyone else? Under previous Kapoks, Leeran, Tellek, even my grandfather, Martal, Prince though I am, I would most likely be confined to darkest holding cell, even sentenced to the Red Leap for such public disrespect of the Throne.'

'I do not find such a thought reassuring, Prince of Tamra. My brothers, especially Davak, and my sister Rebekka, often disagree with Baba, even though he is Kinleader, but he would never take umbrage like this. To act so would undermine his authority far more than an open debate.' She knew the Filane's reputation as a violent people, but to see it with her eyes, to feel it in the flesh of the one she loved, shook her to the marrow of her bones.

He captured her hands and kissed them. She leaned closer and he wrapped his strong arms around her, enveloping her in his warmth and spicy scent.

'It's not the pain, sweet Rasel, but the shame of it that troubles me. Truly, it will soon be over. I am sure to find two-tens double wall duty the more onerous punishment, because every moment we're apart pains me more.'

'It's not right. It's not the way my people do things.' She blinked back the tears.

'That may be, my love. Yet this is the way we do things here.'

He brushed back the long tendrils of dark hair that had strayed over her face and whispered kisses on her eyes, her chin, her neck. Her heart's song hammered in her ears like a waterfall. She pulled his face down and pressed her lips against his. All other sounds receded. Time hushed.

They broke apart at the clatter of dishes. Leesa and another rosy-cheeked maid did their best to hide their obvious curiosity by looking at everything but them while they cleared away the platters and bowls on the table.

Mannok stood, pulling her up. 'I best go, my love. I will return soon enough.'

If he could endure it, then so could she, but she would not let him endure it alone. 'I will come with you, Prince of Tamra.'

'There is no need to distress yourself, dearest Rasel.'

She lifted her chin. 'I am distressed, it is true, but it would distress me more to let you bear this alone.'

He looked set to argue but took her hand instead. 'Walk me to the Palace then, but you need not come all the way, if you do not wish to.'

They strolled together into the courtyard, through the orchards, past the kitchens and entered the vast Palace by a covered walkway and the lower floor of the western atrium.

Mannok led them to a guarded door hallway along the tranquil pool. The eyes of the spear-bearing warriors widened when they saw her, but they saluted Mannok and together, she and Mannok stepped into the room.

A battle-scarred man with leaf-green eyes and closely cropped hair entered the room.

His eyes flicked to her, but he recovered quickly, and bowed low. 'Prince Mannok. Lady Rasel.'

Mannok squared his shoulder. 'Ah, Kaptan Jakan, you know why I'm here?'

'Yes, Your Highness.' The man of war's voice was gruff. He turned to one of the guards, 'Inform His Majesty, the Prince is here.' He looked back to Mannok, not quite meeting his eyes. 'Perhaps Your Highness, your companion ... ah the lady ... would prefer to wait outside until this business is over?'

Mannok let go of her hand but she held tight. 'My preference is to accompany my Prince. Please?'

Jakan's brow creased. 'Your Highness, that is irregular.' Mannok raised a brow. And the man of war subsided. 'As you wish, Your Highness. Come this way.'

Two guards and another man fell in behind them as the man of war led them to the end of a long airless corridor and down a flight of dank stone stairs into a square room dimly lit by three small high windows and smoky torches. No sound reached them except for the tap of soldiers' nail studded boots on the stone floor and their own heavy breathing. The weight of the dark earth straining against the stone-built walls, pressed down on them.

Rasel blinked as her eyes adjusted to the light. A stand holding weapons and other paraphernalia stood to the right side, a wooden stool and bucket full of water on the other. Against the far wall, a sturdy shoulder-high wooden pole with a cross piece stood like a tree blasted from lightning.

They followed the man of war to within a couple of tanis of the pole. Mannok took a deep breath and turned to face her.

'It's not too late to leave,' he said in a low voice.

She shook her head, not trusting herself to speak.

He squeezed her hand and then his arms were around her again, the rapid beat of his heart vibrating against her. He cupped her face in his hand and touched her lips in a long and lingering kiss.

The thud of boots came from the hallway. The light hunter's step of the son of Martal.

Her love pulled back. Behind him, the Kapok stood just inside the room.

'Kaptan Jakan, I obviously haven't been keeping up with recent developments in army discipline,' he said. 'A new preliminary stage perhaps?' He gave Rasel a long measuring look.

The man of war cleared his throat and bowed low to the son of Martal. 'Your Majesty. I … that is the young woman …'

'Never mind, man. Get on with it. That is, of course, if you are ready, Prince?'

Mannok flashed Rasel a half smile. He pulled his hands from hers and faced his father. 'Quite ready, Your Majesty.'

He unfastened his cloak and pulled his tunic over his head, exposing his well-muscled torso, and walked with slow measured steps to stand in front of the pole. A guard tied the Prince's arms, waist and ankles to the frame with wide leather thongs.

A hand fell on her shoulder. 'Stand back, lass.'

She twisted, shrugged his hand off her shoulder and moved a little apart from this man of blood. The son of Martal turned his gaze on his son, face as impassive as stone.

The two guards stood on either side of the Prince and alternatively brought the lash across his exposed upper back one, two, three, four, five times each. The sound of plaited leather on bare flesh was sickening, each stroke raising a red welted line which first bruised and, after the fourth lash beaded blood. Her love grunted at the eighth lash and groaned on the last.

Rasel clenched her hands into fists, her nails digging into her palms. Tears streamed down her cheeks.

The soldier stepped back, and the Kaptan of Tamra threw the bucket of water over the Prince's flinching back. The first guard untied the thongs securing the Prince, as the second guard supported him and helped him sit on the nearby stool. The third man, dressed in a long sleeveless tunic approached and began to apply salve and bandages.

Unable to bear it any longer, Rasel ran to her love and knelt at his feet. She caught his hands into her own. He sat up straighter and managed a smile. He freed his right hand and gently brushed her tears from her cheeks with his thumb.

'No need to cry, my love,' he said. 'It's over with now.'

When the healer had finished tying his bandages, the Prince stood up at once, and staggered forward. She slipped her arm around him and took his weight on her. She helped him put on his tunic and cloak.

'Can we leave this half-buried room?' she asked. 'I really don't like it.'

He laughed. 'I know what you mean.'

He looked at his father standing at the other end of the room, his arms folded across his chest, his golden eyes hooded and a muscle twitching in his cheek.

'Am I free to go, Your Majesty?'

Rokkan Kapok nodded once, then turned and strode from the room.

Mannok and Rasel followed him at a slower pace.

Chapter Forty-Six: Reception

Rasel

'Should we go back to the house in the orchards, my love?' Rasel asked.

Mannok grimaced. 'Yes, but I'd like to rest a few moments first.' He motioned to a long stone bench close to the atrium pool. Above them towered another two floors before reaching the open square of sky.

'What is up there?' she asked. They had no time for the tour he'd promised yesterday.

Mannok settled on the bench. 'Dinnis' favourite haunt. The Great Palace Library of Tarka. Rows and rows and rows of codices, parchments, plaques and scrolls. I'll take you there, but perhaps another day.' He closed his eyes and rested his head against the wall.

Rasel sat beside him and calmed her tumultuous thoughts.

Sometime later, a horn sounded three long notes from the direction of the main Palace Gate.

'Someone important arriving?' Rasel asked.

'Three notes for a Markan. That would be my uncle Lukarn and his entourage arriving from the north.'

The squeal of the main gate opening and the drumbeats of hooves and booted feet drifted into the open atrium from the courtyard at the front of the Palace. The mincing footsteps of the madomo sounded from the Great Hall.

Mannok shifted on the bench and sighed. 'I should greet my uncle. I'd rather introduce you to him before he hears the news from others.'

Rasel frowned. 'Is that wise? Shouldn't you rest, my love?'

'I can rest later.' He stood, swaying a little, took her arm and walked with her through the doorway at the eastern end of the atrium, through a short corridor and into the Great Hall.

Light fell through the sky panels in the lofty vaulted ceiling, painting bright rectangles on the flagstone floor. Near the entrance doors, a great staircase of dark bloodwood she had not noticed two nights before swept up to the balconies and the higher levels above. The entrance doors stood wide open to the blinding sunlight, letting in the sound of horses whinnying, the whistles and hums of yarmas and the shouts of guards and Palace helpers.

Mannok stood still, his face pale and sweaty beneath his tan. Rasel supported more of his weight. She knew the value of family reunions but worried he might strain his back.

A sturdy warrior with headdress of glossy brown and black feathers and a cloak embroidered with gold thread strode into the Hall. His grizzled hair receded at the temples, framing a blunt face and deep-set eyes. The little man, Bitjarnan, ushered in a group of travel-worn people behind him.

Footsteps came from the sweeping staircase.

'Lukarn, old puma.' A booming voice from above. 'You're late. I should clap you in fetters so you can consider the error of your ways.' The Kapok bounded down the stairs and toward the front doors. He clapped the warrior on the shoulder.

The other man sank to his knees. 'Ha, your pardon, Your Majesty. Next time I'll ignore the threat of Nolmec incursions on your northern border for the honour of sitting around in fancy dress and listening to inflated paeans to your young cub's achievements.'

The son of Martal waved him up. 'We skipped the speeches this year. Even so, you missed quite a show,' he said in a dour tone.

Mannok's uncle gave the son of Martal a questioning look, moving forward, making room for a matronly woman of median height and worried eyes. Her dark brown hair sprinkled with grey was partially hidden by a shawl that matched her long peach tunic. A young woman with a soft bloom to her face, a lad of fifteen or sixteen whose right arm ended in a bandaged stump, and three younglings followed them into the Hall.

The son of Martal's face softened. 'Lady Samara, as sweet as ever. And is this blushing beauty Lady Jarrah? No wonder young

Waren looks so pleased with himself.' The young woman, if she hadn't been blushing before, now glowed.

Both women dipped their heads, the older one responding. 'Your Majesty.'

The son of Martal turned to the lad. 'Trasin, your bravery at Pine Gap will not be forgotten.'

'I didn't do much, Your Majesty. Just followed orders. Prince Mannok and Dinnis are the real heroes.'

'Do not belittle yourself, lad. You acquitted yourself well.'

'That he did,' Mannok said, bestowing a warm smile on the young man. 'Glad you could travel, Trasin.'

Trasin turned and grinned at her prince and bowed. 'Your Highness.'

The son of Martal waved his arm toward her. 'Lukarn, let me present to you the source of all the drama. Rasel, daughter of Jazadek and Rutiah of the southern wilderness. Quite the mystery woman, our Rasel. Rasel, this is my brother-in-law, Lord Lukarn, Markan of the Northern Marches and his wife Markana Samara, their young children and their daughter-in-law, the Lady Jarrah and a budding surgeon, I hear. And this young warrior is Trasin, son of Challak and brother to Adjunct Puran of the Puma clan.'

The Markana flashed a kind smile, while Jarrah looked down clearly overwhelmed by all the attention. The sad-eyed lad bowed low, a little off balance.

Mannok sent her a look of love and admiration. 'The Lady Rasel is ... will be my wife. We are betrothed.'

His uncle's jaw dropped. 'Betrothed? Did I hear that right?'

'That your nephew, the heir to the throne of Tamra, has rejected the loveliest flowers of beauty and grace in all Tamra, indeed, in all the Five Lands to pluck the future Kupanna from the southern wilderness?' The son of Martal spread out his hands, palm upwards. 'Why in all the Wide Lands would that surprise you, Lukarn?'

The Markan's eyes remained fixed on Rasel, his resemblance to his sister, the Kupanna, apparent in the coffee-brown eyes and suspicious stare. '"Of the Southern Wilderness"? What sort of title is that? What is her clan? Her family?'

Rasel stood taller. 'I am of the Forest Folk, of Doryn's Kin.' Could she not make it clearer than that? Yet all she saw were puzzled stares. Were the children of Tamrak's memories so short, that they'd forgotten who had welcomed them to the Wide Lands?

Mannok's uncle opened and closed his mouth. He rubbed the back of his neck. 'And you and Marra agreed to this, Rokkan?'

Rasel closed her eyes, fighting a rising tide of anger. For half an alume now she had taken the slights and innuendos of this ignorant and violent people, allowing them to slide past her for the sake of her love. But the brutality of the whipping had shaken her.

'You may mock me, but my people come from an ancient and cultured lineage. We do not love lightly.'

Mannok's uncle scowled at her and she glowered back, her limbs itching to take on her jaguar form. But something, the voice of caution or the nudge of the Maker, held her back.

The son of Martal folded his arm across his broad chest. 'Rasel, daughter of Jazadek and Rutiah, peace. And yes, Lukarn, we have agreed to this madness. Are you questioning my judgement?'

The man of anger nodded, then shook his head. He gripped his hair. 'Ah, no, Your Majesty. I'm sure you have good reasons.'

His partner cleared her throat. 'Begging your favour, Your Majesty, we have travelled many days and are weary.'

The son of Martal turned his eagle eyes onto the woman and she wilted. His sombre face broke into an apologetic smile. 'Forgive me, Samara. In the excitement of the last few days, I seem to have lost my courtesy. Go, take your husband and family. Your suite is waiting.' He rounded on Mannok's uncle. 'I will see you in the council room in a couple of hours, not before.'

The Markan bowed low. 'As Your Majesty commands.'

The son of Martal now turned his penetrating gaze on her love. 'Mannu, go rest. I'll send Galen to check on you later.'

'My thanks, Your Majesty, but I think Dinnis can attend to my needs.'

A look Rasel could not read flitted across the Ruler of Tamra's face. 'As you wish. Your mother plans to hold an afternoon reception in two days in honour of your bride. You and Rasel should both attend.'

'Yes, Papa.'

The son of Martal strode off towards the stables.

Mannok's uncle groaned. 'I hope he is not planning on one of his reckless rides. And he has no guards with him. Perhaps I should go.'

'Lukarn son of Derik, you will not disobey the direct order of

317

your Kapok,' Samara caught his arm. 'Do not poke the angry jaguar with a stick.'

Mannok's uncle looked set to argue, then sighed. 'I go away for a few alume and the whole world falls apart.'

Mannok snorted. 'Hardly, uncle. Some might think it's been set to rights.' He tucked Rasel's hand into his own.

'Well, nephew, you may say so, but you are looking rather wan. Have you been ill?'

'No. I'm sure my father will explain. I'll see you at the reception.'

'Yes, of course, Mannok,' Lady Samarra patted his arm. 'Before you go, where can we find Waren? He'll want to know Jarrah has arrived.'

'No doubt he is on the wall,' Mannok said, his face suddenly as impassive as Dinnis.

'The wall? What is the son of a Markan doing wall duty for?' Mannok's uncle spluttered.

'Double duty to be exact,' the Prince of Tamra said. 'For insubordination.'

'Insubordination? Against whom?'

Mannok lifted his chin and met his uncle's outraged look head on. 'Against this overrated cub, his Prince. My apologies, aunt. Please don't let me hold you up any longer.'

He nodded to his uncle and Trasin, winked at the younglings and bowed to the ladies, though sweat beaded his face and his eyes darkened with pain.

Rasel took a firmer grip on his arm, and together they headed back to the western atrium, to the Silesian residence set among the trees.

* * *

Two days later, Mannok led Rasel up the main stairs that swept up into the shadowed balconies above. The sunlight flooding in from the glass panels in the vaulted roof brought out ruby glints from the rich polished timber, throwing into relief the intricate carvings of snarling jaguars, menacing koraktil and fearsome warriors carved into the balustrades. Everywhere she looked, an item, an emblem, a tapestry, a carving, a banner celebrated the bringing of death.

'Would your father really put your uncle in fetters for coming late to a family gathering?' she asked.

'What? No.' Her love paused on the stairs. 'I mean, the banquet is more than a family celebration. It also commemorates my father's accession to the throne. But Uncle Lukarn has the furthest distance to travel and holds the border against our deadliest foe and is, and has always been, Papa's most loyal liegeman. He and Papa have been friends since they were boys. Closer than brothers, like Garvin and I.'

'So, they were teasing each other.' Like when she and Semian or others of her Kin had mock fights in jaguar form. Yet, the Markan of the north's disdain for her was no playful act.

'The son of Derik detests me. From the moment he saw me. They all do.'

The Prince's eyes flickered. He caressed her shoulder. 'Give them time, my love. When they know you, they will grow to love you.'

How long would it take? 'And will your uncle persuade your father to withdraw his consent for our union?'

'No. Papa gave his word in front of the assembled nobles of Tamra. He will not renege.'

'But he doesn't want our love to succeed.'

Her love frowned then nodded. 'He's hoping one of us will change our minds. But that's not going to happen, is it?'

She smiled, now on known terrain. 'No, it's not.'

'Come, we risk being late.' Mannok tugged her hand and restarted the ascent. Once they reached the first-floor balcony, they headed for a gold embossed door on the far left, from which came a babble of voices like the rush of swift white water over rocks. The guards saluted and a servant hastened to open the doors.

The room, though a quarter of the size of the Throne Room, seemed light and airy with a high ceiling, bright tapestries and whitewashed walls. Three large casement windows overlooked the Palace entrance courtyard and adjoining gardens, and on the opposite wall, three arched doors, led out to a balcony along the side of an open-aired atrium and the open sky. An escape route of sorts. Small marble-topped tables were laden with trays of delicate bite-sized food and curved wooden stools with plush cushions and divans in rich red and gold fabrics were scattered about the room.

Three-tens of courtiers, draped in colourful tunics, cloaks, headdresses and jewellery stood or sat in small clusters around the tables, speaking and laughing and eating. To the right, musicians played a plaintive breathy tune. The light, colour, movement and numerous conversations swirled around her, each grabbing her attention in noisy conflict and making her head spin. She'd rather the known dangers of the jungle than this chaotic warrior ants' nest.

'Stay close, my love.'

Mannok kept hold of her hand and wove his way through the small clusters of nobles, acknowledging many with a nod or slight bow, ignoring their whispering and veiled stares. He came to rest in front of the group of stately ladies standing at the eastern end of the room. Rasel recognised the Kupanna Marra, the Markana Samara, Jarrah, Rizanna and Lumi. The Kupanna continued to speak to Samara and the sleek middle-aged woman with green eyes, Haka's wife and Estolik and Lumi's mother. She'd been introduced as Lady Yuta at the banquet.

'The yarn was definitely inferior. I had to send it back,' the Kupanna said.

'That is too bad, Your Majesty,' Lumi's mother murmured while Samara shook her head with an understanding smile.

Fragments of conversations from other nearby groups clashed and wove between the words swirling around her.

'So it's true, the Prince has fallen for a peasant woman ...'

'Did you see how she is dressed, so plain ...'

'I heard she was beautiful, but the colour of her skin, it can't be natural?'

'Indeed, Markana Yuta, it was very aggravating,' the Kupanna said.

'Have you tried Sumak Pichana in Lower Market Street, Your Majesty?' Samara said, 'I have always found them honest and reliable.'

'She is quite an unknown ...'

'So tall, taller than the Prince ...'

'Very unwomanly.'

'White like of bones, the colour of death ...'

The Kupanna smiled. 'Thank you for the recommendation, Samara, perhaps I will though I do not usually frequent Lower Market Street.'

'Nor would I, Your Majesty. It is very common and hardly the place for a lady of noble birth to patronise,' Yuta said.

'A rank commoner ...'

'What can he see in her ...'

'Perhaps it's a disease ...'

The space between Rasel's shoulder blades itched and her neck tingled at the malevolent stares boring into her back. The air thickened with malice, the voices and thoughts battering against her like moths against a lamp. The room spun around her.

'Could even be a spy ...'

'They say she's enchanted him ...'

'I hope it's not catching ...'

'Rasel ... Rasel!'

She started. Mannok's concerned jade eyes looked into hers. She gripped his arm, took a deep breath, trying to shut out the voices.

The Kupanna tapped her hand with a fan. 'In future I recommend you pay attention, Rasel. I am not used to repeating myself.'

'Please, forgive me, Your Majesty.'

'It is a bit stuffy in here with such a great crowd of people,' her love said. He smiled at his mother, his lips thinning. He turned to Rasel. 'I could take you for a stroll along the balcony for some fresh air, my love.'

It was indeed what she wanted, but she should attempt to win his mother's approval, at least try to lessen the force of her censure. 'Thank you, my love, but I will not drag you away when we only just arrived.'

He bowed his acquiescence, flinching a little as he did so. The raw, bruised strips on his poor back still troubled him.

How are you settling in, Rasel?' Samara asked. 'My first time at court, I was eighteen, about your age, my dear, and, not from one of the great noble houses, I found it all rather daunting.' She turned to the Kupanna, 'I remember, Your Majesty, how you took pity on me. It is a kindness I will always be grateful for.'

Mannok's mother's face softened. 'One's first experience of the Palace can be intimidating.'

'Your customs are different from those of my people, but I am willing to learn the customs of the court,' Rasel said, 'And I am very comfortable in the sleeping place provided.' She smiled unreservedly at Mannok's aunt and then smiled encouragingly at shy Jarrah standing beside her and resting a protective hand on her stomach. Rasel could sense new life within. 'My lady Jarrah, it is good to see you again. Should I wish you a blessing for you and Waren on your delightful news?'

Jarrah blushed and looked down in confusion and Samara looked up at Rasel in surprise.

'What are you talking about, girl?' Mannok's mother demanded.

'Oh, the expected arrival of a new life.' From the growing shock in the women's reactions, she'd said something wrong again, though she didn't know what it could be.

'Samara what is she talking about?'

'I beg your pardon, Your Majesty,' Mannok's aunt placed a hand on her chest. 'We hope to be grandparents by the Harvest Festival, but it is still early days, too soon to show.'

Jarrah's cheeks turned a reddish-brown and she studied the mosaic floor.

Kerri, Lumi and Rizanna tittered. Estolik's mother snickered, hiding her painted mouth behind her opulent hand fan.

The Kupanna heaved a heavy sigh. 'A word, Rasel, a mother's condition is not a suitable topic of polite conversation, especially in present company,' she directed her chin at the Prince, who was looking in any direction other than towards her or the other women. 'It is after all women's business.'

Rasel looked down. 'My apologies if I've offended. When the Maker blesses my Kin in such a way it is the cause of great celebration. And why is it just women's business when men are equally involved in the conceiving?'

The Kupanna's nose pinched together and the other women gaped at her. Her stomach dropped like a stone in a deep pond. She had only made things worse.

The Prince cleared his throat. 'Sounds fair to me,' he said. She gave him a grateful glance. His mouth quirked up and his eyes twinkled with mischief. 'I'm relieved Waren will soon have someone else to baby.'

'Really, Mannok, I don't know what has come over you lately. Or rather I do, more's the pity.' The Kupanna glared at Rasel. Her chest swelled. 'Please, ensure you … your betrothed understands acceptable conversation and behaviour.'

Tears pricked Rasel's eyes. No one had ever treated her like this before, as though she were an irritating seed lodged between the teeth to be tolerated or spat out. She wanted to make peace with these people, to be accepted by them for her love's sake. Yet, no matter what she said or did, her attempts at conciliation only made matters worse, much much worse.

Chapter Forty-Seven: Gifts

Mannok

Mannok pressed his lips together and swallowed the words he yearned to fling at his mother like flaming arrows. Obviously, she was still upset about his decision to marry Rasel, yet she could at least treat his future wife with civility. 'An afternoon reception in honour of your bride,' his father had said. What a farce! Not only his back was on fire, his cheeks flamed with rage.

Rasel, the hint of tears in her beautiful dark eyes, moved closer to him and squeezed his arm. 'I'm so sorry,' she whispered. 'I'm not doing well, am I?'

He shook his head. 'You at least are trying to be polite,' he said, not bothering to lower his voice. 'Unlike everyone else at this reception.' Though to be fair, Aunt Samara had tried to welcome Rasel.

A commotion at the entrance of the reception room drowned out his words. Mama, Yuta and the other ladies turned to look. Noisy conversations stilled mid-sentence and a sudden hush fell over the room.

His father, followed by Uncle Lukarn and Aunt Lakwi, swept through the entrance. Mannok's shoulders tensed. Now for round two of scrutiny and insults, but he and Rasel could weather whatever his parents and his family threw at them. The nobles parted and bowed low as the Kapok strode down the length of the room.

Mannok's eyes narrowed. Was that Waren following Uncle Lukarn into the room? Who had countermanded his orders, undermining his authority in the eyes of his band? Waren would only become more insufferable. Mannok closed his eyes and did his best to master the anger boiling up inside him. Rasel's cool hands brushed against him, like a balm on a raging wound. It would not do to lose control now. There was too much at stake. He took a deep breath and waited.

'My lady Kupanna,' his father said breezily. 'You look stunning this afternoon.'

His mother bowed. 'Your Majesty, it seems you at least are in a good mood.'

He grinned at her, seemingly unfazed by the coolness of her reception. The hum of many voices grew in volume as the courtiers returned to their interrupted conversations.

Papa nodded at Mannok. 'Prince, good to see you looking a little less peaked today. Ladies.' He nodded at the Markanas and their daughters as they bowed to him. 'Ah, Rasel, as beautiful as ever. Have they been giving you a hard time, my dear?'

Rasel lifted her chin and met his eyes. 'Your Majesty.'

There was not even a hint of a smile on her lively face. No doubt she had not yet forgiven his father for the punishments he had inflicted. Yet, weird as it seemed, Papa was their one powerful advocate at the moment. Their wedding would depend on his decision to go ahead regardless of the objections of his mother and uncle and perhaps the rest of the council.

Mannok nodded to Uncle Lukarn and Aunt Lakwi, then turned to his cousin. Waren stood next to the Markan, his normally serious face lit by a pleased smile. His hazel eyes turned to the shy Jarrah. Mannok understood his cousin's eagerness to spend time with his wife, especially given their family situation that Rasel had inadvertently outed.

He suppressed a mischievous smile at a sudden idea. 'Ah, good day, Waren, I see you are off duty. No doubt to celebrate the arr—'

'Mannok,' his mother hissed, 'It is inappropriate to bring up such a subject. You should know better.'

Papa and Aunt Lakwi looked from him to his mother. Waren's cheeks darkened. Aunt Samara frowned while Jarrah put her hands to her glowing cheeks. Yuta smiled disdainfully. Lumi and Rizanna giggled again. Uncle Lukarn glanced at him, an uncertain look flashing across his rugged features.

Mannok glanced at his mother with a puzzled innocence. 'I'm not sure I understand, Mama.' He lowered his voice and leaned in closer. 'You mean we should not speak about our family reunion? I thought the arrival of your brother and family from the north was a happy event.'

The Kupanna stared at him, then frowned, flustered. 'No, that is not what I meant.'

He blinked and slapped his forehead. 'Oh, you thought I meant that other happy event. No, no, I wouldn't mention that. I was just thinking that my uncle was, perhaps, justified in releasing his son from his assigned duty for family considerations.'

Waren gave Uncle Lukarn a startled look, and his uncle shifted his balance from one foot to the other and frowned.

Papa searched the faces, first of his wife then of his brother-in-law, before bringing his eagle eyes to bear on him. Mannok met his gaze with feigned indifference.

'The air is so thick with secrets and insinuations, it's a wonder we can still breathe,' Papa said. 'No, no,' he waved down Mama and Uncle Lukarn as they both started to speak. 'Explanations can wait until a more private occasion.' He turned to Mannok, giving him searching look. 'Next time, son, express yourself with greater clarity.'

Mannok bowed. 'As you command, Your Majesty.'

Rasel leaned close and breathed into his ear, 'Now that is something Dinnis might have done. I do feel sorry for poor Jarrah.'

His cheeks warmed. His little ploy wasn't aimed at gentle Jarrah, but fair point. He looked up to see his father's eyes still on him.

Papa looked away then stroked his chin. 'Now, I was in a good mood. Why was that? Oh, yes, now I remember.' He rubbed his hands together. 'You at least will appreciate this, Mannu. The latest batch of young horses from our cousin, Prince Tannik, arrived just now from Silisea. I thought you might wish to select some for your own use and maybe even a couple for our mysterious Rasel of the southern forests, that is if she rides?'

'I can ride, your Majesty,' Rasel said.

Papa raised an eyebrow. 'A love for poetry and horses. We'll make a Tamrin Princess of you yet.'

'Horses, my Lord Kapok?' Mama said, 'Can it not wait?'

'Well, certainly it could. But that is not my wish. So, Prince Mannok, what say you?'

'I appreciate the offer, but I have had several large expenses of late.'

Papa spread out his hands and smiled. 'Consider it a combined birthday and wedding gift.'

'Then, I would be delighted! My thanks, Your Majesty.' He grinned until he noted the expression on Mama's face. 'If the Kupanna can spare me,' he added.

Mama drew herself up to her full height, the top of her head barely reaching Papa's shoulders. 'We have one thing left to do before I bring this shameless shambles to a close.'

She beckoned and Madomo Bitjarnan appeared from somewhere in the crowded room. He picked up a small hammer and tapped a bronze gong standing beside a long flat rosewood case on a nearby table. At the sonorous notes, the conversations around the room died and all eyes turned toward them.

'Lady Samara can you bring me the case?'

Aunt Samara walked over, picked up the rosewood box and brought it to Mama. Mama opened the lid and displayed the contents to the interested onlookers. Inside, an intricate necklace of obsidian and rubies on the highest quality gold chain, with matching earrings, nestled in the soft cotton cloth.

'For you Rasel, to wear at the ceremony,' Mama said. 'I will have them sent to your rooms at the appropriate time.'

'A generous gift, thank you, Your Majesty.' Rasel let go of Mannok's arm and brought out a plain parcel tied with twine from her sash. Bowing, she presented it to his mother. 'I made you a gift also, a sash in the same fashion as the belt I made the Prince of Tamra for his birthday. I know it is simple but I hope you will like it.'

His mother frowned, probably for the first time reminded that in the confusion and drama on the day, she had forgotten to give him even good wishes on his birthday.

'Many thanks, Rasel.' Mama put the parcel down on the table without opening it.

Rasel stepped back, the smile slipping from her face a moment before returning a little less full. Mannok felt a surge of anger. What was the point of such a grand gesture of the reception and the gift, if Mama then snubbed his love in front of all these people?

'You are full of surprises, Rasel.' Papa picked up the parcel in his huge hands and opened it with care. A long supple sash in blues, yellows, greens, and white cascaded out. Papa spread it out, revealing images of the ocean, grasslands, mountains and forests.

Aunt Lakwi clapped her hands together. 'It is beautiful. Like a song.'

'I wove into the pattern the different terrains of the Wide Lands from the Lapis Sea to the Great Mother River for the mother of the Prince of Tamra,' Rasel said. 'I hope we can make peace between us.'

A murmur ran through the Reception room. Mannok held his breath. Surely, this would be at least the first step in winning his mother over.

Mama rubbed her temples and sighed. 'If I might, Your Majesty, I will withdraw. I feel the onset of a headache and I would not keep you from your beloved horses.'

Papa's brows crinkled a moment before smoothing out. 'As you wish, my Kupanna.'

Mama clapped her hand twice, signalling the end of the reception. With a straight back, she walked toward the atrium balcony, Rizanna following behind her.

Lady Yuta cleared her throat. 'If you would, Your Majesty, I should find Lord Haka.'

'Feel free, Yuta. You too, Lumi.'

Lumi ducked her head and she and her mother moved into the crowd.

Once they disappeared into the crush, Papa brought his hand to his chest. 'If we have been discourteous, Rasel of the Forest Folk, I am sorry on behalf of us all.'

Mannok wondered if he'd heard correctly.

Uncle Lukarn grunted. 'It's hardly your place to apologise, Rokkan.'

'Or yours to lecture, Lukarn,' Papa countered. The two men stared at each other as if resuming an old argument. What had Uncle said in their meeting yesterday? What had Papa?

Uncle Lukarn looked away first. 'As you say, Your Majesty, but your security is my concern.'

'I assure you, son of Derik, uncle of the Prince, I am not a threat in any way to the father of my betrothed.' Rasel bestowed one of her dazzling smiles on Papa. 'Apology accepted, son of Martal, I mean, Your Majesty. Forgive me, I am still learning your customs which seem strange to me.'

The hard lines on Papa's face softened a moment. 'That I understand, Rasel of the Forest. Whether in Silisea, Limar or Nolmeca, it took me time to adjust to different expectations and customs. Such experiences change a person.' His smile widened as his gaze shifted to Waren. 'It appears congratulations are due to you and your lovely wife, nephew, if I guess correctly. Good news indeed.' He winked at Jarrah and clapped Uncle Lukarn on the back. 'So, you old puma, you are to become a grandfather before me? Still, I'm not sure that access to such age and wisdom gives you the right to change the Prince's duty arrangements without consultation.'

Uncle Lukarn spluttered. 'My mistake, Your Majesty.' He placed a hand over his chest and bowed to Mannok. 'Apologies, Your Highness.'

Waren stood a little straighter, his tired hazel eyes on Mannok. 'I am at your command, Your Highness. When should I present myself to Kaptan Kaspin?'

Mannok's mood lifted at his father's unexpected support, his Uncle's apology and Waren's surrender after months of constant criticism or correction. He could order Waren back to the wall to complete his shifts or maybe he could allow him to spend the evening with his family.

Rasel brushed against him, her presence like a gentle breeze and his heart swelled with love and possibilities.

'No need, Waren. Lady Jarrah would appreciate the company of her husband at such a time as this. There should be no difficulties in covering your place, given the shortfall will soon be filled by your Prince.' Twenty days trudging along the wall instead of delighting in his love's sweet company would be a trial, but better than not having her at his side at all.

It took a couple of seconds for the full import of his words to sink in, then Waren's face lit up like a festival beacon. 'You have my gratitude, Prince Mannok.'

Mannok fist bumped his cousin. 'No need to mention it.'

Most of the courtiers filtered out the doors into the Great Hall, emptying the room and leaving the small group standing around his father.

'Well, Mannok, are you coming with me to the horse pens or not?'

'Yes, Papa, and Rasel too.'

'You two do seem to be inseparable! Come on then, we're losing time.' He nodded at Aunt Lakwi, Samara, Waren, Jarrah and the others still standing with them, spun around and strode from the room.

Mannok caught up Rasel's hand and raced after him, with Uncle Lukarn behind them. They followed Papa out of the Palace to the service area in the north-western corner of the royal compound, passing the royal kennels. The sun had moved, hazy blue-white light angling in from the west. Close by, dogs barked. The clang of hammer on metal from the smithery, the scrape of a saw on wood, the whinny of horses, the occasional shout and the bustle of carts being loaded or unloaded near the goods gate resounded in the still air.

Three large hunting dogs bounded towards Papa in a storm of happy barking. Before they reached him, they changed course, veering toward Mannok and Rasel, their barks changing tone. Mannok sighed and stood still, his arm on hers.

'Blasted dogs used to scare me witless when I was a child,' he said.

She did not look frightened as Lumi and maybe even Rizzi would have. As Ista would have too. Before Mannok could stop her, she dropped down in a crouch.

'*Shayla Kelevim. Shayla Elemni.* Peace friends. Look at you. How beautiful you are.'

All three dogs stopped barking. Tracker first sniffed then licked the hand she offered. She laughed as they pranced about her, rolling over or pushing up against her, offering their paws to be shaken. 'Oh, you are so beautiful.'

He squatted down with her, wincing as his back pulled, and patted the terrors.

'Arrow, Chase, Tracker, Come!' Papa called.

The dogs jumped up and ran to him, their heads down, their tails wagging in great sweeps. 'Now you silly mutts, heel.'

The kennel master ran up, gasping for breath. He dropped to his knees before Papa. 'Your Majesty.'

'Turuk, why are my dogs roaming free?'

'They rushed the gate, Your Majesty, when a new attendant unlatched it for a moment.'

'Not good, Turuk. But leave them with me. Let Wasuk know I'm here.'

'Yes, Your Majesty.' The kennel master wiped his forehead and dashed off.

Uncle Lukarn, who must have paused to talk to someone in the reception room, caught up with them.

He eyed Rasel. 'Are you okay, lass?'

She stood up, her eyes shining, 'Yes, of course. That's the friendliest welcome I've had since I've arrived in this city.'

Mannok hooted and slapped his thigh. 'You could be right.' He slipped his arm around her waist.

'They certainly seem to like you.' Papa studied Rasel, his golden eyes hooded. 'That's a point in her favour, Lukarn.'

'Only if you trust your dogs' judgement over that of your advisors.'

'Any day, my friend, any day.' He turned to pet each of them in turn, his face widening into a huge grin, his amber eyes alight with pleasure.

Together, they walked the short distance to the stable complex. Twelve young horses milled around in the far end of a training yard. The head groom, a tall man with greying hair, deep-set eyes and a puny Silesian nose, came hurrying up to his father.

'So Wasuk, what do you think?' Papa asked, swinging himself up to perch on the top fence rail. The dogs settled with a sigh on the ground beneath Papa's feet.

Mannok turned to help Rasel up, but she already sat balanced on the railing, her eyes and face alight as she watched the horses. He met his uncle's bemused expression, shrugged, and wished he hadn't at the sharp grab of pain. He climbed the rail with his back as stiff as possible. His uncle kept his boots on the ground and leaned against the fence.

'Prince Tannik has sent some beauties for us this time, Your Majesty,' Wasuk said with a wide smile. He handed Papa a rolled-up parchment. 'They've had some handling but are otherwise untrained. Silesia breeds the finest steeds in the Five Lands.'

Uncle Lukarn snorted.

Papa grinned. 'I won't argue with you there, my friend. Give me a long-legged Silesian racer over a rugged Tamrin mountain pony any day. So, Prince, which one catches your eye?'

Mannok settled himself on the rail and studied the splendid steeds clumped at the other end of the yard and stirring up the dust with their fine hooves. He sidled closer to Rasel. A fine drizzle of dust settled on her midnight hair and soft silver skin. The scent of pine and mountain snow blossom sweetened the more pungent smells around them.

Papa cleared his throat, 'Not that filly, Mannok. I meant the ones in the training yard.'

He caught Rasel's startled eyes and smiled crookedly. Shifting his gaze, he watched the horses interact and made his choice. 'The grey colt with the dark mane and ... hmmm ... that red roan with the white blaze.'

'Humph, whatever your faults, you are a good judge of horseflesh. They are the pick of the bunch,' Papa said.

'Well then, I suppose ...' He looked the horses over again.

'Consider them yours. Wasuk will train them for the saddle, unless you wish to yourself or have someone else in mind. Your wedding gift from me.'

Mannok raised his eyebrows, then he grinned. 'That is very generous of you, Papa. My thanks.'

'You're both wrong,' Rasel said. 'The burnished gold one with the silver mane standing on her own outshines them all!'

And before he could stop her, she jumped inside the fence and walked towards the filly.

Chapter Forty-Eight: Peace

Mannok

Mannok's heart stopped and then thudded like a sledgehammer in his chest.

'Rasel,' he called. 'The horses are unbroken.'

His love looked back over her shoulder and smiled at him. 'Thank the Maker. Why would you want to break such glorious creatures?'

She continued to walk at an angle toward the golden filly standing midway between the other horses and the people at the railings. It was indeed a magnificent creature, head held proudly with flowing mane, pawing the ground. Not as tall or strong as the grey or roan, but well-proportioned. Rasel stopped a couple of tanis from the horse and began to speak to it softly in a mixture of Filane and words of the ancient tongue that she had used earlier.

His heart hammered so fast he could scarcely breathe. How could she put herself in such danger? What if he lost her? He jumped down after her to protect her from this foolishness.

'By the Pit,' Papa growled.

His uncle called out, 'Mannok, what are you doing? Get back here!'

Mannok kept his eyes on Rasel and the filly. He forced himself to walk with slow, even steps, so as not to startle the half-wild horse or the other eleven watching them from the rear of the training yard.

A rustle came from behind him and the sound of boots hitting the ground.

'Slide it, Rokkan. Not you too.'

'Shush, Lukarn.' His father grunted then called in a low carrying voice, 'No loud noises. No sudden moves. Wasuk, some ropes, sacks and your finest hay or some treats, if you please.'

Mannok steadied his breathing and continued to close the distance to Rasel.

She stepped closer to the filly who sidestepped then stopped. The animal stretched out her neck, her ears forward. She snuffled the air, her coat twitching.

Mannok stood still. If something happened, he'd snatch Rasel out of harm's way, but startling the horse now might only make the situation worse.

She took something from her sash, a sunfruit, and offered it on the flat of her hand. The filly snorted, shook her mane, then took a cautious step forward. Two more steps and then the horse took the fruit in its strong, slab-like teeth. Rasel stroked the long neck, whispering in a soft compelling voice.

Mannok let out his held breath, his legs suddenly weak.

'The filly is yours, Rasel,' Papa called in a low tone. 'Now, come back, lass. She is still half-wild.'

Rasel did not seem to hear. She stepped closer, encircling a silvery white arm around the filly's neck, the other stroking her cheek. She turned and beckoned to Mannok. Her face was alight with delight. He stepped up beside her. The filly inspected him, her ears erect.

'Saharah, this is Mannok, son of Rokkan and Marra, Prince of Tamra. You can trust him.' Turning to him, she said, 'Isn't Saharah, daughter of the wind, beautiful, my love?'

The animal snorted and lowered her head, sniffing Mannok's tunic perhaps in hope of another treat.

'Yes, she is but there are other half-wild horses in the yard. Once she is broken—'

'Broken? Why do you want to break her?' Rasel frowned.

'To train her for the bridle and the saddle. Teach what we expect of her so she learns good manners. '

'Oh, is that what it is called? Well, I don't think that will be necessary. Saharah and I understand each other. I don't want her spirit broken.'

Keeping his voice low with an effort, he said, 'Rasel, you can't just jump into a pen with a bunch of half-wild horses. They are much bigger than you, unpredictable and dangerous. And if you want to ride a horse it needs to be … trained. So why don't you come out of the yard with me. Leave the schooling of the filly to someone who knows what they are doing.'

He took hold of her arm, perhaps a little tighter than he intended.

She pressed her lips together and her eyes flashed. 'Let go of my arm, son of Rokkan. Leave if you want to, but Saharah is the lead horse. She won't let the others hurt us.'

This was a nightmare. 'There is no way you can know that.'

The filly nickered and flicked her tail.

'I do know this. And Prince of Tamra, you are making Saharah nervous.'

'I …' No words formed. He clenched his jaw. 'Rasel, you are making me more than nervous,' he growled.

'Shhh …' Then with a quick twist of her arm, she shook free of his hand. 'Step away and I will show you.'

He didn't move, determined not to abandon her.

She leant forward to whisper in the filly's ear before swinging up onto her bare back. He jumped back as the filly reared.

Two of the other horses, the dun and the grey, advanced a few tanis toward them.

'Girl, what are you doing?' Papa called out. Wasuk stood behind him with a lasso while other grooms circled around the yard.

Mannok stood paralysed, sure that at any moment the horse would throw her, that she'd be trampled by sharp hooves, that he would hold her broken body in his arms, that he would lose her. The horse had no halter, no way of restraining it. How could she be so reckless, so heedless, so wild?

Instead of erupting into a flurry of bucking and kicking, the filly shook her mane and stood still. Rasel leant forward, soothing the horse and speaking to it as though in a conversation with a friend. The horse, Saharah, walked forward, circled around him twice before breaking off and headed towards the railing, following Rasel's direction. She slowed to a stop in front of his grim-faced father.

Rasel bowed to him then sat tall and erect on the filly's back. 'Thank you, Lord of Tamra, for your very generous gift. But I would like to school Saharah in my own way.'

Papa gaped at her, at a total loss for words. The dogs grouped behind him. He ran a hand over his face and looked toward Mannok. 'You can come back out now, son,' he said.

Right! He still stood in the middle of the training yard like an idiot. Keeping one eye on the horses snorting at the other end of the yard, he moved back to his father and Rasel.

Uncle Lukarn stood inside the ring, behind Papa, his mouth set in a flat line.

Mannok eased himself onto the railing, a tremor running through his body.

Only then did Papa stare at his love. 'Who ... or what ... are you Rasel of the southern forests? You are not of peasant stock.'

'I am the daughter of Jazadek son of Korak and Kerren; of Rutiah daughter of Yitzak and Chaviah,' she said still astride the gold and silver filly.

She held her head high, her black hair in a cloud behind her, moving with the restive horse as though they were one being. A magnificent, gorgeous, terrifying vision.

'All of which does not mean very much to me,' Papa said. 'Who is Jazadek son of Korak? You say you are not connected to Tamrin nobility. What of Silisea or perhaps even Shanta, if any of that unfortunate land's nobility still exists?'

'Unfortunate?' A flash of anger crossed her face and Saharah pawed the ground. 'I would say, an innocent and peaceful people betrayed and slaughtered by your grandfather, Tellek Kapok? And that not even the last of a very long line of betrayals by your house.'

Uncle Lukarn smacked his fist into his palm. 'Ha, is that what you seek? Revenge? By placing the Prince's life in danger? You reveal your true motives.'

The hunting dogs stirred, Arrow growling low in the throat, Chase and Tracker bristling.

Mannok frowned. 'Can't such questions wait, Uncle.' At least until Rasel no longer sat bareback on a half-wild horse.

'The Prince's life was never at risk, son of Derek. Nor did I ask him to enter the pen with me. And I've had many other opportune occasions if I had indeed wished him harm. Know this. Revenge is not the way of my people.'

Mannok nodded. 'You see plots under every rock, Uncle. I chose to ...'

'Be silent! All of you!' Papa's voice cut through the air like a whip. The dogs whimpered and dropped to the ground. 'It's your uncle's job to see plots under every rock, Mannok! Lukarn, shut

335

up! And you,' he turned back to look at Rasel, 'have not answered my question. Who is this Jazadek son of Korak?'

'Sir, let Rasel dismount. We can have this conversation elsewhere.'

Papa's gaze swung back towards him, then back to his love. 'Answer me, Rasel, tamer of horses, speaker of the ancient tongue, charmer of princes.'

She leant forward, soothing the restless filly. Only after the horse had quietened under her touch, did she answer his father.

'My father, Jazadek son of Korak, son of Jasalim is Kinleader of the Forest Folk, a great traveller even as far as the great frozen wastes of the south, storyteller and singer, chief keeper of the lore and songs of my people. My mother Rutiah, daughter of Chaviah, granddaughter of Dinah, is Healer and Herbalist, Mother to her people.'

'Kinleader of the Forest Folk?' His father frowned. 'You speak in riddles.'

'Son of Martel, it is not our fault that your people have short memories. If you truly knew your histories, you would know who we are.' She took a deep breath. 'Some once called us Adelphi.'

Papa narrowed his eyes. 'Now you take me for a fool, speaking of myths and legends. A shapeshifter of the shadows? Such things do not exist.'

'We are not of the shadows, but children and followers of the Maker. The man of the west, Akrad the Betrayer, has truly mazed your minds.'

'No. Do not say that. As true as it was of Tellek and my brother Naetok, we rid ourselves of Akrad's poisonous influence, his treachery and lies at the cost of many lives. And he is dead. I buried him.'

'I know. I saw him die. Yet his legacy lives on in the minds of your people.'

'How could that be?' Papa shook his head. 'You may despise me. You may despise my House. You despise my heritage, but if you marry my son, this too will be your children's heritage. Are you sure this is what you want?'

Mannok jumped down into the yard. 'Papa, you would not break your word.'

Rasel looked down, her face troubled. Mannok stood still as if the whole world would break in half if he moved. He didn't know who she was, whether Shanti or of some other strange people, these Forest Folk. What he knew like his own heartbeat was that he loved her and she loved him. He could not, would not forgive Papa, if he drove her away.

'Yes, son of Martal.' His love bent down and whispered in Saharah's ear. Swinging her legs to one side of the horse, she jumped to the ground. The filly whinnied, turned and trotted back to her companions, neck curved and her tail held high.

Rasel took Mannok's hand and squeezed it, before facing Papa again. 'Akrad and your House have done my people great harm, Rokkan Kapok, but that is the past. I do love your son. We are already married by the customs of my people.'

'I am not sure what this harm is, Rasel of the Forest Folk.' Papa rubbed his chin, then sighed. 'Though perhaps I can guess. I regret what happened to Shanta, the things Tellek and Akrad did both to your people and, indeed, to mine. May there be peace between us, Lady Rasel. Shayla Rasel bat-Jazadek.'

'The past is not always so easy to mend, but perhaps it's a start. Shayla Rokkan bin-Martal. Shayla Elemni.'

Papa nodded once. 'Peace it shall be. Let's leave our equine friends to Wasuk's care. Lukarn, join me in the library. And Mannok, since you seem to have recovered so well, best present yourself to Kaptan Kaspin to start your wall duty at dawn tomorrow.'

Mannok supressed a groan. It had been hard enough to get time with Rasel over the last couple of days. Once he started on the wall, it would be harder still. Yet soon they'd have all the time in the Five Lands to be together.

Chapter Forty-Nine: Friendship

Lumi

Lumi paced the tack room in the stables, brushing off the tears flooding her cheeks with the flat of both hands. All her dreams shredded in the winds like mist. It was over a ten-day since Mannok had arrived home from the wilderness with that upstart peasant girl, yet his ardour for her burned just as brightly. Even spending the most part of his days on wall duty had done nothing to weaken his infatuation with the temptress. When not on duty, the Prince and Rasel spent every waking moment together. It was as if no one else existed. No matter how Lumi, Rizzi and the other ladies of the court tried to show her up, Mannok only had eyes for Rasel. Rasel this, and Rasel that! Even poor Garvin was looking as forlorn as a lost puppy. Oh, forget Garvin.

She clutched her hair with both hands, not caring about the damage it did to her coiffure. She was angry. Enraged at that woman with her deceptive charms, with Garvin for moping about and making her feel guilty. She was angry with herself for failing, with Mannok for being so blind, with Rokkan Kapok for agreeing to this farcical marriage in ... what, in fifteen days? Most of all, she was furious with her cold-hearted father for putting her in an impossible position, because her failure to win the Prince's heart meant her father would pursue his other hideous schemes.

Lumi shivered despite the warmth of late afternoon sun streaming through the unshuttered windows. She couldn't allow Father to endanger Mannok's life. To betray the Kapok. But what could she do? Who could she talk to? Not Mama, not Estolik. Not anyone outside the family, for if her father was convicted of treachery, her whole family would surely suffer. And she had no real proof, no real idea of what Father planned to do. Yet if Mannok was killed, she would never ever forgive herself.

Lumi collapsed onto a nearby bench. A soft bundle moved beneath her, emitting a loud indignant meow. She sprang up and turned around. A half grown black and white cat glared back at her, its whiskers bristling.

'Oh, beg your pardon, but shouldn't you be mousing or something?'

She gave a ragged giggle that petered out into a sob. Was she talking to a stable cat now? It pointed its petite nose in the air and turned its back on her to curl up on the soft, sun-soaked sack on the bench and wash itself with studied care.

'See, even the cats dismiss me.'

She sat down next to the animal and settled it on her lap. 'So, kitty, do you have a name? Can you tell me what to do? If only.'

She really should get back to the Palace before someone missed her, though she was tempted to sneak an afternoon ride down to the pine trees outside the city without permission. With no escort, she'd need to stay within the grounds. If only she was home, by the sea.

She really should get going, but the warm weight of the cat was hard to resist. A raspy tongue tickled her fingers. The cat's soft fur and throaty purr comforted her. The sun's warmth felt good on her tear-streaked face. Her eyelids drooped.

* * *

Lumi blinked. Dark clouds swirled around her. She stood on a stony pinnacle. Lightning sizzled through the air, pulverising a nearby ridge. The afterglow of the dying sun stained the trailing edges of the clouds crimson. Around her the mountains fought, crashing into each other, smashing everything that got in between and sending rocks tumbling into dark ravines. The uneven patch of ground beneath her feet trembled, sending small stones slithering off the edge. She gasped for air in the thick, sultry atmosphere. The smell of sizzled air burned her nostrils. Where was she? On one of the mountain trails that led to Akri?

She stood alone on rock, teetering above the abyss. She fell to her hands and knees, grabbing the loose rocks and scrawny grass.

'Help! Please, someone, anyone, please help me!'

The crash and bang of the titanic forces threatening to engulf her drowned out her weak voice. The gravel beneath her sandalled feet slipped and spilled over the edge.

'Help me!' But who could hear her? Who would save her? 'Please. By the Maker's favour.'

'Meow.'

A rough tongue licked her chin. The young black and white stable cat stood in front of her in the fading light. Its eyes seemed to hold the wisdom of the ages.

Weaving in and out of her arms, it said, 'Follow me, child.'

'There is nowhere to go.'

The cat put its nose in the air and began walking on a narrow ridge stretching towards a pure silver point of light. A star perhaps? Too big. Maybe Argenti in full circle.

She clenched her chattering teeth and crawled after the cat. Her elbows and knees shook. The sharp rocks scraped her hands. As the silver light grew bigger, she could see a figure in the middle of the glow. The ledge widened, the crash of rock face against rock face dimmed behind her. She stood up and stumbled towards the light. A beautiful woman stepped forward, her skin glowing like shining silver, like Argenti. She leant over the deep crevasse between them and offered a slender hand.

'Follow me.' The cat jumped onto the woman's shoulder and purred.

She stretched out her own scraped and bleeding hands, and snatched them back. The woman was Rasel.

She screamed. 'Who are you? What are you?'

'A child of the Maker, as you are. Take my hand, Lumi, and you will be safe.'

'No, never.'

She jumped back, her heart pounding in her chest and shoved her hands under her armpits. The ground beneath her trembled and began to crumble. Rocks chimed and cracked against each other as they slid into the abyss.

'Lumi, take my hand.'

She took a step back into nothingness and fell. She opened her mouth wide in a voiceless scream as she tumbled through the air.

* * *

'Lumi, Lumi.'

A rough hand shook her shoulder. She opened her eyes and batted it away.

'No, go away, I hate you. I don't need your help.'

'Lumi, wake up. You're having a nightmare.'

Translucent jade eyes looked into hers. She staggered up, her limbs stiff. The cat bounded away with a reproachful meow.

'Mannok, Your ... Your Highness. What are you doing here?'

His eyebrows lifted. He had a saddle balanced in one hand, tack draped over his shoulder. The sunlight no longer streamed into the dark and chilly room and his face was in shadow. Was she still dreaming? She could hardly breathe.

'I could ask the same thing, my lady,' he said, his head tilted. 'Are you well?'

She put her hands to her glowing cheeks. She was thankful for the dim light, that he could not see what a state she was in.

'I was going to ride but sat down for a few moments. I must have fallen asleep. I would have thought someone else would untack your horse for you, Your Highness.'

'Papa always insisted I do it myself when I was a boy. I've got into the habit of it, I guess. Besides, I enjoy rubbing down Shadow.' He placed the gear on the hooks and shelves provided. 'He needs more exercise though. The ride to the wall and back each day barely stretches his legs. Just another ten-day to go and I've done my sentence. Here, let me escort you to the Palace.'

He stood by the door. She smoothed down her tunic and tucked a stray strand of hair behind her ear. Taking a deep breath, she walked out into the corridor lit by smoking torches. Mannok followed close behind her.

'Are you going to the soiree this evening?' she asked.

'No, I want a quiet night after twelve hours of tramping that accursed wall. Besides Rasel does not enjoy the Palace soirees.'

'Oh, she is not used to so many people perhaps. If she comes from a small village.'

Mannok didn't reply at first. They stepped out into the courtyard lit by the last dregs of daylight. Floating above the purplish haze of the horizon, the snow on the Twin Peaks glowed golden and peach. In the west, a silver star shone bright. Around them, the mixed sharp-sweet smell of the stables, the quiet movement of the horses

341

with an occasional snort or soft nicker. A mournful owl hooted in the rafters. They walked across the yards towards the dark bulk of the Palace, lit from within by the golden glow of a thousand candles.

'It's not that. She says the double messages tire her.'

'Double messages?'

'The hidden barbs beneath the honeyed words. The hints and innuendos. The whispers. I think perhaps she sees and hears more than is intended. She misses her family and is lonely when I'm not able to be with her.'

'She's a bit clingy then?'

'No, I wouldn't say that.' Lumi could hear the frown in his voice. 'But I'm gone from dawn to dusk on the wall and she has no friends. Well, Dinnis, Jarrah and Aunt Samara, but Jarrah is in semi-seclusion due to her delicate condition and Mama tends to monopolise Aunt Samara's time, and Dinnis has his own concerns in the city. Otherwise, no one else takes the time. Rasel spends the morning with her filly, Saharah, and in the kennels, but she says she is not used to so much idleness. She would much rather do the wall duty with me.' He laughed. 'When she asked Papa, he said that if she did then nobody, and least of all his wayward son, would be looking out beyond the wall for peril.'

Lumi's heart twisted. True enough. He only had eyes for her. They walked in silence until they reached the front entrance.

'I'll leave you here then, Lumi.'

'Thank you for your company, Your Highness.'

His teeth flashed white in the gathering gloom. 'My pleasure.' He turned to go, then swung around again. 'Lumi, could I ask you a favour?'

'Of course, anything.' Her heart began to pound again.

'Would you be Rasel's friend for me? I mean a true friend. If you took the time to know her, I'm sure you would like her.'

Her heart stopped, then thudded painfully in her chest. Inside the Palace, someone laughed. More stars winked their bright firefly fires in the darkening sky. Mannok let out a long, wistful sigh.

'Never mind, a silly idea. Good evening, my lady.'

'Wait I ...' She chewed her bottom lip.

He looked at her, his chin titled up in anticipation. What was she about to say?

Yet maybe it made sense. If she pretended to be Rasel's friend, it might open up more opportunities to influence Mannok. To save his life and bring her the happiness she craved. Perhaps that was what the dream meant.

She took a deep breath. 'As you wish, Your Highness. If you want me to be friends with Rasel, I will.'

His eyes lit up, visible even in the twilight. Catching up her hand, he kissed her fingers.

'Thanks, Lumi. You are one in a thousand thousands. I knew you were not as shallow as most of the Palace beauties.'

With a graceful bow, he turned and strode off towards the Silisean Palace, a renewed spring in his step. Lumi put her hand to her mouth. What had she agreed to?

Chapter Fifty: Overtures

Rasel

Rasel ran her hand down the unfamiliar heavy cotton of her tunic and sighed. It was a lovely dark forest green, embroidered in silver with images of fruit and flowers. Exquisite work, but it felt heavy and constricting. Her hair, piled up in some complex design by Leesa, unbalanced her head and made her scalp ache. She longed to shake it free, to let it flow about her shoulders like the waterfall depicted in front of her. A jade necklace lay cold on her chest and bracelets clashed at her wrists. She had agreed to dress like the Tamrin, at least at formal events. She wanted to fit in for Mannok's sake. Yet she doubted it made much difference to these haughty and aloof Tamrin people what she wore. The reception room hummed with conversations from which she was excluded, but for which she often supplied the primary topic. She was learning to filter out the hurtful remarks, to listen to the sounds of the garden and the stables outside or follow her own thoughts. She hadn't wanted to come to this afternoon's reception, but this time Mannok's mother had insisted she come. Then, after the first greeting, the Kupanna had promptly ignored her.

She blinked back tears and looked up at the magnificent tapestry hanging on the lime-washed wall of the reception room. It would have taken the Palace women many circles of golden Alumi to make. A pale beauty stood on the rocks in front of the waterfall. In her arms, she cradled an injured youth dressed in Tamrin fashion. The scene was depicted with delicate detail and glowing colours. Surely this was the meeting of Solik and the beautiful Namu. Namu had saved the Prince's life the day they meet at the waterfall, an act of mercy that cost her own life.

'That was my favourite tapestry as a child. Still is,' a rich contralto voice said from behind her.

Turning, Rasel looked into the silvery green eyes of Princess Lakwi. She was tall for a Tamrin woman and she moved with an unconscious grace.

'When my mother, Kupanna Suraya, was making this tapestry, I fell in love with the tale behind it. I used to beg Rokkan to tell that story again and again till even his patience was quite spent. I even helped a little, see, in that corner, the silver fern and bladeleaf about the rocks.'

Rasel liked the ruler of Tamra's sister. There was always a hint of merriment in her eyes. Her kinship with both the Kapok and her beloved Prince was plain. Up until now, the Princess had kept her distance.

'Your Highness. I had not thought of the Kapok in the role of storyteller.'

Lakwi laughed. 'Then you do not know my brother well. He was my biggest hero when I was little. I lived for his return from whatever mission Papa had sent him on. It was as if a fresh breeze swept through the Palace, breathing new life into the farthest corners, right up to the nursery. But there, I'm probably boring you with childhood tales.'

'No, not at all, Your Highness. I love family stories. I imagine he was a tease.'

'True. He still is. That hasn't changed.'

'Perhaps you could tell me, Princess. I note that neither Lady Samara nor Jarrah are present this afternoon. Is all well?'

'Ah, yes, Jarrah is a little unwell due to her condition. Samara is caring for her.'

'Oh, I hope she is not too distressed. My mother suggests a light tea of wiri root and li—'

'Lady Samara has access to an accomplished midwife and the best medicinal advice.'

Rasel bit her lip and nodded. The Tamrin woman studied her for a couple of moments. She did not seem hostile, but she wasn't welcoming either. Why had she approached her now?

'You are an enigma, my dear. Not Palace-bred but not common either. There is no doubt that you have captured my finicky nephew's heart. And I believe you love him too.'

'Yes, I do.'

'Part of me was cheering the two of you on in the Throne Room that first night, though the more sensible part was totally aghast at your audacity. I would wait for your wedding, but I need to leave for the East tomorrow. I cannot risk staying until the roads become impassable with the rains and travel is impossible for several alume. My mother is frail and will fret if I stay absent much longer.'

'I see. May the Maker keep you safe on your journey.'

'My thanks for your good wishes. Before I left, I wanted to wish you happiness if … when … you marry.'

'If … that's what Rokkan Kapok says too. Do you think we will change our minds because the event is delayed?'

Lakwi smiled. 'Perhaps. Though from what I have seen of you over the half alume, I think that unlikely. Don't underestimate my brother, my dear.'

Rasel lifted her chin. 'I know his reputation for brilliant strategy.'

'Yes, but I mean as a friend, not as an enemy.'

Rasel's brows creased. 'But he is not my friend. Apart from Mannok and Dinnis, no one here is.' It was true that since the episode in the horse yards, the son of Martal had ceased probing her. He acknowledged her presence, was polite, but otherwise gave her little attention. What did his sister mean? Could the Kapok ever see her as something more than a threat to the throne?

'My brother is not the heartless tyrant you may think him.'

'I … he is not exactly what I expected.' Perhaps she had been too free with accusations and presumptions in the first few days of her arrival in this city. Yet the memory of the lash on her love's bare back still woke her some nights. What was she to think? Had she been too harsh judging him? Different peoples had different customs, but some things were just wrong. She was sure of it. She shivered. A veiled menace stalked the corridors of this place and at times it invaded her dreams. Was its source the son of Martal or someone else? Maker protect her, even though she had walked into the jaguar's den with her eyes wide open.

The whisper of footsteps approached from her left. Her eyes rounded as Haka's daughter came to stand beside them. In her

346

hands she balanced a small tray of delicacies, fresh and dried fruits and berries, honeyed nuts and small jellies.

'Your Highness, Lady Rasel, I thought you might like something.' The young woman smiled though her hands trembled a little and she could not hide a simmering resentment in her eyes when she looked at Rasel.

'Thank you for your thoughtfulness, Lumi,' the Princess said, helping herself to a selection of the treats.

Rasel took a few berries and nuts and murmured her appreciation. The Princess turned to Rasel with a warm smile. 'Please excuse me. I'll leave you with your friend. I need to say my farewells to the Kupanna. But think about my words.'

Rasel bowed. 'Indeed, Your Highness. I wish you safe travel.'

As the graceful woman strolled away, the daughter of Haka gave a little cough. She reddened as Rasel looked at her.

'Ah, Lady Rasel.' The girl shifted her feet. Taking a deep breath, she looked Rasel in the eye. 'Can I ask you a favour? I was planning to ride tomorrow morning, but the Kupanna doesn't like it if I ride alone and Rizzi is busy with her family at present.'

'I do not have any influence with Kupanna Marra.' Rasel narrowed her eyes. Why, after ignoring Rasel over the last half-circle of Alume, was this proud daughter of Tamra speaking to her now? Why was she so nervous?

'Perhaps you would consent to ride with me.' The words came out in a rush and Haka's daughter twisted her brown hands together.

Rasel's eyes widened. Was this an offer of friendship? It was hard to know the girl's true intentions. Her silvery grey eyes, so strikingly fringed with long dark lashes, were as turbulent as a stormy sea. Resentment, hope, fear, seemed to toss back and forth in a maelstrom of uncertainty. Haka's daughter probably didn't know herself what she truly wanted.

Lumi straightened her stance, her round face finding its usual haughtiness. 'Of course, if it's too much trouble.'

'Oh, no, it's not. I would be pleased to ride with you. Thank you for asking.' Rasel spoke before the other girl could change her mind. She would love to ride beyond the gates of the Palace. Perhaps she should accept even this tentative overture of friendship. As fickle and conflicted as it seemed, it was at least a start towards winning a friend.

Chapter Fifty-One: Confidences

Dinnis

Dinnis saluted the guards standing at the Palace service gate as he slipped back into the Palace compound. He had spent the fine morning at Anna's, digging up and replanting some of her garden beds. It was his regular day off from his medical studies and Tilli's new husband was safely out of the way at his day work in Hartil's stables. Dinnis gritted his teeth. Though Tujik worked intermittently, he refused to help about the shop and expected Tilli to service his every whim. Even when the lout wasn't there, Dinnis found it hard to forget him. His presence haunted the shop, a discarded tunic in the mending basket, muddy boots left to be cleaned at the kitchen door, empty maize beer pots or broken dishes all brought unwelcome reminders of how things had changed in his former haven. Dinnis had welcomed the arrival of a messenger from the Royal Librarian Raltan requesting his help with some ancient manuscripts. He pulled back his shoulders and took a deep breath. He needed to relax, to let go of past dreams and focus on his future as a physician. That was something that did give him pleasure.

As he sauntered past the stables, a musical laugh rose into the warm afternoon air. Looking up he saw Rasel dismounting. She was dressed in a simple tunic, long forest-green cloak, and boots. Her hair cascaded down her back. Despite the escalating mugginess and, no doubt, a ride on her half-wild horse, she looked as fresh as new snow. Beside her the Lady Lumi sat on her mare. She wore a fancier dark blue tunic and silver-grey cloak, her hair piled up in elaborate palace design, a polite smile on her face. Dinnis slowed his pace. Now that was a surprising combination. What was Lumi up to? Before he could quicken his stride again and slip away unnoticed, Rasel looked up, caught his eye and smiled a welcome at him.

'Friend Dinnis, it is indeed far too long since we have spoken,' she called out to him.

Lumi looked towards him, the smile evaporating.

Rasel walked towards him, the golden filly following behind her even though Rasel did not hold the horse's simple halter. Lumi followed on her mount. As all four came to a stop in front of him, Lumi lifted her chin.

'My ladies.' Dinnis bowed first to Rasel, then to Lumi.

'Since no one else is available, could you help me dismount, fellow?' Lumi held out her elegant hand. Her grey eyes were as hard as frost.

Dinnis' mouth twitched. Perhaps he should be honoured. Normally, the daughter of Haka kept as big a distance between them as possible. After a small pause, he held the horse's head steady with his left hand and took the proffered hand with his right. Lumi swung herself down from the horse with a natural grace.

'See that Caramel is groomed.' She turned to Rasel who watched the proceedings with a bemused expression. 'Thank you for your company, Lady Rasel.' With that, the young Palace beauty swept past, and headed to the Palace without a backward glance, leaving Dinnis holding her restless horse.

He raised an eyebrow. 'That's put me in my place.'

'Oh dear. She can be a bit haughty at times,' Rasel said.

Now that was an understatement. Dinnis gave a lopsided smile. This stirred memories of when the other boys used to leave him holding the horses. Caramel snorted and nuzzled the back of his neck. He stroked the rippling neck muscles, feeling the beautiful mount quieten beneath his touch.

What should he do now? Find a groom or stable boy to look after the horse? He could hardly just hand it to Rasel.

'I plan to rub Saharah down anyway. I can tend both of them.'

A grin curved up his face unbidden. 'Let me help you, my lady.'

'Weren't you on an errand? You had purpose in your stride.'

'I'm sure the Head Librarian can wait a little longer.'

'Library.' She sighed. 'Mannok hasn't shown me the library and of course now he is on the wall day and night, or so it seems.'

'Once we have tended the horses, I can show you the library if you like.'

'Oh!' She skipped a step. 'I like that idea, but what do you get out of it?'

'The inestimable pleasure of your company of course, my lady.' He gave an exaggerated bow.

She laughed. 'You are such a tease.'

Once they'd led the horses back to adjoining stalls, Dinnis fetched a couple of buckets of water and hay and then began to remove Caramel's gear. Taking a stiff hair brush, he began to work the sweaty coat. Raltan would probably begin to steam when he didn't arrive soon, but how often did he get a chance to spend time with Rasel? Just being with her was worth enduring a hundred scoldings. He settled into the rhythm of the brush strokes.

'Tell me, friend, is all well with you?' Rasel said as she finished brushing Saharah's golden coat and began to comb out her long silver mane.

He frowned. 'Why do you ask?'

She stood still for a minute looking at her filly's soft coat. 'I'm not sure. You should be happy since you now can devote yourself to the apprenticeship as you have long hoped to do.'

He nodded. 'I am delighted.'

'Yet, I think something troubles you still.'

He met her eyes. Had he given himself away so easily? After years of practice, he could usually hide his feelings even from himself. He dropped his eyes and continued to groom the silky tail of Lumi's mount, conscious of Rasel's eyes watching him. How could he explain the turmoil inside him?

She had been a guiding light to a young troubled boy. Without her encouraging words and wisdom at North Pass, he was sure he would have walked a darker, more twisted and violent path. She had encouraged him to believe in himself, to hope for something better. He had chosen to heal others rather than to kill or seek a powerful position; to follow the precepts of the silver lady's Maker even though he still found it hard to believe. He had opened himself up to Anna's family and allowed himself to love Tilli only to be rejected. Yet even this loss had not prepared him to see his silver lady in the arms of his oblivious half-brother. Once again, Mannok was chosen, favoured, and he was left in the shadows. What good was it now to realise that what he had felt for Tilli was but a fraction of what he felt for Rasel. Akrad's disturbing presence had once again begun to haunt his dreams, though now it was thoughts of Mannok rather than Rokkan that triggered the nightmares. Not that it was Mannu's fault. Just ... just that it wasn't fair. He shivered and rested his head on the mare's muscular flank. How could he say all that to her?

'Don't fret, Dinnis, if you don't want to speak about it.'

He grimaced. 'You once said to sow seeds of love—at least I think you did. Yet whatever I do, love eludes me. The girl I love chose another.' Both of them. Caramel shifted her weight and continued her contented eating. He picked up her hind hoof and examined it before moving to the next one. 'And why not? I've never fitted in anywhere. I'm a nobody.'

'How can you say that? Mannok told me how you saved his father's life. You alone knew the antidote to the poison and how to administer it. Just the other day, Mannok offered you a high position with great rewards, yet you chose to follow your calling instead. Not many men have that courage. And I've seen how kind you are to those who can do nothing for you. I think the Maker is with you.'

Dinnis snorted. 'The Maker?'

'You hear his song even though you cannot yet see him.'

'Now you speak in riddles. And was the Maker with your grandfather when he died at Akrad's hand?' Dinnis bit his lip. 'Sorry, that was a bit harsh.'

'It's a good question. I know that it was more important to Dababa to do what he thought right than to live betraying all he believed in. Remember, he said to me that day, "Not all songs have happy endings, at least not this side of the Composer's undying Song".'

Dinnis laughed. 'More riddles.'

'Life is not the end and death doesn't have the final word.'

He shrugged and put down the last of Caramel's hooves. Picking up a soft cloth, he began to rub her rich coat until it shone. The horse bent her neck and blew gently into his ear. He stroked her withers.

'Well, I do know that when I allow jealousy and revenge to pervade my thoughts, I feel the power, but I am also most tormented by Akrad's memory. It's as if his spirit is stalking me. I don't like it at all. I would rather die than end up like him.'

'Hold on to what is true, my friend. Your time is not yet, but one day it will be.'

'I don't know about that. There are some powerful people who wish me dead.'

'Yet I think you are protected.'

He frowned. 'Perhaps.'

It had occurred to him recently that his father's seeming indifference towards him may have been to shield him from the ire of Lukarn and Marra. Rokkan was the Kapok, so-called supreme ruler of Tamra. Yet he could not rule without armies and the backing of the clans. Yet surely it had not been necessary to totally disown him as he had in the aftermath of North Pass?

Rasel gave Saharah a final rub, then put her hands on her hips and stretched. Even with her face smudged and her hair unruly, her beauty caught his breath. He laid down the cloth and took a step closer. The Palace gong marking the midday hour chimed in the distance. She sighed.

'Another six hours before my love is released from the wall tonight and another nine days before this onerous duty is over and we can be married.' She turned and caressed her horse, whispering endearments.

He wanted to hold her in his arms and make her his own, but he knew she loved another. He swallowed hard. To act on his longings would be a betrayal not only of her trust but that of his brother, the Prince. As he'd determined at Mist Falls village, even if she had chosen another, he could still serve her and the one she loved. He would give his life for her and all that she stood for. And with that dour thought, he felt at peace.

He coughed. 'My lady, perhaps we should tidy up before entering the Palace. I'll meet you in the Grand Entrance Hall in half-hour and show you the library if you still wish to see it.'

'That's a good idea.' She turned and smiled at him. 'You are a good and wise friend Dinnis, the best I have in Tarka.'

Apart from the Prince. And that would have to be enough.

Chapter Fifty-Two: Suspect

Dinnis

Several days later, Dinnis shifted his position beneath the wind-sculpted pine tree. The stark angular peak of the Elder Twin cut into the sapphire sky, the slopes of the Younger Twin half hiding behind it. Nestling between encircling ridges of the Peaks, Tarka lay distant and golden in the afternoon sunlight. The strong wind blowing from the east carried away the tumult of the crowded city. Not even the sound of yarma bells or the reedy calls of their keepers cut through the silence. Only the moan of wind echoed hollowly across the barren slopes. Perhaps his quarry had taken another route today. Yet this was his favourite trail and the best chance to find him alone. There was nothing to do but wait. Overhead a white-headed eagle keened, silencing the soft coo of the grey pigeons in the branches above him.

A slight vibration tingled the palms of his hands where they rested on the rocky ground. The low thunder of a galloping horse sent pigeons flying up with a whirr-whirr-whirr of panicked wings. The silver stallion crested the small foothill, kicking up a cloud of dust with its sharp hooves. Its rider crouched over the strong neck of his mount. Dinnis tensed but did not move. No other figures followed in the plume of dust. A quick grin curved up his face. Perfect. As the stallion came close to the warped tree, he stood up and stepped out into the middle of the trail.

'What the ... Whoa there, Blizzard.' His father, Rokkan Kapok, sat back, pulling the stallion to a stop with one hand while whipping out his spear from its saddle holster. Blizzard reared, his eyes white, his nostrils flared, his sharp hooves pawing the air. Three hunting dogs emerged from the dust cloud and encircled Dinnis.

Dinnis took two slow steps back and folded his arms, admiring Rokkan's skill in keeping his spooked horse under control. All the while, neither the man's gaze nor his spear's aim waivered.

'Slide it, do you have a death wish?'

Dinnis gave a token bow. 'My Lord Kapok. Forgive me if I startled you.'

'Startled? By all that's holy, Dinnu, I was but a hair's breadth from skewering you. What do you mean by this reckless foolery?' Rokkan sat loosely on Blizzard as the stallion sidled and circled nervously. He lowered his arm, sliding the spear back into its holster.

'Your Majesty, I needed to speak to you alone. A task hard to accomplish in the Palace precincts, but as you make a habit of slipping your guard at this point in the trail ...'

The Kapok's golden eyes narrowed. 'Do I now?' He looked at the empty track behind him. 'Yes, well, it's the chasm. 'Tis rare to find a guard prepared to jump it.' Bringing back his searching gaze to him, he added. 'I believe you enjoyed disconcerting me just now.'

Dinnis could not help the smile tugging at the corners of his mouth. The look on his father's face had been classic. He glanced down at the grey rocks at his feet. 'Perhaps, I misjudged the distance but obviously not your skill.'

'Humph, your mischief making will get you killed one day.'

Dinnis lifted his head. 'And that concerns you because?' Rokkan's gaze did not falter nor did it give anything away. Dinnis continued, 'Besides I'm not the only reckless one. Glad I'm not in charge of your security. It would send anyone grey.'

'That's what Lukarn keeps saying. I'm surprised you agree with him. But let's not waste time. The guards will be along soon enough. Mount up behind me. We will keep moving.'

Dinnis had barely swung up, before Rokkan urged Blizzard into a fast walk along the trail, the dogs falling in behind them. He had not been this physically close to his father for years. Gripping the horse with his thighs, he rested his hands on his legs, keeping a gap between them.

'So, what is this information? Surely, you could have passed it on to Jakan? He told me the chillied castana nuts led to a dead end,' Rokkan said.

'The good Kaptan's been gone from the city the last few of days. He is not due back until tonight. I doubt this will wait till then. You asked me to keep an eye out.'

'Indeed. Go on.'

'Over an argen ago, I was at Upper Market Street on an errand when I noted both Waren and Garvin emerging from Tuson's.'

'Tuson's? The supplier of chillied nuts?'

'Yes, sir.'

Rokkan clicked his tongue. 'This only confirms what we know. You have already established that Garvin likes the treat and we knew Waren buys them though he claims he doesn't like them. Both lads are unlikely suspects. There must be someone else.'

'Perhaps. Garvin then took Ladies Rizanna and Lumi to Zusak's Herbarium.'

Rokkan's back tensed, then relaxed. 'Yes, yes, to get some medicinal herbs for the Kupanna. This is not news, Dinnu.'

'Garvin knew the way to the shop.'

'As does half of Tarka. Come, Dinnis, you need to do better than this. Besides if it has waited twenty-five days to tell me, why is it urgent now?'

'This morning Kusak sent one of his sons to ask Anna for dried bloat fish as he had run out and needed some to fill an order.'

The Kapok paused. 'And this is relevant because?'

'Bloat fish is the source of Breathstill.'

The high-pitched cries of a lone eagle echoed against the slopes. In the distance, the faint sound of travellers and spruikers fluttered until being whipped away by the wind once again. Rokkan moved in the saddle, then turned and looked at Dinnis.

'There are purposes for this poison other than murder,' he said.

'Fishing folk use it to stun and capture large fish of the forest rivers and lakes, and tribal hunters use it to kill prey. But such expeditions are not usually planned during the Heavy Rains.'

The Kapok took a deep breath. 'So, another attack may be imminent?'

'A distinct possibility, Your Majesty. I thought you should know.'

'Hmmm. Thank you. Did Anna supply the blow fish to Zusak?'

'No, but there are other herbalists that might have done so.'

'I'll order a covert guard on Zusak's shop and maybe on the two lads too. And we'll tighten security at the Palace, especially during the reception tomorrow and the wedding.'

'Including the kitchens, sir.'

'Yes, definitely. Maybe I should change up my riding routes too.'

The City Gate came into view. 'That might be a good idea,' Dinnis said. 'And the maids? Did you find which one delivered the tray?' Or was there a woman from outside the Palace working in the pay of the poisoner?

'One of the maids levied from the villages, Binti, disappeared soon after. The other kitchen staff confirm she'd been acting strangely in the days around the murders. Head Cook Sanak has set up measures so no one, not even the maids, will be alone with the serving trays.'

'I hope it's a false alarm, sir.'

'So do I, though I would love to flush our traitor out into the open. He is sure to lead us to Haka.'

'And you are convinced neither Waren nor Garvin have motives? They are the only two that have some connection with the nuts and were present or within easy travelling distance of the ambush and the fire.'

'You mean three. You have a taste for chillied castana nuts, don't you?'

The Kapok's tone was casual, but suddenly Dinnis found it hard to breathe. Was he a suspect? Again? He lifted his chin.

'I can see how one might become addicted to them. I appreciated the bag of nuts you gifted me, which I was able to put to good use. But it's not a taste I want to cultivate given that the cost of a single pot is similar to the cost of feeding a villager's family for a week. I can't afford—'

'Peace, Dinnis. I am not accusing you, son. Both you and Garvin risked your lives to save Mannok's. Just as you risked your life to save mine from Uson's plot.' Rokkan tapped the pommel of the saddle with his strong fingers. 'We're missing something. Some vital piece to the puzzle. On another matter, I understand you are no longer sleeping in the bachelor quarters. Have you and Mannok clashed?'

Dinnis snorted. 'We always clash.'

The Kapok twisted around, his eyebrows raised.

Dinnis hitched his right shoulder. 'He has released me from Palace duties so I can pursue my apprenticeship with Laetil of Greyhaven Street. As a physician.' He kept his face impassive, though cold tendrils of fear twisted about his heart.

'So, did you tell him who you are?'

'No. I've told no one.' Well, no one who doesn't already know or guessed, like Anna. Best not mention that. 'He doesn't know about Ista then?'

'Oh, I've told him about Ista. Had to. I was going to tell him everything, but he wasn't in a listening frame of mind at the time. And perhaps it's for the best. Safer.'

'If you say so.' Safer for whom?

'And you are staying at Anna's then?'

'No, I have a pallet in the storeroom at Laetil's.'

'I see. You have set your heart on being a physician then, Dinnu? Both Jakan and the Head Librarian speak highly of you. Even Sparak thinks you have potential. They are hard men to impress. You have opportunities.'

'To shine? Would that be wise?'

Rokkan let out a long breath. 'Probably not, though the library might be obscure enough to hide you from unwelcome notice. There are few enough who frequent it these days or appreciate its value.'

So maybe his father was shielding him. And his convoluted explanations and apologies a year ago, maybe he'd meant them. 'I want to heal people, not scribble in books. Mannok plans to appoint me as his physician.'

Rokkan pulled back on the reins, easing Blizzard to a stop. They had come to a dip in the road. The raucous sounds of the trade and travel came clearly from beyond the next ridge. Dinnis turned and looked behind him. The twin dust clouds of two guards, still tiny in the distance, were arrowing towards them.

Rokkan rubbed his chin. 'That might work. May the Maker grant you success, but best not to stray too far from the Palace, Dinnu. Let me know if you hear anything further. The Prince's upcoming marriage may give our adversary greater motive to eliminate the obstacles in his way.'

'Do you think Rasel's at risk, then?' Maybe he should be present at all the pre-marriage celebrations planned, to keep her safe.

'I'd say, Mannok and I remain his main targets, but it's possible. I'll drop you off here. You'll be right to make your own way back?'

'As always.'

He slipped off Blizzard and bowed low to the Kapok. Without looking back, he strolled over the rise and merged into one of the groups of travellers heading towards the city gates. Several moments, later the crowds parted as the Kapok rode through, two flustered guards riding behind him.

Chapter Fifty-Three: Brotherly Love

Rasel

R asel walked into the small walled courtyard adjacent to the private living room, balancing the stack of leather-bound books from the Palace Library. At first, she thought the fearsome Head Librarian would not allow her to take a single volume, that is until dear Dinnis intervened on her behalf. She was astounded at the sight of so many books and parchments piled together in serried stacks. Now she spent some time each afternoon in this storied sanctuary, ignoring the pained looks of the clerks and the sharp tongue of Raltan.

The wind scattered the spray of the small fountain across the paving stones and she moved to a stone seat on the windward side. Flycatchers and sulphur chits dipped and fluffed their feathers in the lower bowl of the fountain. An ancient karba tree leant against the wall, its branches soaring into the clear blue sky. She placed the books on a marble-topped table and took a deep reviving breath of the fresh air full of the aroma of green leaves, flowers and the chill of the snowy slopes of the Twins.

After days of grey skies and constant downpours, it was exhilarating to hear the wind sing again and to see the clear blue sky. Now, her love would not be soaked trudging up and down the top of the wall. Loyal Garvin had braved the rain to share Mannok's duty with him and keep him company. And today, it was the Prince's last day of duty.

She raised her arms in an arch, twirling around the fountain.

> *She sang to him in the beauty of night,*
> *Under the stars and double moon light,*
> *She healed his hurts, salved his wounds*
> *And together they sang in sweet delight.*

Five days! Only the pre-wedding reception tomorrow evening, some pre-wedding rituals on the fourth day and then finally the long-awaited celebration.

Far above an eagle keened. The long, wistful note trembled in the air and set her heart racing. She tipped her head back and looked at the speck fighting the wind currents high in the blue, boundless sky. The distant speck turned and circled, dipped then rose again, coming back to the same point. Oh, to be up there flying far above the world. A soft knock sounded on the door behind her.

'My lady, would you like to eat.'

Leesa stood in front of the double glass doors with a tray of cheese, nuts, honeycomb and a selection of fruit she enjoyed—sunfruit, guavas, avocado, cherimoya and succulent slices of green cactus melon. Rasel smiled at the shy lass.

'My thanks, Leesa.' She swallowed the invitation to join her in this bountiful feast, which the girl would refuse. Another Palace protocol she found hard to understand.

The maid placed the tray on a small table next to the books. 'Will that be all, my lady?'

'Yes, Leesa. Oh, wait. Would you remind Palarn it's my love's last night on the wall. I would like it to be a celebration. Do you think he would let me help prepare the food?'

'Oh no, my lady. I mean, I … I guess you could…but…'

'But it's not customary.' Rasel felt some of her joy leak out. It seemed that Tamrin ladies met constraints on every side, like fireflies trapped in glass bottles. She would have to challenge some of those assumptions if she was to breathe, but now was not the time.

'Yes, my lady.' The young girl bowed and backed through the door before turning and hurrying away. Even after an alume, the child was overawed by her and the Prince. Yet Dinnis had been right, she was deft and diligent in her tasks. One day she would win Leesa's friendship.

A swooping whisper of wings came from behind her. She swung around. A white-headed eagle perched on the wall, coal-blacks eyes staring straight at her.

'Semian,' she squealed, shedding her irritation at the constraints of polite Tamrin society like a discarded sash.

The eagle spread his wings and leapt from the wall. His form wavered, stretched and changed, wings becoming arms, talons shortening and legs lengthening until, as his feet touched the paving stones, a young man with silvery-white skin and a cream wrap-around sarum and green sash stood before her. The sight of his familiar and dear black curls, dark eyes and straight-nosed face brought tears to her eyes.

She took two quick steps forward and wrapped her arms around him. After a moment, his arms circled her tight and strong. He lifted her from the ground before releasing her.

'One would think you are happy to see me, youngest sister. I've been looking all over for you.'

'Didn't you see the signs I left you?'

'Well, yes, but I couldn't believe that you would come to this forbidden city, to the stone halls of the Kapoks. I thought you must have continued north.' He looked her over. 'I see they haven't restrained you. Are you injured, Rasel?'

'No, I came willingly.'

His brow creased into a worried frown. He studied her a moment and sighed. 'How long have you been here? Enough to satisfy your insatiable curiosity?' He took her hands into his own. 'Come away now before harm befalls you, dearest sister.'

'I can't leave, brother of my heart. It is too late for that.'

He began to speak, but she put a finger on his mouth and pulled him toward the stone bench.

'Have you travelled far today? You must be famished. Come, rest, eat. The fruit is delicious and you'll enjoy the yarma cheese.'

'Then we'll talk about this?'

'Promise.'

He tilted his head, an echo of his eagle form in his movements. 'I am famished. And I have already eaten Tamrin food, before the Betrayal.'

She steeled herself for the lecture, but instead he took the tray and devoured his way through its offerings. Once a heap of discarded peel and broken nutshells replaced the fruit and nuts, he scooped up the cheese and honey.

Jumping up, she went inside and brought out a bowl of water

and a clean cloth. She placed them beside him and curled up on the bench. 'Long journey?'

He placed the tray on the ground and dipped his hands in the water to wash them. 'Aye, and a couple of shapeshifts. Haven't eaten since last night.'

'Semian! You know how draining shifting is, how important it is to keep your strength.'

He poked her ribs. 'Lecturing me, little sister?' His expression sobered. 'When I could not find you, I feared an accident or worse had befallen you. I could not believe you would be in this terrible place. Only when I'd excluded all other possibilities did I gain courage to enter. By the Maker's tears, please come home to the Great Forest with me, Rasel.'

'I can't. Not without my Prince.'

'This makes no sense, daughter of Jazadek.'

He would not understand. None of her Kin would, but she had to tell him. 'Prince Mannok of Tamra and I are handbound, I to him and he to me.'

'The son of Rokkan and you are joined? How can this be?' Semian frowned, his dark eyes full of hurt. 'You know what these people did to us, to their own kin, the people of Shanta and the people of Mokka.'

'All of which happened before I was born, before my prince was born, before any of the Tamrin now living here were born. They acted under the influence of Akrad's lies. Tellek, Mantil, Akrad have all passed the veil.'

'You think that Baba and Matu have forgotten, that our Kin has forgotten? You know we live longer lives than these younger peoples.' Semian jumped up and paced the small courtyard. 'I may have been a youngling, but I remember the slaughter in Tarka, the massacres and starvation in Shanta, the terrible aftermath. How can we trust these oath breakers?'

She looked down, unable to meet the burning questions in his eyes, and traced the shape of her jaguar brooch. 'I love him, like life itself, and he loves me.'

'But do you trust him not to betray you? Not to harm you?'

'Yes, I do.' She met his intense stare. 'Even though I do not know what the future holds, I trust him with my love and life.'

'Young jaguar cubs don't grow up into long-legged yarmas.'

'I know there will be difficulties. Our ways are so different from theirs. Yet, even we are not without sharp teeth and razor claws.'

'When needs must. But violence should be the last terrible inescapable choice, if a choice at all.' He ran a hand through his dark curls. 'Does your prince know who you are?'

She lifted her head. 'I have told them I'm of the Forest Folk, of the Kin.'

'And?'

'They have forgotten who we are. They think we are the stuff of myths and legends. Frights of the night to scare naughty children.'

'He needs to know, Rasel. If words are not enough, you need to show him.'

An icy coldness seeped through her. 'What if he doesn't understand? If he reacts badly?'

'Then his love, if he loves, is not as deep as you think. You can't truly be joined as one if you keep such a truth hidden.'

The words at the banquet floated in her mind. What the Tamrin knew of her people had been twisted, as if the storytellers had blackened her Kin with their own guilt, their own darkness. Would Mannok recoil from her in horror if he knew? Would he break his promises and spurn her? Yet, her brother had the truth of it, she could not hide who she truly was. She had to show him what she was and hope he still loved her.

Semian moved closer. 'I can't persuade you to come home with me?'

She shook her head. 'I will think about what you've said. Will you tell Matu and Baba for me?'

'I will wait at Bridal Veil Falls three days. If you haven't come by them, I'll return to the Great Forest and tell them.'

'They and any of our Kin would be welcome—'

'Daughter of impetuosity, who of our Kin could come here, to this place of great sorrow?'

'I could bring my love to my Kin in time.'

'I'm not sure that would be wise. Farewell, sweet sister.' Semian pulled his sarum tighter around him. He looked to the sky, his legs tensing beneath him.

She jumped up and caught his arm. 'No, stay a little longer at least.'

'Can you not hear the ground cry?'

She quivered. 'Yes, but I can hear the laughter too. New life, new songs.' She let go of his arm and blinked the tears from her eyes. 'You have not told me of our Kin. How Baba and Matu are. Whether Metizbah has birthed her baby. Where the Kin group has moved with the coming of the rains. Whether Davak has returned from his latest journey. And I have so many stories to tell you, if you would hear them.' She pointed to the books on the table. 'For a start, they have a vast library with rows upon rows of books.'

Semian stood still, sucked in a deep breath. 'For you, I'll stay an hour or two until the sun touches the horizon. Be careful, sweet sister, for I fear for you.'

Chapter Fifty-Four: Revelation

Mannok

Mannok tramped the long, weary length of the City Wall, the wind whipping his cloak against his legs. Garvin trudged beside him, a welcome if silent companion. Hazy blue shadows lengthened across the city below as the sun slipped further down the sky. Mannok rubbed his hands in the cooling air.

The staccato blast of a horn echoed across the valley, warning that the city gates would close at sundown. Merchants in Lower Market Street shuttered their booths, while the more transient traders on the flats outside the wall packed up their stalls. In the fertile valley below, villagers wended their way home from the fields of swaying maize.

'Our last shift. Maybe even the last time we march this wall,' Garvin said.

Mannok play-punched his friend on the upper arm. 'You didn't have to, my friend. This was my punishment to bear.'

'It's about the only way I can see you, these days.'

Mannok lifted his eyebrows, though perhaps Garvin had a point. In the past, he and Garvin were inseparable. Now, the little spare time he did have, he chose to spend with Rasel.

A group of warriors with Puma insignia cantered down Royal Parade toward the Gate. Puran, son of Challak, rode at their head. Once through the gate, they took the road to the north, no doubt heading back to Nakri and the border. Many nobles had already left, not willing to stay even another five days with the increasing risk of flooded rivers, landslides and broken bridges as the heavy rains set in.

Mannok shifted his spear and swung around to tramp back along his assigned section. Surely, he'd worn a runnel in the stone by now. From the wall it was possible to see the life of the city and the surrounding district ebb and flow with the cycle of sun and seasons. A song of the city, Rasel would say. The hours on the wall wouldn't be a punishment if Rasel walked beside him, but no doubt that was the main reason Papa vetoed the idea. Earlier this afternoon, Papa rode out with two guards scrambling to keep up. He and the guards had returned an hour later. At one point, Mannok thought he had seen Dinnis slipping through the crowds and into the city, though he hadn't seen him leave the city earlier.

'I love the view from up here.' Garvin echoed Mannok's own thoughts, as his friend often did. 'You can see so much. Sorry to be late this morning. I had to take care of some family business.'

'Not a problem. You are coming to the pre-wedding reception tomorrow, though?'

'Wouldn't miss it. And I'm really looking forward to the day before the wedding.' A wolfish grin split Garvin's affable face.

Mannok made a face. By custom, the groomsmen blindfolded the groom and whisked him away to overcome challenges of their devising. Not unlike the Trial of Tears, though only one day, not five. Was Garo plotting some particularly gruelling test in revenge for his Prince's neglect? Mannok needed to find a new balance in their friendship. They'd always be brothers, but Rasel had become as important as life itself.

The sun slid further down the red-flushed sky, kissing the distant mountain peaks in the west. A golden rosy glow illuminated the snow on the mountains on the Elder and Younger Twins. The wind died down.

In the south, a lek away, a rider cantered along the valley floor, scattering anyone in front of him on the road. A long dark cloak streamed behind him. Even at this distance, Mannok recognised the lean figure. He lifted the small horn to his lips and blew two short notes followed by three long ones. A few moments later, Kaptin Kaspin bounded up the stairs from the guard house, barely puffing despite his years and white hair, and angled towards them.

'Report.'

'Master Sparak, sir.' Mannok pointed with his spear towards the dark rider who was now within a few hundred tanis of the City Gate.

'Good call. You two, go down and escort him to the Kapok.'

'Yes, sir. And my changeover to the next shift?' Mannok asked.

'I'll see to it. Once the Kapok dismisses you, you're released from duty.'

'Your command, sir.' Yes! He brought his fist to his chest. 'It's been an honour.'

Garvin saluted his father. 'Sir.'

Kaspin clapped them both on the shoulder. 'And a pleasure to have you serve under my command, Prince Mannok. Many blessings on your coming nuptials.'

'My thanks, Kaptan.' Mannok wasted no time jogging toward the stairs and then bounded down them three at a time, Garvin followed at a slower pace behind him.

* * *

Mannok and Garvin strode behind the silent, taciturn Master Scout through the Great Hall and into the complex of corridors and offices near the Throne Room. The duty officer, Lutan Tavin, ushered Sparak toward the Council Room and rapped on the massive seiba-wood door.

Sparak turned to face Mannok. 'I'll take it from here, Your Highness.'

Mannok and Garvin saluted. Garvin turned to go, but Mannok did not move.

Sparak scowled, the old scar running from chin to brow creasing. 'You are dismissed, warrior.'

Mannok stuck out his chin. 'Which means I'm off duty now and no longer under your command. If your information relates to what I think it does, I, as Prince of Tamra, intend to stay.'

He moved toward the door and Sparak blocked him.

The spymaster returned a stare that could freeze the Sha River in full flood. 'My duty is to the Kapok and no one else. The information I carry is for his ears only.'

Not if it was about Rasel. This man terrified Mannok as a child. Still did, if half the rumours were true, but he wasn't retreating.

The door swung open and a shadow fell over him. Papa loomed in the doorway, his feather headdress scraping the lintel. 'You are off duty now Prince Mannok?'

'Yes, Papa.'

Papa glanced at Sparak and then lifted a shoulder. 'Come in, the both of you.' He beckoned with his head and stepped back into the room.

Sparak's lips tightened, but he said nothing as he slipped into the room after Mannok.

Garvin stepped toward them.

Papa turned, smiled. 'Garvin, son of Kaspin, we will see you at the reception tomorrow.'

Garvin nodded. 'Yes, sir.'

Papa raised his dark eyebrows.

Garvin's face fell. He shuffled his feet and bowed. 'Your Majesty.'

His best friend hurried away. Mannok frowned. When was Garvin not welcome to join them? His chest tightened. What news did Papa expect Sparak to deliver?

The casement windows blazed with a fading red-fire, and blood-red shadows shrouded the high-ceiling room. A massive table, scattered with maps, charts, reports and old candles dominated the room. High-backed chairs, a side table and a small hearth added small comforts.

Papa threw himself into one of the chairs. 'You're late, Sparak.'

'Roads aren't so easy to travel this time of year, Rokku. Nor was the task you charged me with an easy one to pursue.'

Papa laughed. 'What! You want easy, old fox? Maybe it's time to retire.'

The taciturn man's teeth flashed in a smile so brief, it was gone before it started. 'Can't get rid of me that easy. Do you want to hear what I've found or not?'

'Spit it out, man.'

'My scouts searched the Shanti wilds and the towns and villages of the Southern Reaches, but we found no trace of the woman's family. No village exists within fifty lek of the Hunting Lodge and no one in many hundreds of lek around recognised the woman's description. It's as if they and she don't exist. She isn't who she says she is.'

'Then who is she?'

Sparak spread out his hands. 'My best guess? She's of Shanti descent, through the eldest daughter of Sil and Akrad.'

Papa jumped up and stalked the room. 'The histories say none of my Shanti royal cousins survived the siege. It would fit many of the facts about her, but not all.'

'More to the point, Your Majesty, does she seek to spy out your treasures and your weaknesses? And if she claims Shanti descent, does she seek to exact revenge for past harms? What. Does. She. Want?'

'Ha! Our Prince's heart. She refused a generous offer of treasure and has withstood every move to encourage her to rethink her choices.'

'So, she plays a long game. Whoever she is, she's not a simple villager and probably not Tamrin.'

Mannok swallowed hard, heat bubbling from his gut to his head. He'd thought Papa had called a truce. His stomach twisted. A truce until his spymaster found evidence to discredit her? No wonder Sparak didn't want him in the room. But they'd found nothing. Nothing at all.

'Papa,' he wet his mouth and marshalled his arguments. 'If she was one of Sil's children, then she's of royal blood. And even if she isn't, you yourself have admitted her courage and wit. Why is it so hard to accept that she is what she seems? That our love for each other is real?'

'Nice sentiments,' Sparak said with a curl of his thin lips. 'I gave up on romantic codswallop the day the Nolmec burned my village and slaughtered every last woman, man and child. Every yarma, horse and dog. And all because they trusted in a truce with the enemy.'

Mannok folded his arms. 'What has that to do with Rasel?'

'Can you imagine the damage she could do if she were a Shanti spy?'

'But you found no evidence of that. Nothing. All you have is suspicions. Rasel said her family would be hard to find, unless they wished it.' Mannok spun to face his father. 'Papa, you gave your word that we could marry.'

His father stared back at him as though reading reflections on the surface of a lake. His mouth was set in a flat line, his eyes hard as bronze.

Mannok's hands went cold. He had submitted to his father's list of punishments and conditions. His father could not withdraw his support now. 'If you have doubts, then I'll swear surety for her loyalty and good wishes.'

Papa snorted. 'That rather defeats the purpose, Mannok, don't you think? I might as well hand the Throne to Haka on a golden platter and retire if she is found to be treasonous and your life is surety for it.'

'You could adopt a son. Trasin or Hasuk,' Sparak suggested.

'Not helpful, Sparro, or even likely to work.' Papa barked a laugh. 'Tempting though. Yalik would be a more strategic choice.'

'Papa!' Mannok ignored the cold-hard ache in his chest and squared his shoulders. 'Your Majesty, if I disappoint you to that extent, I can renounce my birth claim and leave Tamra with my wife, Rasel.'

The hardness in Papa's face melted like a layer of frost in sunlight. 'Mannu, I don't want you to go into exile and not only because your mother would never, ever forgive me. You should know that you have never disappointed me. Reckless and stubborn you may be ...'

'Like father like son,' Sparak muttered.

Papa sent the scout a 'shut-your-mouth-you-yarma' look and continued, '... but you make me proud in a thousand different ways. It's not just the realm that keeps me awake at night, that I long to keep safe. It's you, my son, the newborn babe I held in my hands eighteen years ago.'

Mannok blinked. Had he heard correctly? Papa proud? Of him? It was all he ever wanted to hear as a child. And then with his grief and anger over Ista and now the tension between them because of his love for Rasel and the punishments meted out, he'd forgotten how much his father meant to him. He'd grown to see Papa as the enemy. He'd thought his father was angry with him, but perhaps what he saw was his own anger, not his father's.

The raging heat snuffed out of his limbs, his heart, but that didn't change how he felt about Rasel. 'Papa, I love her. She loves me. She doesn't mean me harm. She doesn't mean you, or anyone else harm either.'

Papa shook his head and sighed. 'If you believe so, then she best stay, for good or ill.'

Sparak jumped forward. 'Your Majesty.'

'Mannok is right, Master Scout. You haven't found any evidence against her. You haven't found anything at all.' Papa held up his hand as Sparak opened his mouth. 'I'm not saying we shouldn't be cautious, but over the last thirty days, I cannot fault her despite some strange ways. So, in the absence of tangible evidence that she means harm, I will accept the Prince's judgment on her motives and character.'

Sparak scowled. 'Naetok—'

'—not Mannok. Not one of my children is.'

'Your problem, Rokkan, is that you're an incurable romantic. It will bury you one day.'

'A fate none of us can avoid in the end, Sparro. I've made my decision. It's final.'

Sparak shook his head with a mournful look. 'A softness that comes from reading too much poetry as a child. But who am I to argue, oh mighty Kapok?'

'By that token, Ralton should be a paragon of high sentiment and cuddly kindness. And you argue every blasted time.'

Sparak snorted, then let go of a rusty laugh. 'True.'

Mannok squeezed his eyes shut. Each moment he stayed was another stolen from his time with Rasel. 'My thanks for your trust in me and in Rasel, Papa. Now, if you would give me leave?'

Papa waved him off. 'Go, go. I'll see you tomorrow at the reception.'

* * *

Stars had winked into existence against the deep turquoise sky by the time Mannok reached the outer courtyard of the Silisean Palace. The welcoming glow of candlelight flickered through casement windows and mouth-watering smells mixed with the scent of wood sap and flowers enticed him inside.

The two guards saluted him, and Palarn greeted him at the door, bowing low.

'Your Highness, Lady Rasel is in her rooms. Your meal will be ready to serve soon.'

'My thanks, Palarn.' Mannok nodded and continued towards the private rooms. In the small intimate sitting room, the candles were lit and a small brazier glowed in the corner. The double glass doors stood half-open, letting in a night breeze. Rasel's white-clad figure was visible through the cloudy glass diamonds. She stood close to the central fountain.

'Rasel,' he called.

He blinked. Did a dark figure stand behind her in the deep shadows of the karba tree?

Mannok stepped into the courtyard, the door swinging shut behind him. Rasel stood alone in the gloaming with her back to him, her head tilted back as if looking into the purpling sky. A snowy owl lifted into the air, landing on the highest branch of the tree.

Rasel turned towards him. Tear tracks shone on her cheeks, shining like silver streams. She took half a step towards him, slipped her slender arms around his waist and rested her head upon his shoulder. Her ragged breathing trembled against his chest.

'What's wrong, my love?' he asked.

'I miss my family and my home,' she replied, her voice muffled.

She pushed closer into him, her body warm against his. The now familiar scent of pine and mountain flowers filled him with tenderness. The owl hooted from the top branches of the ancient tree.

Rasel stepped back and held his hands. He freed one and leant forward to brush the tears off her face.

She smiled back through the trembling of her bottom lip. 'Sorry.'

How hard would it be to separate from one's family and home, to be alone among strangers? 'Do you want to go to your family?' He didn't want to ask. Didn't want to hear the reply, in case she said 'yes'.

'No, not without you.'

'What do you see in me?' he asked.

She arched her eyebrows, her long lashes still dewy with tears. 'I do like your library, but …' she traced a finger over the jaguar design on his golden pectoral chest plate and on to the muscles of his shoulders and chest. 'I love your courage, your strength, your love for life, your loyalty to your friends, your capacity to let go of anger and forgive.'

'As always, you praise me more than I deserve.' Mannok caught her fingers and pulled her closer. 'Soon we'll have more time together.' Three more nights. He had to do this right. He could not afford to do anything that would reflect badly on her honour, if his family was to respect her.

The low mutter of voices, muted by the walls and doors, permeated from the inside, where Leesa and Petrak readied the smaller dining room for the evening meal.

Her hands trembled in his.

'My love, you're cold. We should go inside,' he said.

She took a deep breath of cooling night air. 'Before we do, I have something to show you.' Her voice quivered, she who had faced down his father without flinching.

'After the meal, perhaps?'

'No, now.' She stood taller. 'I told the son of Martal, your father, that I am of the Forest Folk, an Adelphi as your people term my Kin, a shapeshifter.'

'A joke, yes?'

'No, son of Rokkan, not a joke. I know only one way to convince you of the truth.'

'How?'

She put a finger to his lips. 'Hush my love.'

Pulling her other hand free, she stepped back and stood a moment thinking. Then with a nod, she stretched out her arms and pitched forward.

'Rasel!' He went to catch her, but found he could not.

Before his eyes, her form shimmered and wavered, her silvery skin took on golden fur with black rose-ringed spots, her fingers grew dagger-like claws, her face shortening and broadening and taking on long white whiskers. A full-grown jaguar crouched in front of him, the black tip of her tail twitching.

A dream. He'd wake at any moment. He reached out a hand and touched her fur, soft with the glide of powerful muscles bunched beneath the velvet skin. The wild feline smell filled his nostrils. His legs turned to slurry like a half-frozen river.

'Mannok! No! It's me, Rasel.'

He blinked, looked at the hunting knife in his hand that he didn't remember unsheathing. He dropped it and sat down on the dew-cold paving stones and tried to make sense of what had just happened.

Not a joke, then. Adelphi, shapeshifter, his love.

He licked his lips. 'Did I hurt you?'

'No.' She butted her great head against his shoulder. 'Just a scratch.'

He buried his hands into her fur, felt the heat radiating out from her, this jaguar, his Rasel. 'I can understand now why my tale of the mother jaguar distressed you,' he said. Babbling because he didn't know what else to say, what else to think.

'Taking on the song of another creature creates a certain kinship,' she said.

He lifted his head and met her dark, wide eyes. 'Is that why you sympathise with humans?'

She laughed, though it was more like a guttural cough. 'My Kin, like your people, son of Tamrak, are descended from the first parents, Aduma and Kai-eema, though our people and yours separated paths many eons ago.'

She crouched, her form shivering once again until his Rasel sat before him.

'This is my natal form. I am a woman just like your cousins. In recent times, your people and mine were friends and allies until the Betrayer turned you against us, though perhaps the seeds of distrust had already been sown as you became lovers of stone mansions and gold and status. And my people withdrew more from your palaces and cities.

He believed her. 'And your reason for being here?'

'You invited me, Prince of Tamra. You asked me to marry you and I said yes, because, heart of my heart, I love you.'

'And you mean me, my father, my people, no harm?'

'No, no harm. You need not fear me. But now that you know what I am, do you want me to leave?' Her voice quivered on the last word.

'No!' He knew the truth of it, like he knew his own heartbeat. 'I ... you're more wonderful than I could have imagined.'

A brilliant smile spread across her silvery-white face and danced in her dark eyes. 'I will show your father, your family.'

'No.' He caught her hand, Sparak's lean face flashing before his eyes. Papa's eagle-eyes. What would they do to his love if they knew? 'It's enough that I know.'

She frowned, then nodded. 'As long as there are no secrets between us, my love.'

Pushing himself to his feet, he took her arms and pulled her up into a tight embrace. Their lips met, fierce and bruising and full of passion. He never wanted to let her go or come up for air.

Moments later a latch turned. 'Your Highness. My lady. Oh! Forgive my intrusion. Should we delay serving dinner?'

With an effort, Mannok stepped back. He caught his breath. 'No, Leesa, we will come now.'

Rasel tucked her arm in his and whispered in his ear. 'Five days and no one shall interrupt us.'

The gust of wind came sobbing around them, pulling at hair and garments. In the west, the final glow of the sun faded from the sky. With a mournful call, the owl rose slowly from the low branch of the karba tree and, with powerful strokes, circled around them. It dipped a wing and then glided over the wall and into the night.

Together, he and his beloved followed Leesa into the golden glare of candlelight.

Chapter Fifty-Five: Collapse

Lumi

Lumi swallowed against the lump in her throat. How had it come to this? In three days Rasel would marry the Prince. Now he stood with Rasel at his side, welcoming the guests as they came through the Throne Room doors. Mannok looked regal in gold cloak, jade-green tunic and breeches, gold accoutrements and headdress. He held Rasel's hand as though cradling a precious treasure and, between guests, sent her looks of pure adoration. Someone had dressed her in a long forest-green tunic embroidered with leaves and birds, a jade-and-gold-encrusted sash and long crimson and gold cloak. Jewelled combs held her midnight hair, piled up in the latest Palace fashion. A jade necklace and dangling earrings framed her radiant face.

The highest nobles of the land, or at least those who had not yet returned to their own clan lands, clustered around the room. Lumi wished her family had already left the city, but Father had insisted on staying to the bitter end. But then, with typical highhandedness, he'd set off with Estolik on a short expedition, supposedly to inspect a nearby alabaster quarry. This morning a messenger came to say Father had been delayed and wouldn't arrive until tomorrow. His absence at this high occasion made her nervous. Did Father have plans in place to harm Mannok? Or the Kapok? She should warn them, but what evidence did she have? And if the Kapok didn't believe her, if nothing happened, who knew what Father would do to her. No matter how often she swallowed, the lump in her throat wouldn't shift.

Kerri, standing on the other side of Rizanna, reached over and tapped Lumi's arm with her fan. 'Just because she is dressed up like a princess doesn't make her one. What does he see in her?' She scrunched her small nose with the same disdain she'd showered on Lumi, Rizzi and the rest of the Tamrin court earlier in the year.

Rizzi tinkled with nervous laughter. She twirled a tendril of chestnut hair then clasped and unclasped her hands. 'She's mazed his mind.'

Kerri sniffed. 'That must be it. I cannot see one thing to recommend her, don't you agree, Lumi?'

'As you say, Princess.'

Even as the words left her mouth, Rasel turned and looked straight at her, as if she'd heard every word above the babble of voices in the room. Lumi flicked her fan to cover her face. Kerri would be miffed that Mannok had rejected her in such a spectacular fashion only to choose a woman with no family, no name, no position or wealth to recommend her. After riding out each morning with the woman, Lumi was all too aware of Rasel's qualities. She combined a shapely statuesque beauty with knowledge of the classics and a sparkling wit. She rode her filly even in the busiest city streets without saddle or bit. And her welcoming smiles and soft words could trick one into thinking she meant to be a friend. Yet how could she be anything but a fake and an imposter? Perhaps Rizzi was right that she was an enchantress.

A sad, disappointed look flashed across Rasel's face before she turned to welcome another guest, this time Kaptan Kaspin and his wife.

Rizzi leant over and whispered something into Kerri's ear. The Limarian princess covered her rosebud mouth with lacquered nails and simpered. Her pale eyes gleamed as they fixed on Garvin strolling past. He balanced a small tray with a tumbler of guava juice and two beakers of birch wine. Their eyes met and his face broke into a smile.

Lumi looked away, her cheeks warming.

'Lackey, do you have a drink for me,' Kerri said, her petite chin in the air.

Garvin's heavy eyebrows climbed up his forehead. He looked behind, to the sides and back at Kerri. 'Beg pardon, are you speaking to me, Your Highness?'

'Garvin only fetches and carries for Mannok and his wench,' Rizzi said. 'I do assume the guava juice is for that woman.'

Waren turned around from where he stood with Jarrah, Trasin and a couple of others some paces away. He sent a disapproving-big-brother frown in Rizzi's direction.

'Oh, not a servant, but a personal attendant of our esteemed Prince then.' Kerri sniffed. Her multiple golden bangles clashed as she put her hands on her hips.

Garvin looked from one to the other, a crease between his brown eyes. His jaw tightened. 'Yes, the juice is for the Lady Rasel. The wine is for the Prince. But I can certainly fetch you some drinks if you desire, Lady Lumi.' He glanced at Lumi, then looked away with a flat smile. 'Lady Rizanna ... and you too, Princess Kerri. Birch wine perhaps?'

'Birch wine would be adequate,' Kerri said.

'Nothing for me,' Lumi managed against the increased tightness in her throat.

'Nor me,' Rizzi said.

Garvin presented the Princess with the spare cup, perhaps meant to be his own. 'Now, if you ladies have had your fun, I have an errand to complete.'

Rizzi stepped forward and caught his arm, leaning in close. 'Sorry, Garvin, if we were discourteous. Friends still?'

Garvin gave a sharp nod, disentangled himself, and walked toward the Prince, his back as stiff as a frozen waterfall. Waren separated from his cluster and walked up to Garvin. He put a hand on a shoulder and spoke a few hushed words. Garvin nodded and smiled, some of the tension easing, before continuing on his way.

'Why tease poor Garvin?' Lumi said, a sour taste in her mouth.

Rizzi shook her head, her lips a little parted, her eyes fixed on Garvin as he made his way to the Prince. Had Rizzi transferred her affections to Mannok's loyal shadow? A strange way to flirt with him, though it certainly got his attention.

Kerri giggled. 'Oh, but he is just a soldier's son, is he not?'

'Garvin is an honourable warrior of Tamra, his family comes from an old lineage, well-respected in the city and Palace. But even if it wasn't so, that was poorly done.'

All three of them jumped at Waren's reproving words.

Rizzi put her hand to her chest. 'Brother dear, don't scare us like that.'

Across the room, Mannok took the guava juice and handed it to Rasel before taking a sip of birch wine. Rasel smiled and said something to Garvin and he smiled back, though it looked a little forced. Something troubled him, but Garvin son of Kaspin was the least of her concerns.

The woman took a long swallow of the juice. Moments later, her fine brow creased. She looked up at Mannok wide-eyed and gripped his arm. The tumbler fell from her fingers, crashing to the mosaic floor. Her legs crumpled and, with a soft moan, she fell like a wilting flower drifting from a tree.

'Rasel!'

Mannok's agonised cry carried throughout the reception room, stilling conversations and laughter. Heads turned to look. Mannok crouched down and took Rasel in his arms. She did not stir, her face waxen, her limbs limp.

Had the woman fainted in the heat and humidity of the room, made worse by the throng and standing still at the door so long? Afterall, she was unused to the weight of formal clothing.

'Now she makes a spectacle of herself.' Kerri made a small noise of disgust.

Rizzi grasped Lumi's arm.

'She's ill.' Jarrah pushed forward through the staring, whispering crowd, Waren hurrying behind her.

'My love, wake up.' The sound of fear and loss and agony in Mannok's voice tore at Lumi.

By the Maker, was she dead? Lumi rushed toward the group at the door, not sure what she could do.

Rizzi grabbed her arm and pulled her back. 'Let Jarrah help her.'

Lumi shook off her friend's hand, sinking dread clawing at her belly. Was this Father's work? But why target the woman, not the Prince? So that she could have a chance at winning Mannok's affection? Sudden relief flooded through her that it wasn't Mannok lying lifeless on the floor and then, surprising her, a wrench of grief for this strange woman who'd brought a dash of fresh air and an overture of friendship with her from the wilderness.

Jarrah stooped and loosened Rasel's sash and tunic. 'Stand back, all of you, give her some air.'

Rasel's eyes fluttered. She was alive, thank the Maker. She reached out, her slender hand shaking like a leaf in the wind. She gripped Mannok's tunic. He bowed his head and she put her lips to his ear.

Bright tears started in Mannok's eyes. 'I love you too,' the words wrenched out of him. 'Jarrah, save her please.'

Rokkan Kapok strode towards them, Markan Lukarn on his heels, so close he almost tangled with the Kapok's cloak. Kupanna Marra, with Mama and Lady Samara, approached from another direction.

'Stand back and give her room,' the Kapok boomed. 'Jarrah, what is wrong with her?'

Lumi stumbled back a few steps, but she could not drag her eyes from Rasel's still form.

Jarrah put her ear to Rasel's chest, examined her eyes, mouth and limbs. Do you feel any pain Rasel?'

The woman shook her head, her chest straining with the effort of breathing.

'Apoplexy perhaps, Your Majesty, though she's young for it. Or ...' Jarrah swallowed and her voice quavered. 'Maybe poison. I'm a surgeon in training, not a physician.'

'Breathstill,' the Kapok said, rubbing his chest.

Lumi followed his eyes to the fallen tumbler, pink guava juice spilling out over the floor.

'No,' Mannok whispered. He rubbed Rasel's hands, patted her cheek, but she slumped against his chest. 'Rasel. Wake up.'

'Your Majesty, I'll find Galen or Fulik,' Garvin said.

The Kapok roused himself and caught Garvin by the shoulder. 'No lad, stay here. Bitjarnan, find Fulik. Kaptan Jakan, move all but family to the back of the room. No one else leaves until I say so.' The Kapok's blazing gaze swept over the clumps of nobles as though looking for someone.

The white-haired man saluted and hurried off, shouting orders. A rising murmur of half-hearted protests swelled through the room then petered out. Once the tottering madomo left, the guards barred the doors. More guards moved the courtiers to the other end of the room, leaving the group clustered around Rasel isolated.

A tall figure pushed his way through the crowds from the edge of the room, a leather satchel slung over his shoulder. The Nolmec, Dinnis.

'Let him through,' the Kapok's voiced boomed out.

With a grumbling murmur the crowd parted.

Rasel gave a soft sigh and her hand slipped from Mannok's. Her head lolled backwards. Mannok let out a long keening cry that sliced through Lumi's heart, leaving it in jagged pieces. She had wanted her rival gone, defeated, but not like this.

Chapter Fifty-Six: Broken Trust

Mannok

She couldn't die. She couldn't die. She couldn't die.

Mannok cradled his beloved Rasel's head against his chest, studying her limp form for the smallest signs of life. Her face was translucent, her hands, white and unmoving, cold as ice. Only the slightest rise and fall of her chest showed that she still lived.

He had seen this deathlike stillness before, when Uson had poisoned Papa a year ago. But Uson was dead and buried. So, who could have done this? His breath rasped against his throat as a long thin wail threatened to push past his lips. He clenched his jaw and took a ragged breath. Please, by all that's good, all that's precious, please don't let her die.

People crowded around—Jarrah, Lumi, Waren, Trasin stood close, eyes wide and staring, behind them others of his age-mates. Lukarn and Garvin stood on the other side of him. His father and Mama beside him. Which one was to blame? Who in this room, in the Palace, had done this to his love? If it was Papa, he'd never forgive him.

As moments seeped by, she seemed to stiffen, the soft touch of her breath fading like morning mist. If he knew of a way to give her his breath he would. Instead, she slipped away from him like desert sand through an open hand, like a reed boat in a flooded river's fierce current.

Dinnis dropped down beside Rasel, his breath rasping.

'What is he doing here?' Mama shrilled.

'Peace, Marra. Let Dinnis help unhindered.' Papa's voice was pitched low so only those standing close could hear.

'He is my physician,' Mannok croaked. And the man knew poisons. He reached out and grabbed Dinnis' arm. 'Save her, please.'

'I will.' Dinnis pressed his finger flat against Rasel's slender neck and then put his ear close to her mouth. He checked her eyes and mouth, tested the suppleness of her limbs.

'Lay her on her side, flat on the floor.' Dinnis helped Mannok place her. 'Support her chin like this.' Dinnis guided his hands.

Satisfied, he reached for the beaker and swirled the remaining liquid. He then dipped his finger in the dregs at the bottom, sniffed it. He grimaced.

'Breathstill?' Papa asked.

Dinnis nodded. 'Yes. Though there is something else I can't place.'

'You have the antidote?'

'Yes, Your Majesty. I need a cup of birch wine.'

Papa grabbed a beaker from the abandoned tray and thrust it at Dinnis, who then tested it.

With a nod, he opened his satchel and removed a small packet. He crumbled some of the dried grey-green herb into the beaker, using a metal rod to mix the potion. Then kneeling over Rasel, he dribbled the liquid into her mouth, his eyes fixed on her face.

This mixture saved Papa's life. Surely it would save Rasel's.

'She's taken a large dose,' Dinnis said. He continued to dribble the mixture into her mouth at intervals.

Rasel gave a faint sigh. Her breathing grew stronger. She coughed. The antidote was working. She opened her eyes, wide and dark, and stared at the lean lad attending her.

'*Chava* Dinnis,' she said, her voice the faintest whisper. '*Tova rabal.*'

She slowly turned her head and looked at Mannok. Her eyes were like dark pools in her silver-pale face. Her fingers curled around his as soft as feathers. '*Ahavi*, my love.'

She struggled to catch her breath and a series of harsh coughs left her panting. Mannok ripped off his cloak and folded it under his sweet love's head. He removed the jewellery and combs from her hair, to make her more comfortable.

Her breathing become steadier and stronger. Mannok closed his eyes for a brief moment. Surely the danger was past.

He looked up. Papa and Uncle Lukarn were in deep conversation a few steps away. Kaptan Jakan moved in and joined them. Guards stood at all the exits. More guards moved the astounded courtiers to the other end of the room, leaving the group clustered around Rasel isolated.

Papa returned to their group; his golden eyes fixed on Rasel's face. Kaptan Jakan and Uncle Lukarn followed.

'Mannok, do you remember who gave Rasel the juice?' Papa asked.

'Garvin got the drinks but ...'

Dinnis threw a lightning glance at Papa.

His father met the look and shifted his eyes to Garvin. 'Is that so, Garvin?'

'Yes, Your Majesty, but I didn't know. I wouldn't. Surely you don't suspect me?'

Papa's face didn't soften. 'Where did you get the juice from, Garvin?'

'I poured it from the pitcher on the table over there and brought it straight here.'

A cold chill shot up Mannok's spine. 'If someone tampered with the pitcher, others would have felt the effects of the poison.'

No one else had collapsed, only Rasel. Garvin was his earliest and most loyal friend. There was no way he would be involved in an attempt against his life. But against Rasel? Did his friend resent her because he felt neglected? No, if he couldn't trust Garvin, who could he trust? Not the Garvin who tramped by his side at the wall, even when it wasn't his duty.

Papa nodded. 'Yes, and a guard was positioned at the table. And no one else touched the tumbler, Garvin?'

'No, sir.' Garvin stared at the floor, his tan face taking on a greyish hue.

'This is ridiculous. Garo wouldn't hurt my love. With the press of people, someone could have slipped the poison in the drink.' Mannok looked at Rasel's wan face. 'Must she stay on the floor?'

'I'd like Lady Rasel to regain a bit more strength before we move her. She isn't recovering as fast as I expected.' Dinnis stayed close to Rasel, a worried frown on his normally calm face.

Papa tapped Jakan on the shoulder, and the Kaptan cleared his throat. 'If I may, Noble Garvin, you bought chillied castana nuts from Tuson's recently?'

Garvin lifted his blunt chin. 'Yes, I purchase them when I can afford it, which is not that often. I didn't know that was a crime.'

'We believe that a number of attacks, including those on the Kapok and the Prince and the murder of Uson and Asik, are connected. And fragments of this unusual treat were found near Uson's body.'

'Further attempts on the Prince's life? I hadn't heard of this,' Rizanna said. 'I thought those lads were responsible for the attacks.' She picked at the knot in her sash. Kerri and Lumi hovered behind her.

'For reasons of security we haven't made this common knowledge,' Uncle Lukarn said. 'But yes, the attempts didn't stop with Uson's murder.'

Jakan nodded. 'Most likely, Uson and Asik did not work alone. They were killed because of what they knew. Whoever is behind the attacks may have promised wealth, power, position and maybe even marriage.'

Lumi gasped.

Garvin shot her a look. He dropped to his knees and his eyes widened, like a cornered deer held at bay by a pack of hunting dogs. 'Your Majesty, I didn't do it. I would never betray you.'

Mannok scowled at Papa. 'That seems a lot of perhaps and maybes. Garvin was in as much danger at the ambush at Pine Stand Gap as I and at the fire at the Way Station.' Though, now he thought of it, Garvin's clothes had seemed less ashy than the others.

'I agree, Mannok.' Papa glanced at Kaptan Kaspin and Lady Taraya, standing a few tanis back, faces slack with shock. 'But it is beyond dispute that Garvin was the one with access to Lady Rasel's drink. No one else had the opportunity. We need to take him into custody.'

Chapter Fifty-Seven: Forgive Me

Rasel

Each breath tore through her, like a club studded with a thousand teeth. She could move her limbs now, no longer imprisoned in a traitorous body that would not respond to her directions. But something still wasn't right. Some foreign and malicious substance worked its way through her tissues, turning her lungs to fire and her muscles to water. If her mind could focus, perhaps she could eliminate it. But never had she felt so weak, so helpless, so at the mercy of others. She gripped the Prince of Tamra's hand, drawing strength from his presence.

Filane words swirled around her, words of anger and accusation. What were they saying now?

'No one else had the opportunity. We need to take him into custody.'

She propped herself up, her breath whistling at the effort.

'Rasel, lie still,' her love murmured. 'You need to recover.'

'I can breathe easier sitting up,' she gasped.

Dinnis looked at her intently. 'That could be.' He pressed a finger to her wrist. 'Maybe ...'

Mannok put his arm around her shoulders, supporting her weight. People clustered around them with strained faces. Mannok's loyal friend knelt in front of the son of Martal, head bowed, shoulders slumped. Bewilderment, hurt and fear flittered across his open face.

The son of Martal heaved a sigh. 'Jakan, search him.'

Two guards advanced on Mannok's friend. He held up his hands. 'Let me.'

The son of Martal nodded, and the guards stepped back. Mannok's friend took off his headdress, unfastened his pectoral plate and cloak, handing each item to the guards.

'Knife, tunic and boots,' the man of war, Kaptan Jakan, said, his face a tight mask of regret.

Garvin wordlessly complied, removing his scabbard, pulling his tunic over his head, shucking off his boots to stand in his breeches, bare chested and barefooted on the war-patterned floor. He held his arms out from his sides.

A guard stepped up and ran his hands over every tinas of the lad's body. 'Nothing, Your Majesty.'

The son of Martal gave a curt nod. 'Search the room, starting with the area between the jug and here. And Jakan, get Lutan Tavin to make a list of our guests, and all but family should be cleared from the room. No one is to leave the Palace until I say so.'

The Kaptan gave the orders. Lutan Tavin and several guards took charge of the guests, while other guards spread out and searched the crevices of the divans, under the tables, behind tapestries and in the ceramic pots holding the plants.

The son of Martal turned back to Mannok's friend. 'Think, Garvin, did you stop or speak to anyone along the way? Did anyone brush up against you?'

'He stopped to talk to us,' the daughter of Haka said, a quaver in her voice.

The son of Martal turned his eagle gaze on the girl. 'Who do you mean by 'us', Lumi?'

'Princess Kerri and Lady Rizanna and me. Lord Waren also had a word with ... with Garvin.'

'While he carried the tray?'

'Yes, Your Majesty.'

'Ridiculous. You can't accuse me. My father—'

'Hush, no one is accusing you, Princess Kerri,' the Kapok said. 'But we need to exclude all possibilities.'

A warrior came up to the Kapok and bowed. 'Your Majesty, I found this in one of the plant pots.'

He opened his hand to show a small bag of dyed yarma leather with a golden design stamped on the bottom. The Kapok took it and loosened the draw strings. Nestled inside, were two small glass bottles.

Dinnis jumped up. 'Be careful, sir. Don't touch the vials. There may be traces of poison left behind.'

The son of Martal handed the bag to friend Dinnis who placed it on the floor. Taking a soft cloth from his satchel, he picked up and examined first one vial and then the other.

He gave Rasel a worried look. 'Two vials, maybe two poisons. It would explain the slow recovery.'

'There's a puma on the bottom of the pouch.' Rasel whispered the words against the growing tightness in her chest.

'Impossible.' Mannok's uncle scowled at her.

Dinnis carefully turned the bag over, displaying the emblem embossed in gold. A puma, as she'd said.

The Markan of the North's face dropped, but he recovered quickly. 'A misdirection then, like the black-fletched arrows at Pine Gap Stand.'

The Kaptan stirred. He darted a look at the man of frowns, Mannok's uncle, then widened his stance. 'Your Majesty, Lord Waren also purchased the nuts from Tuson's and, like Garvin, was in the vicinity of the other incidents and could have interfered with the juice when he spoke to Garvin.'

Waren's eyes widened. 'I'm loyal.'

Samara gave a little cry while Jarrah looked up and shook her head.

'You can't be serious. What motive would he have?' Mannok's uncle roared.

'The animosity between the Commander and the Prince is …' Jakan's voice faltered under Mannok's uncle's withering stare.

'This … this is silly,' Rizanna said. 'Waren never breaks the rules.'

'Maybe you should look to the one with the most motive to undermine the Throne.' The Kupanna looked directly at Dinnis.

'No, Mama.' Mannok shook his head. 'Waren has no reason to buy chillied nuts, he hates them, same as me. And Dinnis saved my life at Pine Stand Gap. He has no reason to poison Rasel.'

'Unless you were the actual target, Mannu.'

Dinnis remained kneeling beside her as though the discussion did not concern him. He drummed his fingers on his satchel, his eyes shadowed by thought.

'Peace, Marra.' The ruler of Tamra turned to the son of Lukarn. 'Do you deny you bought the nuts, Waren?'

Waren looked at the Kapok, then bit his lip and looked away. 'I bought them, yes.'

'For yourself or someone else?'

Waren folded his arms and studied his boots, his mouth in a hard line and conflict written across his face. He was protecting someone. Rasel sighed, her breath catching into a flurry of racking coughs.

The Princess of Limar's bangles chimed. 'So, imprison and question all three, I'm sure you'd get answers. Such a fuss and she's not even dead.'

She gave Rasel a scathing glance. No love there and no furtive glances of regret or guilt either. More telling perhaps was the lack of a covert triumph in the spoilt Princess's manner.

'Kerri!' The daughter of Haka hissed and sent long troubled looks toward Garvin, as though she felt responsible in some way. And despite her recent overtures of friendship, the daughter of Haka viewed her as a rival, perhaps one to be eliminated. She hid her thoughts better than most Filane.

'Rokkan, you can't mean to imprison your own nephew? Dinnis did it.' The Kupanna wrung her hands. 'He contrived it somehow.'

Dinnis looked up at that, replaced the vials in a bag. His mouth twitched into a wry smile. 'I would be speechless in admiration for my own ingenuity, except I am not the puppet master in this charade.' He gripped the Prince of Tamra's shoulder, but spoke to her. 'Lady Rasel, breathstill is common enough, and the antidote well known. The second poison is harder to determine. I think, given your symptoms, it's a coral toxin, not something often seen in the mountains. It would be imported from the coast.'

'You know the cure though?' her love demanded.

'Maybe. We should give an emetic as soon as possible, to remove any remaining poison, and then a koka bean brew, bladeleaf and pasak blossom to help with the symptoms.' He hitched his shoulders. 'Perhaps, a room nearby would provide a better environment for treatment.'

Her love nodded. 'I can carry her to one of the guest suites.'

'Or, if His Majesty would permit, send for a litter.'

'Jakan, see it done,' the son of Martal commanded.

The Kaptan signalled some guards who rushed from the now almost empty room.

Rasel leant forward. 'My thanks, man of the north.'

'Thank me, when you are returned to full health, my lady.' He stood up, pulled down his tunic and surveyed the room. 'I do hope any arrest can wait until then.'

'By the pit, I should hope so. Or not at all,' the Prince of Tamra growled. He looked straight at the daughter of Haka. 'Did you do it, Lumi?'

'No! I wouldn't.' The daughter of Haka's silver eyes widened in shock.

'Mannok! How can you say such a thing?' Lukarn's daughter moved restlessly beside her. 'It has to be Garvin.'

'A bit closer to the blood, I think,' Dinnis muttered.

'Rizanna.' Rasel whispered. The signs of guilt were there, the nervous energy, a certain furtiveness, the guilt-tinged thoughts. But why, except that from the moment Rasel entered these halls, they all despised her. Was the daughter of Lukarn jealous, as Dinnis had suggested?

The Kapok drew in a long hissing breath.

Lukarn's neck bunched, the veins in his temple throbbing. 'What? No child of mine would do this ... this thing. On what grounds do you accuse her? She's a child. Not yet seventeen.'

Something clicked in Garvin's face. Confusion flashed into a sudden certainty. He sent the daughter of Lukarn a burning look. 'It was you. You asked me which drink was the Lady Rasel's and, while I spoke to Kerri and Lumi, you touched my shoulder and huddled close. You set me up to take the blame for murder. Said nothing while your brother remained silent for your sake. After all, what's one life more on your conscience? No, no, we are not friends.'

Rizzi broke into shrill laughter. She pulled a hunting knife from her tunic and pushed the daughter of Haka out of the way, her hazel eyes wild. 'What if I did? I'm not going to be shackled like a commoner in that stinking yarma stall of a prison.'

'Rizzi,' Markana Samara cried out. Waren buried his face in his hands and groaned. 'No!'

The guards rushed toward the daughter of the Markan of the North.

Rizanna backed away. 'It was his idea. He said I had to for the sake of the realm. I ... I didn't know about the attempts on Mannok's life. I would never have agreed if I had. He made me do it.'

The Kapok waved the guards back and took a step towards the troubled lass. 'Who said, Rizzi? How could he make you? No one was holding you at spear point.'

'I did a terrible thing. He said they were a danger to you, Uncle Rokkan, and to Mannok. He said they knew something and they might talk to me because we'd been friends. If I took the tray, I could get in to see them,' Rizzi looked at the Kapok, her eyes bright with tears. 'I didn't know it would kill them.'

The son of Martal took a step closer. 'You poisoned Uson and Asik?'

Rizanna lowered the knife a fraction. 'Yes, they deserved it, maybe. Maybe they had to die.'

'The guards would have seen you, Rizzi.'

'I was dressed as a maid. No one recognised me. I even stopped to talk to Uson for a while. Offered him some nuts until ... until he began to moan and writhe. It was horrible.' A shudder ran through Rizzi's taut body. Her hand dropped a ninas or two further.

The son of Martal took another step towards her. 'And was poisoning Rasel your idea?'

'He suggested it, to save Mannok from her. She is a wicked enchantress. He said she is a threat to the Throne and he'd reveal my secret if I didn't do it.'

'What do you know of the ambush? The fire?'

'He said nothing about that.' Tears welled up in her hazel eyes. 'I would never harm Mannok, I swear Uncle Rokkan, I never would.'

'But this man, he lied to you Rizzi. He played you. He has tried very hard to harm both me and Mannok. Who is he?' Where is he?'

'He left the city days ago.

'His name,' the Kapok said, his face grim.

The girl shivered. 'He said I should keep the thing we did a secret, or bad things might happen to me.' With all the spite and envy and subterfuge drained from her face, only terror and stark truth remained. 'Will I be lashed? Will I have to jump the Red Leap? I don't want to die.'

Rasel's heart fluttered. Just a child, yet she had killed and had wanted to take her life. Regrets but no real remorse, so many shadows filled one so young. How could this be?

Mannok's uncle gave a soft moan. He rubbed his face. 'Rizanna, you have to tell us his name.'

'Adjunct Puran, son of Lord Challak of the Puma tribe. I thought he was working for you and Uncle Rokkan, Papa.'

'Puran? Are you sure? Does he work for another?' Rokkan asked.

Rizzi shook her head, tears streaming down her face. 'I'm so sorry, I don't know. I didn't know. Please forgive me, Uncle.' She turned towards Lukarn. 'Papa.'

Lukarn opened his mouth, then closed it, his face anguished.

She turned away from her father, stretching out a hand to Mannok. 'Mannu, please forgive me.'

Her love's body stiffened, his arm tightening around her. 'Never.'

Rasel looked at him, placing her hand on his arm. 'My love …'

Rizanna laughed, a high-pitched eerie sound. She shifted her grip on the knife, pointing it at her breast. The Kapok took two strides and grabbed her wrists. The sharp blade clattered to the floor, gleaming in the late afternoon light, and she collapsed into his arms. Sobs wracked her body.

'It's Lady Rasel you need to ask for forgiveness. If what you say is true, with the boys you were duped, but you intended to kill her without qualm,' Rokkan said. 'And you were content for others to take the blame, even your own brother or Garvin. Lady Rizanna, you will face the Royal Council's judgment for your deeds against the Throne. I can only thank the Maker that your plan and that of your oath-breaking cousin have failed.'

Rasel sat up straighter. 'I do forgive you, daughter of Lukarn.' She turned to the Kapok. 'Please, let this be the end of it.'

Rizzi only snarled at her.

'If only it were so simple,' the Kapok said and sighed.

Chapter Fifty-Eight: Friends

Lumi

Lumi stared at the embossed double doors of the Silisean Palace. The sun, angling through the green foliage of the surrounding trees, singed her shoulder blades and highlighted the fine details of the carving on the door panels in searing white light. A fine mist of sweat beaded her top lip. Already white clouds were pillowing on top of one another in the sultry blue sky, like dreamier reflections of the distant mountain peaks. Hopefully it would rain later today.

She reached out to push open the double doors. A happy laugh from inside stilled her movement and her arm dropped to her side. Looking down at her sandaled feet, she smoothed an imaginary crease in the fine cotton of her deep blue tunic. What was she doing here anyway?

The soft trill slid into a sustained cough. Lumi's forehead furrowed. Had Rasel not fully recovered? Mannok's anguished face as he looked at his betrothed lying motionless on the floor had haunted her dreams last night. Who was she kidding? His love for the peasant girl would not easily be broken. This was no passing infatuation and in two days' time, they'd be married. A sob caught in Lumi's throat and she bowed her head in defeat.

'Your pardon, my lady, but were you going in?'

Lumi jumped at the sound of Garvin's voice. She spun around, her hands flying to her cheeks. Two young men stood before her, arms folded across their chests. Garvin's thick eyebrows hitched up in bland query while Prince Mannok's stormy green eyes matched his downturned mouth.

'I'm sorry,' she stammered. 'I ... I wanted to see how the Lady Rasel was faring.'

The Prince's expression lightened a little, though he said nothing.

Garvin tilted his head to one side. 'Just a suggestion, but you could try entering the building to make inquiries.' Then his face widened into a friendly smile. Stepping past her, he pushed the doors and then swept his arm towards the opening with a flourish. 'My lady.'

Her cheeks burned hotter as she looked towards the Prince. Protocol demanded that he take precedence. 'I ... I don't wish to intrude or get in the way.'

A small smile stole onto Mannok's face. 'I think it would speed matters up if you went in, Lumi.'

She nodded and stumbled through the small hall and into the shadowed receiving rooms, Mannok and Garvin following behind her. Shutters on the front windows repelled most of the late morning sun, with only spots of light dancing on the cool mosaic floor. As her eyes adjusted to the relative dimness, she saw Rasel reclining upon a divan at the far end of the room. A tall man leaned over her, an arm around her shoulders. Beyond her, serried doors opened out to a shaded courtyard and tinkling fountain.

Mannok pushed past her as the man stood back and placed a cup upon the small table next to the divan. The Nolmec, Dinnis. Rasel turned towards the Prince and smiled, her whole face lighting up.

'Prince of Tamra, I am glad to see you.'

The Prince smiled back. 'My love, how are you? Here's Lumi come to visit and wondering after your wellbeing.'

The enigmatic Nolmec busied himself with some vials and small pots, putting away medical paraphernalia into a worn leather satchel.

'I'm well enough, thank you, though both Dinnis and Laetil insist I rest for a couple more days. Anyone would think I was an invalid.' Her laugh ended in a cough.

Dinnis moved towards her, offering her the cup. After a few sips, the spasms began to subside.

'Wretched cough.' Rasel sighed, her silver brow creasing. 'But really, I am feeling much improved this morning.'

Mannok sat down beside her. Rasel leaned against him, slipping her arm around his waist. Lumi looked away, small twinges of compassion fighting with the swirling jealousy.

'I don't like the sound of this cough, Dinnis,' the Prince said.

The tall fellow nodded. 'Nor I. Master Laetil confirms my suspicions that a coral toxin was added in addition to the Breathstill. A slower-acting poison, but one that also takes longer to clear from the body. Which is why rest is required, Lady Rasel. You are not a good patient.'

'This is a new experience for me, Friend Dinnis, but I will do my best to bear it well.'

Mannok's eyes narrowed and his lips thinned. 'Rizanna has much to answer for.'

Lumi's throat tightened at the coldness in his voice.

'Poor Rizanna.' Rasel's dark eyes looked sorrowful.

Either the woman cared despite Rizzi's actions against her or she was an adroit actress. Lumi sighed. The events of last evening still snagged her thoughts, not least that her best friend had been scheming murder. How could she have had no inkling of what was troubling her? No doubt Puran had put Rizzi up to it as she claimed, but was Puran acting on his own? The sharp memory of the young Adjunct in deep and agitated conversation with her father tightened the knot in her throat.

Mannok snorted. 'Poor Rizanna indeed! She tried to kill you, my love. She almost did, and she did kill Uson and Asik.'

'I know, Prince of Tamra, but she is young and was troubled and deceived.'

'So she says.'

'It is possible to be manipulated and intimidated into doing things you would not normally do.' Lumi bit her lip. Why had she said that?

Mannok's nostrils flared and his hand formed a fist. 'And you think that makes it right?'

She shook her head.

'Easy Mannu, Lumi's not to blame for Rizzi's foolishness,' Garvin said.

The Prince scowled at his friend for a few seconds before his face began to relax. Lumi shot Garvin a grateful smile.

'I'm sorry, Lumi. I'm out of sorts this morning, especially since Rizzi gets off with a light sentence. The Council agreed on indefinite exile at Chiba working as a common maid under the oversight of Aunt Lakwi.'

'Then the Council has already made their decision?' Dinnis asked.

'And you asked for leniency, as I asked? Thank you, my love.' Rasel bent forward, placing a light kiss on Mannok's cheek. 'She is still young.'

Mannok growled. 'Yes. Let's not talk about it anymore. It depresses me.'

'Well then, let's talk about our wedding.'

'Humph. Papa is talking about postponing until you are completely well.'

'But I will be well enough in a day or two. Do you think we can persuade him to leave the day unchanged?'

Lumi collapsed on a nearby chair and suppressed the urge to shout. Delay. Delay. Delay. Not that any amount would separate these two now.

A grin transformed Mannok's face. 'We can certainly try. Dinnis do you think you or Laetil could add the weight of medical advice?'

The Nolmec hitched his narrow shoulder. 'If the Lady Rasel's health continues to improve, but only on the condition that the lady agrees to complete rest over the next couple of days.'

'My friend, you drive a hard bargain.' Rasel smiled, her expressive eyes shining. She leaned forward. 'Can I ask you a favour, Lady Lumi?'

Lumi's eyebrows drew together. 'If I can ... perhaps.'

'Now that Jarrah is not affected so much by morning sick—' Rasel stopped, looked at the three young men, then sighed, 'I mean, now that she is feeling better from her indisposition, both she and Lady Samara have agreed to be my wedding attendants. But I understand it is usual to have another at the ceremony. Lumi, I was hoping that you would agree to be my companion.'

Lumi blinked, not sure if she'd heard right. 'You want me to attend you, Your Highness?'

'That's a great idea.' Mannok beamed at her. 'Rasel has greatly enjoyed the rides you have shared each morning, dear Lumi. I'm happy that you have taken time to be her friend.'

'And it's a great honour too—a companion at a royal wedding,' Garvin said. He looked at Lumi, his head tilted to one side and grinned at her. 'Waren, Hasuk, Trasin and I will be among the Prince's attendants.'

'And Dinnis,' Mannok said.

'Oh, I thought you had forgotten about that,' the Nolmec said. 'Must I?'

'I'm holding you to it.'

Lumi looked from one smiling face to another. Well, why not? What did she have to lose? She nodded.

Mannok jumped up and gave her a quick hug.

'Let's celebrate.' He clapped his hands. 'Palarn, some food for my friends.'

Chapter Fifty-Nine: Alone at Last

Rasel

Rasel woke to the sound of the birds heralding the sun. Shadows still shrouded the room with a hint of light bleeding through the shuttered doors. Today was the day when her marriage to Mannok, already performed by the customs of her own people, would be confirmed by the customs of his. Yesterday, after a ritual bath, Mannok's Aunt Samara had taken her to one of the smaller temples. Here, as was traditional or so she was told, she had spent the afternoon in quiet reflection. Apparently, Mannok also underwent a different ritual of a more boisterous nature involving challenges devised by his age-mates.

Sitting up in the bed, she hugged her long legs, her stomach fluttering. She didn't doubt that the day would be long and filled with rules and rigid Tamrin protocols. Still, once it was all over, she and Mannok would finally be married in the eyes of all. She smiled, her breath catching, as she thought of her splendid Prince.

Approaching footfalls came from the living areas beyond the bedchamber followed by a soft knock on the door. Pulling a cotton shawl over her shoulders, she glided to the door and opened it. Markana Samara, Samara's daughter-in-law Jarrah, Lumi and the young maid Leesa, entered the room.

'May the Maker bless you on this special day, Lady Rasel,' the Markana said with a bow. Jarrah, Lumi and I will be your companions today, if you so desire.'

Rasel smiled at the older woman. 'Indeed, I do.'

Leesa, her soft brown eyes lowered, offered her sunfruit, yarma cheese and frothy koka drink on a small tray.

'It may be a long time before you get a chance to eat again,' Jarrah said.

Lumi had moved across the room to open the shutters, letting in the pearly grey light. The horizon was blushed with salmon and gold. Samara waved two serving women carrying clay water pots into the small room used for ablutions beyond the bedchamber. Rasel could hear the splash of water being poured into the sunken bath. She allowed herself to be led into the room, undressed and submerged in the flower-scented water. The women chattered and laughed, teasing her about the nuptial night, as they scrubbed her with soft soap, sluiced the cold water over her and rubbed her down with scented avocado oil. It felt strange to have these women she had only met a few ten-days before, helping her with intimate tasks she had been doing for herself even since she was a young girl. She closed her eyes and forced herself to relax. Leesa with gentle hands combed Rasel's dark curls that fell beyond her waist.

Once the women had dressed her in a simple white tunic, they led her back into the bedchamber. By now, golden sunlight was streaming into the room. Her eyes widened as she noticed a bloodwood tray full of small pots, brushes, boxes, containers and an intricately carved bone knife. On the bed, brilliant clothes and jewellery were laid out. Soon, more solemnly now, the Markana, Jarrah and Lumi were busy applying a thick red and black paste in detailed patterns on her forehead, cheeks and arms. Using cochineal, they reddened her lips and nails. She breathed in sharply when Samara took the bone knife and began to cut her hair at the shoulder.

'Why?' she asked, watching her dark curls falls softly to the ground.

'To mark the end of your life as a maiden.' Samara swiftly wove her remaining hair into multiple braids tied with red and black beads.

'It has never been cut. It is not the tradition of my people.'

Jarrah carefully saved one lock and placed it in a carved wooden box. 'This we give to the groom after the wedding night for him to treasure.' She gave a shy smile.

Then they dressed her in a long white tunic with a wide woven waist band, a thick red sleeveless robe embroidered with gold thread and jewels, ruby-encrusted slippers and a long cloak embroidered with gold. Then came the jewellery; gold bands on her arms, the ruby and obsidian necklace and ear pendants the Kupanna had given her when she'd first arrived in the Palace, and an elaborate golden circlet with an arc of nodding red and black plumes.

'Mannok will not recognise me.' Rasel held her head steady, the weight of the finery pressing down on her.

'Don't worry, he will,' Lady Samara said with a gentle pat. 'You look beautiful.'

Rasel could hear a riotous noise in the distance. Lady Samara carefully led her out through the public rooms, the tight skirt of the tunic forcing her to take small petite steps. By the time they reached the reception room, the noise of reverberating drums, horns, flutes and raucous shouts drowned out the birdsong. A loud knock at the door and there was Prince Mannok, in a rich tunic, robe, cloak and headdress of green and gold. His face was painted in black swirls. She knew him by his lucid jade eyes and quick enthusiastic grin and smiled back unabashedly.

Without a word, he took her by the hand and led her at a stately pace to an awaiting litter carried by six strong men and surrounded by a noisy crowd of the Prince's age-mates and retainers. She could see Garvin, Dinnis, Waren and the others she knew. He handed her up and when Samara, Jarrah and Lumi had settled in beside her, he drew the thick embroidered curtains, enclosing her in darkness.

The litter swayed and jolted as they progressed from the Palace grounds, through the streets crowded with cheering people, to the great temple at the pinnacle of the city. Stifled by the heavy perfume of the furnishings and languid air, she could not shake the feeling of being trapped. When the Prince opened the curtains and helped her out of the litter, she almost kissed him in front of all these people.

He squeezed her hand and led her up the stairs to the top of the pyramidal structure to stand before with a man with wrinkled face, snow-white hair, a man who she now knew to be Chief Priest Kaifak. His golden staff and gilded robes caught the sun. Markana Samara, Jarrah and Lumi stood to her left while Waren, Garvin, Hasuk, Trasin and Dinnis stood to Mannok's right. Above them was the blue sky with the sun behind them and the gibbous orb of Alumi hanging above the western horizon.

Standing by the side of her love, longing to touch him, she soon lost the thread of the long interminable ceremony with its prayers, incense, admonitions, vows and rituals. She spoke when prompted, walked three times around the altar and bent her head forward so that the Prince could place the golden three-stranded necklace over her braided head, all the time afraid she would lose the heavy headdress.

The priest gently turned them to face the semicircle of nobility surrounding them, with the Kapok and Kupanna standing at the centre.

Holding Mannok's and her hands up high, the priest's voice boomed out, 'The Prince Mannok and his new wife, Princess Rasel. May they be blessed with long life, prosperity, progeny and happiness.' The man placed the Prince's strong hand in her slender one. The air vibrated with yells, cheers and a cacophony of music.

She smiled happily, beginning to relax, relieved that the ordeal was surely over. The sun was now high in the azure sky. Far overhead, she thrilled to see an eagle drifting in the thermals. Semian, surely. Maybe her brother would dare enter the city of the Kapoks to visit her.

'Have we finished, my love?' she whispered to the Prince of Tamra.

He did not turn his head but whispered back, 'Afraid not, my love.'

She caught sight of Kupanna Marra staring at her with cold disapproval. A small hard-to-read smile played at the corners of her husband's mouth.

'We are not supposed to talk until we are finally alone later tonight,' Mannok whispered, his lips barely moving.

'Night?'

She exhaled slowly and steeled herself. Her head was already aching from the noise, the smells, the crowds and the heavy clothes and headdress. And she still felt a little weak after her poisoning ordeal. She longed to ride off on Saharah, with Mannok on Shadow beside her to seek an extended time alone together, as was indeed the custom of her own people. Yet, she had always known that marrying him meant she was marrying into his family, the life and traditions of these strange Tamrin. It was a price she was still prepared to pay.

The rest of the day passed in a blur. After bowing low to his parents, Mannok led her back down the long stairs while the guests and crowds pelted them with maize kernels, flowers and sweets. Then they were carried back together in an ornate open litter. They made even slower progress, with mothers lifting their babies to them to be blessed and the Prince scattering handfuls of gold pieces among the crowds pressing up to see them. Once at the Palace, they followed the Kapok and Kupanna Marra into the Throne Room. After a light meal, they sat next to the royal couple while an endless parade of gifts was presented, admired and the givers thanked.

The feast that followed in the Banqueting Hall was a fiendishly formal affair in which the bridal couple had pride of place. Rasel barely touched the food. Following the numerous courses of extravagant dishes, the company was entertained by musicians and acrobats. Then there was the dancing, so unfamiliar with its rigid, formulaic movements. Towards the end of the banquet, a group of young men attempted to steal Mannok's shoes while his companions ran interference.

'They stand in for your family,' Dinnis whispered, appearing to her left.

She was glad to see a familiar friendly face, though Mannok turned and gave his sardonic friend an appraising look.

'But don't they have shoes of their own?'

'It's a tradition. If they steal your groom's shoes, he won't be able to steal you away from your loving family.'

'Too late, he has already stolen me!' She looked at Mannok and he grinned back at her.

At last, the feast was over, but now they were accompanied on their way to the Silesian quarters by Mannok's parents, close family and friends carrying long tapered candles and torches. There was a lot of hilarity and joking, most of it bringing a blush to Rasel's painted cheeks. Soon they were crowding into the bedchamber after them. Markana Samara sprinkled flower petals on the bed with a blessing. Then with Rasel standing on one side of the bed and Mannok facing her on the other side, their companions divested them of all their finery until only the simple white tunics remained. Rokkan Kapok clapped his son on the shoulder.

'Well, into bed with you. Best keep your rash promise, Prince of Tamra and make her your wife.'

He left and everyone else poured out into the adjoining public rooms. Even though she could still hear the babble of their merriment, at last she was alone with her love. She wasted no time in moving to his side. He caught her up in his arms.

'Rasel.' He closed his eyes and laid his forehead against hers. 'Prince of Tamra.'

She shivered at the touch of his hands. She could feel the pounding of his heart against her chest. Fear and excitement chased each other in her tumultuous thoughts.

'My love, you are so beautiful,' he whispered opening his eyes and looking deep into hers.

She lost and found herself in the green depths of his intense gaze and she wasn't afraid.

Chapter Sixty: New Beginnings

Dinnis

The hilarity and celebrations in the Silisean Palace went on long into the night while the Prince and his Princess did what brides and grooms do when left alone on their wedding night. The Kapok and Kupanna had departed sometime after midnight, though Mannok's age-mates were in no hurry to leave.

As the first light of day began to creep through the shutters, Dinnis smothered a yawn and disengaged himself from a raucous discussion on the merits of different breeds of hunting dogs. Laetil would be expecting him to help with the usual round of sickness and injuries following too liberal celebrations throughout the Palace and across the city. There would be feasts and entertainments for the next ten days in honour of the royal wedding. But his time at the Palace was over. As he sauntered towards the main door, he saw Trasin sitting on his own in a corner looking miserable. He clapped the lad on the shoulder.

'Would you like something to drink or eat?'

'In truth, I think I have already imbibed too much.' The lad sighed.

'No one blames you, Trasin.'

Trasin looked up, his boyish face scrunched into a frown. When he caught Dinnis' eyes, the scowl crumpled into a woebegone expression.

'Don't they? Who will trust me now? How could Puran have dishonoured our family like this? Papa would be ashamed that he broke oath against Rokkan Kapok. Why would he do it?'

'I don't know, though it's not just Puran. The Kapok's own niece, the Lady Rizanna, has been implicated. It's a great shock to everyone, not least to Markan Lukarn and Kupanna Marra.'

'A sad day for the Puma clan.' Trasin's young face lengthened. 'Do you think my uncle's Markanship is at risk?'

'He and the Kapok are closer than brothers and there is no evidence either he or Waren are involved. Look Trasin, the sun already rises on a new day. No matter how dark the night is, don't give up hope. Maybe you should put those idiots over there right about hunting dogs.'

The lad laughed, though his eyes were sad. 'Maybe I will. One thing is for sure, you are a good friend Dinnis. I won't ever forget that.'

They bumped fists. Trasin walked over to the group sprawled around a table crowded with tumblers, dishes and platters now empty of food. Waren looked up and beckoned him in and Garvin clapped him on the shoulder.

Dinnis smiled and nodded and slipped out of the door. Blushing clouds formed ladders climbing the vault of the grey sky. The air was fresh and full of birdsong carolling the red dawn.

So Mannok had kept his promises and Rasel had won her Prince. He was glad she was happy, yet he grieved the loss of something that perhaps had never been his. Maybe one day he would find a woman to match her, but for now he was free. Free from Palace duties and Palace intrigues. Free to pursue his own goals. Perhaps he should take his own advice to Trasin and look to the future. He toyed with the idea of going over the wall for old times' sake, then thought better of it. As he walked through the fruit trees, he began to hum an old soulful tune—the old lay about the tragic love story of Prince Solik and Namu of the waterfall.

'You are in a relaxed mood.'

The deep voice brought him to a standstill, his heart pounding. A tall, powerful figure in the shadows, leaning up against the rough grey bark of a Marosa tree. Rokkan! The Kapok pushed himself off the tree trunk and stepped towards him.

'I wanted to thank you. It's a tangled mess, but we are perhaps closer to unravelling it due to your wit and diligence. And I owe you the Prince's life and now Rasel's.'

Dinnis bowed. 'I was glad to help the Lady Rasel, Your Majesty. Lord Lukarn must be relieved his child is spared.'

405

'Well, Haka and Duran wanted the full punishment to be exacted.'

'The Red Leap?'

'Yes. A shameful and brutal death. No doubt they hoped to create dissension between us, but Lukarn exempted himself from the decision. As my Master of Horse, he could only concur with those two hypocrites, but as her father he could only ask for mercy. He is devastated. He even offered to stand down as Markan, which I refused. But Mannok spoke in her favour, very reluctantly, I must say.'

'Because Rasel insisted on forgiving her.' Which was so like her. 'But Rizanna is to remain in exile?'

'At least for now. I can't ignore what Rizzi did, though I do believe her story that she has been duped at least in part. Sending her to the east, into Princess Lakwi's keeping, is the best I could come up with, at least until I can confirm her story about Puran.'

'He could have been responsible for the attacks on the Prince,' Dinnis said. 'He even had injuries consistent with such an attack following the ambush and was close enough to reach the village the night of the fire. Jakan says Puran fled to the north with some of his cronies.'

'Yes, it's plausible. And Waren admitted that he bought the nuts for his sister. And she has admitted to taking the tray to Uson and Asik.'

'Loose ends neatly tied. By the way, Trasin is concerned he is implicated in his brother's probable treachery.'

'He needn't be unless he gives me cause. I think I'll keep young Trasin close in Tarka for a bit. As for Puran, it seems he has been brooding on his father Challak's untimely death for some time. I understand why he might have sought revenge against me, for perceived wrongs during the rebellion, yet he couldn't hope to be Kapok. Somehow, I don't see him as the shadowy mastermind, more likely another puppet like Rizzi. This isn't over, I fear.'

Dinnis gave a tight smile. 'More of Haka's doing is my guess. Perhaps he promised Puran the Markanship of the North, which his father had under Naetok or some other high office.'

'Most likely. If we capture Puran, he could lead us closer to Haka. But we will have a bit of breathing space for a while.' Rokkan stroked his chin. 'You are very like your mother, Dinnu. She followed her own course, resistant to Akrad's influence even though he was her guardian, her Arkon. She too was intelligent and brave. She would be proud of you. As I am.'

Dinnis met his father's eyes, overwhelmed. 'I'm not sure what to say. That sounds suspiciously like a compliment.'

The corners of his father's mouth tugged up. 'Don't get used to it.' Pulling something out of the folds of his tunic, he threw it at Dinnis.

Dinnis reached out and caught it without thought. It was a small bag with something heavy inside. After an almost fatherly moment, was Rokkan paying him for services rendered?

He felt the weight in his hands, then threw it back. 'I don't need your metal, Your Majesty.' He lifted his chin. 'I can make my own way.'

Rokkan raised an eyebrow and threw it to him again. 'Just take it Dinnu. It's a small gift, not a payment. The Maker knows that I owe you more than I can repay. More than I can say.'

Dinnis hesitated. After a moment, he opened the drawstring of the bag and drew out a red painted pot of chillied castana nuts.

He smiled at Rokkan's teasing humour. Those nuts had led them on a rather convoluted trail but, in the end, they had exposed the culprits. And he had developed a taste for them. He put one in his mouth and bit down on it, savouring the rich creaminess of the nut's heart and burst of fiery chilli flavours. He extended the pot towards the Kapok who took a couple of nuts and popped them into his mouth.

Over the last several alume, he had earned his father's trust, working in tandem with him to foil Haka's schemes. He had even been given the freedom to pursue his own dreams. And Mannok now respected him. There were still those at the Palace who did not trust him, and his father would never acknowledge him publicly as his son, but they were forging a new relationship, one he could live with.

'I'm thinking I'll go for a ride. Want to join me?' Rokkan interrupted his thoughts.

'The way you ride, I'll pass. I do hope you are not going without an escort!'

'You know, it's depressing how like Lukarn you sound at times.'

'He can't always be wrong.'

Rokkan laughed. Clapping Dinnis on the back he turned and strode towards the stables. Dinnis extracted another nut and chewed. A breeze ruffled his hair. Who knew what the future held? Haka wasn't defeated. Yet today was a glorious day and he had work to do.

Author Note

If you've enjoyed this foray into the world of Nardva, please leave a review on Amazon, Goodreads and/or your favourite reviewing site.

Keep up to date with new releases, giveaways and events, sign up for *Jeanette O'Hagan Writes* email newsletter http://eepurl. com/bbLJKT and receive a short story set in the world of Nardva.

You might also like

Akrad's Children–the first novel in the *Akrad's Legacy* series.
Heart of the Mountain–the first novella in the Under the Mountain series.
Ruhanna's Flight and Other Stories–a collection of short stories, mostly set in Nardva.

Coming Soon

Lumi's Allegiance, Book 3 in Akrad's Legacy stories
Mannok's Betrayal, Book 4 in Akrad's Legacy stories
Space Triage and Other Stories
The Chameleon Protocols trilogy

Character List

Akillis, Palouma of the a Nolmec phalanx at North Pass.

Akrad, Arkon of the Nolmec (also call the Betrayer or the Westerner by the Forest Folk and Deceiver by the Tamrin) of unknown origin but who has dominated the politics of Tamra and the Five Lands for over to seventy years.

Amaruk of the X clan, wife of Princess Lakwi and Markan of the Eastern March.

Anna, the old Herbalist in Crooked Street, Tarka; mother of Tilli, Nikki, Aska and Norak.

Old **Anton**, domestic servant at Nakri; he lost a wife and two of his sons to a Nolmec raid and three brothers in the rebellion.

Lutan **Atorak**, a warrior in the Palace Guard and sent to the Border Patrol with Mannok; a minor noble from the northern Puma clan.

Asik son of Lutan Turak, orphaned in the war and given a position as Prince Mannok's companion.

Binti, a kitchen maid.

Bitjarnan, the madomo (head of palace staff, household steward) to Martal Kapok and his son Rokkan Kapok

Challak, son of Waruk, cousin of Lukarn and Marra, Head of the Puma clan, who sided with Naetok.

Durak, father of Durrin and Markan of the Southern March.

Durrin, son of Markan Durak, best friend of Estolik.

Dinnis, the son of a Tamrin warrior and of Kiprissa Gaia, granddaughter of Akrad.

Estolik, son of Markan Haka and Markana Yuta and older brother of Lumi.

Fulik, one of the garrison surgeons of the Royal Guard.

Galen, royal physician.

Garvin, the son of Kaptan Kaspin and childhood friend of Prince Mannok.

Haka of the Dolphin clan, the grandson of Tellek Kapok and cousin of Rokkan Kapok. He is Estolik and Lumi's father and Markan of the Eastern March.

Hasuk son of Kaptan Maikwi, orphaned in the war and given a position as Prince Mannok's companion.

Ista, younger sister of Dinnis, and daughter of a Tamrin warrior and of Kiprissa Gaia, granddaughter of Akrad.

Kaptan **Jakan**, a warrior, Kaptan of the Palace Guard.

Jarrah, Waren's wife and a surgeon.

Jati, daughter of Princess Lakwi

Jazadek son of Korak and Kerren; Kinleader of the Forest Folk, father of Rasel and Semian.

Chief Priest **Kaifak** of Tarka.

Kaptan **Kaspin**, Kaptan of the City Guard and father of Garvin.

Kimsak, a younger son of Markan Lukarn

Kontar, second son of Durak and Durrin's younger brother.

Korak, Kinleader of the Forest Folk and grandfather of Rasel and Semian.

Brigan **Kolik**, son of Derik, Markan Lukarn's younger brother and a Brigan in the Kapok's armies.

Lakwi, Princess of Tamra, younger half-sister of Rokkan Kapok, and son of Martal Kapok and Kupanna Suraya and married to Markan of the Western March.

Lantil, a Palace guard.

Lukarn of the Puma clan, son of Derik, older brother of Kupanna Marra, nephew of Kupanna Suraya and best friend of Rokkan Kapok. Rokkan appoints him and Markan (or governor) of the Northern March after Prince Naetok's treachery.

Lumi, daughter of Markan Haka and Markana Yuta and younger sister of Estolik.

Mannok (Mannu), Prince of Tamra, son of Rokkan Kapok and Kupanna Marra

Marra of the Puma clan, Kupanna of Tamra, wife of Rokkan Kapok, mother of Prince Mannok and sister of Markan Lukarn

Martal Kapok son of Tellek Kapok and father of Rokkan Kapok, Prince Naetok and Princess Lakwi.

Mattik a royal scribe, originally a villager

Prince **Naetok** (Naetu), younger half-brother of Rokkan Kapok, and son of Martal Kapok and Kupanna Suraya. Before he dies, Martal appoints him Markan (or governor) of the Northern March.

Keloumen **Nikoris** the commander of the Phalanx of Nolmec supporting Akrad. Nikoris is under the command of the Nolmec General Nuktis.

Ninak, retired Kaptan of the Palace Guard, nephew of Pirak and father of Redrik.

Palarn, Prince Mannok's camp master and madomo.

Pirak, son of Kusin, of the Grey Fox Clan spoke against Rokkan at Nakri

Adjunct **Puran**, son of Challak, brother of Trasin of the Puma clan.

Ralton, head librarian in the royal library.

Rasel, youngest daughter of Jazadek and granddaughter of Korak of the Forest Folk.

Redrik, youngest son of Kaptan Ninak and grand-nephew of Pirak

Rizanna (Rizzi) of the Puma clan, eldest daughter of Markan Lukarn and Markana Samara, brother of Rizanna and Prince Mannok's cousin.

Rokkan (Rokku) Kapok son of Martal Kapok and Kupanna Tula (princess of Silisea).

Rutiah daughter of Yitzak and Chaviah, granddaughter of Dinah, Healer and Herbalist of the Forest Folk and mother of Rasel and Semian.

Headman **Saluruk** of Mist Fall Village in the Southern Marches.

Markana **Samara**, wife of Markan Lukarn and mother of Waren, Rizanna, Kimsak etc.

Sanak, Head Cook at the Golden Palace of Tarka.

Semian son of Jazadek and brother of Rasel, one of the Forest Folk

Princess **Sila** of Silisea, wife of Tannik and mother of Tolteal; Sila is also Rokkan's cousin as her mother and his (Tula) were sisters.

Kupanna **Suraya,** second wife of Martal Kapok, stepmother of Rokkan Kapok and mother of Prince Naetok and Princess Lakwi.

Queen **Suza** of Silisea, mother of Princes Tannik and Asok

Tamak, Markan Lukarn's chief surgeon in Nakri.

Prince **Tannik** of Silisea, husband of Princess Sila and father of Prince Tolteal.

Lady **Taraya**, Kaptan Kaspin's wife and mother of Garvin

Tilli, daughter of Anna the Herbalist.

Toban, a young ruffian and leader of a street gang.

Prince **Tolteal** of Silisea, son of Prince Tannik and Princess Sila.

Trasin, Lord Challak's second son and age-mate of Mannok.

Tujek, a worker at nearby Hartil stables.

Turuk, Royal Kennel Master.

Uson son of Lutan Yanak, orphaned in the war and given a position as Prince Mannok's companion.

Valen, garrison surgeon at Kaja and Jarrah's father.

Waren (Waro) of the Puma clan, eldest son of Markan Lukarn and Markana Samara, brother of Rizanna and Prince Mannok's cousin.

Wasuk, head groom of the royal stables, originally from Silisea.

Yalik, son of Markan Amaruk and Princess Lakwi, a member of the Prince's band.

Markana Yuta, wife of Markan Haka and mother of Estolik and Rumi and a good friend of Kupanna Marra's

Markana **Yuta**, wife of Markan Haka and mother of Estolik and Lumi and a good friend of Kupanna Marra's.

Zaven, Lutan in Rokkan Kapok's guard and later in the Palace Guard.

Peoples, Time and Measurements

People, Titles and Words

The Filane people consist of the people of the Five Lands (Mokka before the invasion by the Nolmec, Tamra, Shanta, Silisea, Limar). The Five Lands are in the southern hemisphere of the world of Nardva.

In Tamra, the king and queen are called Kapok and Kupanna while in Limar they are called Sulkan and Sulkana. In Tamra, the Lords of the Four Marchs (North, West, South, East) are known as Markan and their wives as Markana. The major household steward is known as 'madomo'.

Among the Nolmec a princess is called *Kiprissa*, a prince Kiprisson or more commonly *Alfeas*; a commander of a Phalanx (or Brigade) is a keloumen; *kuree* is a general honorific meaning 'sir'; *moros* means idiot or fool; *pioni* is foot soldier or servant; *chia* is a term of endearment.

Some Eldar words: *rakka* means fool or idiot, *saba* means grandfather, *baba* is father and *matu* is mother.

The Moons and Time

Nardva has two moons, the bigger golden hued moon Alumi and the smaller silver hued moon Argenti. The Filane (unlike the Nolmec) base their calendar on the cycle of Alumi with 12 months of 30 days. Thus an **alume** is 30 days (the cycle of Alumi); an **argen** is 20 days or two ten-days (the cycle of Argenti). Time is also divided into tens (e.g. a half-ten; a ten-day; two ten-days etc.)

Among most of the Filane nations at that time, **the day** is divided in two sets of ten 'hours' each - sunset to sunrise, sunrise to sunset. Thus, the first hour begins at sunset while the tenth hour ends at sunrise, and so also during daylight.

Filane measurements:

A **lek** (plural also lek) is the equivalent to 1.2 kilometres; a **tana** (plural, **tanis**) is equivalent to 1.2 metres; nina (plural, **ninas**) equals about 1.2 centimetres.

Map of the Five Lands

Genealogies

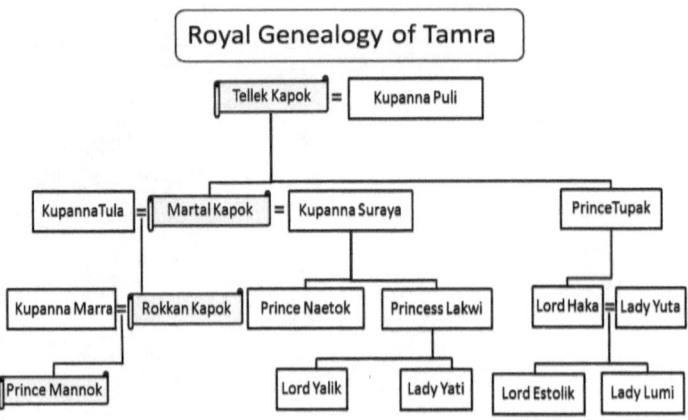

Royal Genealogy of Tamra

Tellek Kapok = Kupanna Puli

KupannaTula = Martal Kapok = Kupanna Suraya — PrinceTupak

Kupanna Marra = Rokkan Kapok — Prince Naetok — Princess Lakwi — Lord Haka = Lady Yuta

Prince Mannok — Lord Yalik — Lady Yati — Lord Estolik — Lady Lumi

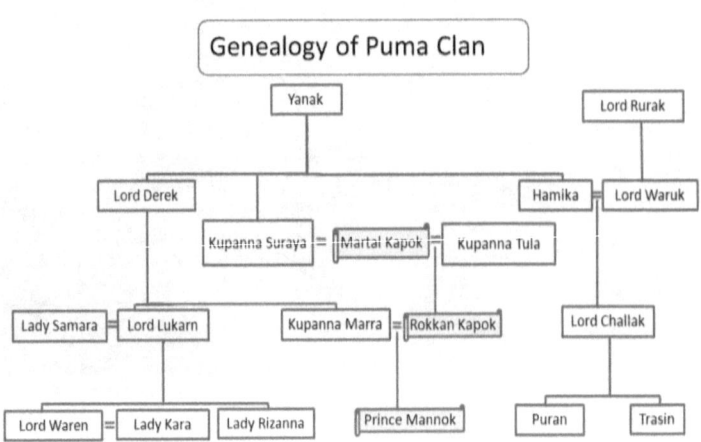

Genealogy of Puma Clan

Yanak — Lord Rurak

Lord Derek — Hamika = Lord Waruk

Kupanna Suraya = Martal Kapok — Kupanna Tula

Lady Samara = Lord Lukarn — Kupanna Marra = Rokkan Kapok — Lord Challak

Lord Waren = Lady Kara — Lady Rizanna — Prince Mannok — Puran — Trasin

Acknowledgements

Rasel's Song is the second published novel in the *Akrad's Legacy* series. The series follows the lives of four young people caught up in the unrest and political machinations following a bitter war. In *Rasel's Song*, the story focuses on Mannok, Dinnis and Rasel.

For readers of my other stories, the events of Rasel's Song occur immediately after *Akrad's Children*, but many, many years after those recorded in 'Ruhanna's Flight' and the *Under the Mountain* series and even the *Tamrin Tales* ('The Herbalist's Daughter' and 'Lakwi's Lament'), though a savvy reader may recognise some familiar names and references.

My heartfelt thanks to my wonderful and much valued editor, Nola Passmore (of The Write Flourish), and for valuable feedback from Nicky Nugent, Christine Barrett, Mazzy Adams, the members of the Year of the Novel class, the Sparkly Badgers Writers group, especially Claire Buss, and my sister, Kathleen Hillenberg.

I'm especially grateful for my family—my loving husband Tony, my precious children Kathleen and David, and my parents Tom and Jean Curtis—who instilled in me a love of faith and fantasy— and siblings, Tom Curtis, Frank Curtis, Chris Curtis and Kathleen Hillenberg, with whom I've shared many wonderful adventures.

As always, I'm grateful to my Maker in whose creative and imaginative footsteps I can only hope to follow.

Jeanette O'Hagan, April 2021

About the Author

Jeanette has spun tales in the world of Nardva since the age of eight or nine. She enjoys writing high fantasy and science fiction, poetry, blogging and editing. Her Nardvan stories span continents, time and cultures. Many involve courtly intrigue, adventure, romance and/or shapeshifters and magic. Others, like 'Space Triage', are set in Nardva's future and include space stations, plasma rifles, bio-tech, and/or cyborgs.

Since the publication of her first short story in 2014, Jeanette has published five novellas (*Heart of the Mountain, Blood Crystal, Stone of the Sea and Shadow Crystals* and *Caverns of the Deep*) in the *Under the Mountain* series; the first two books in the *Akrad's Legacy* series, *Akrad's Children* and *Rasel's Song*, a collection of short stories, *Ruhanna's Flight and other Stories*, as well as a plethora of short stories and poems in twenty anthologies, more recently *Space Triage* in *Challenge Accepted* (proceeds go to the Special Olympics), *Shadow Queen* in the *Starlit Fantasy Anthology* and *The Princess and the Messenger* in A *Glimmer of Uncommon Fairytale Retellings*.

Jeanette has practised medicine, studied communication, history, theology and a Master of Arts (Writing). She lives in Brisbane and loves reading, painting, travel, catching up for coffee with friends and pondering the meaning of life.

Website

Jeanette O'Hagan Writes at jeanetteohagan.com

Social Media

Jeanette O'Hagan is most active on
Facebook, Instagram, GoodReads, and Bookbub

Publications

Novels & Novellas

Akrad's Legacy series

Akrad's Children (By the Light Books, 2017)

Under the Mountain series:

Heart of the Mountain: a short novella, (By the Light Books, 2016)
Blood Crystal: a novella, (By the Light Books, 2017)
Stone of the Sea: a novella, (By the Light Books, 2018)
Shadow Crystals: a novella, (By the Light Books, 2019)
Caverns of the Deep (By the Light Books, 2019)

Short Stories:

Ruhanna's Flight and Other Stories, (By the Light Books, 2018)
'Broken Promises' in *Another Time Another Place* anthology, (Swinburne Students, 2015)
'Shadows of the Deep' in *Tales From the Underground*, (Inklings Press, 2017)
'Full Moon Rises' in *Like a Woman* anthology, editors Mirren Hogan, Jeanette O'Hagan & Christina Aitken, (Mirren Hogan, 2017)
'Project Chameleon' in *The Quantum Soul*, (Sci-Fi Roundtable, 2017)
'Stasia's Stand' in *Crossroads* (Birdcatcher Books, 2017)
'Treasure in the Snow' in *From the Edge*, (WAG, 2019)
'Wolf Scout' in *Tales of Magic and Destiny*, (Inklings Press) 2019
'Maroon's Sanctuary' in *Gods of Clay*, (Sci-Fi Roundtable, 2019)
'Space Triage' in *Challenge Accepted*, (Stephanie Barr, 2019)
'The Shadow Queen' in *Starlit Realms Fantasy* anthology (Elizabeth Klein, 2022)
'The Princess and the Messenger' in *A Glimmer of Uncommon Fairy Tales* anthology (Elizabeth Klein, 2023)